"Arguably superior to the Buffy franchise . . . Wildly creative and invents a totally new and refreshing milieu."

—*Fangoria*

"Banks spins a head-bendingly complex tale of passion, mythology, war and love that lasts till the grave—and beyond."

—Publishers Weekly Online

This title is also available as an eBook

SURRENDER THE DARK

L.A. BANKS

POCKET BOOKS
New York   London   Toronto   Sydney

Pocket Books
A Division of Simon & Schuster, Inc.
1230 Avenue of the Americas
New York, NY 10020

This book is a work of fiction. Names, characters, places, and incidents either are products of the author's imagination or are used fictitiously. Any resemblance to actual events or locales or persons, living or dead, is entirely coincidental.

First Pocket Books paperback edition April 2011

POCKET and colophon are registered trademarks of Simon & Schuster, Inc.

For information about special discounts for bulk purchases, please contact Simon & Schuster Special Sales at 1-866-506-1949 or business@simonandschuster.com.

The Simon & Schuster Speakers Bureau can bring authors to your live event. For more information or to book an event contact the Simon & Schuster Speakers Bureau at 1-866-248-3049 or visit our website at www.simonspeakers.com.

Designed by Leydiana Rodríguez-Ovalles
Cover design by Lisa Litwack
Cover illustration by Gene Mollica

Manufactured in the United States of America

10 9 8 7 6 5 4 3 2 1

ISBN 978-1-4516-0778-9
ISBN 978-1-4516-0897-7 (ebook)

As with all things, my first thank-you goes to The Creator, for allowing me to have the opportunity to craft a new series.

But there are so many people who are in my corner too—a blessing in and of itself: my daughter; my wonderful Street Team of friends, who always urge me on; and of course the readers who keep hitting me on Facebook and email me, asking, "So what's next, Ms. Banks?" (Big smile.) Thank you for all the love!

Acknowledgments

Without Sarah Crowe, my agent, who is a positive force of nature, this wouldn't have been possible. I also want to give special thanks to Jennifer Heddle, my editor, and her wonderful staff and colleagues at Pocket Books, who made this project a joy. No book is a solo effort; it requires a solid team of people all pulling in the same direction to birth a novel, let alone a series (or at least twins, otherwise know as a sequel, LOL!). I might have been the one "carrying," but I had a great book obstetrics team—*thank you*—and the baby even came out with a very pretty cover! Big hug!

SURRENDER
THE
DARK

Azrael squeezed his eyes shut more tightly when the light around him dimmed behind his lids. As the Angel of Death, never had he imagined that he would fear the return to darkness as terribly as he did now.

Yet he refused to lose sight of the fact that to be chosen was the highest honor imaginable. The sacrifice would be great, but that was what made being selected so deeply revered. It would be soon, he could feel the energy around him changing, could feel the anticipation of the others as he remained poised between the edge of one realm and the descent into the other.

He was a being of pure light who would now be reconstructed into the heavy density of earthly flesh and matter . . . a process that hurt like hell. Most of his kind didn't make that full transition into flesh, avoiding the pain and temptations wrought by that earthly condition.

Instead they reached out to humanity through the veil between worlds, entering human space without actually becoming a part of it. In the world but not of it . . . a delicate balancing act to be sure.

And while most of his fellow warriors hadn't fully returned to the plane of sensation since the first big battle that had emptied the realms above, some of his brethren had actually been trapped in the earthly realm following their clash with the fallen. That war had been Azrael's only time incarnate; fighting directly and valiantly for the primary heavenly cause—routing out evil—and his fearlessness in battle had earned him his title as the Angel of Death. The murmured rumor was that if the Most High was calling upon him now to actually manifest on earth, then things were worse than originally imagined.

Visions, dreams, whispers, the quick rearrangement of matter, or other forms of intervention were how angels of the Light most often made their presence known to humans. But desperate times called for desperate measures. The cosmic clock was ticking, and this mission required forces on the ground. It also required an acute understanding and compassion for the human condition that could only be acquired through human experience. That was the directive he'd received from the inarguable Source.

If the Remnant failed to shift the course of human history toward the Light, then the planet would plunge into darkness forever. The human project would be lost and the Source of All That Is would create it again somewhere else in the universe.

Based on that premise, the order from On High to save humanity by experiencing humanity, the most revered creation of all, made his predecessors and mentors warn Azrael that this mission was particularly dangerous. If he failed, the dark side would win and the balance between the darkness and the Light would forever be tilted in the favor of demonic forces. Humanity would be swallowed up in that darkness; the Most High's most cherished creation, humankind, would be lost. It was a battle no warrior of the Light could refuse.

Still, he had to prepare himself for the requisite pain. He'd been told to expect the adjustment period to be awful; the memory blackout and loss of knowledge could last for interminable human days until his bio functions synced with the spheres of Light once more. Until that happened, he'd be vulnerable—and this time, they'd warned, the excessive human population, environmental damage, and the proliferation of electromagnetic interference would slow his reintegration.

The planet was struggling under the weight she was carrying, and the negative vibrations strangling the earth had actually thickened the density that his kind would now have to wade through. It wasn't like the first war he'd fought, when the planet was still light and the density of it was in its infancy. Penetrating eons of darkness now defied comprehension, and he would feel that in his flesh so viscerally that the pain alone could weaken his resolve.

He hated being vulnerable to the dark side.

In that first raging battle between the Light and the fallen, angels tumbled from the heavens to fight without the loss of cognition or strength. That was when the earth was young and pure and the density between the realms was a gossamer energy.

Azrael quieted his mind. It was time for his descent, his fall back to earth where he'd be propelled from the Light into the heavy density of the human world.

Unnatural warmth crawled over his skin, rising like a tide of agony until he cried out. Then came the fall; a hellish plummet that ripped the breath from his lungs and felt almost as though his flesh was being shorn from his bones. Only faith sealed his sanity within him as tears stung his eyes and pain wracked his body. Mercy was all that he asked. That request became a bleating refrain inside his spirit as the pain intensified before his cells finally shattered into a million pieces of light. Then, just as suddenly, the pain was gone, but the terror had only begun.

Sucked through a weightless vortex he was conscious of being, yet without form or substance, hurtling through the icy blackness, the blessed Light from the Source of All That Is so desperately far away. He wept without eyes or tears. He reached out with phantom arms, immediately regretting his mission. But it was too late. He had been chosen and it was time.

Rebirth into the human world was no different from what he imagined a human birth to be; frightening pressure and the dawning realization that one is being torn away from the comforting source of all one has ever known.

He hit the ground with a thud in a fetal position, naked, shivering . . . disoriented and cold. Earth stench and dank wetness stung his nose and forced him to lift his head. Something skittered by him in the dark. His body demanded breath, and he inhaled sharply, gagging and coughing at the abomination called air. What hell had he been born into? Wonder and disdain filled him. How could mere mortals survive such ruin?

Steel tracks pressed into his skin; a dark tunnel loomed before him. Fragments of knowledge tried to take anchor in his embattled mind, coming in fits and starts. Languages, cultures, eternal wisdom, tried to savagely force themselves into his brain, the human-replica organ that held knowing within his skull. Information stabbed at his mind too quickly, dredging an agonized wail up from his body-trapped soul.

A light barreling toward him made him scramble to his feet and smile. Anticipation and hope almost made him giddy. Hands on either side of his head, he slowly looked up. Tears streamed down his face. Please . . .

His shoulders throbbed as though deep, bloody gashes crisscrossed his back; he realized his wings were gone. But when he reached over his shoulder with one hand to gently touch the burning area with his fingertips, amazingly his skin was whole. Only the pulsing ache and what felt like a thick, raised keloid scar remained where his missing appendages should have been. Every muscle in his limbs trembled to hold him upright. Nausea roiled within his stomach. *My wings are gone.* Amputated by the fall to earth?

Azrael swallowed hard as his hand dropped away from the wreck at his back, for the first time realizing how much he'd taken for granted without even realizing he'd done so. Maybe this, too, was part of his lesson, his growth, and why he'd been chosen to search for one of the Remnant.

But the light careening toward him made him focus.

Was the Source taking him back? he wondered. Then knowledge whispered the horrible truth. No. Seek safety or be broken.

Intuitive gifts of second sight and clairsentience told him he couldn't outrun what was hurtling toward him. Sacred understanding made him aware that, although immortal, if he met this light, it would definitely hurt like hell.

Azrael quickly flattened his body against a slight depression in the wall, and the train passed, whirring by him like a howling dragon.

Panic sweat covered his body as he ventured out of his hiding space once the danger had passed. For a few moments he stared at the retreating metal nightmare. A train. The humans called this thing a train. Right. He had to align his understanding with modern terms and languages. That would be a part of his survival; it would also help determine the success of his mission. Comprehension of this world during this era was paramount. He had to remember, had to restore his knowledge. They'd told him to reach out to his brethren through prayer—the same way humans accessed angelic assistance. Hayyel, his brother who ruled the province of wisdom, would know what to do.

"I call upon you, Hayyel, my angel brother in the Light, the guardian of true knowledge, please help me," Azrael whispered, then began walking. "Can you hear me from down here in this cesspool?"

He rubbed the nape of his neck and released a forlorn sigh. If *he* wondered whether his angelic brethren could hear him from earth, then how did fragile humans ever endure? No wonder the dark side was winning. But he refused to give in to despair so quickly. With strengthened resolve he lifted his chin and kept walking. Hayyel would eventually hear him. All prayers penetrated the veil between worlds and got to where they were supposed to be. Hayyel would send him the information he needed; he had to believe that.

Azrael moved toward the subway platform with purpose. He would learn this world quickly, and his mind would soon absorb all he needed to know; the more human contact he had, the more he would blend into this world in this era.

Yet he had to remember to simply be in this world and not of it. That was what the ancients had said. That was also what Hayyel now began whispering into his mind. He could hear a faint voice inside his head trying to help him make sense of where he was and to help him gather his wits. Then just as suddenly as he'd been given that small comfort, the knowing voice ebbed. It was as though the messenger was too far away to be heard distinctly or the density was too much to allow the message to get through clearly. Maybe the limitation imposed by his human brain could also have made the message from Hayyel so fleeting? he wondered. However, he'd also felt Hayyel's message of encouragement within his spirit, and that bolstered him.

The platform just ahead stole Azrael's attention again. Hayyel was right; he had to reach it before the next howling light came. Abnormal heat emanating from one of the rails made Azrael stop. He stared at it for a moment, sensing deadly current running through it, and stayed clear of it, then took off jogging toward the diffused light illuminating the platform.

With little effort he reached up and placed his hands on the edge of the cement and pulled himself to safety. He felt strong now, but he sat on the ground for a few seconds reviewing the whole concept of motion here on the earth plane. One couldn't just think where one wanted to be; it required intent and then physical action? So inefficient.

When he stood again, he frowned, studying his palms. They were dirty. He glanced down his body. His skin was dirty. Plus his feet hurt. He lifted a foot, staring down at his upturned sole. Here he bled like a mortal? The new experience was odd indeed. And filth could cling to an angel's corporeal form?

If the dross of existence could cling to an angel's exterior down here, then what in Heaven's name could cling to an angel's spirit? Memory slowly returned as his body and mind adjusted to the new environment. The warnings were then true. Temptation, seduction, excess, decadence, were all things that could weaken him while he searched for the girl.

Small stones and glass had lodged in the soft flesh of his foot, and as he picked them out, more blood rushed from the open cuts. Azrael stared, fascinated. A round, flat aluminum ring made him wince as he extracted it from the tender wound. Now he had to put down his injured right foot to examine his left.

"Yo, would you look at this crazy, bare-assed motherfucker down here! C'mon, son! I know you homeless and all, but at least put on some drawers! Damn!"

Azrael snapped his attention up from his injured foot to look at the young men that had entered the station. He stared at them and they laughed at him. One had thick, woolly hair and even brown skin like Azrael's—the hue of walnut bark. Azrael needed to understand what tribe, what ethnicity, this young male came from. It stood to reason that if their skin and hair were similar, then this would also be the tribe of the Remnant he sought. It had been this way since time immemorial; even though all angels were from all human tribes, his kind appeared to humans the way they could best comprehend and accept the manifestation of an angel before them. It would be less scary if the angel that manifested to deliver a message looked like them.

"Bless you," Azrael said quietly. The young man had given him a clue, despite his obvious insolence.

"Bless me?" The young man came closer to Azrael, peering at him as though he were some strange creature. "Check it out; G.I. Joe here is also a preacher. Bless me— fuck you!"

"Man, if I was you, I'd fall back. Homeboy is cut up like he's been lifting weights for a decade and might could do some damage. Looks like he's a crazy vet or somebody that snapped once they let him off the prison yard, feel me?" another, much darker, ebony-hued male said.

"Ty is right, man," a pale, slender youth with golden hair added in a nervous tone. "If I was you, I'd definitely fall back."

"What? Y'all scairt? Dude ain't *that* crazy to try *me,*" the first male said, laughing. "I got something for 'im, if he wanna try a brother."

They were kids. Just boys. Azrael stared at the three-some, assessing if they were indeed humans and not demons, then relaxed. They were just misdirected humans filled with unspent rage. Young boys, maybe two decades old or perhaps a little less. Time here for him was still difficult to judge. They also spoke an odd language—English, but in a dialect impossible for him to immediately place. But he knew that their dialect would provide yet another clue, once he heard it again and matched it up to a source tribe.

Azrael glanced down his body and slowly lowered his foot, suddenly realizing they were robed, and he was not. Emotions he had never experienced slammed into his spirit. Embarrassment, confusion, anger, all of it tinged by wariness and fear. Sensing danger, he covered his groin with his hands and backed away, then turned toward the wall, ashamed to be seen.

"Man, leave the bum alone," the darker youth said to the group leader. "Look at his back, bro—seems like somebody already knifed him up good . . . so if you ask me, he's bat-shit crazy. Don't go near him, is my advice."

"Yeah, man," the other youth agreed. "You don't know what he's carrying if he comes at you, and he definitely ain't got no money—least nowhere you wanna touch it when he pulls it out."

"Where your clothes at, son?" the tall, walnut-hued kid shouted at Azrael, then gave the angel a menacing grin.

"I have none," Azrael replied calmly, turning to face him. "Will you help me? I am not from the enemy of mankind."

All three young men burst out laughing. The tall one brought a short, white object to his lips, then lit it with a small blue cylinder that produced a flame when his thumb clicked it. He shook his head and took a long drag, passing the strange-smelling white stick to his pale friend first.

"You in the wrong part of town to be begging for clothes and talking like Shakespeare and shit, son. That's a real good way for a brother to get beat down in North Central."

Frustration and a jolt of confusion shot through Azrael. "If we are indeed brothers—more importantly, our brother's keeper—then why would you not help me cover myself? I have done you no harm, and hidden within your raiment you have more than enough resources, not to mention knowledge, to assist a being in need. I can sense it, therefore I do not understand." Azrael stepped forward, emboldened by the new surge of human emotions pulsing through his veins. The injustice of it all made him irate. "In fact, I do not understand why my shame and heartbreak at being separated from the Source is so amusing to you. Where is your compassion?"

"Oh, shit . . . this motherfucker is straight trippin', man!" The pale kid handed off the glowing white stick to the darker of his friends as he blew smoke out of his nose and began coughing.

"Awww . . . man," the darker kid muttered, shaking his head as he accepted the pungent offering. "You done did it now, son. Don't nobody clock my boy's cheddar."

The leader thrust a hand in his jacket and pulled out a metal object and pointed it at Azrael, laughing. "You know what we got for beggin' fools round here in my territory, son? We got a cap to bust in your crazy ass—so you better take that bull to somebody who's trying to hear it. That's what I got hidden in my whatever you call it, a nine, aw'ight!"

"Yo, man, this bum ain't worth the hassle from po-po or doing time for, even if he is stupid. Don't shoot the bastard . . . you gonna seriously blow my high if we gotta run or dump a body." The darker kid took another drag on the disappearing white object in his hand and shook his head again. "This train needs to hurry up and come on before some real sick shit goes down."

Instinct told Azrael that what was pointed at him was a weapon that could do him great harm. Fury flooded his veins. He was unarmed! Defenseless, as far as these young wolves knew . . . yet they would threaten him with death simply for being a poor vagrant. A beggar in need, as far as they knew.

"Temper your words and your actions with wisdom or die!" he shouted, his voice a sudden, booming echo off the tile walls as he pointed at the young men before him.

The three boys looked at each other for a second, then burst out laughing.

"Oh, shit," the leader said, walking in a circle, raking his fingers through his wild, woolly hair. "This bitch is straight crazy!"

Something fragile snapped within Azrael. Time felt as if it stood still as he moved between the temporal beats of earth moments to cross the platform and grab the offending leader's wrist. Supernatural strength arced through him like a sudden current. Never had he felt so alive.

Twisting up the leader's wrist quickly, he lifted the

man-child off his feet with the weapon still in his hand and pointing toward the ceiling. A loud sound discharged as time snapped back into normal earth rhythm and a harsh sulfuric smell bit into Azrael's sinuses. The scent had come from the weapon and now lingered. The boy he held above his head continued twisting and yelling, as his friends ducked down, shouting.

"Watch the gun, man!"

"Stop shooting!"

Now Azrael had language to describe what was happening. He also had a weapon in case more human evildoers crossed his path tonight. He closed his eyes for a moment, summoning discipline: *Thou shalt not murder* had always been mistranslated as "thou shalt not kill"— and on this mission against the darkness, a righteous kill for self-defense was indeed allowed.

The desire to end their lives was so seductive, so tempting, as adrenaline thrummed through his system. But a small voice inside him reminded him of the elders' warnings: The taking of a human life should never be enjoyable. These boys' deaths would not be necessary, unless they decided to attack again. Azrael opened his eyes. His mission came back into focus.

Stripping the weapon away from the leader, Azrael yanked the young man's jacket from his body as though disrobing a child, then shoved the offender hard. The kid hit the ground and scrambled away from Azrael with new terror and respect in his eyes.

"Each of you who have much to repent, be Good Samaritans and donate to my righteous cause," Azrael said in a threatening murmur, slapping his chest with a broad, flat palm. "Or take a glance at where you are headed if you continue on your current path of murder and mayhem." He stared into their eyes, watching them recoil in horror as he gave them a glimpse of the dark side within their minds. "It is your choice. It is *always* your choice."

Chapter 1

Celeste could feel the darkness within the apartment closing in on her as she watched Brandon roll a joint on the cluttered coffee table before him. An old soda bottle, several beer cans, an ancient Chinese-food carton, charred reefer seeds, and an overflowing ashtray littered his makeshift weed-prep area.

His eyes were hard as he glared at the baseball game on television and licked the edge of the rolling paper he held. She absently stood and went over to the small kitchen pass-through and squeezed a nearly empty pack of Newports, glad that a couple cigarettes were left in it. The stench of aging garbage filled her nose, but given his foul mood, asking Brandon to take it out would be suicide. If she took it out herself, he'd start yelling about where she was going and would no doubt accuse her of trying to sneak out or something stupid. She'd deal with it tomorrow, like everything else.

She cut Brandon a sidelong glance. A joint wasn't going to chill him out tonight. It rarely did. Two years of Friday-night fights told her that. History was what it was and rarely changed unless something drastic went down. No, a joint wasn't what he wanted and it wouldn't keep him mellow. Only a few things would, and she wasn't one of them anymore. Hadn't been in a long time.

As quietly as possible, Celeste extracted a cigarette from the pack. The last thing she wanted to do was start a big argument over whose pack she was taking a smoke from. It was hers, but Brandon never seemed to remember anything that she contributed to their so-called household. And reminding him was dangerous, depending on his mood. She'd decided after their first really bad fight that it just wasn't worth the risk. Tonight it definitely wasn't worth it.

Dampening down her anger, lest she say something to ignite his rage, she walked over to the cabinets to find a glass for what was left of the vodka she'd purchased. She didn't turn on the lights. That would only hurt her eyes and make the roaches scatter. Right now she didn't want to see them any more than she wanted to contend with Brandon.

"You got any money?"

Celeste barely responded. "No. I told you before, I'm broke."

"Then what good are you, bitch? You never have any money, like I'm supposed to always take care of your skinny ass." He shot her a withering glare over his shoulder but didn't get up. "You got money for your goddamned liquor, though, right?"

She didn't reply, just fetched a short rocks glass from the cabinet, waiting a beat while whatever was crawling around scurried to a new hiding place.

"Don't have an answer to that one, do you?"

Celeste didn't tempt fate by looking up at him. He would have caught the flippant attitude in her expression, which would have been enough to propel him off the sofa for a confrontation. Instead, she kept her head down and her lips sealed. If there had been no threat of a severe beat down, she would have had plenty to say—like, "If you go to work every day washing dishes at the pizza shop and don't pay nary a bill around here on a regular basis, then why doesn't your mangy ass have any money?" That was the silent question.

But it would have been foolish to ask that question out loud even on the best of days. Her five-foot-six, 130-pound frame was no match for his six-two, 180-pound one. Simple math said to suck it up and shut up.

"Thought so, bitch."

She remained mute and just went to the freezer, extracted her bottle, and poured a little more vodka into her glass than originally intended, then as quietly as possible added some ice.

Muttering obscenities under his breath, Brandon went back to the game and his task of managing his weed. "Yeah, your crazy ass ain't stupid enough to say something back to me. I know that much."

Keeping Brandon in her peripheral vision, Celeste tucked the stolen cigarette into a loose fold she'd created under her tank-top hem and soundlessly poured a little more of the clear, potent remedy into the glass to top off the ice. Trying to move as quietly as a shadow, she edged her way toward the kitchen threshold to head down the long, dark, narrow hallway.

"Where you going?" Brandon's attention suddenly snapped in her direction again.

Celeste froze. "To pee," she said flatly, without any change in her inflection.

He turned back to the game again and lit his joint. She relaxed and edged her way out of the dark kitchen to hurry down the hall before he decided to change his mind and pursue her. Baseball wasn't all that interesting; fighting with her had become his national pastime, especially on a Friday night before the first of the month.

If her SSI check had come to her aunt Denise's house, then she would have been guaranteed some measure of peace. Aunt Niecey, who didn't believe in direct deposit or technology, would have cashed the check for her as she always did and then paid Celeste's rent and utility bills directly with a money order off that—right there at the check-cashing agency, something Brandon couldn't say jack about. Her aunt, a robust woman who was built like a tank and didn't play, was the only living relative in the family responsible and compassionate enough to take on the challenge of being Celeste's guardian as long as Celeste was claiming mental disability.

Celeste took a cool sip of vodka and kept walking. At least somebody had her back, even if her mama was dead and her daddy was in a crack house or dead somewhere.

Besides, Aunt Niecey would take out her earrings to scrap over a principle in a heartbeat as if she were still fifteen years old, if it came to that. They said her aunt was the wild one of all the Jackson girls. But Denise Jackson was the only one who'd lived to see her three score and plus some and at eighty-odd years old was still spry and in her right mind. Strokes, heart attacks, diabetes, and bad living had taken everybody else's parents. Celeste took a deeper swig from her rocks glass as she walked through the darkness, feeling the warming effects of the vodka. She didn't care that some of her cousins said auntie was too mean for the devil to take. Her cousins didn't know Auntie's kind heart.

It was simply that Aunt Niecey didn't brook no bullshit, as her aunt so colorfully claimed. Celeste's cousins, and all their badass kids, had plenty of drama going on 24-7—not that she could talk. But one had to respect her aunt's position and proclamation. Denise Jackson could back up whatever she said with authority. That's why they didn't like Aunt Niecey so much, even though every last one of them was too much of a punk to say that to her face.

So, who else but fearless Aunt Niecey was gonna be the legal guardian of someone diagnosed with schizophrenia, chronic depression, and substance abuse after a violent nervous breakdown? That woman was prayed up, had raised up all the broken children in the family, and also packed heat, just in case her Jesus was a little slow to intervene or respond. According to her aunt, God helped those who helped themselves.

But regardless of all that, the feds and the state required a guardian in matters such as these, and her aunt had stepped up in return for a small, monthly inconvenience fee. That was fair, the way Celeste saw it. Not even freedom was free.

The thing that really scared her was the question of what she would ever do if Aunt Niecey was gone. Her aunt was a lifeline. Yet her aunt was moving slower year by year. It was only a matter of time. Fatigue was written all over the poor woman's face, just as *Arthur* was twisting her hands and feet into knots. Arthritis was the only thing to slow down the pure force of nature that her aunt had been.

Celeste took a huge gulp of vodka and shuddered as it went down. It was bad enough coming home to her mother dead on the kitchen floor from a stroke when she was in middle school. She didn't want to be the one to find her aunt like that, too. It was a fervent prayer, not that she thought God ever listened to her. If He did, then He wouldn't have allowed half of the things that had happened to her.

She just hoped for the sake of her aunt that whoever was in charge up above would make her aunt's passing smooth and easy. Denise Jackson, a weary warrior who claimed to be a soldier for God, deserved some respite from this cruel world. That was one of the reasons Celeste didn't tell her aunt half of the crap that Brandon pulled. It would probably give the auntie who'd raised her a heart attack where she stood.

That thought frightened Celeste as much as the things she sometimes saw looking at her from behind people's supposedly normal faces.

Brandon got up from the sofa and went into the kitchen to bring the entire bottle of vodka back into the living room with him. The pungent smell of reefer wafted down the hall to surround her. Celeste paused, judging whether it was safe to move. He didn't seem to notice how much she'd taken for herself and just turned the cold, freezer-stored bottle up to his mouth. Rat bastard. That was *her* bottle.

For a few moments she drew silent comfort from knowing that all she had to do was say the word, and her aunt would get Brandon put out. The big question she wrestled with was, what was stopping her from going that extra mile?

Fear claimed her as she timidly sipped her drink and then continued walking toward the bathroom. It was almost as if a dark force had tethered her to someone that clearly despised her, yet she couldn't break free of him even when everyone from her doctors to her family said Brandon Jacobs was part of her addiction. But it was deeper than that; only she couldn't talk about it. Not without their thinking she was crazy.

She hugged the wall as she edged toward the bathroom, half-terrified of the dark, half-terrified of what she might see without her meds. Her footsteps were light and unsure, like those of the mice that used the cover of darkness to keep them safe while they pillaged the cabinets.

Brandon wasn't a demon, just a sick bastard she lived with. She had to believe that to hold on to a fragile thread of reality. Celeste mentally repeated the things her doctor had told her in their last session. She had the power to make changes in her life, including leaving Brandon . . . even if he swore he'd kill her, though? She never talked to anybody about that part. Not even to her aunt Niecey.

That was the $50 million question that neither her therapist nor the psychiatrist could answer. Brandon had even come to a session and passed their scrutiny in a way she had never been able to. Like a Boy Scout he swore he never said the things he said, and they'd strangely believed it along with every other lie he told. She'd gotten so outraged that she'd screamed and shouted; that only made them believe him more, since he remained calm with tears in his eyes, pretending to be innocent and claiming that he'd cut his own arm off before ever hitting her. Yeah, right.

Silent fury swirled within Celeste as she kept walking and praying for a night of peace. Most times she was so confused that she couldn't tell whether Brandon had said the things she thought he did. All she felt was terror when he spoke to her. How did one explain that to people who lived so far removed from her reality?

It was impossible to make them understand that sometimes Brandon's voice sounded like growls and his eyes seemed to glow red in the dark. Celeste glanced over her shoulder and hastened her quiet footsteps. Everyone told her that was crazy and impossible. That it was her illness making her imagine things. Worse yet, when she'd try to show them her cuts and bruises from his attacks, by the time she got to the hospital there was strangely never any evidence that he'd hit her.

No one believed her except her prayed-up aunt, who claimed she knew a demon when she saw one. But both the psychiatrist and the therapist were almost ready to commit Aunt Niecey when she'd once admitted that, so she never talked about it again, leastwise not to jeopardize the SSI check coming in—$1,144 a month was nothing to sneeze at.

Celeste rounded the threshold of their tiny bathroom and shut the door, quickly clicking on the light. *Just breathe and don't look in the mirror.* Demons lived in the mirror.

She opened the medicine cabinet, grabbed a disposable lighter, and sat on the windowsill with her sneakers on the toilet, leaning out of the window to light up. Carefully balancing her rocks glass on the radiator top, she cupped her hand against the cool, early-September breeze and brought the end of her cigarette to the flame.

Taking a long, satisfying drag on the menthol butt, she glanced at the open medicine cabinet. Would have been nice to have a little something to go with the vodka to take the edge off. But Brandon had long sold her meds. He did every month. Haldol and Cogentin had street value. She was so morose now that she almost laughed, thinking maybe she should just go all the way out of her mind and let them put her on Paxil and lithium, which fetched an even better price in the hood. But common sense told her that if she wanted to keep Brandon off her back, it was better not to even trip about her missing meds, and she wouldn't as long as his selling them chilled him out.

Still, she was nobody's fool. Celeste reached down behind the radiator and checked a flat of bills that were duct-taped to the tile wall. Only her hand was small enough to reach the thin fold of five $20 bills. Since Brandon never cleaned, the likelihood of his spotting it way back there was slim to none.

Satisfied that her stash was still intact, she sat back and took another long drag off the Newport, allowing the smoke to slowly filter out of her nose. Vodka chased the angry smoke, cooling her throat and burning her stomach when it hit bottom. She couldn't remember the last time she'd eaten. After he left tonight maybe she'd go out and get something quick and would be sure to hide all evidence that she'd had any money available to feed herself. Celeste took another slow sip and closed her eyes. This was no way to live.

If she killed the bastard in his sleep, she'd do life in a lockup for the criminally insane. Her mental-health record already damned her. If she claimed self-defense, who would believe her? If she said she'd snapped because he'd stolen her meds and sold them, the DA would probably get one of her doctors to pull out one of Brandon's old lies he'd told her family therapist at a goal-setting meeting about how she was selling her own meds, turning tricks, and stealing from him to get crack. For someone like her, she doubted patient-client confidentiality would hold up in a court of law.

Nobody except Aunt Niecey seemed to believe that crack was Brandon's drug of choice, not hers. Alcohol soothed Celeste's savage beast. Crack and meth had somehow passed her by, despite that prescription meds hadn't. Crazy what the system deemed acceptable or not.

Celeste opened her eyes and inhaled again deeply, then blew the smoke out in a huff against the full moon. "A full fucking moon," she murmured, staring up at the blue-white orb, mesmerized.

But Aunt Niecey had told her they had to be practical, that they could deal with ousting a demon behind closed doors their way. The wise older woman, the eldest sister of Celeste's dead mama, had counseled her to just agree with whatever the doctors said in the goal-setting meetings.

Aunt Niecey hadn't gotten to be her age with her own property without knowing something.

All the rehab-clinic docs and therapists said it was simple. Celeste shook her head again as she polished off her drink, mentally recounting the goals they'd set forth: Celeste will identify triggers that lead her to run away and to act with violence. Celeste will become more comfortable seeking support from family or other trusted, responsible adults when she feels like fleeing. Celeste will decrease impulsive reactions to conflict-based situations. Celeste will verbalize the need for nurturing and support in her close relationships. Celeste will set reasonable boundaries. Celeste will identify a path forward as well as identify strategies and lifestyle changes necessary to avoid substance abuse. The case psychologist will work with the hospital psychiatrist before the next session to identify additional strategies for Celeste's success.

"Meanwhile," she murmured in a sullen tone between drags, "Celeste will figure out how to kill a demon if it jumps on her again in her house."

If Brandon and Aunt Niecey ever got into a real confrontation, she knew her aunt had no problem telling him where to get off. The problem was, he seemed smart enough to avoid that and to always make her word questionable in front of a third party.

Why did they all think they knew what was best for her, anyway? Her shrink from the hospital provided the meds, while the substance-abuse counselor did the monitoring, and half the time the left hand didn't seem to know what the right hand was recommending or doing. It was all a sham, as far as she was concerned. But her monthly checks hinged on her playing by their rules, and on her elderly aunt's word that bills were getting paid and toxic behaviors were decreasing. Even Brandon was smart enough to play the game. Maybe the demon inside him was, too. Everything needed somewhere to live, as a practical matter.

Damn . . . she wished this had been the first of the month. Things were always so much more chill, then. As soon as the check came and the bills were paid, and after her aunt took her "monthly management fee" off the top, Aunt Niecey would then give her the rest of what was left to manage. From there, she and Brandon could scrap over the measly couple hundred dollars that remained after rent had been paid.

Celeste narrowed her gaze at the moon. How in the hell was he claiming to take care of her so-called skinny ass? She paid all the bills from her SSI check via her aunt. *She* once had a decent receptionist's job at the university before things got all messed up in her life. *She* had waited on and qualified for Section 8 housing. *She* bought any groceries, such as they were. *What was she doing with this man?* And, it was *her* pack of cigarettes.

Celeste tossed the spent butt out the window and stood. Being afraid to live alone or to be by herself had brought her to this place, and she knew it. For the first six months of being with Brandon, she felt something close to hope. Brandon's presence chased away the shadows and made her feel almost normal again. She was able to go out in public without seeing insane images in people's faces. She could get away from Aunt Niecey's strict rules . . . could even have sex again. Then something began to wither in her spirit.

New tears formed in her eyes. She allowed the fat

droplets to rise to the edge of her thin lashes and spill down her cheeks. Maybe it wasn't Brandon's demon, maybe it was hers? Maybe the doctors were right. Confusion once again made her unsure. Constant emotional battering left her with no self-esteem as an anchor. Maybe she was everything Brandon said she was—a skinny, know-nothing bag of bones, crazy and made that way from depression and not eating and drinking way too much. Maybe it wasn't demons that she was afraid of seeing in the mirror; maybe she was afraid of seeing what she'd become. That was her therapist's take on it—that she didn't like what she saw so she'd created mirror monsters.

It was true, in a way. She did hate what she saw when she was brave enough to look into the mirror. Her skin was acne-scarred and her complexion off. Even Aunt Niecey said she looked gray. What was there to look at in the mirror, really? A bag of bones in old jeans and a raggedy orange tank top, with jacked-up skin, no makeup, and hair breaking off so badly that the only style she could keep was a ponytail brushed back into a scrunchie. Pathetic. She didn't even want him touching her, hadn't submitted to that in almost a year. Didn't understand why he'd want to, if she was all the horrible things he'd regularly called her.

Maybe that's why Brandon had come to hate her, because she was that crazy bitch he'd claimed she was. Celeste picked up her glass, about to go for a refill, then remembered that he'd also claimed her bottle. Now the question became, was another drink worth getting her ass kicked over? No. At least not at the moment. He'd go out soon, she hoped.

Everything would have been fine . . . if only it had been the first of the month. But the check wasn't due until then, and nobody in Section 8 housing ever heard anything. Definitely not a woman getting her ass kicked down in Mantua. That was just a run-of-the-mill occurrence, part of the environment that one took for granted. To survive, everybody had to be smart and stay one step ahead of what could happen next—men, women, and children, young and old. The bottom was no respecter of age or gender. Escaping from a beating was better than enduring one or even winning—because if she won, she'd go to jail for either battery or murder.

A loud bang made her jump back into the corner by the toilet and the window, accidentally dropping the glass. Splinters from the door flew at the same time shards of glass exploded on the floor as the door slammed against the tub, hinges hanging. Brandon stood in the doorway, his full six feet two inches of dark rage contorting his face, his fists balled at his sides. Celeste's heart beat erratically like a trapped bird's.

"You stealing my cigarettes down to the last one in the pack now?"

He leveled the charge at her almost snorting like a mad bull. For a moment, fear sent new tears to her eyes as she shook her head and wrapped her arms around her body.

"Don't lie, bitch!" he shouted, now pointing at her. "You know I can smell you've been smoking in here! You think I'm some kinda fool? You think I'm just gonna allow you to steal from me and that won't cost you?"

A prayer flitted through her mind. This time he was

going to kill her; she could feel it in her bones. *God in heaven make it quick. Save me from this demon.*

But as soon as she'd said the prayer, an eerie calm overtook her. She slowly unwrapped her arms from her body. There had been enough heartbreak, enough pain, enough tragedy. She no longer cared. There was no escaping the beast or the hell her life had become. They didn't have a drug or a new therapy that could fix this. Surrender . . . and let it all end here, she thought, then swallowed hard. Tonight was as good a night as any to die.

"I didn't steal your cigarettes. They're mine," she said, baiting him, wanting death to take her.

"What did you say?" His voice was a lethal rumble.

"I said," she repeated, with attitude in her tone, "I brought those cigarettes, just like I paid the fucking rent, the gas bill, the electric bill, and put food in this joint. All you pay is cable. So, if you're gonna kill me, do it—and stop playing."

"Bitch . . . I will—"

"Man the fuck up and kill me, then, asshole, and stop telling me what you're *gonna* do—or get *the fuck* out of my house! Get thee behind me, Satan! In the name of the Most High I command you to get out of my house, demon! I'm so sick of your shit; just get it over with already!"

He'd crossed the tiny space in a blur and had her by the throat. She could hear glass crackle and pop under each of his angry footfalls. Her head banged the wall as he shoved her against it, then somehow with her feet off the floor he slung her against the open medicine cabinet. He was so much stronger than she'd remembered. Her eyes bulged and the stinging warmth at the back of her skull told her that her head was cut. But no breath entered her lungs, which burned from air deprivation.

Gagging, she held on to Brandon's thick biceps as he thrashed her back and forth like a rag doll. Her vision winked with black floating orbs the closer she came to passing out. That was when she saw his irises change to a gleaming red. She began praying in her mind the way her auntie had once taught her. Something shiny glinted in the corner of her tear-filled vision, catching in the blur of it as the medicine-cabinet door fell to the floor and shattered.

The object was short and metallic. Salvation was a pair of Dollar Store tweezers. No, she didn't want to die like this. She wanted to live! Scrabbling for them as her head and back slammed against the tile, she got the tweezers in her fist. Two seconds later they were lodged in Brandon's right eye. He fell back, yelling in pain, releasing her. She dropped in a slump against the wall, gasping and heaving as his screams rang out.

"Demon, I command you in the name of God to flee this house," she croaked, quickly edging her way past Brandon's body to get to the window.

Then suddenly a second shadow separated from the one Brandon's crumpled body cast. It was misshapen with horns and stood slowly on two hoofed feet. Long, spidery claws spread across the bathroom tile toward her.

Celeste screamed and pressed herself into the far corner of the bathroom for a second, heart racing. Where Brandon had fallen, he and the foreboding shadow now blocked the door as an exit; the window was the only way out without passing him—it—them.

She stripped the duct tape off the wall, the money

instantly in her hand. The ominous shadow immediately synced up with Brandon's shadow and disappeared. Brandon lifted his head with a snarl; one bloody, dead eye stared at her around the deeply lodged tweezers, the other one red, gleaming, and promising that her death would be pure agony. For a few fragile seconds, neither of them moved. She was paralyzed where she stood by what she thought she saw. Time stopped. Then suddenly Brandon's mouth became a distorted forest of crooked, razor-sharp teeth.

Instinct propelled her out of the window with a bleating mental prayer. Something she couldn't explain kept her from breaking her legs from the two-story fall. She hit the ground with a soft thud, sticky money still in her fist, then she got up and ran hard and fast.

Celeste looked back only once to see the window slam shut by itself and then saw the lights go out. Brandon's loud, panicked voice bit into her ears, tortured her mind, and arrested her conscience. It was a desperate plea, an interrupted wail of her name filled with terror, not anger. That made her hesitate, slowed her escape, and kept her staring over her shoulder at what she should have been flat-out running from. Before she could turn away, Brandon's bloody face hit the glass. She knew he was dead by the vacant look in his one normal eye.

She ran in earnest as if the very devil were chasing her.

Chapter 2

Out like a shot, Celeste took off running hard and fast again, nearly blinded by tears. Money got shoved into her back jeans pocket, a scream lodged in her throat. Something invisible in that bathroom had slammed shut the window, then smashed a 180-pound man against it as if he were a small child.

The night was too still, as though the darkness itself were a predator. A partially uninhabited block faced Celeste as she fled across the street heading toward Mantua Avenue's train tracks. Between the abandoned buildings on Aspen Street, the crack house on the corner, and the apathy of the people who were hunkered down in tiny, vermin-infested rental units up the block, there would be no witnesses to declare her innocence. And there were definitely no heroes where she lived.

Something unknowable had killed Brandon. But all evidence pointed to her. The truth, if she told it, would have her committed and imprisoned. Truth was rarely a reliable witness.

Her decision about which way to run had been made in a split second. Dilapidated homes leaned against the darkness like a snaggletoothed grin. Open lots between what should have been an unbroken chain of row houses provided a haven for whatever wanted her dead. Although dirt, and not concrete, had broken her fall, the overgrowth of huge weeds and abandoned tires only added to her terror. A stitch caught in her side as her smoker's lungs caught fire. But she kept running.

Adrenaline and panic propelled her across one desolate street after the next. Yet, there was no escape from the wasteland of blighted houses and rusted-out cars. A few disinterested, drug-numbed neighbors sat on their porches, oblivious to her peril.

Instinct drove her in the opposite direction of the universities. Penn and Drexel were behind her, an escape into a shield of deeper poverty was before her. She knew she had to stay away from where the police regularly patrolled. Had to stay away from those whose job it was to zealously protect society's more important citizenry. She had to go deeper into the hood, go underground and get lost in the throng of what the authorities considered throwaway humanity. Maybe there she could blend in.

Train tracks created a natural barrier at Mantua Avenue, forcing her into the open street, the high guard wall and power lines impassable. That sent her eastbound up a slight rise to Thirty-fourth Street Bridge by the zoo, where she could hang a quick left and cross the bridge, a good escape route beneath a canopy of trees once on the other side.

Sweat stung her eyes. Gasping, she pushed on to Girard Avenue, a full three additional blocks, until she had to stop. Celeste clutched the wire fence that was supposed to keep would-be jumpers from hurling their bodies into the river, suddenly bent, and vomited.

She stood slowly, wiping her mouth with the back of her wrist, then stared out at the blue-black water and the odd beauty of the downtown skyline framed by light-pollution haze and dim stars. As much as she'd despised Brandon, in the last few moments of his life she knew that he'd been as frightened as she was. Something had been in him, something evil that had finally taken his life.

Faraway sirens caused her to look over her shoulder and once again contemplate the river, this time for its swiftness in taking a life. Her life. Suicide was a possible answer, she thought. It would end the pain, would end the horror that had followed her all her life. Tonight she was at the breaking point.

Out of shape, beaten, and weary, her legs and body ached so badly they felt numb. Her head throbbed; her chest burned. The stitch in her side felt as if she'd been stabbed with a short, wide blade.

New tears filled Celeste's eyes as she threaded her fingers through the wire Cyclone fence again and held on tightly. She couldn't go to her family; that would be the first place the cops looked. Nor could she drag Aunt Niecey into this to be possibly set up as an accessory to a murder somehow.

She'd rather die than be locked up and drugged for the rest of her life, trapped in a living hell. If she was going to go to hell, then it would be one of her own choosing and on her own terms. As tired as she was, she was fairly certain that she could climb high enough to pitch her body over the top of the fence.

But why was this happening to her? Why hadn't any of her prayers been answered? She didn't care what Aunt Niecey said, she had been forsaken!

Celeste bit her lip as a sob fractured her. She couldn't go on, couldn't take living like this a moment longer. If the river would just be swift . . . if the river would just be merciful. It might hurt briefly on impact; maybe she'd be scared for a few seconds as she fell, but she'd been hurting and terrified for what seemed like her whole life. At least after the few minutes of pain there'd be peace.

However, a low growl in the overgrowth near the corner made her back away from the fence. The instant she saw what it was, she pivoted and began running.

On the border of the park, a feral, stray pit bull and his foraging mate had stopped their snuffling for zoo tourist garbage along the edge of the concrete bridge barrier to contemplate her, a decided interloper in their territory. Abandoned park mansions and overgrowth from the lack of city funds were a haven for the animals tossed out of moving vehicles after pit-bull fights; that made them a city menace that bred almost as quickly as rats.

Until they'd begun growling, she hadn't even seen them. It was as though the strays had appeared out of nowhere. To die of a fall into the river from one's own free will, a planned suicide, versus being savaged to death in the street by pits, wasn't something she even had to think about.

The strong, fast animals would overtake her in seconds.

A passing trolley crossing the wide boulevard was her salvation. Remembering how to hop a trolley from her youth, Celeste zigzagged through light traffic and jumped on the back of it, knowing the dogs would follow—knowing Philly drivers from the hood could give a shit about a stray mutt.

The screech of a car, a thud, and a conclusive yelp all happened behind her. Curses confirmed that one dog was down, the other had fled. If the driver's car had been damaged, the surviving dog risked getting shot. Life in the city was what it was, sometimes brutal but oddly consistent.

She jumped off the trolley as it slowed to a stop for the light on the other side of the Girard Avenue Bridge at Thirty-third Street. All she had to do now was run a few blocks through the park over to Oxford Street and she'd be in North Philly, where she could hide until she figured out what to do.

Trees grew up and around a strange white building. One thick branch exited what should have been an intact roof. Azrael stopped for a moment and stared at it. Many hundreds of humans had once worked there. The dilapidated factory was a full block long and several stories high. Windows were missing, broken out of the frames to make the structure resemble a ragged smile. He'd been walking for what felt like a long time, trying to sense anything remotely close to the energy pattern of the Remnant he'd been assigned to protect. He had to find her. He could sense that evil had launched another attack on her tonight, and her will and faith were crumbling.

Azrael closed his eyes and allowed his head to drop

back, taking in the environment. So much pain . . . so much anger . . . despair and fear. Still there were glimmers of love . . . flickers of compassion, higher frequencies making a stand against the Ultimate Darkness. That meant there was still hope, still time.

Trying to get his bearings, he inhaled deeply and read the broken letters on the building he faced: PYRAMID ELECTRIC SUPPLY.

Slowly but surely, impressions from the environment entered his awareness. He could begin to feel the lives that had passed through this building and had walked down this street, just as he could slowly begin to feel the woman he sought. Her pain stood out from the other dim pulses of life force around him. She was close, he could feel her, but her inner light was so dim now that it had almost gone out. She'd nearly tried to kill herself. A barb of pain entered his chest and made him briefly cover his heart with his hand. Time wasn't on his side; she was on a path of self-destruction.

Azrael glanced around, noting that he'd been walking along the street labeled Glenwood Avenue, and then it had become Oxford Street or had merged into it, but which way did he need to search now?

The massive vacant building he'd passed along the way also had no roof. It took up the length of one named street to the next. Just as with all the other empty businesses and factories he'd passed, spirits rose from this one, disoriented and moaning, and incapable of giving him any directions. Livelihoods and lives had been lost there. The pain of economic blight that filled in behind those losses was too intense to ignore.

A crooked sign hung on the corner of the building with the broken word EASTERN. The rest of what it said was unreadable and missing. A large vehicle stopped on the corner and picked up a tired-looking woman. He wondered what this area and all the lives it contained would have been like had darkness not fallen upon the land.

"Go to the Light," he murmured, and in his mind envisioned a long, crystal cylinder of swirling white light. "Go into the peace that surpasses all understanding," he urged, then began walking as one by one spirits fled the abandoned structures, gravitating to the divine portal he'd opened for them.

But a long echo of spirit wails stopped him in his tracks. He turned to watch in horror as gnarled, shadowy claws reached up and snatched at the rising souls. Darkness gripped them, trying to keep them lost and anchored inside the abandoned factory. The building was clearly infested. The open, dank structure was a perfect demon roost. But these innocent souls had to be freed.

Hurdling the wire fence in two hard pulls to flip himself over the top of it, Azrael entered the building through a broken window, shoulder lowered. Instantly the darkness released the screaming souls and began to converge on him. Stray dogs stood and growled, their eyes suddenly gleaming red. Bats that scuttled along the hanging metal ceiling pipes turned away from their feast of mosquitoes to look at him, eyes glowing as shadows loomed and gathered in the corners, all perched for an attack. Drug addicts that had been in the far corners slowly lumbered forward, eyes now blacked out and vacant.

Quickly glancing around for a weapon, Azrael picked

up a pipe and said a silent prayer. He would not stand by while the darkness tried to claim souls that belonged to the Light.

As his grip tightened and his gaze narrowed, everything that had been in the shadows rushed him all at once. In a double-handed swing he fought off the first feral creature that lunged. It exploded on contact with what had been a lead pipe but which now glowed with white-hot angel energy. Something savaged him from behind, and in a deft spin, he gored it, then turned again to respond to the aerial attack of demon-infected bats.

Releasing a battle cry, he grabbed at a shadow creature to his left while his right hand speared a creature that leaped out of the shadows with dripping fangs. His voice sent a shock wave into the cloud of bats, blowing them out of the opened roof to rain down as singed confetti.

Then just as suddenly as the attack began, the empty building became eerily quiet. Everything that had rushed him receded into the shadows like a black tide. Azrael ran to a bank of windows to see if the cylindrical light portal he'd opened was taking up lost souls without attacks from the darkness. He watched them rise, relaxing as no evidence of demon interference seemed present.

Sadness filled him as he wondered how many places on earth had innocent spirits trapped by the darkness, keeping them aimlessly wandering and haunting locations that had been familiar to them while they were alive. But he couldn't dwell on that now.

Azrael climbed through the window and walked to the fence, again flipping himself over the six-foot wire enclosure to land on the curb. He had to get back to his mission to find the girl. The archangels were tasked to deal with larger global issues; guardian angels were tasked to protect individuals. He was a warrior, tasked to fight demons once he found the human who would lead the Remnant.

"You're not supposed to get involved in fighting every human battle along the way, brother. You'll wear yourself out before you've even found her."

Azrael quickly spun to meet the voice. "Gavreel . . ." Instant joy filled him as he clasped his fellow warrior in a warm embrace. "What tribe am I to search for my chosen? I can sense that she is near, but was thrust into this abomination of condition without enough—"

"Peace," Gavreel said in a low rumble, but shook his head, stepping back from Azrael. He held Azrael out from him with strong, wide palms, his silky jet-black hair lifting from his broad shoulders on the breeze as he stared at Azrael with intense, dark eyes. "You've only been in the flesh here for a few hours and you're already about to alert the darkness of where they can find and injure you. Be wise, my brother. But I cannot shorten your learning curve, for to do that would be to rob you of some of your lessons. We are here to learn as much as we are to protect. The more we learn, the greater our effectiveness. We must know the pain of mortals to understand and have compassion for those we serve."

"I am aware of our mission and the rules of engagement. My apologies, old friend."

"As I said, *peace*. Then if you know the rules, you are aware that you must learn the language and customs of the tribe your Remnant hails from on your own, as each of us is here to search within the tribe of human manifestation we most identify with."

Duly chastised, Azrael's shoulders slumped and Gavreel smiled.

"Take heart, old friend. Should demons attack again, I am there at your side in battle as I have been for millennia. Beside death is always peace, when there is order in the cosmos."

"But how will we—"

Gavreel laughed and began walking away. "You sound like a mortal—many questions and short on faith, O dealer of death. Your powers will strengthen as you adjust to this hostile environment. I didn't intervene earlier because, even though I knew you had the strength to defeat the enemy, *you* needed to know that you did. It was good to see you rush in, not even knowing if you could prevail. But you did so on behalf of those souls that touched your heart. For every act of kindness, your strength in this realm will increase. You're not alone. They sent many of us down here and I'll know where to find you, just as you'll know where to find me. You will hear me and I will hear you, in time."

"Our wings . . ."

"Are not necessary here and would ruin the human disguise," Gavreel said quietly. "I was told that what is created in the spirit cannot be taken away in the flesh. . . . They are still there, I suppose, in our auras. This density is deceiving. See yourself as whole in your mind. Do not dwell on the loss. We have much work to do and grieving will steal your peace."

"You do not sound sure . . . and I do not fully remember

all that I was told." Azrael released a breath of frustration. "The adjustment period is . . ."

"More difficult than imagined." Gavreel nodded. "But it will ebb. Connect to human centers of learning, and once you connect to your Remnant, your disorientation should ebb . . . I am told. I have not located mine yet."

Azrael nodded and then jogged forward to catch up to Gavreel, stopping his retreat. "It is strange. I remember ancient history, like the names of the fallen—the names of our enemies, yet I do not know the very basics of this plane."

"Short-term memory loss," Gavreel said flatly. "Happens when they configure us for a human body." He shrugged with a half smile. "But remembering who can cause you great pain and injury is not a bad thing to have instant recall about, true?"

"Truth," Azrael said, clasping Gavreel's hand in a warrior handshake. "Then, have you encountered Asmodeus?"

"No, and pray that you do not meet up with that archdemon while on your mission, brother. He is fully consumed by the temporal world . . . the name he has chosen in this culture is Nathaniel, the literal translation meaning 'gift of God'—arrogant! Be on guard. His watchers are many, and Forcas, our fallen brother who rules the province of invisibility for the demons now, has joined his legion and is always lurking in the shadows. Asmodeus is also guarded by Lahash, the one who interferes with Divine will; as well as Pharzuph, a principality of lust; plus Malpas, who appears as a crow; and Appollyon of destruction. Six strong fallen and their legions will be set against you. Remain ever alert."

"That is good to know. You are a trusted friend."

Gavreel nodded. "As are you. I only arrived here a human week prior to your manifestation. Thus, I am still learning as well. Seek Bath Kol, our brother of prophecy, to maintain your peace. I have offered you as much as I am allowed tonight. I cannot even tell you where to begin your search for him. Trapped here on earth as a Sentinel, he is in constant motion for good reason. Every passing day he grows weaker to the temptation of an ultimate fall . . . always test him when you encounter him, brother. He may not be himself by the time you reach him. His choice is unknowable until you face him, and every encounter with him requires shrewd discernment on your part. That is the risk; but our Sentinel brothers are very wise about this world, indeed." Gavreel seemed sad as he started walking again.

"Indeed," Azrael said, following him. The thought of being trapped on earth as a Sentinel for all of eternity because he'd violated Divine Law sent a shiver through him. Sentinels had been on earth twenty-six thousand years, since the last battle against the darkness, and because they fell victim to the temptations of the planet, namely lying with human females and siring children, they were now banished from ever returning home.

The two angels shared a meaningful look filled with understanding.

"Don't get trapped here, my brother," Gavreel said in a quiet tone. "You know the rules. Get to your target, complete your mission, and get out. The longer you're in this human body, the harder it will be to stay focused, and the easier it will be to slip and fall."

"Thank you, brother. Godspeed on your mission as well."

"*De nada;* it is nothing, but you're welcome." Gavreel stopped and turned, holding Azrael's gaze. "Haven't you wondered yet why the Angel of Death was sent here in this location, along with me, the Angel of Peace? Why here, in this place called Philadelphia of the United States, and not the highly contested for Holy Land that the humans call the Middle East? Would that not seem to be a more logical place for death and peace to manifest side by side?"

Azrael rubbed the nape of his neck. The questions left him mute but lit a torch to the edges of his mind.

"You look hungry, thirsty, and weary, *sí?*"

"*Sí?* Wait . . . that is Spanish. Just like the words *de nada*."

Gavreel nodded with a smile. "Yes—*sí? Comprende?* Understand? The human-world languages will start to adhere to your human mind. The first one to come in like a baby's teeth is the one your chosen speaks. Patience, brother. It is the very basis of peace."

Azrael nodded. "Yes. You, above all, would know how to maintain one's peace. I stand humbled in your wise presence. Thank you for your counsel. And it is true that I am feeling the effects of being in this uncomfortable human form. No flight . . . no instant anything. Every little detail of movement bound by the physical."

Gavreel laughed. "Ah, yes, gravity and what the mortals aptly call physics. These are the laws of manifest matter. You will get used to it. Go have a cool drink of wine for a few human resources called dollars at the human watering hole they call a bar. I see you have already adopted their clothing, although you could use a longer pair of pants and a bigger pair of shoes." Gavreel's smile widened. "I take it you have resources?"

"Yes," Azrael admitted slowly. "I will use the human dollars to make the raiment adjustments soon."

"Clothes," Gavreel said, underscoring the new word for Azrael. He then pointed to his feet. "Shoes . . . this variety of foot apparel is called sneakers, sometimes referred to by the maker's name as well. Pick up the human slang quickly so you do not stand out. Camouflage and blend in. That will help both you and your chosen survive demon incursion."

Azrael heard Gavreel's warning but was still thoroughly fascinated by the name he'd seen beneath the maker's mark inside his shoe when he'd put it on. "Ni . . . ke—is then the maker this would be named for . . . what I would ask for when I required a new pair? How is this pronounced?"

"Nike—pronounced *Ny-Keee,*" Gavreel said, laughing. "By the way, your entire foot should comfortably fit into them, not hang out the back as though it were a slipper or sandal. Think back on the original owner's way of wearing them, and you must find your size, albeit difficult."

"Clothes . . . and shoes. Sneakers." Again Azrael nodded, thinking back on how the boys' pants lapped over the cloth strings in their shoes and how their sneakers fit over their entire foot. Gavreel was right; even their coat sleeves reached the full length of their arms. The boys were much smaller than he in length, breadth, and height. He would make the adjustment as soon as he could, now that he had resources—dollars. "I will amend my choices."

"Good. You will also need to rest, though not as much as the mortals, and eat *clean* food and drink plenty of *clean* water, or you'll be sick as a dog. Do not ask me how I know this. Everything that smells good and appeals to the human eye or palate is not necessarily good for this body temple we briefly inhabit. There is a bar not far down that street, but go easy on the wine without food. In fact, you may want to avoid the wine altogether and just have some water there until you can eat." Gavreel pointed out the direction, then turned and left Azrael to sort it out for himself.

Azrael stared after his brother Light warrior, watching him walk away into nothingness, knowing that his brother had asked him several questions laden with clues—trying to help answer his confusion without violating the rules by giving him all the answers. All warriors were to experience the human conditions of fear, confusion, learning, pain, hunger, emotion—all to become stronger and more compassionate for their charges and what the humans they were to guard had faced. He supposed even the loss of his wings was a part of the lesson. But to help him, his friend was teaching him in riddles, in the old form of the parable. Gavreel had also pointed out a haven; it was in his peaceful, intense eyes that simply said, *Trust me*.

Chapter 3

Celeste veered off Oxford to head down Jefferson Street, avoiding entire abandoned blocks of looming darkness. At this hour and in her condition, no one would suspect that she'd have money on her. That was her best defense to avoid a mugging—by looking like a crackhead. Everyone with an ounce of sense knew that pipers at this time of night who were trolling the streets were trying to hustle up more cash. Worse case, some hard up asshole might ask her if she wanted to make some money. But it wasn't as if they'd go to the trouble of grabbing her.

Still, roving bands of young males were as unpredictable as the feral pits. The last thing she wanted to be was the potential victim of a gang-bang initiation. That meant she couldn't go down the street as far as the towering projects where young guys gathered or over as far as Daniel Boone School, where the basketball courts and rec center would draw teens slinging dope all night.

A block-long, redbrick beacon stood out against the night. The bar's sign was missing and impenetrable steel grates were pulled down over all the windows, but the front door was open and the blare of R&B told her it was an old-head joint.

Perfect. Old-heads just wanted to get their drink and their swerve on. It was the young hip-hop crowd that always had beef in the streets about women and turf, or dumb shit like gang colors. Old-heads just wanted relief through life in a bottle.

Celeste entered the dark, narrow establishment and felt the smooth crooning of Isaac Hayes enter her bones. Cigarette smoke stung her eyes. She relaxed a little. This was obviously a place where the city's rules didn't apply, which meant authority was nonexistent, except for whoever manned the pump shotgun on the other side of the bar.

She quickly scanned the dimly lit surroundings. Black and red stools with some ripped seats showing pad innards; old Christmas-tree lights strung along the top of the walls added winking ambience. A blaring jukebox stood in the corner. Damn, she wanted a cigarette, and they had a machine. Good.

A few scattered round tables lined a grimy wall with animals-painted-on-velvet hangings. No off-duty cops, just as she suspected. She could smell old cooking oil wafting from the back—probably wings and shrimp and fries were available. That was also good, even though her stomach was a wreck. A few open seats; it wasn't crowded. If she put a twenty on the bar, they'd let her stay and drink and use the bathroom to clean up. Nobody here would see jack if the cops came looking for her. This place was safe. Celeste walked in deeper toward the bar.

"Yo, sis. Hol' up, hol' up. You gotta buy to stay," the hefty bartender said in a loud, no-nonsense tone, seeming more like a bouncer than a barkeep. "What you looking for we don't sell. Not up in here."

"You don't have vodka?" she replied with attitude, then pulled out a twenty and slapped it on the bar.

"My bad, sis," he said, taking up her cash and then running a marker over it to check it. "Smirnoff all right?"

"Yeah," Celeste muttered, and hoisted herself up on the stool. "And gimme some change for the cigarette machine." She grudgingly accepted her drink, collected her change, and angrily pushed a dollar tip toward the bartender.

"Like I said, my bad." He offered her a sheepish grin that she didn't return.

"Can I use the bathroom or I gotta pay for that, too?"

"No, pretty . . . you can use the restroom. I'll watch your drink. And if your ole man is hitting on you . . ."

"Yeah, whatever." Celeste knocked back the drink, feeling it burn on the way down, then slid off the barstool to go get a pack of smokes. "Set me up with another when I get back."

The bartender nodded with a smile and began cleaning a glass with a filthy rag. "Cool. I'll save you a seat."

She didn't answer him, just collected her Newports and matches, then headed down the narrow aisle toward the ladies' room, such as it was. Shoving her box of smokes in her pocket, she eased her way into the tight confines, hit the light, and locked the door behind her. What was supposed to be a mirror was a warped piece of metal whose sheen had long gone. God did answer some prayers.

Celeste bent and splashed cold water on her face and washed her hands without the benefit of soap. She let out a weary sigh. Of course there were no soap and no towels or toilet paper, what had she expected?

Using water, she smoothed her hair back from her face, adjusting her scrunchie with a wince as she tried to avoid the tender spot caused by the deep gash in the back of her head. At some point, she'd have it looked at, maybe . . . but not here, not in this city. She had to get as far away from Philly as possible. One more drink and she had to get a plan together. Buses ran to New York regularly for like eighteen bucks. From there she could figure out how to head north, maybe . . . or was it better to get lost in the dirty South?

"North," she murmured, wiping her hands down her jeans to dry them as she extracted a cigarette from the new pack, glad she no longer had to fight about something so simple.

She struck a match, leaning the tip of the butt into the flame, and pulled hard. Smoke filled her lungs, creating an instant buzz that the drink hadn't. She closed her eyes for a moment and let the smoke slowly filter out through her nose. Yeah . . . north was best. In the South you had to have a vehicle. If she headed to New York, she could get around on their public transit system and probably hop another bus that would take her somewhere like Buffalo or even out to Detroit—then she could cross over to Canada and be out . . . But not all on $80. "Shit!"

Frustration claimed her as she flung open the bathroom door with a cigarette between her lips. There was no way she could hang around Philly until her check came, and even when it did, the moment she and Aunt Niecey cashed it, the law would come down on both of them—which all got back to the point that she couldn't involve her aunt, who would then be an accessory to a fugitive's flight.

"Damn, damn, damn," Celeste muttered, and found her barstool.

The bartender slid her vodka straight-up and an ashtray; in here, no one cared about the smoking ban in bars. She pushed a ten in his direction, this time without a tip.

Azrael stood on the corner looking at the place that Gavreel had identified as a bar. It was suddenly difficult for him to breathe. Pain blossomed within his chest and spread through his limbs. It was a deep down soul cry that brought tears to his eyes. The urge to weep was so profound that he looked up toward the sky and blinked back the moisture and swallowed hard. He knew it was her; it was her soul signature that he felt. As the pain ebbed, knowing followed it. The things she'd been subjected to . . . the abuse. Demons had entered her father and pulled him into a vicious drug addiction; they had attacked her mother and finally killed the poor woman through a stroke. Hardship had plagued this young human female, giving her multiple guardian angels nearly more than they could handle—yet his side, the heavenly Light, was still covering her.

He walked into the bar and watched her slowly self-destructing on a barstool, adding toxins to her already overburdened body. Soon, her human liver and kidneys and lungs would fail. Her mind was already teetering on the brink of mental collapse. Men had used her body until it had been left a limp rag. Her pretty cocoa brown face was bruised, her once even lush mouth swollen and her lip was split. Her hair was thin and brittle from years of poor diet and stress, plus what was left of it was wild and matted with blood. From the haggard look of her dirty clothes, it was clear that she'd been in a physical struggle. She'd been beaten and attacked and practically held hostage in her own home. Azrael briefly closed his eyes. The forces of darkness were insidious and experts at torture. But they could no longer have this one. Not on his watch.

Brooding over her drink, Celeste sipped it slowly between long drags on her cigarette. No one bothered her. Everyone here seemed to be in the same state of mind, working out problems too massive to handle. The only thing that changed was the music as a new song dropped, this time Marvin Gaye. A body slid into the open barstool beside her and she didn't even look up until he ordered water.

Celeste lifted her head and froze. The guy's complexion was too clear and his jaw military-square. This was a cop if ever she saw one.

"Water—that's all?" the bartender said in a skeptical tone. "Bottled or outta the tap, man?"

"The cleanest," the man beside her said, staring at her now.

Celeste took another drag off her cigarette and started to climb down off her stool.

"Those will kill you, you know," the stranger said.

"So I've read on the warning label." She was out of there.

"Don't leave. You have nowhere to go."

She froze. Damn . . .

He picked up her glass and sniffed it. "This isn't water."

"No shit, Sherlock," she muttered, and eased her way back onto the barstool. What was the use of running to get tased or shot? If she'd been made, then so be it. Resisting arrest wasn't gonna do much good.

"This doesn't help you. Why do you do it?"

She let out a hard breath. "Helps my nerves. And what?"

The bartender set a cold bottle of water down in front of the stranger. "Couple things: One, this costs just as much as a regular drink. We in business to serve liquor. Two, can't have you upsetting my paying customers, feel me? You making the lady nervous. So, if y'all got some domestic bullshit between you, take it outside—but while y'all up in here, know I got a peacekeeper for anything that might jump off. We clear?" The barkeep looked at Celeste. "You want another drink, baby?"

"No. Thanks," she said calmly. "I was just leaving, if that's okay with him?"

She watched the cop pull out a huge wad of bills and slide a C-note across the bar.

"You ain't got nothing smaller than that?" the bartender argued. "You ain't gotta come up in here flashing."

Something wasn't right. She watched the guy with the

bankroll look down at it, seeming confused as he pulled the rubber band off of it and laid it out on the bar.

"Pick the denomination that is appropriate," the stranger said in a pleasant tone.

Celeste watched as the bartender sifted through what had to be several thousand dollars to find a five.

"You ain't have to be a comedian, man," the bartender said with an attitude.

She watched the cop's brow furrow with what seemed like a combination of confusion and annoyance. But the transaction gave her assessment time.

He was undercover, that was obvious, but badly so. His sneakers didn't fit; his fatigue-jacket sleeves were way too short. His pants were high-waters . . . but his long dreadlocks were salon immaculate, just as his smooth, dark-walnut-hued skin was flawless. His face was so handsome it made her want to squint. Plus, he was G.I. Joe fit . . . had to be like six-five, 220, all muscle and zero body fat. Long cords of sinew ran up his forearm and she watched it move, mesmerized by it, as he handed off his cash.

How they thought they could pass him off as some homeless dude in the hood was beyond her. His diction was too perfect, the whites of his eyes too clear, almost crystalline clear . . . and he smelled fresh, like a baby's newborn scent. For a few moments it was so weird that she couldn't stop staring at him. Regardless, she had to figure out a way to seem as if she were going along with him, then give him the slip.

As though he'd read her mind, the cop suddenly looked at her. "We need many more of these containers of water. She is dehydrated."

"No problem," the bartender said with a satisfied grin, and put five more bottles of water in front of the stranger, then took an obscene amount of cash for what could have been purchased for under ten bucks at a supermarket.

Celeste narrowed her gaze but said nothing. It wasn't even a name brand of water, some knockoff brand that was probably bottled tap. But what did she care? It wasn't her cash.

"Here," the weird cop said, handing her a couple of bottles as he stashed the rest in his huge jacket pockets and folded away his money. "This is better for you than what you've been drinking."

Wary, she accepted the offering without comment, surveying him with skepticism. Who was this dude and what did he want? Maybe he wasn't a cop. But he damned sure didn't seem like any drug dealer she'd seen—not dressed like that.

"You need to come with me. Let's step outside."

"Am I under arrest?" Celeste cocked her head to the side in a challenge. "Because if so, you need to start reading me my rights and I definitely want an attorney."

Rather than a snappy comeback, he seemed puzzled for a moment. "Let us leave this place. Too many earthbounds are here, too much low-frequency energy that draws the darkness. I also understand that I have not properly identified myself and you are right to be skeptical."

"*What?*" Still clutching her water bottles, she rested her fists on her hips. Just her luck to have been picked up by a dealer or some undercover dude who was strung out on his own shit. But it was a relief to know she wasn't going to be arrested. "You know the first rule is not to use your own product, right?"

"What is she speaking of?" the odd stranger asked the bartender, who was chuckling as though watching a sideshow.

"C'mon, son . . . my name is Bennett and I ain't in it." The rotund bartender just shook his head and wiped the bar off with the same rag he used to clean the glasses.

"Thanks for the waters," Celeste said, moving away from the bar. "You have a good night."

"Wait," the stranger said. "It's dangerous for you to be out there alone."

She hesitated and folded her arms over her chest, still holding on to the water he'd given her. "You're not from around here, are you?"

He shook his head.

Just what she needed, some foreign drug dealer or wannabe rookie cop trying to mack her. She wasn't sure which was worse, somebody looking for a green card or a cop.

"I don't need any money and I'm not no ho."

He frowned. "A what?"

"Whore, prostitute, trick—"

"Oh, no, no, you have misjudged my intentions in the most profound way. I am here to protect you. I am your angel."

"Okay . . . I'm out. That line is way too corny." Celeste spun on her heels and headed toward the door as several men at the bar as well as the bartender burst out laughing.

"But he's fine as hell, girl!" an old female barfly called out behind Celeste.

"You can be my angel with a bankroll and a body like that," another shouted behind them. "The young be missing their blessings—but I got something for you, daddy!"

Cool air pelted her face. Annoyance made it flush warm when she sensed him behind her. Of all the nights she couldn't cope with a crazy, it was tonight.

"I have no interest but ensuring your safety," he said, rounding her and stopping her progress down the dark block.

"I said to get out of my face. What part of I'm not interested didn't you hear?" Celeste shot back.

"But what about the demons? The one that choked you and hurt your head? I know what happened. I know it wasn't your fault. You have never taken a life."

She stopped and stared up at him. Now he had her attention.

"I am Azrael. You are Celeste. We must help each other." He looked down at his clothing. "I am poorly dressed, and in order to help you, I need to look like I belong to your tribe. Will you help me?"

"Why are you fucking with my head?" she asked in a lethal whisper. "If you heard or saw what happened at my apartment and think you can blackmail me, you've got more money in your pocket than I could ever dream of . . . and if you want a booty call, with the cash you're carrying, you can hire a very enthusiastic pro. The gentlemen's clubs are—"

"I don't want a prostitute, I want you."

"Excuse me?"

"No, no, no," he said quickly, now gesturing with his hands as he spoke. "My use of the language is still imperfect. I am not trying to garner sex from you or lure you into an untoward proposition. You would *never* have to fear that from me."

Celeste closed her eyes for a second, then let out a weary sigh. A foreign gay man wanted a wardrobe consultation in the middle of the night, or else he'd go to the cops? *Only in America.*

"Are you serious?" Celeste opened her eyes and considered the plaintive look on the handsome man's face. Now some of his immaculate appearance made sense. "And, like, none of your, uh, brothers in the family would help you get fly?"

Azrael shook his head no. "I can no longer fly and my brothers cannot help me do that."

She looked at him for a moment, wondering what country he was from. He didn't get any slang.

"Wow . . . that's cold," she said after a moment. "I thought all the kids—you know, gay guys—stuck together, just sayin'. But then again, what do I know? Sorry for stereotyping. My bad." She let out another weary breath. "But it's really not cool to try to use something against somebody to get them to help you."

"I would *never* do that to you, Celeste. And I am not happy at all . . . why would I be gay about something as serious as this?"

She shook her head and waved off his misunderstanding of what she'd meant. It didn't matter anyway. She had more important questions. "How do you know my name? Were you a friend of Brandon's?"

"I was not his enemy, but I was certainly not his friend." Azrael folded his arms over his stone-cut chest. "I did not approve of the way he treated you, and his use of inebriants opened him to the portals of darkness. A spirit attachment easily latched on . . . then it climbed inside him. There wasn't enough Light within him to repel it. He is lost and that is always a sad thing . . . always a waste."

"Wait a minute," she said quietly, backing away. "You really do believe in . . ."

"Yes," Azrael said without shame. "I told you, I am your angel. We all work for humankind—those of us who have not fallen. In this, the end of days, we must all surrender the darkness within to allow the Light to prevail. Even some of us have not made it."

Celeste turned and began running. This dude was crazier than she was! But he caught up to her, calmly jogging beside her as she ran as fast as she could.

"We should find hallowed ground to rest," he said.

She darted down a desolate street and he was right on her flank.

"Who do you think sent the dogs? It was not the darkness, but the Light."

She stopped running, winded, and simply stared at him.

"The Light heard your cry. You wanted to end the glorious gift called life. Your guardian angels—and, yes, you are blessed to have more than one of them—sent two half-starved animals to save you. We must pray for the poor beast that gave his life. The male, sadly, got hit by a metal vehicle. And . . . you have two women who love you dearly—your mother and your aunt, and they pray—"

"Stop with the bullshit!" Celeste shrieked, tears streaming down her face and not knowing why. "My mother is dead!"

"I know," he said in a gentle tone, touching her cheek, but she shrugged away. "You were only twelve."

"Right. I was only twelve, so if you're gonna run game on me—"

"This is not a game, Celeste. It is deadly serious. You are one of the chosen. The Remnant. Your mother is in spirit and still watches over you. Demons attacked her. She didn't have a stroke from natural causes, nor was she mentally ill. And you are not mentally ill, either . . . what you have seen is real."

Fighting back a sob, Celeste stared at this strange man. "Then what do you want from me? First I thought you were a dealer, then a cop, then some gay dude wanting me to buy women's clothes for him—"

"I want us to get out of the danger of the streets. Can you lead us to a temple, a mosque, a church, somewhere there is protective Light for the night?"

"Look around," she said in a sad, far-off tone. "Every two to three blocks there's a church or a mosque, but things are so bad the doors are locked."

"I have the keys," he said, his voice a gentle balm. "No door can be locked against me, especially not where humans come together to pray to the Source of All That Is."

She released a sad, sarcastic chuckle as she wiped at her face with the backs of her wrists, still holding fast to the water he'd given her. "Take your pick around here. We're short on temples, synagogues, or Catholic cathedrals in this end of town, but you can probably find a Pentecostal church, Seven-Day Adventist, Baptist, AME, Jehovah's Witness, or pick any masjid or mosque."

"The one closest would be best."

With her shoulders slumped in resignation she trudged ahead of the strange man who was even crazier than she was, but who had nonetheless struck a nerve. Might as well take him where he wanted to go.

"Tell me, Celeste, why is it so easy for you to believe demons exist but not a being like me? You even saw a demon take a man's life . . . the trauma is still in your aura. I can read that as if it is an open book. Thus, would it not stand to reason that, if there is extreme darkness, there must also be extreme light? Yet when I tell you I am an angel, you doubt."

She stopped on the steps of a large Baptist church, the nearest sanctuary she could find.

"Because, for one, if you haven't noticed, miracles aren't an everyday occurrence around here. And, two, I thought angels had wings. And because people just don't walk up and say, 'Hey, I'm your angel and I'm gonna make all your troubles fade away.'"

His expression became sad. "Miracles are an everyday occurrence down here . . . but humans do not understand what a miracle is any longer." He reached up and rubbed his shoulders. "Angels do have wings in the upper realms of Light. Here . . . they don't." He turned toward the door and rested both palms against it. "And we cannot make all your troubles fade away because of the free-choice rule . . . we can only offer a defense against the darkness. Sometimes we can save a life, heal a body, turn around a bad situation, or reveal the truth—but we must be called upon by you in order to act. We are your servants. That is what the war was about in the beginning. Some of us disagreed with our role in relationship to humankind."

Celeste jumped back as his palms began to glow with blue-white light against the door. Within seconds the lock clicked and then the door gently creaked open.

"Come," he said. "Do not be afraid. We will refresh ourselves with food and water here, and if you will allow me to tend your wound, I will."

Chapter 4

Celeste stood just inside the door of the sanctuary, coaxed in by the fear of demons and the human authorities that were no doubt searching for her, but now terrified to be trapped inside with the strange man or entity that was before her.

"How did you do that thing with your hands?" she asked breathlessly.

"Intent," he said. "All intention is energy; energy moves the atoms of the material world. This is why thought is so important. What we believe can be made manifest. What we speak is a vibration. Thought and sound are a harmonic convergence."

" 'First there was the word and the word was God ...,' " Celeste murmured, staying close to the door.

"Yes."

The being didn't elaborate as he walked deeper into the building. He just stopped for a moment, closed his eyes, took a deep breath, and released a soft sigh. "You said there may be food here . . . and possibly other resources."

"This is deep," Celeste replied under her breath. "A freakin' angel stealing from a church. Go figure."

Azrael tilted his head. "Are not the houses of worship supposed to feed the hungry and clothe the poor? Isn't all that they collect to be in the service of humankind?"

"Yeah, so they say . . . but I guess you haven't seen televangelists. That's just my politics, what can I say."

Becoming convinced that the man before her meant her no harm, she pointed to the alarm box by the door. "That should have gone off. Could be a silent one calling the cops as we speak, so whatever you need from here you'd better hurry up and get it, then be out."

Azrael shrugged. "I am not here as a thief nor are you, therefore no alarm should sound."

"Yeah, well, if po-po shows up, I'm out, and I suggest you follow my lead. You'd better hope they haven't paid their bill and that's why bells aren't ringing." Edging away from the wall, she glanced around. "The sanctuary is that way, nothing there but books and the altar . . . usually all the 'resources'" she added, making air quotes with her fingers, "are in the basement or in the office."

"Show me . . . please."

She stared at him for a moment, distrustful but considering. "I don't think you'll find your size in the clothing-donation bins they probably have. What are you . . . like six-four, six-five? What size shoe do you wear?"

"I do not know." His expression became pained. "When we come into the flesh, we come as a member of the tribe of the one we seek, but also are formed from the energy our essence emits."

"Wait, so you're still trying to tell me that this is the first time you've been—"

"Incarnate, yes . . . although I came to earth before to battle, but not hampered by human form. Why are my words so doubtful to you? I have done nothing to show myself as a liar."

Celeste shrugged and thrust a bottle of water under her arm, twisting off the cap of the other bottle. She took a deep sip, then screwed the top back on. "It isn't you. Don't get your boxers in a bunch. I'm just not sure that I haven't had my final nervous breakdown and this isn't all some psychotic-break trip. Like, who sees demons and angels? Just saying. Besides, I did bump my head—or rather had the living shit knocked out of it."

"In time I hope to earn your trust," he said quietly. "Let us be hopeful and search the donations."

His forlorn tone almost made her feel sorry for him. Almost. But she kept him in front of her, pointing the way down the dark stairs, just in case he was a lunatic. However, the thing that made her timidly follow him was the low, resonant hum and blue-white light that seemed to frame his body as he walked into the complete darkness.

"Whoa . . ." Her voice was a low rush of awe. With the streetlights on outside she hadn't noticed the eerie illumination, nor had she seen it in the bar. She hadn't even noticed it just inside the foyer, as the streetlights and moonlight made a pool of light where he stood—but now the light was coming from him.

She rubbed her eyes and held on to the banister, staying several steps behind him as they reached the bottom landing. He crossed the floor, then with a wave of his hand the basement lights came on.

"These donations, where would they be?"

Celeste just stared at him, staying near the exit in case she had to bolt. "What are you?"

"I have already told you who I am as well as what I am." He frowned, folding his arms.

"Okay . . . then if you really are an angel, have you ever met . . . you know," she asked just above a whisper while pointing toward the ceiling. "Him?"

"Him?"

She relaxed and walked across the open rec-room floor. "Figured you were just messing with my head. If you don't know who the big Him is, then stop playing. You ain't no angel." She went to a series of plastic bins stacked in the corner, trying to see if there was any rhyme or reason to the way they'd sorted the secondhand clothes.

"Celeste, the Source of All That Is cannot be defined as male or female. The Source is both, is all . . . and, no, only the most evolved of us have ever been in that Ultimate Light." He looked off into the distance, staring at nothing in particular, then closed his eyes. "The peace that fills you, even in the most remote reaches of that Light . . . the love that surrounds and bathes you, I cannot describe."

"Then what are you doing down here in this hell—by comparison," she asked offhandedly, setting her water on the floor and hunting through the bins, discarding children's gear and old-lady dresses until she found men's clothes.

"Searching for you—one who can sway the balance."

"Yeah, okay," she muttered, rummaging through old-men's suits and ties. She stood and let out a huff of breath. "You gonna stand there or help, O cosmic one?"

"Why do you mock me?"

"Aw, don't be so melodramatic. I'm not mocking you. If you say you're an angel, then cool. You're an angel. I'm supposed to be on meds, and when I'm not, I see a lot of weird shit. So I accept who I am. Embrace your inner nut job and see if there's anything here that'll fit."

He came closer, but then turned away with tears in his eyes.

"What's the matter?" Celeste shook her head. "For the love of Pete . . . Okay, I'm sorry if I hurt your feelings. You're not crazy. All right?"

"It is not your words. It is what has happened to the owners of these clothes. The donations of male clothing . . . these men have died. Old men . . . but they do not disturb me, nor do the donations from the elderly women. That is the cycle of life—the widows or widowers bring in the raiment of their husbands and wives so that others in need may have them. That is good. But the far bin. Do not open it. Young boys . . . adolescents. Murdered by other boys in the prime of their lives. I cannot understand."

Beyond freaked-out, Celeste slowly dropped the clothes she'd been holding and went to the far bins. She watched the stranger named Azrael walk away and place a palm against the wall and drop his head. Tears streamed down his handsome face as he squeezed his eyes shut. She popped the top on a bin and pulled out a basketball jersey, then a pair of jeans, then a FUBU jacket. Everything her hands landed on was an article of clothing that could have been worn by any young urban male.

"Please, Celeste," Azrael whispered. "Can we go from this place to somewhere not filled with so much heartbreak? Mother's tears have stained each garment. I cannot wear any of it. All those boys shot by one another . . . and for what? Foolish disagreements, egos, for territory that they could never truly own."

"You're an empath," she said in amazement, closing the bin and staring at him as he wiped his face with broad palms. "I saw it on a show once . . . about people who have special extrasensory gifts."

"We're all empaths where I was made."

She nodded. "Deep. All right. Maybe drink some water or something."

He let out a long, weary sigh and pushed away from the wall, then dug a water bottle out of his pocket and opened it, then downed it. "The angels wept in Heaven, and now I know why," he murmured, opening the second water and downing it in a long guzzle.

"When's the last time you ate?"

"Never," he said calmly.

She sighed again and picked up one of her water bottles from the floor, opened it, and took several sips. "They have a soup kitchen, a food mission, here. I could go find us some grub if you want?"

"It must be clean, like the water."

"Oh . . . my God . . . a vegan."

"Don't use any of the names of the Source of All That Is in vain," Azrael said in a soft murmur. "Please. To call that much power should be for a good reason."

"My bad. I respect whatever your belief system is. My aunt always says that, too." Celeste finished her water, then picked up the second bottle to save for later. "Look, this is a food mission and a round-the-way Baptist church. Dollars to doughnuts, they've collected a bunch of canned goods from folks who are poor themselves, have white flour, white refined sugar, low-grade cuts of meat in the freezer, if they have that. This is the kinda place where women like my aunt Niecey come and cook for the people who are poorer than the food donors out of love and duty, but it's not gonna be politically correct vegan fare, feel me? Expect mac and cheese, collards, chicken, and nothing organic. This isn't Whole Foods. There will be chemicals in it, plenty of processed goods loaded with sodium, preservatives, pesticides, and whatever else—but guaranteed those old dolls will make it taste so good you won't care. So your choices are these: Either wait for the morning when we can go downtown or let me see what's in the pantry that I can nuke."

"I must have clean food," he said, lifting his chin. "So must you so that your light remains strong."

"Brother, I have never been a vegetarian or vegan and have more chemicals in my system than the law allows, literally. Which reminds me, I could really use a smoke, so can we go now?"

"Will you let me heal you first?"

"I need stitches, your hands are dirty, and I'm really not feeling going into a bathroom with a guy I don't know, especially if there's mirrors. Don't ask; it's a long story."

"I will cleanse my hands thoroughly and promise you no harm."

"Bathroom's over there, judging from the sign above that doorway. I'm going outside for a smoke. If you're not out by the time I finish my Newport, then it's been nice meeting you. With everything going wrong in my life, I cannot take care of a disoriented foreign dude and risk getting blamed for breaking into a church on top of everything else—I ain't hating, I'm just being real. You seem like a really nice guy . . . one with a lot of problems, but who am I to talk?"

"I will not be long."

"Yeah, whatever."

Celeste fled up the steps without looking back, crossed the wide foyer, and slipped outside into the cool night air. She tucked a bottle of water under her arm and dug out her pack of smokes, pulled one out, and lit it.

What the hell was she doing? This guy wasn't a cop and definitely had a screw loose. Fine as all get out, too—which made it all the more of a shame. But he wasn't her problem. She had major issues of her own, yet she was wasting time hanging out in a church, listening to a story that was so bizarre it made her condition almost seem normal. Then again, the brief stint she'd spent in a psych ward had already shown her there were worse cases than hers.

Celeste took another long drag on her cigarette and began walking. Her life was so jacked up. "Good-bye, Mr. Fine Crazy Angel," she muttered as she crossed the street. "I wonder how many tours of duty you did in Iraq to wind up like this?"

"Only one," a now familiar deep voice said next to her. "But that was a long time ago and the region was called by a different name."

Celeste jumped and began violently coughing. "Oh, shit! Don't do that! I didn't even hear you roll up on me!"

"The water helped," Azrael said calmly. My body needed it to start to adjust. Can we find the place that sells clean food without poisons?"

"Whole Foods is closed, dude," Celeste said, still coughing, then flung her cigarette butt down. "They definitely have an alarm and paid their bill *and* keep their lights on all night."

"I can get us in and have money to pay for what we eat. We will not abuse the hospitality of that way station."

"Dude," Celeste said, growing annoyed. She opened her water and took a long sip to help her stop coughing. "That's all the way downtown on like Twenty-second and the Parkway."

"Can we take the train . . . or those large carriages that stop at the corners?"

"A bus. Yeah. But—"

He held out a yellow blouse and a Windbreaker to her. "Let me heal your wound," he said in a gentle tone. "Come back into the church, bathe so you feel better. There are clean clothes there that will fit you. In the pastor's office is a well that runs water. My word as my bond, I will never harm you."

She just looked at his outstretched hand for a moment and slowly took the clothes offering, but still kept her distance. This had the ring of a really cheesy horror movie to it, and it was definitely how serial killers operated. No way was she going to be the stupid chick that trusted the handsome stranger.

"If you can heal my head *out here* without hurting me,

then I'll see about going back in there for a shower. Deal?"

He nodded. "You are right to test me in this, the end of days. I accept your shrewd discernment."

She finished her water and tossed the bottle into a pile of trash, noting his slight frown. "What?" She put both hands on her hips. "They don't have recycle cans anywhere nearby, if you haven't noticed."

"They do inside the church. Respect this planet. It is one of the greatest gifts that—"

"Okay, okay, I get it." She picked the bottle up off the ground. "You green people so get on my nerves. I don't see what my one little bottle could hurt."

He stared at the trash-strewn street and held out his hand until she gave him the bottle, which he quickly shoved into one of his deep pockets. "It would appear that no one here thought their one little bit of refuse would hurt either. Just as so many do not realize how the actions of one person can make a difference." He looked at her with his intense gaze. "Celeste, you can make a difference."

Celeste rolled her eyes, then shook her head. "You are really working my last nerve, brother. So, what's this healing thing you can do?"

"May I have permission to touch the site of the injury?"

She looked at his hands. "Yeah, I guess so, but go easy, all right? That sucker hurts like the devil."

"Do not mention the Unnamed One," Azrael said, glancing over his shoulder as he walked toward her. "It would be better to be inside on hallowed ground."

"No dice. I want to be outside if you put your hands on me."

"Very well," he said in a patient tone, then placed one hand on her forehead and the other gently at the back of her head, cupping it.

She stared at him, watching his dark eyes as he held her head. They seemed so sad, so filled with empathy that she wanted to weep and wasn't sure why. Soon a slight tingle radiated along her scalp, making it itch as a low, buzzing sound filled her ears. Fatigue suddenly made her legs wobbly as the warmth that covered her scalp slowly spilled down her arms and along her back and breastbone, flowing down her limbs until the tips of her fingers and toes tingled.

Out of nowhere a bitter sob broke free. She couldn't breathe as wave after wave of emotional pain roiled inside her, followed by acute nausea. All of the suppressed memories came back with a vengeance. She could remember each body blow, actually feel each viperous word that was ever shouted at her as though she'd been stabbed. Suddenly, just seeing herself smoke or knock back straight vodka made her want to hurl. It was all coming back, coming up, coming out. She wanted to scream and cry at the same time. But more than anything, she wanted this ugly review of her life to stop.

"Get off me!" she shrieked, twisting to get away, but he held her fast and kept his voice steady.

"Give me all the pain, Celeste—everything they did to you, give it all to me."

Crying and pulling against a hold that she could not break, finally she just held on to his shoulders and wept. "I'm just so damned tired."

"I know," he whispered, then suddenly hugged her to

him hard, resting his cheek against the crown of her head.
"I promise you I will not harm you or forsake you. I will
be your Light until your inner light is repaired. Lean on
me, ask of me, I am here to serve you."

She yanked away and hurled on the pavement, heaving up only bile and vodka.

"Let the poison come out," he said calmly, rubbing her
back. "We will go get more water, after you bathe. The
addictions are gone. Throw away the smoke poison, too.
The cigarettes."

She stood slowly and slapped his face. Then she
quickly backed up, expecting him to punch her. "Who
the fuck gave you the right to do whatever you just did
to me!"

"You gave me permission to heal you, so I did. It all
had to come out, not just the physical wounds but all the
harm done to you emotionally and mentally . . . and spiritually. I pulled the sickness out of your emotional, mental,
physical, and etheric bodies. The cut on your scalp was the
least of what was wrong."

"I'm out. Don't follow me. Get away from me," she
said, flinging the clothes on the ground.

"Many times mortals are so used to the pain that it
frightens them when it is gone. Feel your head. The cut
is sealed. All that remains is the dried blood. It is the same
with the wounds on your spirit."

"That is bull . . ." Celeste's words trailed off as her fingers slowly tested her scalp.

Carefully removing the blood-soaked scrunchie, she
allowed her hair to fall to her shoulders, then parted back
sections of it, sure that she would find a deep gash. After

several minutes of thoroughly separating crusted clumps of hair only to find unbroken skin, her hands fell to her sides.

"There's no cut."

"No . . . it's been sealed."

Again she stared at him for several long moments. "Why did I get sick?"

"The poisons had to come out."

"The alcohol and nicotine . . . meds and food toxins?"

He nodded. "The more poisons that are in the body, the harder it is for the higher vibrations and messages from the divine to reach you or for you to reach them." He paused for a moment, appearing to struggle for the right words to make her understand.

"The human spirit is pure ether, Celeste. But the human mind and body function on billions of nonstop electrical currents and chemical reactions . . . and everything on the planet that is living has an electromagnetic pulse or life signature. Even the earth and every planet and heavenly body has a signature pulse—a sound that we can pick up on. That's how we also know that this bountiful planet is sick and dying. When that pulse is muted or weighed down by corrosive toxins, it takes much longer for the signal to reach the upper realms of light. It also makes it difficult for the human mind to interpret angels' voices trying to give you guidance and assistance. This is why the dark side wants humans to weigh themselves down with toxic waste."

"So . . . a prayer is sort of like a satellite signal? And if we're polluted with toxins, any messages we receive will be like the static on an off channel on the radio or digital dropout on cable TV?"

He paused. "I am not sure of this satellite you speak of . . . or about a radio and TV device you mention? But your prayers and wishes and thoughts are an electromagnetic signal, yes. A pulse of energy. So, when someone with a very strong signal sends up a request or a group sends it up in unison, then it gets to us faster. When two or more—"

"'Are gathered in His name . . . ,'" Celeste murmured, staring at the strange man before her.

He nodded. "Correct. Conversely, when someone with less biological, mental, spiritual, or emotional interference becomes still in meditation, they can hear us more clearly."

"Yeah, well, your so-called healing hurt like hell," she whispered. "Not my body, but . . ."

"Your spirit had been so damaged, Celeste," he said quietly. "What they did was so wrong. The only thing they weren't allowed to commit outright was your direct murder, but there are a thousand ways to kill a human spirit and to make that person either slowly or quickly destroy themselves."

"You keep saying they. Who—Brandon, the men before him, the doctors, the—"

"The demons. Dark-consciousness entities and elementals, dark principalities, those whom we have waged war against since time immemorial. You are a key that fits a lock that they seek to open." His voice was low and serious and his eyes never left hers. "We should go onto hallowed ground for this conversation. You should shampoo your hair and completely change clothes to feel renewed. I will go into a nearby store and get the appropriate clothes and shoes, which I will leave money for on the counter.

We will not steal. Then we will catch a cab to the place to eat without poisons . . . and then we will go to your aunt Niecey's home to allow her mind to be at peace and to put an additional protective barrier around the good fortress of spirit she's already erected. We shall sleep there for the night. A veil of protection will keep the human authorities from her door. Then we shall seek Bath Kol."

"Your voice sounds different . . . you're speaking like you know the city now—I don't understand. How do you know my aunt! Who are you really?" Celeste bit her lip and held her head with her hands, feeling both confused and terrified.

Azrael stepped closer to her and cupped her cheek with a warm, gentle palm. "There is no need to fear me. I am only different now that I've been given permission to touch your aura as well as your body temple by the laying on of hands . . . and now that you've invited my spirit to help yours. Healing always helps both the giver and the receiver. We are both stronger now for it. Your knowledge is my knowledge, just as down inside the deepest core of who you are . . . you now know who I am. And there's no turning back from that truth."

Chapter 5

Street-survival instinct warred with the gut-level trust she now oddly possessed. The two internal compasses had violently dueled since the stranger named Azrael had crossed her path. Now another variable entered the fray—the incredibly weird sensation of being crystal clear in thought.

Powerful emotions roiled within her as she walked next to the man who called himself an angel. Fury was the first thing to surface; if demons had actually plagued her life, had been the slithering monster within her father . . . enough to drive the man into an abyss of addiction . . . if they had killed her mother and entered Brandon . . . if these beasts had invaded her life and plagued her aunt Niecey with illness and arthritis, then she wanted every single last one of them blown to smithereens!

Guilt quickly followed when she thought back on all the things she'd done that she wasn't proud of. But it seemed so much easier, then, to numb the pain with whatever inebriant she could get her hands on. But knowing that she'd been played by the dark side made her get angry all over again, angry enough to cry.

"It's going to be all right," he said, not looking at her and keeping his eyes fastened on the church ahead. "This I promise you, Celeste."

She wiped at her tears in angry, jerky motions but said nothing. Something in the tone of his voice, the sureness with which he'd made the comment, made her want to sob. But she refused to allow him to see her do that again, even though she'd never in her life had a guy tell her it was going to be all right—and made her feel that it was anything but a sweet lie told just to get into her panties. This was something different . . . something strange and way out of her field of comprehension. She hadn't been clean since she was a kid, and the newness of that alone was making her hands shake. Being numb was a shield, had always been her trusty crutch. Now she felt vulnerable and exposed, a state much more terrifying than walking through life in her previous half-zombie state.

Celeste wrapped her arms around herself as she walked down the street. When she was a kid, not having anything in her system such as drugs and alcohol meant she could see what others couldn't see. She wanted to be blind to the demons, didn't want to see dead people or any other crazy shit that normal people didn't see. How was that some fucking gift?

Plus, it didn't make sense to rely so heavily on what she felt, given the many mistakes she'd made in her life, trusting her so-called gut. Yet she found the lure to follow

Azrael back into the church too great to resist. Somehow she wound up down in the basement again, this time hunting and pecking through the clean women's clothes in the donation bins for something more her taste, as though she were at a Saturday flea market.

He was also right about one thing: A level of clarity within her told her he wasn't violent or sick, even if she still wasn't sure about the whole angel bit. For certain, he was a healer . . . maybe a crazy psychic dude or an empath that saw himself as an angel, she wasn't sure. But she was sure that he wouldn't harm her, and from some deep reservoir of survival instinct within, she knew that as solidly as she knew her name, even though she wasn't sure why.

Celeste glimpsed him from the corner of her eye as she picked through the donations bins. It felt so odd not to be slightly buzzed. The jaded part of her wanted to laugh at the irony that being straight felt as if she were high, and being high felt as if she were straight. This was some backward, script-flipped *Alice in Wonderland* crap if she ever felt it.

Clean jeans in her arms along with a light gray sweater, a pair of socks, and an unopened pack of new panties from the underwear bin, she stared at Azrael, who had thankfully kept his distance.

"I will be in the sanctuary in meditation," he said quietly. "Seek me there once you have bathed."

"Okay," she said in an unsure tone, and kept her eyes on him as she crossed the room, then turned and ran up the steps.

Flattening herself to the wall in the dark, she listened

hard for Azrael's footfalls, but relaxed somewhat when she didn't hear him come after her. With a bit of effort, she was able to enter the dimly lit sanctuary and follow the emergency exit lights back behind the side pews to the minister's private office.

The moment she entered the room, she clicked the lock behind her and pressed her back to the door with her eyes closed.

"Please, God, don't let me be a fool," she whispered. "Protect me from all harm. If nobody else in the world believes me, you know I didn't kill Brandon . . . and that I'm not trying to steal from the church or from a minister." She dug in her pocket and placed a crumpled ten and a few singles onto the minister's desk, then clicked on the desk lamp. "I don't know who this guy Azrael is or if he's some kind of freak or killer and if my internal radar is off, but if he is, please let me escape through a window again or something. Thank you, Amen."

Looking around nervously and listening hard, Celeste entered the private pastoral bathroom and turned on the light. For a moment she just gaped at the white-on-white tiles and full glass shower encased in white Italian marble. Every possible amenity greeted her, down to fluffy, white towels to shower gels and soaps. Gold-toned fixtures made her feel as if she were inside a five-star hotel. Even the toilet was pristine.

As she placed her loot down on the floor in a neat pile and shed her filthy clothes, she couldn't help but wonder why the office and bathroom were so well-appointed, while the rec room where children learned was ill equipped with old folding chairs and ancient blackboards, a piecemeal offering of dusty books on the shelves, and linoleum square tiles that were cracked and peeling.

Celeste turned on the water and shut off her mind, listening for potential danger, which didn't come barging in. The hard pelt of warm water felt so good, the fragrant lather almost brought tears to her eyes as she washed dried blood out of her hair. It had been years since she had a shower where the pressure was so perfect, only once really, where the bathroom was so clean, where just the soap alone smelled so good.

The sad memory made her turn her face into the spray to wash the tears away. It had been in the hotel with her mom . . . the only time she'd ever experienced luxury like this. They'd gone to Atlantic City and hung out for the day doing the boardwalk rides. Her mom had hit on the quarter slots for $500 while Celeste was enjoying Skee-Ball. They had a meeting place at a specific time so they wouldn't miss the return bus to Philly. But instead of saying it was time to cash in all her red Skee-Ball tickets, her mom came with a big surprise—they were going to stay overnight at the Tropicana and were going to eat at the seafood buffet.

Celeste stepped out of the shower and cut off the spray, then saw the lotion and mouthwash and tiny Dixie cups on the sink. She couldn't dwell in the past, had to keep it moving, had to go forward. Drying off quickly, she pumped lotion into her palm and slathered it on her body, then hastily dressed. As soon as her sneakers were laced, she poured a cup of mouthwash into a fresh bathroom cup and knocked it back as if it were a shot of strong liquor, gargling and spitting it out, still avoiding a glance in the mirror. Finally towel-drying her hair, she finger-combed it as best she could and made one fat plait, knowing that she could find a rubber band in the minister's desk.

But staring down at the filthy clothes on the floor with the bloody hair scrunchie, something within her took pause. The clothes seemed grayer, dirtier, than she'd remembered, as though everything sick and old and toxic within her had absorbed into the fabric. Slowly she removed the cigarettes from her back pocket and dropped them into the pile on the floor. Tonight her life had to change, and she wouldn't leave that filth for the pastor to encounter as a violation of his space.

Hunting under the sink, she found a small plastic bag and gathered up everything old and worn, then used the towel she'd dried her body with to wipe up any water that she'd inadvertently left on the floor and on the sink. Folding the towel neatly along with her used washcloth, she placed it on the radiator top, hoping to minimize her offense.

"Thank you," she murmured, then backed out of the bathroom and cut off the light. The low-watt desk lamp was still on. The door to the office was still locked. Azrael hadn't barged in to attack her. The money was still on the minister's desk where she'd left it.

She found a rubber band in a small tray with paper clips near where she'd dropped the bills. Borrowing one for her hair, she then smoothed out the bills, found a pen and a Post-it note, and scrawled a brief message.

Thank you for saving my life. An angel came to your church tonight with me. May God bless you and all who worship here.

Celeste stood back from her note. "You have totally

lost your mind, Celeste Jackson," she murmured to herself, then turned out the light and left.

Azrael was where he said he would be, in a pew in the sanctuary—*but he had changed his clothes.*

She approached him warily and slid into the far end of the second-row pew next to him, then stared at him. His head was bowed, his wide, thick hands spread against the wooden pew before him, hands so graceful they almost blended into the dark-walnut hue of the polished wood like an ornately carved flourish. Somewhere, somehow, he'd found a brand-new red-blue-and-yellow-striped collared shirt, jeans that fit, and sneakers that covered his feet. But the tags were still on them. Soap scent wafted toward her as though he'd also showered. He even had a new navy blue Windbreaker lying beside him, instead of the old combat fatigue jacket that he'd been wearing, which had been way too small.

However, she would not interrupt anyone in mid-prayer. So she waited until he finally looked up. Initially he stared at the ceiling, then he brought his attention toward her.

"What's it like to be perfect," she asked, no sarcasm in her tone. "Like . . . to know everything?"

"There is only One Source that is perfect, only the One knows all. That is why we can fall."

"Even angels . . . supposing for a second that I believe in them?"

Azrael nodded.

"Where'd you get the clothes and the shower so fast?" She studied him hard now, needing to know that she wasn't coming unglued again.

"I learned many things tonight," he said in a far-off tone. "I learned that if my brother Gavreel of Peace could walk through the folds of human time and space, then I could, too, if I settled down. The Source of All That Is does not play favorites, is not capricious. The Source loves all the children it has created. My fear of being here and my anger at my perceived loss blocked my ability to know that. Coming to understand that, and experiencing loss just as any human would, was my lesson. Being here in this sanctuary gave me enough stillness to mediate on the essence of this truth."

Azrael let out a weary breath. "In this density, there is so much distraction and so much distortion that it is hard to stay connected or to hear without deep concentration—that is something else I learned."

Celeste nodded, but he still hadn't answered her question to her satisfaction. "But the new clothes, dude . . ."

"When we touched, I saw much of your knowingness. I found a place nearby that sells these items. I went in and found my size and left them money."

"Oh . . . man . . . how much money?" Celeste shook her head. "I hope you didn't leave it all?"

"Three of those with the numerals one zero zero on it. I still wasn't completely sure how to make sense of the payment system here."

She reached out and looked at the shirt tag that still hung from his sleeve, then guesstimated the cost of the jeans. "Well, you left them about a fifty-dollar tip—which I guess is cool for shopping after hours. The sneakers alone in your size were pretty expensive, so I guess it's all good."

"Is it customary to wear this marker on your items of

apparel?" He lifted his arm to show her the antitheft device affixed to his sleeve at the armpit, then pointed out the alarm on his shoe. "It is very uncomfortable. Is this only for new items? If so, I'd rather try the secondhand items."

She smiled. "Here, let me pull the tags off for you— but just like you did on the door, you have to get the alligators to come off your sneakers and jacket and jeans." She pointed to the heavy plastic alarms. "If I yank them, they'll tear holes in your clothes."

"Oh," he said, seeming amazed. "I suppose if the shopkeeper was there, he would have done this once I made my decision?"

"Yeah . . . that's definitely how it works."

Celeste swallowed a smile, but it faded on its own as she watched him take off a huge sneaker and apply blue-white light from his fingers to open the store alarm and remove it. He did it two more times on his other garments, then released a long, satisfied sigh.

"Thank you, Celeste. This feels almost as good as the shower."

"Which you took where?"

"Oh, at someone's home on the way back to the church. They were not there using it. I left them a payment to help their household and then put on my clean clothes and came back here to meet you."

She simply stared at him.

"But I have a confession to make," he said in a quiet tone, then looked away from her.

She waited, mute, almost holding her breath.

"I learned about rage when I first came here. It is a

very low frequency vibration . . . frighteningly so. I also learned about ego and loss . . . and I am ashamed of my actions."

"What did you do?" she whispered, feeling all her muscles readying to help her bolt.

Azrael closed his eyes. "Three juveniles were poised to attack me for no reason, simply because I was naked and confused and defenseless. I got angry . . ."

"Oh, my God," she said without censor. "Did you kill someone?"

"No!" he said quickly, turning in his seat fast enough to make her jump. "But I asked them for their clothing— only . . . that is not accurate. I demanded that they help me and we are only supposed to request. Then I used force to take what I needed. I am so ashamed. I had no right to the things I took . . . I traumatized three youths and even stripped them of their weapon and their paper resources." He produced the gun for her and held it out to her in the flat of his palm.

For a moment, she recoiled, but calmed down a bit when he hung his head.

"Celeste . . . what am I to do to make that offense all right or—"

"Okay, first off, put the nine away," she said in a firm, steady tone. She waited until he'd once again stashed it under the jacket lying on the pew. "Second of all, part of what went down is what I'd like to refer to as karma."

Azrael looked up at her and she watched awareness slowly dawn in his dark brown eyes.

"Those young-boyz were slinging rock on the corners, or they wouldn't have had a cash knot like that in their pockets. Either that or they were stickup artists. You were minding your business and they decided to mess with you—but tonight, let's just say they also learned a lesson about picking on the seemingly helpless and defenseless. Let's hope that you did traumatize them enough to make them think twice about victimizing someone weaker than them again. The Almighty has a plan, least that's what my aunt told me. Sometimes I believe her, sometimes I don't. But I do know this—wallowing in guilt for something already done is of no use. It wasn't like you'd jacked some old lady's pocketbook or stole from a hardworking family's household. For about two bucks worth of soap and water, you gave a needy family a hundred bucks. Besides, a nine-millimeter in your hands is probably better than one in theirs. Who knows, you might have kept them from shooting another kid their age by stripping them of their weapon. So walk away with the lesson and say a prayer and keep it moving, if it's really worrying you."

He just stared at her.

"How did you become so wise, Celeste? I have been truly troubled about the three boys since it happened."

"You learn down here to let some stuff go or you'll lose your mind." She chuckled sadly. "Ask me how I know. What am I saying, *down here*?" She shook her head. "See what I mean, I am certifiable."

"No, what you're saying is completely true." Azrael nodded and spread his hands along the pews. "People come in here all suffering from loss. I now understand why they took my wings in such a visceral way. Had I not known loss, I could not be compassionate to human loss.

Had I not known fear or anger, I could not know why people succumbed to that."

Suddenly he stood and stripped his shirt over his head, revealing his stone-cut chest. Celeste was out of the pew as if a bee had stung her.

"Hey! You crazy? I'm not even about to—"

"I must show you what I lost," he said, oblivious to why she'd fled the pew. He turned around before she could fully bolt. "Look at my back . . . I have never known injury or loss or imperfection like this in my existence."

Riveted to the floor, her gaze traveled over what should have been a smooth, athletic surface of muscular splendor. Wide, broad shoulders and a proud straight posture revealed thick scars raised on otherwise flawless skin. Someone had hacked into his beautiful back as though trying to create a horrible wood carving. Tight cords of muscles formed a deep valley along his spine that gave rise to a tight, spectacular ass covered in jeans, but her eyes remained on his scars.

"Dear God in Heaven . . . ," she murmured, slowly going to him. "Az . . . who did this to you?"

"The Source," he said quietly, and hung his head, still facing away from her. "It brought me humility . . . made me more humanlike in my understanding. Gavreel says we all lose them in the rebirth to teach us this lesson. It was a practice begun after the Great Fall, I'm told, to make sure that those of us who come to earth remember to serve humankind, that we remember where our true Source of power comes from, and to give us greater compassion for the weak."

The tragedy visited upon his back made her walk

forward. This man had obviously been tortured or abused as a child, and she couldn't just stand there and witness his pain saying nothing. If this horror is what had broken him, she could understand. All she could offer was human touch in the form of a hug. Her aunt Niecey had taught her that a gentle hug spoke volumes, especially for someone who felt ugly and unclean—something she'd felt for most of her life.

She placed her fingertips on his back, gently testing whether he'd whirl around and draw back as many injured souls might do, or if he'd allow her close enough to the old wounds to let him know that on a human level she cared that he'd been mistreated by this cruel world.

The moment her hands rested on the scars, she felt him relax under her gentle touch. Maybe he was from Africa, a person tortured in Somalia or the Sudan . . . or maybe he was an ex-vet who had been a POW, or maybe he'd been knifed in prison and was just out of the joint, but this gentle soul had been scarred so terribly by someone hateful, and it broke her heart to see it.

"I don't know who this Gavreel bastard is, or what kind of gang initiation he performed on you or whatever the story behind this guy is . . . but this isn't right. No one should be allowed to do this to another living being."

"It wasn't him," Azrael replied just above a whisper.

"All right—it doesn't matter. We all have scars . . . some can be seen with the naked eye, some are hidden. You're still whole, no matter what they did to you."

She laid her cheek against his right-shoulder scar and briefly hugged him before she stepped away. "Let's go get you something clean to eat," she said in a gentle tone. "Okay?"

They walked to Broad Street and caught the subway to Fifteenth Street, then jumped a cab the rest of the way to Whole Foods right off the Parkway. The entire time Celeste's mind stayed with Azrael's scars. He'd said he'd gotten them upon his rebirth, which she could only take to mean he'd been a victim of unspeakable child abuse. Maybe Gavreel was his father, a sick stepdad, or his mother's screwed-up boyfriend, or even an older brother or uncle. No wonder Az had made up an elaborate past and mental shelter that he was an angel. Who was she to judge? She'd been to enough therapy to know a safe-place denial story when she heard one.

The only thing she couldn't figure out was how he did the blue-light healing thing and how he opened doors with no alarms going off. Same dealio with removing the alarms off his clothes. Maybe he did have a little paranormal, extrasensory thing going on like some psychics she'd heard about and seen on TV. Maybe that's why some sick adult had either burned a small boy or lacerated the child so badly that all he could believe now was that he was an angel fallen to earth. Maybe his grandmother had told him that, no matter what, he was an angel. The possibilities were so sick and so sad that she wanted to weep for him, then she reminded herself that there were 8 million stories in the naked city.

Besides, the bigger problem was that she'd forgotten that a police substation was right around the corner from Whole Foods!

"You know," she said carefully as they climbed out of the cab, "this is probably a very bad idea."

"Why?" Azrael asked, his gaze as open and seeking as a child's.

"There's a police station around the corner, dude. If your alarm thing doesn't work or if they have a paid night guard in there, we're screwed . . . especially if you've got an unregistered weapon that could have been used in multiple felonies—none of which you know about. Just sayin'."

"Ah," he said, nodding as though he fully understood the gravity of their situation. "Then I will have to really concentrate to be sure that we remain undetected."

Just like that, it was clear that the problem was solved in his mind, and he walked toward the bright store lights.

Hanging back but close enough to watch him, she stared in awe as he closed his eyes and placed his hands against the locked doors. When they swished open, she ducked behind the chained row of shopping carts. However, after a few moments, when no alarm sounded, she slowly stood and timidly came forward.

"This place is more than I could have imagined," he said, calling out to her. "Celeste, come join me!"

"Shsssh!" she cautioned, hurrying to enter the doors behind him and hoping they closed quickly. "You make a terrible thief."

"But that is because I am no thief, nor are you. We will pay."

"Okay, okay, but technically, we are not supposed to be in here. And, you've gotta watch for motion-detector alarms and whatever."

"Ah . . . then you will teach me what to disable as we find nourishment."

"Yeah, yeah, yeah," she said, nervously looking around. "Okay, and here's how you tell clean versus anything with pesticides. Organic is the stuff you want, Conventional—not so much." She pointed out the labels over the produce, but his attention ricocheted from one bright stand of fruit to the next.

"Look at these . . . ," he murmured in awe, taking up fat, succulent strawberries and opening a plastic case. He closed his eyes briefly and turned his chin toward the direction of the ceiling. "Thank you," he murmured, then opened his eyes.

She couldn't help but laugh as he bit into a berry and moaned as though he'd never eaten in his life.

"Oh, Celeste . . . the things of this temporal world are truly divine."

"Yeah, well, lemme open up a ripe mango for you, brother, and you'll pass out," she said, laughing. "But go easy on the unwashed fruit. We might need to take them into the bathroom and at least rinse them off."

"Whatever small amount of dirt is on them will not compromise my system, I do not believe," he said, steadily eating the strawberries as they walked.

"Yeah, well, keep eating all that fruit like you're doing and you'll have to visit the bathroom anyway, sooner than you think."

She kept low, even though Azrael strolled leisurely behind her with perfect posture, and found a pile of stacked mangoes. Carefully selecting one, she dug into it with a thumbnail, then peeled it, standing back from the juicy mess that splattered the floor.

"Here, take a bite."

He accepted the offering with wonder, then smelled it as though about to sip a fine wine, and bit into it. She laughed out loud when his eyes crossed and his knees buckled.

"Watch it, there's a pit in the center."

"Can we take some of these with us, Celeste?"

"Sure." She went through the pile and selected several to load into his jacket pockets, careful to avoid the pocket that had the gun. "But get some green vegetables in you, too—like, you can cook kale and collards—"

"Cook," he said, seeming confused. "Why cook anything? Raw, natural, is best."

"Okay, you are a hard-core naturalist, aren't you? Hmmm . . . well, they have raw bread, probably raw pies—made with almond or cashew crust, nothing baked . . . melons, I don't know. Supplements and stuff. Nuts . . ."

"Can we try nuts and seeds?"

Celeste chuckled as she took him to the canisters of raw cashews and almonds, grabbed a plastic bag, then showed him how to lift the spout to fill the bag. Again she watched him chew and emit a low, satisfied moan of satisfaction. Laughing as she went down the seemingly endless row of choices, she loved every moment of his sampling.

"Okay, I am addicted to Kettle chips, I admit it—and, no, they aren't good for the human body. You can have these natural, uncooked flax chips, which are okay . . . but me, I'm still hard-core."

"Can I taste one?" he asked, seeming curious as he followed her.

"Notice I didn't give you an apple—I'm not trying to

be in Eve's position of handing an angel temptation that you'll never be able to resist."

He smiled and hastened his steps behind her. "That is mythology, you know . . . one woman could not cause the fall of humankind. Men made that up when they wanted to create a reason to separate the Source into a male dominant role and then required an excuse to steer human society into patriarchy. Besides, I just want a little taste of what you claim to be so irresistible."

Celeste laughed. "Yeah, that's what all guys say when they want something they aren't supposed to have. Suddenly Eve was framed and they only wanted a little bit." She grinned and gave him a wink over her shoulder as she found a big bag of plain Kettle chips, popped it open, and stuck one in her mouth.

"Aw . . . man, I love these," she said, crunching. "But I'm a purist—I don't go in for the exotic flavors. Plain is da bomb."

He eyed the bag in her hand, then eyed the aisle. "These are all bad for you?"

"Yep," she said, laughing and popping several chips into her mouth.

"Can I try just one?"

"Nope—because you can't eat *just* one."

"You are teasing me," he said, laughing.

"Yes . . . I most certainly am," she said, offering him the bag.

She watched him as he took out one lonely chip, smelled it, studied it, and then placed it in his mouth, initially seeming as though he didn't know how to actually chew it. But once he crunched down on it, he frowned.

"Celeste . . . these are incredible."

Again she burst out laughing, this time so hard she had to bend over and wipe her eyes. "Oh, no, I've corrupted an angel with Kettle chips—you are cut off, brother!"

"No . . . just one more?"

His request made her sit down hard on the floor as he swiped the bag from her and ate several more.

"Read the label, dude!"

He stopped munching, jaws filled like a squirrel's, and tilted his head to the side in question. She got up, still laughing, and turned the bag over, showing him the ingredients.

"Okay, I guess these aren't too bad, like some other stuff. But if there's a word on here you can't pronounce, it's a chemical that's slow poison. You're lucky; these don't have any."

"I think I understand," he said, still chewing.

"Well, while we're in here, I might as well show you pure crack . . . that would be the ice cream aisle. But I'm not gonna let you make yourself sick, if your system is clean. That much I would do for a friend. Nothing dairy, or behind all the fruit you'll definitely get the runs . . . but they've got this coconut-milk ice-cream-substitute stuff that one of my rehab buddies swore was off the chain. She said the chocolate was the best."

"Thank you, Celeste," he said, walking quickly behind her, grabbing another bag of chips.

He stopped behind her as she stopped in front of a freezer case.

"Here, try this—scoop some out on your finger. We can get some plastic spoons and forks and napkins and stuff on the way out. In fact, since we're really shopping, lemme go get us a couple paper bags. I'll be right back."

She knew she had to be out of her mind when she rounded the register and decided to take four recycled cloth bags, then filled two of them with large bottles of water, napkins, and plastic cutlery, and headed back to meet Azrael as though they were a couple shopping on a bright Saturday afternoon.

But as odd as this night had been, this was the most fun she'd had in years. Seeing the wonder of something new spread across his handsome face was positively captivating. His perfect, brilliant white smile was magnetic, and his laughter was a balm to her battered spirit.

When she found him, he was sitting on the floor with chocolate ice cream all over his hands and face like a naughty child, dipping a chip into the ice cream, eyes closed, head back, dreadlocks dusting the polished floor.

"I never knew it could be like this," he said in a thick rasp of pleasure. "If this is just a sample of what is here . . ."

"Watch it, man," she said, her smile fading and not sure why. "Be careful not to OD on the good stuff."

"You are right," he said, opening his eyes. "Temperance and moderation."

"Yeah, something like that or you'll have a bellyache." But her smile returned as she looked at his sticky face and hands. "Don't move; don't touch anything, especially not your new clothes. Let me go get you a Sani-Wipe from the food court, okay?"

"I trust you implicitly, Celeste, my guide."

Again, he'd made her smile, even though she'd rolled her eyes at him and sucked her teeth. It was a corny line, but cute nonetheless. As promised, she returned and knelt before him, wiping his face as he cleaned off his hands. Something in his eyes made her linger as she rubbed chocolate and potato-chip crumbs away from his full mouth and off his square chin. A thick droplet of chocolate was in the cleft of it, and chocolate stained the beautiful dimples in his cheeks. He was a shade darker than the ice cream she wiped away. She didn't know where he came from and knew he was crazy, but there was no denying he was a divine work of art.

"Do you want anything else?" she asked more quietly than intended.

"Yes," he said in a low rumble. "But I do not know how to describe it or name it."

She sat back on her heels, then stood up. He got to his feet without using his hands, just put his feet flat on the floor and stood. As a diversion, she picked up the empty carton and jammed the soiled Sani-Wipes into it before closing the lid, then held it up to him.

"Just like back in the street, I should probably go find all the trash we left while grazing and chuck this stuff." She looked away from him, feeling the intensity of his stare. "Uhmmm . . . why don't you take these bags and get whatever you want for later—no ice cream, though, it'll melt."

"All right," he said, gathering the bags and unloading his pockets into them. "Then can you show me where the bathroom is?"

Chapter 6

She sat on the floor in the vitamin aisle and waited for Azrael, cautioning him to be careful not to be seen in the huge plate-glass windows near the small cafeteria section that had eat-in tables and chairs by the bathroom. A full fifteen minutes had passed before Azrael returned with a delighted look on his face.

"It was simply amazing in there," he said, gesturing wildly with his hands.

"TMI," she said, laughing and cutting him off before he could go into details she did not want to know. "Way too much information."

"No, but you must hear me out, Celeste," he said, eyes alight with wonder. "Initially I had to really think hard to go through the knowledge you'd allowed me to access from your mind in order to figure out the logistics that went with the sensations."

"Az, man, I really don't want to know about this."

He beamed at her. She simply stared at him.

"But I figured it out! Then I figured out what that big roll of paper was—"

"Tell me you washed your hands *with soap* and water."

"Yes, yes, of course," he said, pressing on. "But when I stood up, the thing had a mind of its own, and whoosh, everything went down and new clean water filled back up. Then I was stumped looking for soap . . . and I could smell it on the wall. When I tried to figure out the little box that contained it, somehow I waved my hand in front of it and a big glob squirted out."

Now she was laughing in earnest and sprawled out on the floor. "Oh, Azrael . . . I swear you are so crazy."

"No, but it took me several tries until I had the coordination to master the soap—but did you know the water comes on with a wave, too?" He began to pace, face alight with excitement. "All one has to do is get the soap on one's hands and then present them under the well spigot and it splashes fresh water into your hands!"

"Did you figure out the hand dryer?" she said, wiping her eyes.

"Yes! Quite amazing! I saw the hieroglyphics and—"

"Hieroglyphics?"

"The drawings . . . the images on the silver box."

"Yes," she said, wheezing from laughter.

"I pushed it and hot air blew out!"

"Well, I'm glad you're back," she said, standing with effort. "For a moment I thought you'd fallen in."

"Is such a thing possible? Would it suck me into the tube? Why would humans create something so dangerous? What if I were a small child?"

"Relax, it's just a saying," she said, shaking her head as she waved him away. "I'll explain later. But how come if you can pick up things from touching a person or an object, you just don't get the full picture or the full comprehension? I don't understand that about your gift."

His brow knit as though he was in deep thought for moment, and she watched him closely. Although she was somewhat going along with his self-delusion that he was an angel, she was also quietly trying to help steer him toward the logical fact that he wasn't. The man was way too fine to be this tripped out. Besides, after tonight it was probable that she'd no longer be able to babysit him, and it would weigh heavily on her heart if she didn't bring him a little closer to reality so that he could function. Someone ruthless could take advantage of such a gentle soul, yet at the same time, he had the body power of a lion. People like that could be dangerous if they had a sudden fit of anger—so she kept Azrael always within bolt distance.

"I think it is because we absorb so much so quickly that it is all tightly packed into our human minds, and then as we need it, we can access it . . . but we still have this difficult density here to contend with. It creates a delay."

"Oh," she said, playing along. "Then I bet a library would blow your mind."

"What is a library?"

"The biggest one in the city is around the corner—the Parkway Central Library of Philadelphia, which is down the street from the Franklin Institute, where they have all types of scientific stuff, and then there's the Philadelphia Museum of Art, the Rodin, all of that would blow a fuse."

"Huge repositories of knowledge," he said in a hushed

tone. "Celeste . . . would you please show me those places?"

"Come on, dude," she said, shaking her head. "I don't know how you do this lucky break-in thing, I'll give you that, and maybe you do have a gift. But there's such a thing as your luck running out. You don't have enough time in the world to read all the books and stuff they have in there, anyway."

"I can't read," he said, looking away at the shelves. "I just perceive."

"You can't read?" Her question was gentle, not accusatory, as she looked at his massive, athletic frame. He wouldn't be the first guy from the city that had a ballplayer's body that coaches and a parent wanted to exploit at the sacrifice of the fundamentals. Then again, if he was from a foreign country, maybe he'd only learned the language by ear and never had a chance to be taught written English.

"No," he said quietly, walking down the aisle. "When you gave me the bag of crunchy temptation food, I could not read it. But I knew where you pointed and could touch the words and perceive if there was poison in it or not."

"Now that's deep," she murmured, watching him stop at the beginning of the vitamin-and-supplement aisle.

He took a deep breath and laid his palms flat against a row of bottles, which slowly began to glow. "For example . . . I can perceive that what is in these herbal cures is something that will feed my cells and help nourish every iota of my being. And because they are all natural and plant-based, I can literally ask the plant they were made from if it would allow me to absorb some of it."

"Whoa . . . but if you touch all the bottles—assuming what you say is true, then people shelling out thirty bucks a bottle or more for some of this stuff won't get what they bought."

"No," he murmured, closing his eyes, and making more bottles light up as he felt his way along the shelves as if he were reading braille. "Lack of abundance in the universe is a myth. If you ask the herb to share itself, it will give me what I need and will give the person who selects a bottle for purchase what they also need. I do not understand why humans battle over resources. There is enough to go around."

She had an argument ready but it fled her mind as she watched the shelves light bottle by bottle, then watched the thin rimming of light around his body get wider and wider the more bottles he touched.

"This feels so rejuvenating, Celeste," he said, breathing out the words. "I feel some of my original strength returning. . . . Why don't all humans eat like this and take in nutrients that will help them? You can all do what we do, if you still your spirits and clean out your temples."

She wrapped her arms around her waist and hugged herself. It felt so strange to actually be clean, and her hands were slightly trembling.

"All humans cannot afford to eat like this," she said resentfully. "Not the way the system is currently designed," she added, knowing that it was important for him to understand. "If you hadn't noticed, we're in a different part of town. This is the high-rent district, bro. We've got about three hundred dollars' worth of food in these bags, and I haven't even thrown in meats, staples, cleaning supplies, or whatever. Plus, if you were to buy all the vitamins you just touched, you'd have to add like another three to five hundred bucks. Most poor people, especially single moms or grandmoms with kids, can't come into a place like this and keep all the bellies in their household full. So they've gotta opt for cheap, and cheap means low-quality stuff that'll kill you. Basic economics."

Azrael looked up, studying her gaze with a disquieted frown, then stared at the last shelf again. "This knowledge you are sharing is troubling, Celeste, but very important."

"It's true," she said, relieved that he'd accepted her words without argument. It had been a long time since anyone, especially a guy, had allowed her to share what she'd learned without blowing her off or telling her she was stupid.

"Don't get me wrong, though," she said, feeling the freedom of speaking out with her own truth. "Some real political resistance, go-green folks from the neighborhood, have figured it out, and some poor folks have made the lifestyle change for religious reasons. But by and large, the general public remains unaware of just how much of what they find in their normal supermarket and fast-food joints is killing them. Cheap, dirty, processed food is less expensive. People with limited resources are forced to buy it. Nice markets like this are not in impoverished neighborhoods. Fact. The big food corporations make a mint on that cheap food crap, and so do the hospitals and pharmaceutical industry when you have to come to them like a junkie to take meds to correct what the food they sold you all your life gave you."

He looked at her with a pained expression. "That isn't fair."

"No," she said with a sad smile, "but it is what it is. You

asked why humans fight and war over resources—they do because in some parts of the world, just like in some parts of the city, you have such inequity that it will numb your mind. Right next to a five-star restaurant where they throw out thousands of dollars of food every day, a homeless person can starve to death. In India, they walk over dead bodies in the streets of Calcutta. The places in the hood you probably visited today are mansions compared to the squalor some folks live in overseas, man."

"How do you know this?"

She smiled. "I'm currently unemployed, and the two bills that Brandon paid without fail were his cell phone and cable. You can learn a lot that way."

"Cable is what?"

"TV—moving pictures . . . shows."

Azrael stepped away from the shelves. "Can the library show me these things you speak of?"

"Way better than TV, if you feel from a book and learn from the pages."

"Then, we must go to this library."

Celeste let out a hard breath. "Okay," she said in a weary tone, wondering why she was humoring this sweet but crazy man.

"Thank you, Celeste. I know all of this must be very unsettling to you . . . but if you hold my hands, I have a gift for you."

She arched an eyebrow, but then relented, deciding that allowing him to hold her hands inside the brightly lit Whole Foods aisle was much less daunting than when she'd allowed him to touch her wound on a desolate street in North Philly. Hell, she'd even taken a shower with him lurking around in a deserted church. Plus the cops were around the corner, even though that was the last place she should run to, given that she was no doubt wanted for murder.

After a moment of hesitation, she tentatively slid her hands over Azrael's outstretched palms. Warmth immediately radiated into her hands as his massive fists gently folded around them. Soon the aftertaste of pungent vitamins coated her tongue, and even the lights in the market seemed brighter. New energy pulsed though her system, making her practically high. Light-headed, she took deep breaths trying to keep from passing out.

"Your cells are so depleted and in such need of regeneration. Your skin and hair will benefit from this sharing, so will every blood cell and your bone marrow, ligaments, muscles, and tissue. Repair begins from the inside out. First we got out the toxins and healed the inner pain and outward injuries trapped in your energetic bodies. Now we will replenish you down to the cellular level."

He let go of her palms and her ears were buzzing. He picked up a liter bottle of water in each hand and held them out to her. "Drink both down and then go to the bathroom." He opened the cap on one of the large bottles of room-temperature water and pressed it into her hand, not taking no for an answer.

"Okay, okay, I get the point."

He looked up quickly and that made her stop drinking. "Coconut water," he said.

"Huh?"

"Your electrolytes are off, as are mine," he said, staring at her without blinking for a moment.

He dashed away from her, returning with a full liter carton of coconut water in each hand and one under each arm. "Hayyel is much easier for me to hear now that I'm cleaned out and strengthened. He says we must flush— does your aunt have a juicer? If not, we should also buy one of those and mix the dark green leaves of vegetables for added strength with carrots and items he told me to get."

"I'm still on the first liter and never was a big water drinker. I feel sick to my stomach."

He opened the coconut water and watched her down it. "Okay, now water."

"This is insane," she muttered, but complied. "Now I really have to pee."

"Good. That is the purge cycle. Drink the other bottle of water, too. I will go get the rest of the items we need, and then you'll tell me how much money to leave so that we aren't stealing."

How they managed to get out of the supermarket unde-tected while weighed down with enough produce to open a vending stand, along with a Vitamix blender, was beyond her. But Azrael insisted they needed it.

Thankfully, he lugged the heavy items and gave her two small bags, then insisted they *had* to go to the library. Better judgment told her to flee while there was still a chance that she wouldn't get locked up, but complete fas-cination had a stranglehold on her.

Just as in all the other venues, he stood at the back door of the Main Library of Philadelphia on tiny Wood Street, bags at his feet, pressing his hands against the door with his eyes closed. But the moment the door clicked open, he slowly slid down to the ground and to his knees.

"What's wrong?" she whispered, looking around nervously. "You tripped an alarm this time, didn't you?"

He simply shook his head no with his eyes closed, stroking the door with his palms. "No . . . oh, Celeste."

"What, dude—like, we have seriously gotta get inside before a cop car rolls by or some conscientious citizen calls 911."

He looked up at her with tears shimmering in his eyes. "Do you know what's in here . . . the knowledge that this vault stores?"

Fear of discovery made her grab him by the elbow in an attempt to hoist him to his feet. "Later, inside and out of sight, you can get all philosophical. Right now, we'll be going to the Round House on Eighth Street, if you don't haul ass. Then you won't get to see anything but the inside of a jail cell."

That got him on his feet. "I will not do anything to jeopardize an opportunity to learn."

"Good," she said, hoping that recent city budget cuts meant that the only thing monitoring the library was a security camera instead of patrolling guards.

They hustled inside and Azrael set his bags down on the first long table they came to. "Celeste," he said, like a kid right before Christmas. "They have cuneiform tablets in the rare-book collection!"

"Okaaaay . . ."

"Do you know how far back those tablets date?"

"No . . . but I thought you couldn't read?"

"I can't . . . but I can *feel* the ancient civilizations through them, I can actually sense history, I can smell the old lands!"

Then he did something that both shocked her and took her breath away. He kissed her hard on the mouth and hugged her up off her feet before she could protest, then dropped her and took off toward the stairs.

Celeste set down her bags and ran behind him. That fool was going to get himself shot by a night guard or trip an alarm! But she couldn't keep up with his taking two steps at a time up the huge marble Romanesque staircase, then up the exit. She was huffing by the third landing and he was still loudly urging her onward.

Only the coded door to the rare-books collection stopped him for a moment, and again she watched in awe as it seemed as if an electrical charge from his body transferred to the door through his hands, popping the substantial combination lock.

"Dude . . . if you ever decided to go into banking, you would make an awesome vault manager—you could retire in less than a week."

He didn't dignify the comment, but went straight to a large, mahogany cabinet that had brass locks on every drawer, then systematically opened each one. She watched him carefully, reverently slide out the special cases that held what looked to her to be bits of broken pottery. Just as he had touched the vitamins in the market, he closed his eyes, shaking his head, quietly murmuring to himself as he held each piece.

"I've never been in this part of the library," she said offhandedly, reading the signs. "They've got ancient manuscripts from the medieval period . . . like really old Bibles, Qurans, and a Torah. All sorts of stuff."

"Please show me," he said with tears of joy glittering in his eyes. "I am understanding so much. Hayyel, my brother who presides over wisdom, is so pleased."

"Okaaaay . . . ," she said as respectfully as possible. Everyone had the right to his own delusions, she supposed, and she'd given it the old college try to bring him a little dose of gentle reality.

"Seriously, Celeste," he said, now holding her gaze with intensity. "So much is coming into my direct consciousness so quickly that it is as though the entire Akashic Records from On High are thrusting themselves into my human mind. Maps, science, literature, history, art . . . novels, it is as though by being here you have helped me unlock what was already inside my head, but trapped in this new organ I've acquired with my new body. Humans use only ten percent or so of their brains, and yet I have enough knowledge from my angel existence to fill two of them to the hilt. This is why my knowledge seems so slow—there was simply too much information crammed into my head until it was stuck. The thick density of the earth plane made my synapses fire slowly . . . but now that I'm absorbing knowledge again down here, I'm remembering, Celeste!"

"Okay, that's cool," she said, beginning to walk. "Soooo . . . like . . . whatever this record is that's downloading into your brain . . . is that why most people only use like seven to ten percent of their minds—because we don't have more direct access to this cosmic repository thing you're talking about?"

She rubbed her palm down her face. Man, if touching cuneiform had set him off like this, the Internet was gonna blow his mind. They could skip the Franklin Institute; she'd probably have to put a spoon on his tongue as he went into an information-pleasure convulsion.

"No," he said, gently closing a drawer and relocking the cabinet. "The Akashic Records are there for all. But if you only have two strands of your original twelve DNA strands turned on, and if our body temple is unclean, then it makes it almost impossible to hear angelic advice or to tap into the truth provided by the Source. That is why, even with all of the misinformation and dogma out there, all of the old religions across all tribes are very, very specific about diet."

Azrael let out a frustrated sigh. "But even with all that is against them, and even sometimes with a bad diet or even addictions, somehow the miracle and wonder of our younger siblings, you that are human . . . some of you humans break through . . . inspired artists, musicians, scientists, those they call your geniuses in all areas—they've found the flow and tapped in, and what they've created cannot be destroyed. It remains a part of the Records for all of eternity."

She looked at him like he'd just spoken Greek. "What?" Nothing he'd just said made any sense to her whatsoever. And it annoyed her to no end that he began gesturing more emphatically with his hands and speaking more loudly and with more authority in his tone, as though that alone was supposed to improve her comprehension.

"Wait, back up," she said, now walking beside him as they went deeper into the collection. "Twelve strands of DNA? I thought we had the double helix thing they taught us in high school science? What memo did *I* miss?"

He drew near to her, then looked around before leaning down to whisper in her ear. Now his proximity in a semidark library wasn't as unnerving; she wanted to hear what he had to say and found herself hanging on his every crazy word.

"That's what the war is about," he whispered. "The earth is the free-will zone. Originally humans were made just as we were made, in the image of The Source . . . just with less power until you had spiritually matured. You were to acquire wisdom before knowledge, then your power would be available to you."

"Okay," she said. "That makes sense. We had to learn to be responsible and then we'd get the juice. Sounds like a plan because, believe me, we have plenty of examples of very powerful people who are very stupid."

Azrael nodded. "That hasn't changed since the beginning."

"Okay, at least we have the same politics, but what do you mean twelve strands of DNA? I'll go along with a conspiracy theory in a minute, but, dude, there's hard science that—"

"No," he said, cutting her off. "Angels have twelve strands, and you humans were originally given twelve, just as there are twelve scattered tribes, and the entire cosmos is not some random accident. It is mathematically exact. The grand design is more fantastically beautiful than you can imagine, Celeste. But here, on earth, at the height of the war some twenty-six thousand years ago, a battle we're still fighting, the darkness won a two-thousand-year period of time within this struggle to sway humankind . . . and the first thing they did was to turn off the extra strands of DNA in your bodies to make you unaware of your spiritual majesty . . . to make you more prone to excess and violence. Only a few brave souls have mastered their double helixes that were left and are able to turn on the dormant helixes in their bodies. You call them masters, yogis, and highly evolved spiritual leaders. Then there are those like you, whose twelve strands could never be turned off. You are rare. You are a member of the Remnant."

Again, she just stared at the man. "Maybe I'm in the slow class, but I don't get it."

He released a sigh of frustration. "Like I said before, it's complicated. These theories of energy and Light are simplified in the old spiritual texts, hence the use of parables and—"

"Okay, okay," she said, cutting him off with an impatient wave of her hand. "I get that part. We humans with our ten-percent brain functions aren't gonna understand all of this, unless we're Einstein or something. But all I wanted was a simple answer to a very simple question."

Azrael just looked at her. "That's what I've been trying to tell you, Celeste. Your question wasn't simple, and neither is the answer."

He stood tall and looked around again before leaning back down and continuing in an urgent, warm whisper into her ear. "Only having access to the two strands of DNA encoded in your body, and not even the full strands at that, because much of the coding on even the double helix has been turned off, makes you humans more likely to be ruled by the animal side of your natures. That base nature is nothing to be ashamed of. It is inherent in all natural beings—even us—but it must be transmuted to the higher frequencies. Without anchoring to higher ideals, you spiral into darkness instead of gleaning to the upward spiral flow of energy into the Light. That is how you are so easily controlled. You are being drugged with the food, mind-numbed by misinformation, and having your worst passions and fears stoked."

"Wait," she said, pulling away from him, her mind reeling. "Turn off some of the pieces of a person's DNA . . . I don't—"

"Your own science now shows that tones, actual sound, can activate certain dip switches on the DNA strands . . . some turned on can create superior healing and superior IQ, some can activate helpful T cells in the body and can create disease barriers and immunity, while others turned on or even turned off can create congenital diseases and birth defects. Human scientists are studying DNA encoding now, and one day they will know how to turn on the best attributes within the double helix. They are experimenting with sound waves as well as medicines and genetic engineering to switch on good genes. The problem is, humanity is running out of time while they struggle to find the clues to healing."

"Oh, forget it," she muttered, blowing a stray wisp of hair up off her forehead.

"I'm not trying to be evasive or confusing," he said more gently. "Just honest. You'll just have to trust me and have faith in what I've told you."

"Yeah, I figured that at the end of all this circle logic, when I didn't understand, you'd tell me to have faith." What else was there for her to say? "Do you know how old a line that is? How sick and tired people are of just being told to believe?" She stared at him hard and then shook her head, defeated when he lifted his chin as though to object. She didn't want a rebuttal or to argue the point further. "Don't answer that. It was just a rhetorical question."

He leaned down toward her again and spoke low and fast and directly into her ear. She could almost feel the tension crackle in the air between them as he drew a breath and continued with his wild theory.

"The Unnamed One is the Prince of the Airwaves," he said, and then cautiously looked around before speaking again. "Sound travels that way, through the air, and that is how the Ultimate Fallen were able to slowly dim the human light—they used sound—oratorical propaganda, rhetoric filled with hate. They began this campaign of turning off the lights within humans eons ago and managed to turn off all but the central double-helix strand of DNA, allowing only the very basic-level coding that would let humans reproduce and function to remain. It was power unchecked at the highest levels of human society and governed by hell. That is why humans use only ten percent of their brains now . . . except for some. And in hate and fear-inspired campaigns, anyone who went against the norm was ousted, stoned, crucified, burned at the stake, tortured, punished, or imprisoned until the human flocks were manageable and docile."

Azrael stared at her hard now, his gaze intense and

riveting. His unease was making her feel jumpy. If he was scared, then she was thoroughly freaked out.

"We need those that have access to the full set of twelve strands of their DNA to begin to turn on the lights of the masses," he said in a low, firm tone. "Someone like you, along with other sensitives, can begin to turn on the lights within your fellow humans through sound—the use of your voice, your message of truth, your resistance to the darkness. When we gather the Remnant together, you will create a powerful movement that will become the tipping point within human nations. And the dark side finds that very dangerous . . . because once people know the truth and they see how they've been manipulated for centuries, they will demand worldwide change. My job as an angel is to bring the Remnant together and to protect you as this occurs."

Okay, now he was truly scaring her. Not because she feared attack or murder, but because the last thing she wanted to deal with was a religious extremist. Perhaps more scary than that was that everything he was telling her resonated deeply within her as every old parable she'd ever heard zinged through her mind. Make a joyful noise unto the Lord. Speak no evil. Words have power. Celeste hugged herself and stared up at Azrael.

"Okay, say for a second I believe you . . . then how did mine stay on when everybody else's didn't?" she whispered, now glancing around nervously the way he had a few moments ago.

"That is a longer story than time allows us in this building. We must still go to your aunt's home and rest for a long journey away from this city. Do not be troubled," he said, monitoring her sobered expression. "This is why I was sent to protect you before the date of no return. I am sure Nemamiah and Gavreel will meet us there, as well as Barbelo and Hayyel, if they are manifest yet. This is also why we have to travel far to seek Bath Kol to better understand the prophecy."

Chapter 7

Celeste walked beside Azrael trying to figure out the best way to make a break for it, as room after room in the library drew his attention. He found levels of floors between floors that had stacks she didn't even know existed of dusty, manually cataloged periodicals of the most obscure nature.

But she didn't give a damn what he said. If he was some jihadist, she would call the feds on his crazy ass in a New York second.

Plus, there were just some facts she couldn't ignore—facts that a few laughs in Whole Foods couldn't make go away. His name sounded foreign, as did the name of every one of his friends. He spoke like somebody from another country. Now he was talking about the two of them going on some long trip to find more foreign-sounding dudes, plus some head honcho named Bath Kol? Who in the heck from Philly named their kid freakin' Bath Kol? Aw hell to the no.

And she had to be stone cold out of her mind to even for one minute consider taking this guy to her aunt's home. To what? Drag her aunt Niecey into a terrorist plot? She'd heard about bull like this on the news.

Then there was the whole spooky thing with busting locks with blue light . . . probably some spy shit they'd rigged, and with all the cameras they'd passed, no doubt Homeland Security would swoop down on her any second now.

Celeste stopped walking, her mind racing a mile a minute as her heart began to beat erratically. Wait a minute . . . how could Azrael have known about all that shit that happened to Brandon? What if Azrael and his terrorist crew had staked her out and picked her because of her unstable record that anyone in the neighborhood would have told them for five bucks . . . murdered Brandon— then showed up like her savior?

"Celeste, are you all right?" Azrael turned and looked at her, his frown one of concern.

She spun and bolted. He might be bigger than her, might even have a gun, but this huge building had a lot of places to run to and hide in.

Zigzagging through the stacks, her goal was to head toward the open door on the first floor. Worst case, she could break into an office and call 911, or just punch it in at the Information Desk at the first floor and pray that somebody at Philly's Finest was on point and doing his job.

Half falling, half jumping, she held on to the banister as she stumbled closer and closer to the street level. Panic sweat coated her, making her clothes stick to her skin. She couldn't hear him behind her, which was just as unnerving as hearing him thunder after her.

She hit the first-floor panic bar on the stairwell door and raced across the wide marble floor toward the Information Desk and skidded to a halt as he calmly stepped through the folds of nothingness with a placid look on his face.

"I thoroughly apologize," he said in a soothing voice. "Celeste, I allowed my own anxiety about this entire situation to transfer to you, and that should have never happened."

She held her heart with one hand and clung to the edge of the desk with the other. "How did you do that?" she gasped. "You drugged me—the water. You used a hypodermic needle and tainted the coconut water when I wasn't looking, that's why you made me drink it!"

"On my honor, Celeste—"

"That is bullshit!" she shrieked, now clutching the telephone receiver and trying to figure out how to place an outbound call on the complicated system. "I don't give a rat's ass if you shoot me! You Al Qaeda motherfuckers aren't the only ones who will die for a cause! Family is my cause! You ain't gonna go to my aunt's house to freak out an eightysomething-year-old woman, and I'm not helping you blow up innocent people here for twelve strands of light or whatever you were babbling about! Take that back over to where you come from! It ain't perfect here, but it's home!"

He reached into his Windbreaker and she dropped the telephone and braced herself, knowing she couldn't outrun him, but she could damned sure play dead if she wasn't fatally shot. But he did the most outrageous thing—pulled out the weapon, then turned the handle of the gun in her direction and slowly approached her.

"Here. Take it, if it will help you trust me. Pull the trigger, if you need to. It will hurt but I will not die. It will complicate things when they find me here in the morning bleeding all over their floors . . . but you have already seen that, if they imprison me, I can simply open the locked doors. But the one thing I told you is true: I mean neither you nor your aunt any harm."

Azrael set the gun down cautiously on the edge of the Information Desk and backed away with his hands up.

"These are perilous times, Celeste. You have lived a life of suffering. There are those in the world doing unspeakable things in the name of the Source of All That Is in every country and under the aegis of every religion. I am not one of those misdirected humans. I am Azrael."

"All of your names sound foreign," she said, grabbing the gun and glancing quickly at the telephone. "And you're talking some end-of-days war bullshit . . . uh-uh. Sounds like a jihad or some kind of fundamentalist evangelical holy-war crusade to me, brother."

"Each of our names is translated into this language with the tonal sounds that vibrate with our spirit essences and thus sound—"

"Cut the crap!" she shouted, trying to get the phone to work.

"Yes, cut the crap, Azrael," a deep, sinister voice said behind her, making her spin around to meet it.

Celeste trained the gun on the new intruder, but he didn't seem to care. He was tall and willowy, almost seemed delicate, but she could feel an aura of pure danger waft from him as he smiled. A pair of steel gray eyes so clear that they seemed wolflike fixed upon her, and a preternatural wind from nowhere, one that she couldn't feel, lifted his long, platinum blonde hair off his shoulders and made his black leather coat billow out around his leather-clad legs. His complexion was nearly the same hue as his hair, and were it not for his gray irises, she would have thought him albino. But her eyes left his gaze to study his mouth and the unnatural line of his teeth that seemed to be slowly lengthening.

"Forcas," Azrael said in a deep, angry boom. "Know that I will have your head before this war is over!"

"See, Celeste," Forcas said, smiling. He pushed a long spill of silky blond hair over his shoulders as his gray eyes became pure black. "No more Mr. Nice Guy when you make him angry. The first thing he does is threaten to take my life. He will take yours as sure as we are standing here."

"Liar!" Azrael shouted, rounding the desk.

"Ask him what his name *means,* sweetheart. Bet he didn't tell you that."

Celeste's attention jerked between Azrael and the man in black leather with black eyes. A supernatural current seemed to flow between the men as a howling wind kicked up inside the library, scattering papers off the Information Desk and sending pens and paper clips airborne.

"His name means Angel of Death, and he has hunted his own kind for millennia! He is no respecter of free will amongst his *own brothers,* but is a blind soldier doing Michael's bidding! So why would he allow the free will of humans, girl? Be smart and choose to run away from him as fast as you can!" the one Azrael had called Forcas said.

"I do the bidding of Archangel Michael because he has not fallen! Archangel Michael of the Light, like Archangel Gabriel, and Archangel Raphael, and like all the others at the highest echelons, is still linked to the Source of All That Is, just as he will always be! As I will always be! Humans have free choice, it is *law*! Angels have one choice—the Light—or they cannot be allowed to use their power against humans! Do not attempt to twist her mind with your deceit—half demon! You have obviously learned too well from your new Dark Lord, Satan. Your choice to follow the darkness of evil instead of the Light is what plummeted you into the fall from Grace."

Forcas smirked. "Why not join us? Our leader, Lucifer, which means 'Light-bearer,' if you want to get technical, is much more understanding than the first master I had, so I traded down, shall we say. It was less stressful."

Suddenly Azrael let out a furious war cry, stretched out his hands, and the thick wrought-iron grate that protected the front of the library from intruders tore off the wide front doors. Each sharp rod of the ornate iron grate ripped apart, forming into huge spears that crashed through the outer glass doors as Azrael pointed toward the being named Forcas.

Iron whizzed over Celeste's head. She could feel the hot breeze they left in their wake. Instantly Forcas sent glass cases, tables, and marble slabs from the wide staircase hurling toward Azrael to deflect the iron bars and then disappeared.

Sirens were near. Celeste was crouched down beneath the Information Desk panting. Two strong hands that were so hot they nearly burned pulled her gently out.

"I'm sorry you had to see that, but we have now attracted unwanted attention. We must collect our bags from the back table by the door and leave this place at once." Azrael shook her gently when she only stared at him. "We must get to your aunt's home before the demons do—do you understand?"

Numb, Celeste clasped the two bags of food that Azrael thrust into her hands and allowed him to tug on her arm to hurry her out the door and down the back street. He'd said it was important to bring a food offering to her aunt, but she was so freaked-out that she could barely think of her own name, let alone some damned groceries.

After a block of brisk walking, he closed his eyes, and suddenly a cab came around the corner and stopped.

"Hey, you people looking for a cab?"

"Yes," Azrael said. "Thank you."

"No problem," the cabbie replied, as Azrael helped Celeste into the vehicle. "I was just about to go off shift and it seemed like all hell just broke loose on the Parkway. Cops were flying down the street like crazy, and you two kids don't need to be out in all of that. So—where can I take you?"

Both men looked at Celeste. She hesitated, but then it suddenly dawned on her that this couldn't have been a psychotic break with reality if the cabbie said he heard sirens. If this cabdriver actually saw physical evidence of a major disturbance on the Parkway, then that had to mean that she really was sitting next to some sort of supernatural being—because based on the shit she saw in the library lobby . . .

"Fifty-eighth and Baltimore," Celeste said quickly, now staring at Azrael dead on.

"Okay, you got it," the cabbie said, veering away from the curb.

During the entire ride to West Philadelphia, the cabdriver tuned into different radio bands trying to find out what happened, speculating about the nature of mankind and crime and delivering his take on life as he knew it. Azrael spoke pleasantly but remained noncommittal when he interjected. Celeste kept her focus out the window, too freaked-out to talk, let alone discuss anything mundane.

"You all have a blessed night and be careful out here," the cabbie said as he collected his fare and they exited his vehicle.

Azrael touched the roof of the cab and leaned down. "You also be blessed and may your fortune multiply and your health improve. Thank you for going out of your way to answer a prayer to give us a ride tonight."

Celeste watched the roof of the cab glow blue-white and tightened her grip on her bags.

"Aw, it wasn't nothing but the right thing to do," the cabbie said with a wide smile. "You two seem like good people, and after all, ain't we supposed to help each other? If everybody did that, we wouldn't have the crap going on in the world that we do now." The cabbie wiped his brow. "Y'all have a good one."

Azrael shut the door and met Celeste on the curb.

"You did something to him, didn't you?" She stared at Azrael and waited.

"The man had a lot of problems, most of them being financial and health-related. He didn't have to answer my prayer for a fast deliverance from the site of danger, but a good soul in proximity picked up on it and did. His problems were easy to help repair. I just answered a few of the requests he'd sent out."

"Before we go into my aunt's home, I really need to know who and what you are . . . because the things I saw . . ." She backed away a bit. "The other dude's eyes turned full black and he lifted off the floor. Was he a vampire or something really crazy? I know better than to invite death into my aunt's house."

"Do not say his name, as the vibration carries on the wind. But the other you saw is one of our fallen. He has gone dark, now more demon than angel. He rules the principality of invisibility for the legions of darkness—does the bidding for the demon world. At one time he used his gift to help humans remain unseen on the battlefield, to help hide the enslaved from bounty hunters or to protect the innocent from witch hunts and searches. At one time his ability to cloak people from danger would have helped keep Roman soldiers from seeing villages of people they might round up for their horrific gladiator games . . . or would have hidden men, women, and children from ethnic-cleansing roundups of the many holocausts this world has seen. We would have called on him to hide the innocent and little children from predators. But he no longer uses his abilities for good. He once warred on our side hiding the legions of the Light during battles. He and the others with him commingle and corule with all manner of demons—but I am not one of the fallen."

Her heart was beating fast and her eyes were so wide they were drying out from not blinking. "He called you the Angel of Death."

Azrael nodded. "For those angels of the Light that fall. Yes. Most assuredly I am that. But I have never been beset upon humans. That is not my charge, nor my mission."

"Then why would they send an Angel of Death looking for me?" Her voice quavered as she asked the question, still trying to absorb what she'd seen and what she was hearing.

"Because I am one of the more feared champions from the first wars . . . and those that direct my mission must have known that to find you required sending in an able destroyer of the fallen. Now that I have seen one of the adversaries, I know this to be true." His gaze was furtive as he studied her face. "Celeste, you must have faith in me until I can further prove to you who I am, but it is not safe for you or your aunt that we tarry outside of an unblessed structure."

He didn't have to tell her twice. Somehow Azrael's words again connected to that pit of knowing way down deep in her belly. She turned and headed north a half block to Ellsworth Avenue, then motioned with her chin. "Fourth house in."

She said nothing as they trudged up the steps. Initially it had been her plan to get near her aunt's home but not show him the address, give him the slip down the many narrow West Philly streets, then loop back and get in.

However, after what she'd just seen and heard, Celeste simply knocked on the door.

After several tries, an upstairs light came on, and then she could see through the steel-grated window of the security front door that her aunt was headed down the steps. Celeste clutched the supermarket bags she held while also holding her breath. It had to be close to four or five o'clock in the morning, and her aunt was gonna have a cow.

Multicolored head scarf on, pink robe securely wrapped around her robust frame, Aunt Niecey blinked behind her glasses with a frown and talked through the security door as she opened the inside door.

"Chile, have you lost your ever-livin' mind showing up on my doorstep with some man you done dragged in off a street corner somewhere at this hour of creation? You best not be on them damned drugs, 'cuz I swear 'fo Jesus Hisself I will—"

"Ma'am . . . I helped her get away from someone who is on drugs and who was beating her," Azrael said in a calm tone. "Your niece is clean of any drugs and she has even brought healthy food to your home. We apologize for the hour, but if you open the door, we can explain everything."

Celeste just stared at Azrael as her aunt released a grunt of annoyance but turned the locks. She now understood why he'd said they needed to bring the food along; it was evidence, and the only evidence that would have made Aunt Niecey open up. Drug addicts didn't waste money on food.

"Well, I thank you kindly," Aunt Niecey said, peering at the bags. "I never could stand that fool she was going around with from the pizza shop. He was a demon, I tells ya—had somethin' wrong with that boy."

Azrael nodded as Celeste's aunt stepped aside to allow them in. "Your fruits of the spirit are accurate. The poor man was possessed."

Aunt Niecey cocked her head to the side and folded her arms over her ample breasts after she locked the door. "You speak like you've had a little church up in you . . . you in rehab?"

Azrael smiled a slow half smile. "No, ma'am, but I do know most scriptures from the old texts pretty well."

"Ain't nothing wrong with that," she said, going to Celeste and holding her out to inspect her. "She looks better than I've seen her in a long time. Don't smell like an ashtray, either." Then slowly her aunt pulled her in close. "You say that fool been hitting on my chile?"

Celeste nodded, tears suddenly rising in her eyes as her aunt Niecey's thick arms enfolded her into the only safety she'd ever known. A rough, arthritic hand petted Celeste's hair as she buried her face against her aunt's shoulder.

"Hush, chile, it's gonna be all right. I done prayed night and day for you to be delivered home like this to me . . . whole, healthy, and away from a fool. You still young and pretty and got your entire life ahead of you—so don't you get no crazy ideas about cutting your life short, you hear me? I can take a lot of things, but losing you after I done lost your mama . . . my dearest and best sister, no. That would put me in the ground."

Clinging to the warmth and the wisdom, Celeste tried to steady her breath, but it was impossible. Aunt Niecey's hug dredged up the sob that had been waiting since her world turned upside down.

"Aw . . . baby, you jus' go on and let it all out and give it to me."

Her aunt's words only made her cry harder, as she remembered Azrael saying those exact words when he'd healed her cut.

"This po' girl done been through a lot," Aunt Niecey said, looking at Azrael as she rubbed Celeste's back. "I don't know who or what you are to her, but if you hurt this baby girl after all she done endured, ain't no power high enough in Heaven to keep me off your ass, son. You hear? This is *my baby*. My baby sister's only chile. This one here is special. This one here is anointed—jus' like every door and windowsill and floorboard up in here is anointed, I done put down special prayers on this one. An' jus' like the devil can't come up in this prayed-up house, can't nobody who ain't right stay with this special chile to bring her down. She ain't like all them others out there, so if that's what you want, you best get to steppin'. Knew it when I first held her in my arms, so ain't no fool gonna mess with one of God's children, we clear?"

"Yes, ma'am, and I couldn't agree more," Azrael said in a respectful tone.

Celeste lifted her head and looked at him, slowly understanding that for all these years, her aunt's fierce prayer-warrior nature had been the only thing that stood between her and whatever was hunting her. Azrael subtly nodded. Celeste wiped her face quickly and kissed her aunt, then hugged her hard.

"I love you, too, baby," her aunt said in a tender

murmur, cupping Celeste's face with thick, meaty palms. "That's the most powerful thing this side of Grace, so you never forget that. Your mama loved you hard like that, too." Releasing Celeste's face, Aunt Niecey stared at Azrael. "What's your name, son?"

"Azrael."

"Hmmm . . . ," Aunt Niecey said in a skeptical tone. "Main thing is, you promise me you won't be beatin' on her or get her caught up in no drugs, then you'll be all right with me." Then she hesitated. "You got a bunch of babies in the streets by different women?"

"No, ma'am, on all counts," Azrael said with a slight smile playing about his mouth.

"All right then, so long as we clear," Aunt Niecey said, frowning at Azrael, but some of the bluster had gone out of her tone. "I'll make us some tea, lest you a coffee drinker?"

"Tea will be fine," Azrael murmured. "And we brought you some things for your kitchen."

"Much obliged, and I thank you for bringing my chile home—that was all you truthfully had to bring to set my mind at ease . . . so we gonna pray before we do anything else."

"Thank you," Azrael said solemnly, then closed his eyes.

Aunt Niecey smiled and gave Celeste a quick wink. "I think I like him already."

Chapter 8

*H*ospitality won out over any potential hostility Celeste's aunt may still have had, given the hour of their arrival. Bags of food offered meant peace in Aunt Niecey's world—no matter what time of the day or night it came. Her aunt's motto was "Make the kitchen right, then we all right." This simple, old-school gesture was imprinted in her aunt's generations-ago, North Carolina roots. Azrael had therefore passed her aunt's sniff test by observing three basic rules as a man—he'd come in the door with respect, showed he wasn't foreign to prayer, and had offered the lady of the house groceries. It didn't get any more basic than that.

"Look at these vegetables," Aunt Niecey said in awe as she fawned over the gorgeous produce. Carefully extracting lush bunches of greens from the bag as though lifting a newborn, she shook her head and clucked her tongue in full appreciation. "I don't know what to say."

"There's a juicer, too, ma'am . . . with a little book-let about how to use it to get the most nutrients from the plants."

Aunt Niecey waved Azrael away. "I know what to do with kale and collards. By the time I finish with 'em, you'll think you done died and went to Heaven."

Celeste gave Azrael a look, which he caught. Later she would explain that there'd be no way to tell an eighty-something-year-old African-American woman that she couldn't cook her collard greens until all the nutrients were in the water—or the pot liquor, as her aunt called it. That Vitamix was most likely going to gather dust on top of the refrigerator, but Celeste didn't have the heart to tell him so. Somehow his slumped shoulders and sad eyes let her know that he'd probably figured that out.

"Y'all sit down and let me fix that tea," her aunt said brightly, going to the stove to turn on the kettle as they took seats at the aged table. "Since y'all health nuts now, talking about juicing and such, I guess you can drink this green tea one of my grands came in here with. Me, myself, I like the old-fashioned kind—Tetley. I don't know what to do with this new-fangled Chinese tea. It don't even have a string on the bag so you can dip it. But you all are welcome to it."

"Thank you, Auntie," Celeste replied. It was impossible not to smile. Her aunt was so set in her ways. "But do you have honey?"

"Of course, suga. You know I keep it around here for colds."

Celeste glanced at the big tub of white sugar on the counter. "Well, can we have just a little of your cold remedy? Az doesn't eat anything refined, like white sugar."

Aunt Niecey gave them a puzzled look over her shoulder as she filled the kettle with fresh tap water. When Celeste opened her mouth to stop her, Azrael interjected.

"It's all right . . . it'll be boiled."

"Somethin' wrong with my water?"

"No, ma'am," Azrael said, trying to deflect any potential insult.

Celeste stood. "Aunt Niecey . . . Azrael is real funny about what he puts into his body. He only drinks purified water." She bent and extracted a large liter bottle of water from one of the bags. "Can you make the tea with this?"

"If you like it, I love it," her aunt said, shaking her head as she accepted the bottled water. "Now I see why you all come a'callin' with bags in your hands . . . unless all your friends eat like hippies, you're gonna have to go everywhere toting your own food. Seems a little extreme to me, but who am I?" Aunt Niecey released a small grunt and went about putting a flame under the kettle and hunting through her cabinets for an old jar of honey. "But I will say this. Leastwise if you that particular about what you eat, I don't have to worry about you taking no crazy drugs. Now I'll sleep good once I go back to bed, if Arthur leaves me alone."

This time when her aunt turned back to the stove, Celeste could see a slight blue outline frame her aunt's hip. The strange light covered her aunt's left foot, too, as well as both of her hands, where most of her pain usually resided. Then just behind the bright yellow curtains Celeste saw the same glow going across the windowsill, and it was at the back door.

Leaning up slightly, she peeped out the window. The blue glow seemed to extend down the side perimeter of the back of the house where the rows were no longer joined. Azrael cut Celeste a glance and she sat back down.

"All right, let's see what else y'all got up in these here bags," her aunt said, snapping Celeste's focus back into the kitchen.

Aunt Niecey came back to the small, yellowing, white linoleum table and bent to peer inside one of the bags that sat on an ancient chair with white, cracked plastic padding.

"In the bottom of that one," Azrael said in a tentative tone, "are just some things I thought you would personally like . . . some of it is for Celeste, too."

Aunt Niecey cut him a questioning gaze for a moment, then smiled as she dug deeply into the bag. "You must really care about my baby." She lifted out sweet-smelling vanilla lotion and fragrant homemade lavender soaps. "This had ta cost you an arm and a leg . . . but that chile always loved this kind of stuff ever since she was little. She'd always get into my good lotions and perfume."

"Az . . . ," Celeste murmured. "With everything going on, you went back to get me soap?"

"When we were at the church, I felt how much you liked soap."

"I ain't even gonna ask," her aunt said, waving one hand at them while pulling out more items. "But at least you all was in church, so I know it wasn't nothing untoward." Then her aunt straightened up and put the bounty she'd scooped out of the bag onto the table with both hands. "Aw, now look at this . . . all kinds of barrettes and combs for your hair, too, suga . . . uhmmph . . . uhmmph . . . uhmmph."

"I did not want you to have to continue to use a rubber band and damage it," Azrael said quietly, staring at Celeste. "I want you to only have things that will make you happy and that will help you heal."

"Thank you," Celeste said in a soft murmur. She was stunned that in the midst of all the insanity, mayhem, and pure chaos, he'd perceived her shower . . . was that much of an empath that he'd picked up on such a silly little nuance of hers and had addressed it in a way that was so unbelievably sweet.

"It is my duty, but more than that—it is my pleasure to make you happy." His gaze was too intense now and she had to look away. She found the edge of a napkin in the plastic holder to pick at. No man she'd ever known had cared enough to do something so nice, much less one she'd incorrectly judged as a cop, a homeless vagrant, then an apparition from her own nervous breakdown, then a drug dealer, then a terrorist. She'd believed Azrael to be so many different things all in one fragile night—everything but what he probably really was, which was something almost impossible to wrap her mind around.

"That one's a keeper," Aunt Niecey announced with a chuckle, then went back to the stove to turn off the kettle.

Long, quiet minutes passed as Celeste's aunt fixed their tea and returned to the table, setting down two steaming mugs before them. Celeste watched her aunt as she pulled down a box of loose tea from a high shelf, then hunted through the drawers for a long-lost tea ball and found it.

"Well, you young folks can rest yourselves on the

couch to have your tea and can keep the TV on low, if you ain't tired. . . . Keisha brought a new computer in here—it's in the dining room all twisted up with my phone lines somehow. She said it was called a laptop and told me I needed it for all the kids to use when I watch 'em. What them kids need is a switch to their bad little butts, if you ask me. They be in there fighting over that thing half the time, and I wanna know why can't they just read a danged book? Don't ask me how to use it, but they play games and do homework—you can amuse yourself with that, too, if you want. Makes me no nevermind. I'ma take my tea up and say good night."

However, before she left the stove with her mug, Aunt Niecey gave Celeste a meaningful glare. "But you know my rule about hanky-panky. I don't care how old you are, if you ain't married, it ain't happening under my roof."

"No, ma'am . . . it's not even like that," Celeste said quickly.

"Yeah, well . . . you sleep up in your old room. Mr. Azrael can have the couch. Might not be like that at this moment, but I've lived long enough to know that things have a way of getting *like that* on the *spur* of the moment. Anyway, you know where I keep the blankets and towels."

Aunt Niecey looked from one to the other but then gentled her expression. "But I'm glad you met someone who seems nice." She smiled, revealing large gaps between her teeth where her dental plate went. "He's gonna be high maintenance to cook for, but so far, my hunch is he's one of the good ones."

Celeste smiled. "Good night and thank you for opening the door."

Aunt Niecey just clucked her tongue and took a sip of tea. "Ain't no bother. What else was I doing? You young folks keep things interesting. But y'all get some rest."

Azrael stood when Aunt Niecey headed for the doorway. "Ma'am, thank you."

She turned to him and set her hot tea down on the table and took up both of his hands. "I might be half-blind, but I can tell a good soul when I see one. You feel it inside your heart. As long as you treating my chile like this, you always welcome here."

Azrael nodded and Celeste watched the blue-light white cover her aunt's gnarled hands.

"You got honest eyes and a healing touch . . . your skin is clear as a baby's behind like you ain't never took a drug or a cigarette in your life—probably not a drinker, either."

"No, ma'am," he murmured.

"Warm-blooded, too. Your hands are burning up, son."

"They're always that way . . . but again, I thank you for your hospitality. This won't be forgotten and you definitely will have a star in your crown. Be blessed, Ms. Jackson."

"You, too, son," Aunt Niecey said quietly, then did something she'd never done to any of Celeste's other boy-friends—she hugged Azrael hard, then touched his face. "I don't know where you came from, but I'm pretty sure the Good Lord sent you."

When the elderly woman pulled away from their embrace, Azrael stepped aside so Aunt Niecey could pass by him in the narrow space between the table and the doorway.

"Good night and thanks again for everything," Celeste said behind her. "I love you."

"Good night, baby . . . and you know I love you. Goes without sayin'."

Both Celeste and Azrael stared after the elderly woman and watched her go up the stairs. Once Celeste heard her aunt's bedroom door close, she turned to Azrael.

"Thank you for healing her."

"I just took away a little of the pain."

Celeste became very, very still. "Then you didn't heal her all the way . . . because . . ."

"Celeste," he said in a sad tone and then sat down slowly. "For everything there is a season."

Celeste picked up her tea and stared down into it. "I thought angels could do everything."

"We can do what we are asked if it is in accordance to Divine will."

"But I saw the blue light touch her, then it was on the doors and the windows and—"

"The light on her body was my intention to siphon away the pain from her . . . the light at the windows and doors and along the perimeter of the property was her doing. She anointed this house with her prayers and love. We answer those prayers. There is a corps of us that are dispatched solely to address human prayer. Her home is blessed. Her home is protected, and no demons can enter. This house will be passed over. I added my prayers to strengthen hers."

"That is so deep," Celeste murmured. "But how come I could see it? I never saw that before, and Aunt Niecey didn't just start praying tonight."

"The scales are beginning to fall away from your eyes, Celeste. Your temple is clean, the toxins are gone from your system, and you have literally been touched by an angel. The Light inside you, in your special DNA, is beginning to repair itself; therefore you can see the Light in others and you can also see any prayer light covering inanimate objects."

He hesitated as though searching for a way to make her understand. "Just like before I touched you and before we went to the library, I didn't know how to address your aunt properly as 'ma'am.' I didn't know the culture, the dialect . . . but the longer I remain in your company, the more my resident knowledge is released. It is no different with you. The more you are in my presence, the more you will comprehend about the higher realms of existence. Death is not final, it is not separation. The spirit is eternal. As long as there is no separation from the Light, humans are also immortal. Only the body dies."

Celeste took a slow sip of her hot tea, not angry, simply weary and knowing the truth inside her soul. Her aunt had lived a long life. Her aunt had raised generations. Her aunt was due divine respite from it all soon. She's said it many times before, her aunt was tired.

"I guess the Angel of Death isn't exactly the one to consult on life-extension requests then," she said with a sad smile, looking at Azrael as her vision blurred with tears.

Her tone was gentle and had a faraway quality to it, sounding more like a soft plea than a sarcastic statement. For some reason, her calm resignation about what he was trying to tell her seemed to draw him to her. He knelt down on the floor in front of her and clasped her hands in his, then slowly laid his cheek against her lap.

"This is why you brought me here tonight, isn't it, Az?"

He looked up at her as though speaking now would make the words cut his throat. He only nodded.

"When?"

"I do not know, but soon," he replied softly. "The time and hour is not my province. But it will be a gentle slip away in her sleep. Denise Jackson deserves no less than that. My brother who sees to such things has whispered that promise to me."

Celeste's entire body stiffened, and through his tender gaze she could tell he was trying to send as much love and Light into her being from his heart as he could.

"Not tonight," Celeste said in a quavering whisper. "I cannot be the one to find her."

"You won't," Azrael said, squeezing her hands tightly. "And it will not be tonight." He looked up at her and repeated the promise. "Not tonight. . . . I just wanted you to have a chance to tell her how much you loved her and to show her you were all right before you left this city on your quest, because I know that your spirit would never be at rest if you didn't."

Celeste extracted her palms from his, wiped her face, and reached for the honey, pouring some on a teaspoon with shaking hands. "I've cried more in this one night than I have in a lifetime. Have seen things that should have really sent me into a mental ward. But of all of it, knowing what you just told me about my aunt, is both a blessing and a curse." She dipped the spoon into her tea and stirred it slowly, then returned her focus to him. "It must be hard to know in advance . . . to see death coming to those you love. I can't imagine. How do you deal with *knowing*?"

Her honest question and the intensity of her gaze seemed to be almost too much for him to bear. He glanced down at her lap for a moment, then drew in a steadying breath before he continued to look deeply into her eyes. She could tell that he was trying to impart the truth through the confusion within his spirit. How did one deliver news like this? she wondered. Had to be as hard for the giver as the taker.

"I have never had anyone to specifically love," he said in a quiet rumble. "Only the entire amalgam called humanity. Of course I love the Source of All That Is with the very foundation of my spirit, but I mean loving an individual part of the Source, loving one human in particular, is new to me."

"It's something most of us here spend a lifetime searching for and sorting out . . . loving family or not, loving children or not, figuring out all the dynamics of love struggles. It occupies a lot of our time here." Celeste released a long sigh. "All I know is that my aunt Niecey made loving somebody an art form . . . she loved family hard and true. She claimed you and made no bones about the fact that you were hers. And all I know is that she was mine. *Is* mine. Will always be that."

"Your aunt is so very, very dear. When I held her hands, I felt generations of people she's touched, a cascade of help that she flung out into this world not caring where the net of love she'd cast landed . . . and it went on and on to even those she'll never know. And then I knew her work was done and I almost wept for joy, but also for the sadness that her transition will cause so many, especially you."

"I don't even know how old Aunt Niecey is," Celeste murmured as another large tear rolled down the bridge of her nose. "But you're right, she helped so many, especially me with all my drama. . . . Will she really go to a good place?"

Azrael grasped Celeste's hands again and brought them to his heart. The swift motion made her lean in close, their faces only inches apart.

"Celeste, she will go to a most beautiful place of freedom and love. No corporeal form to feel injury or pain, no hatred or guilt, or anger or fear. There is no hunger or lack . . . and everyone she ever loved is there, just as she will be able to still be here for you."

"Thank you," Celeste murmured, then brushed his forehead with a gentle kiss. "I believe you in a way I've never believed what they told me growing up. You've shown me things in one night that . . . I don't even have the words for."

"You saved my life, too, Celeste." He looked up into her eyes, and soon she could feel all the compassion and warmth of his spirit radiating from his soul source within.

"I didn't save you," she whispered. "You're . . . the angel, not me. I was the one messed up and on the run that you picked up in a dive bar, remember?"

"Were it not for you," he admitted quietly, "I would have been found before I fully understood this world. My enemies thought that they would find me weak and vulnerable, which is why they only sent one of theirs after me. Had they known I had become strong, there would have been a more uneven attack."

"The guy in the library?"

"Yes . . . from my initial manifestation, my energy signature was weak, my mind confused. . . . Gavreel said I had possibly tipped them off by trying to send earthbound spirits in pain into the Light. So, they sent one of their more insidious beings to break my human body before I could become strong, clearly hoping that I would be delayed in finding you."

"But I didn't do anything but scream and run and give you a hard way to go," Celeste murmured, her gaze searching his. "What could I have possibly done in the short couple of hours we've known each other?"

"You trusted me when everything in your human experience indicated that you should not have. You brought me to hallowed ground so that I could meditate and still my mind to hear my nonmanifest brethren more clearly. That gave me direction and grounded me. You fed me, Celeste—took me to where I could rejuvenate this physical body I am so unused to with proper food . . . then you fed my spirit and made me laugh, made me happy so that I could understand how profound and so very simple human joy can be. That fed my spirit. And then you fed my mind, took me to a place where I could learn so much so fast that it made me dizzy, and at the very end of that, you stood your ground and did not forsake me, even though you had every reason to flee."

He looked at her with a gentle expression, rubbing the backs of her palms with his thumbs. "You taught me your words and customs with a touch . . . you hugged me in a church, laid your cheek against my scars, and had compassion for my injuries even while still half-frightened of me—yet you became righteously indignant about the injuries you'd witnessed and you were ready to fight those who you thought had scarred my back and had taken my wings. You have a righteous soul, Celeste, one that cannot abide seeing another being abused, and that is a sacred thing."

He looked away again and swallowed hard, seeming to struggle for words that would convey the depths of his emotions. "You trusted me enough, even after what you saw and despite all your fears about what I might be . . . that you brought me to your sanctuary. Here. And it has taught me of the loving, trusting, beautiful nature of the human spirit. Until now, I had only heard of this. Until this moment it was all theoretical, and although I never fully understood why the Source wanted us to fight so valiantly for humanity, I knew there had to be good reason. Then I came here, filled with disdain for the horrible conditions that this supposed beauty was to flower within. As I looked around and felt the worst deprivation I had ever known and witnessed lost souls too many to even count, I almost began to give up hope. I could not understand what I was witnessing and therefore began to even question the reasoning of the Source."

Azrael closed his eyes and brought her knuckles against his cheek. "Oh, Celeste, don't humans know that if we angels give up hope once we have manifested on earth, that is the end for us? That is how we die . . . once we are separated from the Light, if we lose hope, then we are fallen for good."

"Then the fallen?" she asked in a tight, frightened voice. "Are they dead?"

"They are dead to the Light. Their spirits consumed by the darkness they've surrendered to, even though their physical forms remain . . . which means they are dead to love, compassion, healing, or joy."

"Then don't die, Azrael," she murmured, brushing the crown of his head with another soft kiss. "There are places so much worse than here . . . children and adults all over the world experiencing famine and horrors that I can't even imagine, and yet, beyond my ability to even understand how, they have hope."

"In the library I learned this," he said, nodding as he looked up at her again. "India, Africa, Central America, the Middle East, Asia . . . Russia . . . the children, Celeste . . ."

She nodded and tightened her grip on his hands. "Yes. The children. Here, too."

"It is all over the world," he whispered, sounding horrified. "And what has happed to the waters—blackened with oil, just as the air is blackened with smoke. The animals and the fishes and the birds . . ."

"You pulled from the recent newspapers and videos," she said, as tears spilled over his lashes.

"How do you maintain hope? You have no understanding of how to bend energy or how to manifest change within the laws of nature . . . humans are so small against the perils so large, yet you hope."

"Because most of us know, somewhere way down deep inside us—without being able to explain why—we know that there's something bigger than us, something stronger than us, something that doesn't want this horrible thing that is happening to us to happen."

"But you are mortal," he said in a quiet rush. "Your time here is finite to the human senses, and there is such fear among you of crossing over into the unknown."

"Even though we argue about the path and whose way is the so-called right way, and every religion swears theirs is the only answer, we know inside us that even if we die, there's someplace we can go to be at peace, and that we can see our loved ones again, or we can come back to help right the wrongs ... we *know*, Azrael, no matter what logic dictates. No matter what evil men and women do, we know that truth and right will prevail in the end ... even if we don't live to see it. Even if it will take generations to make it right. That is the only way I know of to survive as a human being, a weak and small thing in a very hostile world."

"They never could kill all the Light ..." Azrael stared up at her.

"If by 'they' you mean the dark side or demons, then no," she said in a strong voice. "They couldn't."

"For millennia they've tried, Celeste. That is why I am a warrior for the Light and against the darkness. They've used every evil means they could employ ... from famine, to pestilence, war, and oppression. They've razed whole villages, done unspeakable crimes against humanity and the earth. But they couldn't turn off all the human Light. ... And they couldn't find all the Remnant, like you."

"Why?" she murmured, clasping his hands tightly and needing to understand.

"Divine intervention," he said in a firm but quiet tone.

Celeste nodded. "I believe that. My aunt Niecey will tell you that the devil is a liar. They couldn't make people stop praying during the Holocaust, they couldn't make people stop praying while they were in the hulls of ships being carried away in slave chains. They couldn't make people stop praying when they marched them across the country on the Trail of Tears, and like many a vet will tell you, there are no atheists in foxholes. As long as one person does the right thing, keeps praying, keeps believing . . ."

"Yes," he said, squeezing her hands. "That is why you are so important. But the trials and the tribulations that have come against humanity, that is not God's doing. The Source loves you and would never just toy with humans for capricious, egocentric reasons. That is the big lie."

She leaned in closer, bringing his hands within her fists against her heart. "Don't you see, Az, the more they do against innocent people in the material world, the more we hold on tighter to what we can't see . . . because when everything around us in the natural world is totally without hope, the only place to go is somewhere out there to a Higher Source and to ask for supernatural help. And time and time again, history proves that, something nobody can really explain happens to make things right."

Chapter 9

As Forcas approached, beautiful, drug-limp women pulled away from Nathaniel. He tossed back the remains of his Bowmore single-malt Scotch and surveyed his lush surroundings, bemused by Forcas's worried expression. Life was good and the human world was well on its way to going to hell in a handbasket. Comfort and wealth surrounded him. Lucifer had placed unlimited resources at his disposal; what was there to worry about?

Nathaniel smiled and studied his manicure, waiting for the so-called distressing news from one of his sentries. The temporary waterfront-warehouse roost that he'd selected for his fallen angels had been transformed into a lush, ultramodern sanctuary filled with priceless originals from Salvador Dalí, Picasso, and Warhol stolen from the collections. Sumptuous art deco furnishings and red and black leather sofas and chaise longues were draped with heroin-dazed models while still others toked on pipes filled with rock cocaine. He watched one beauty snort her brains out along a kidney-shaped glass table, then lick the tiny coke crumbs left behind. She was as good as dead.

He took a hit of coke and smirked as he stood, enjoying the freak show of naked bodies writhing on the floor before an open fireplace pit. He loved the body he now inhabited and thoroughly enjoyed the way it responded to the sensual earth environment. He had exquisite Roman features, lush dark hair, was tall, muscular, equipped for battle and for sexual prowess, with humans groveling at his feet—this world was good to him.

Four strong, dark angels, each with the body of a gladiator, and representing tribes to the east, to the west, to the north, and to the south, guarded the cardinal points of the warehouse. They nodded at Forcas as he passed.

Nathaniel lifted a decanter of the single-malt Scotch and tipped it in Forcas's direction as Forcas dropped to one knee in front of him. "You look like you need a drink, brother."

"He was stronger than we expected."

"We?" Nathaniel said with a sinister smile. "I told you not to underestimate the Angel of Death. I battled him many times in the first war, and he is still in existence, as am I." Nathaniel poured two short glasses of Scotch, slid one across the kidney-shaped glass table, and motioned with his hand for Forcas to rise and sit on one of the art deco, black leather chairs. "We cannot waste time bickering amongst ourselves, but next time do not be so arrogant. Take Appollyn with you . . . but tell me, where did you find him?"

"In a library."

Nathaniel held his glass in midair and burst out laughing. "Oh, that is so rich and so like Azrael!"

"He had eaten clean foods, too, milord. Not only is his will strong, but his human body energy is also very strong. He attacked without hesitation, and I could tell that he owned no fear."

"Of course he didn't," Nathaniel said in a low, ominous tone as his eyes turned pure black.

Forcas looked down at the geometric-design rug, clasping his hands between his knees. "He found the girl."

"What!" Nathaniel was on his feet in an instant and hurled the glass at the far, exposed-brick warehouse wall. As it shattered, his long waves of brunet hair lifted from his shoulders on an unnatural wind.

"She took him to the library. She must have been the one who fed him," Forcas said quickly.

The dark angels who guarded the four corners of the large, open space now turned their focus inward to stare at the dispute. Nathaniel reached back with both hands, spun hard, and flung a dark orb of black energy against the windows, shattering the floor-to-ceiling panes. Humans shrieked, and he waved his arm, rendering them unconscious. But instead of the glass exploding outward, it imploded to cover the floor with glass that suddenly blackened.

"Demon centurions!" he shouted. "Come forth!"

Every shard of glass sprang to life, drawing together until they formed six writhing masses. Each squirming black essence soon transformed into a grotesque figure of human deformity, with gargoyle features and red, gleaming eyes. Each demon's mouth was twisted and distended by jagged teeth, hands contorted into bone-crushing claws. Gray-green flesh the pallor of death pulled away from their semi-exposed muscles. Naked and sexless, they looked up at Nathaniel, gazes narrowed.

When they stood, Nathaniel's stature grew taller and he ripped off his black biker jacket. As his rage escalated, a pair of enormous, glistening black wings tore through his back. Blood splattered the table and across Forcas's face from the violent ejection. Nathaniel pointed at the demons, which had begun to back away from him.

"How in Lucifer's name could this happen? The last report I received she was broken, on the verge of suicide, and had been driven mad! How in so short a time can this be?"

"Asmodeus, as you are aware, we are not allowed to kill her, so commanded the Dark Lord," one bold demon hissed.

"Nathaniel," Asmodeus corrected in a lethal whisper between his lengthening fangs. "How many times have I instructed you to call me by the name of this culture's translation, lest you slip in tongue before the wrong party?"

"Milord," the demon corrected with a sneer and a be-grudging bow. "Fallen angels and demon principalities cannot trump angels from the higher realm of Powers, where warriors like Azrael are made. Only one from the angel legions of Light can take her life. Remember the edict: We are not allowed to outright murder a member of the Remnant, only drive them mad or make them want to kill themselves. Otherwise, if we kill the girl, upon her death the Light essence of her soul will go to strengthening our enemy's side. She went beyond our sight—"

"Because he took her onto consecrated ground! Where is she now?"

"We do not know, milord. We are currently blind to her whereabouts . . . perhaps she is still on consecrated ground."

"Don't you have a tether to her addiction? Haven't you kept her tempted by drugs and alcohol enough to make her soul weak and to question her own judgment! Use the shadows to send dark spiritual attachments to leach her Light from her spirit, to drive her further into self-destruction—give her cancer, goddamn you! Something, anything, but she cannot pair with the Light's fucking Angel of Death! Make her life even more of a living hell so she'll commit suicide and be done with this folly!"

"She is no longer addicted," the demon said in a hiss, stepping forward to challenge Nathaniel with a narrowed gaze. "He cleaned her out; that much we know. He used a power that you no longer own, the power to heal, to break our bonds and to remove all spiritual attachments that ravaged her soul. Do not blame us. You were to keep your kind, your brothers in the Light, away from our work . . . and you did not. This is what we will report to the Dark Lord. How you fallen angels suddenly became our overlords instead of Lucifer is something yet to be sorted out in Hell. But we did everything to make her—"

"Silence!" Nathaniel shouted and hurled a black energy orb that splattered the demon that had spoken against the brick wall. Nathaniel then turned to the remaining demons, who hissed dissatisfaction over their midlevel commander's extermination. "Because you did not do your jobs, my brother in darkness encountered a fully prepared Warrior of the Light! A Powers-level angel!" His booming voice shattered the crystal decanter of Scotch.

"Forcas could have been made to cease to exist. Now he must take Appollyon with him, my Angel of Destruction, or perhaps Malpas, or even Lahash and Pharzuph—none of whom I want to risk this close to the date that the veil will be lifted between worlds. What about this do you not understand? December twenty-first, 2012, is but a few short months away. A few short months! The last time we fought this war, the dark side won only because legions of us took the fall! That will not happen again. Without us, original demons born of Lilith would have been crushed—are there any questions about this history?"

Nathaniel walked a slow, threatening circle around the silent demons. "Get the girl away from Azrael. Drive a wedge between them, break her spirit, make her distrust him, do whatever it takes so that he may not claim her. Find this girl and bring her to me. If you cannot turn her dark or break her, I will do so myself!"

Azrael sat very still in the dim, modest living room, contemplating the human female that disquieted him so deeply. Tonight a pair of soft, gentle hands had caressed his scars. Something he'd never felt before slowly lit inside his chest as she'd unexpectedly attempted to heal him with her touch.

He'd felt her soul weep as she'd stared at his destroyed

back. Then came her anger, the pure fire of her righteous indignation and readiness to protect him against whatever had caused his butchering. The warrior-defender in her spirit had risen in a snap call to arms as her mind wrestled with who could have abused him so.

She cared so intensely, so deeply, yet didn't even know him. But to her, that didn't matter; in her mind, what had happened to him was wrong, and she didn't care who he was or what the circumstances, it caused her pain to see another being harmed. Then her soft, soft cheek rested against his shoulder in the sanctuary of the church for a few moments while her hands stroked away his shame. This after the woman had been beaten, starved, trauma-tized, humiliated, chased by dogs and demons, and other-wise abused. But she still had room in her heart to see the pain of another, even used her own pain, her own tragic experiences, to identify with his.

What was this glorious capacity of the human spirit? What was this capricious thing called free will, where some of them could commit the worst abominations against each other, while still others could reach out past their own agony, past their own best interest, to help someone they perceived more in need than themselves?

Celeste had sensed disorientation and fear in him, while she was terrified herself. Azrael looked at the stairs, remembering watching her footfalls as she'd said good-night. He'd relaxed under her sweet touch, even while unable to sort out how she'd made him feel, just as it was impossible to grapple with the emotions that roiled within him as she fed him fresh mangoes and potato chips and ice cream, then wiped his sticky face. Some level of tenderness belonged to the nurturing angelic realms, but Celeste owned that same divinity here on earth.

After being in her company and then being introduced to her aunt, and experiencing how a woman who'd lost so much still gave so much, he finally understood the lesson in the loss he'd experienced. Human beings could also heal. They were indeed Divine beings. Perhaps that was what he had to understand before he could ever go forward with his mission.

He'd looked into a pair of weary but gentle brown eyes and had seen that through all the scars Celeste Jackson had endured her spirit still had innocence, hope, and a plea that fairness and justice prevail. He'd seen that goodness, her pristine core, and felt as if his heart would shatter as her voice broke and she bit her lip when he had to deliver the hard truth that her aunt's days were numbered. His sworn code would only allow for the truth, and he didn't know what to do to stop Celeste's pain. And he so desperately wanted to stop her pain. But wisdom that profound was something he did not own.

Part of him was compelled to hug her, while another part of him wanted to just lie and avoid her question altogether. Conflicted, he'd opted for the inadequate words and had told her what he now wished he hadn't, all the while his arms strangely aching to embrace her.

He released a long sigh and dragged his fingers through his hair. Even with the bitter truth, she didn't blame him or lash out at him when she easily could have. Instead her eyes had glittered with unspent tears and the passion of conviction. Celeste's gorgeous brown eyes were the eyes of a human woman who had endured much but still believed. She'd made his fingers tremble as he'd traced the lines of her tears and beheld her pretty face. She had taught him something else tonight, something just as important as hope—faith when all hope is lost.

And what he was feeling right now for her was so damned dangerous. She had the potential to become an addiction, something more than a passing bad habit. He knew the rules, but could also feel rational thought evaporating within him. It was imperative to wrest back control. When he'd seen Forcas, something fragile within him had snapped.

Azrael rubbed his palms down his face. Yes, he was a warrior, but tonight he'd felt murderous intent. What he'd felt was about more than simply protecting a valued asset of the Light; listening to Forcas try to coax Celeste into the darkness had ignited a level of rage that he'd never known . . . just as she had, in her honest assessment of life, somehow ignited brand-new passion within him. It was terrifying.

Azrael stood and walked away from the sofa into the dining room. He had to shake this feeling and do something constructive to occupy his mind.

Left to his own devices within the new wonder of a twenty-first-century human home, sleep evaded him. That's what he told himself. It was the newness of the environment; it was the threat of ever-present danger. He would not attribute his restlessness to persistent thoughts of her.

Azrael looked down at the computer. It made him sad that by truthfully answering her question he'd brought her pain. He wondered if that was really the source of human lies—not wanting to cause pain, not wanting to experience pain from the other person's reaction, or a mixture of both.

Those kinds of human choices he was beginning to understand, just as he was becoming aware of just how much he didn't really know. Every emotion had a trigger, had a price, and exacted some toll on his spirit and even his body. He'd felt emotional pain as though it were a heaviness in his chest. He'd felt rage zing through him so hotly and quickly that it had made his ears ring. He could now also identify tenderness and caring; it felt warm and soothing, just as laughter caused everything within him to instantly lighten.

Then there was this strange and deeply disturbing emotion that he felt when he looked into Celeste's eyes, when she touched him gently and let down her guard. He wasn't ready to identify the component parts of that emotion yet, or to address where it manifested in his body.

He moved to the dining room table as quietly as possible, remembering that Celeste's aunt had offered him use of this thing called a laptop. As he sat down, he remembered Celeste had also said that the Internet would blow his mind. He stared at the lime green device, knowing that somehow this and the place called the Internet were linked.

Stilling his thoughts, he called on any impressions of the relationship between the laptop device and the Internet that he could glean from the library and from his mind-bond with Celeste. Afraid that he might accidentally break it, he gently lifted the unit and turned it over, careful of the long wires connected to the wall as he tried to figure out how to open it. But the moment he touched it, children's mirth filled him and their open knowledge gave him all he needed to know. He could feel the laughter and excitement from the children that Mrs. Jackson babysat. They'd touched the computer; they enjoyed playing games on it. They were experts on how to use it.

Eagerly popping the unit open, he quickly turned it on, bypassed the easy password, *Nana,* and logged on to a Web browser. Instantly his consciousness went out into a black void, then images and information careened into his mind so fast that he drew away from the unit, panting.

Azrael pushed the off button and slammed down the top, appalled and amazed. Although his eyes were tightly shut, images continued to career through his mind in millisecond intervals, causing his lids to flutter. He was almost near a seizure, but the images slowly began to abate and he spread his palms out wide and pressed them down hard against the wood table to ground himself.

Slowly opening his eyes, he wiped his brow and sat back, staring at the small, flat neon green box on the table. Celeste had been right; the Internet nearly blew his mind. Millions of humans had come together to create what was like a human replica of the divine Akashic Records. And this coming together had no filter. It was as though the gates of Heaven and Hell collided here; you could find great good or great evil on the Internet . . . it was wideopen, which made sense to him as he pondered the issue— this was the free-will zone. Both Heaven and Hell did reside here on earth, too, and that was what the battle was about—which side was going to prevail.

But the difference between what was in the human

worldwide database and what resided in the Akashic Records was that truth and lies and misinformation were allowed to reside side by side.

"Interesting," Azrael murmured, peering at the laptop, but not ready to touch it again just yet.

What had almost shut down his mind was the instantaneous filtering required in order to sense and weed out the dark-consciousness aura around information created for harm. The library had much less of that; it was as though some responsible humans had decided against allowing in things such as child pornography and hate-filled newsletters calling for armed violence, even though adult subject matter was permitted. But in this elusive place called cyberspace, anything and everything was allowed.

Deeply inspirational things, such as messages and websites of uplifting purposes and beauty, were right next to satanic worship and ritual killings, and things that no human was ever meant to do with an innocent animal.

What was really unnerving was that the sites took him through the full gamut of human emotion. Some sites made him want to laugh, some made him want to bitterly weep. Some were provocatively arousing, while others revolted him with indescribable disgust. The need to protect came as quickly as the urge to kill. And all of it shot through his mind faster than his feelings could process. That, too, was what had almost caused the information seizure. The Akashic Records modulated to the being's frequency, unlike the Internet.

Still, for all its human imperfections, it was a wonderland of options that taught him music, languages, and even how to speak and understand Celeste's dialect. He hoped she would be pleased. But he had to get the horrors he'd seen out of his mind . . . the dark side of the Internet was definitely no place for a being of Light.

Azrael shivered and then focused his mind again, now realizing that he possessed entirely too much knowledge— there were things he was quite sure he never wanted to know. However, he was pleased to learn of the wealth of information in the human consciousness about energy and the Light. He'd also begun to understand that it wasn't wise to do a general search. One had to be specific.

Tentatively opening the laptop again, this time when he turned it on, he spoke his intention out loud.

"Maps . . . find me maps of the places I need to go to seek Bath Kol and any balance keepers that will guide me on my mission."

Again he closed his eyes as Google Maps seared his brain with satellite images of streets, apartment buildings, warehouses, transportation options, and monasteries. Azrael drew away from the computer, breathing hard. He shook his head as he stood up on wobbly legs.

"Wow," he murmured. "What a rush!"

Serenity claimed Celeste and she felt oddly refreshed as the sound of deep, booming male laughter mixed with her aunt's husky-timbered mirth awakened her with a smile. She hadn't felt this calm and safe waking up since she'd been a kid, and even then she'd never felt this completely at peace.

A blender whirred . . . and she could smell pancakes?

Celeste swung her legs over the side of the bed and gathered together the robe she'd borrowed to sleep in. She dashed down the short hall and down the steps and found Azrael at the stove making spelt pancakes and her aunt seated at the table looking through an old scrapbook.

"We didn't mean to wake you up, suga," Aunt Niecey said, wiping her eyes. "But Az gonna make me need diapers if he don't stop cutting up."

"Huh?" Celeste looked from Azrael to her aunt completely confused.

"He's been telling me all kinds of crazy mess about why you gotta cook a certain way, then is trying to get me to eat these here pancakes with no eggs in 'em with tofu whipped cream—whatever *that* is—and then he had the nerve to swirl up almost all them good collards in a danged blender! Who eats collard greens raw from a blender?" Aunt Niecey started laughing again and wiped away tears of mirth. "The boy done lost his natchel mind, even though his pancakes with mango and strawberries look good."

"Try these," Azrael said with a big smile, setting down a plate of pancakes topped with fruit, pure maple syrup, and what looked like whipped cream. "I've already blessed the food, so dig in and tell me what you think."

"You let him cook on your stove?" Celeste stood in the doorway, slack-jawed. Nobody but serious family, and not even all of them, got to cook at Aunt Niecey's stove!

"We had a bet," Aunt Niecey said, taking a huge forkful of fluffy pancakes. "I bet him he couldn't make breakfast as good as my Roscoe used to, and he bet me I couldn't make him laugh."

For a few seconds, Celeste simply stood in the doorway amazed. What had happened during the six hours she'd been asleep?

Azrael had changed clothes and had clearly showered; his long locks left a damp spot down the back of his fresh royal-blue, collared T-shirt. He also now wore a different pair of jeans and smelled as if he had on cologne—and had what look like barber-trimmed five-o'clock shadow. He had to have gone back to the stores alone at night to gather more supplies. She glanced at the bags sitting in the corner on the floor. All-natural pancake mix and syrup were definitely not in the bags before. She glanced back toward the sofa and saw a bulging men's gym bag and a women's backpack.

"What do you think?" Azrael said, giving Celeste a measured glance before he offered Aunt Niecey a wink. "You want to call it a draw?"

"Might have to do that," Aunt Niecey said, seeming oblivious to the exchange between Celeste and Azrael. "Son, you can burn, even if you got some hippie kitchen ways."

"I'll take that as a compliment."

"Was meant as one," she replied, chewing a mouthful of pancakes. "These are really good."

He set down a glass of fresh-squeezed orange juice in front of Aunt Niecey. "We'll work our way up to green juices, how about that?"

"Yeah, well," Aunt Niecey protested, laughing. "You gonna have to work your way up a real hard row to hoe if you think I'ma be drinking no collard greens."

"She's tough," Azrael said, looking at Celeste and laughing. "Are you hungry?"

"Yes," Celeste replied, as the smile she'd been wearing widened.

"Then come join us and have a seat." Azrael turned back to the counter, then brought her a glass of the green juice that her aunt had rejected. "But since you didn't place an earlier bet, you'll have to abide by the cook's rules and get something green in you first."

Celeste sat down laughing as her aunt let out a whoop and slapped the table. She couldn't remember when she'd seen Aunt Niecey in such a good mood.

"Tell me how nasty it is, chile, and don't lie," her aunt said, wrinkling her nose.

Picking up the tall glass and scrutinizing it under the light for dramatic emphasis, Celeste took a deep sip, then drank down the entire glass. He'd obviously put something sweet in it to cut the pungent collards, and it tasted like thick apple juice with a bit of a bite to it. Celeste allowed the mixture to roll over her tongue, trying to figure out his recipe. "It's really quite good. What did you put in it?"

"Oooohhh, girl, you need to tell the truth and shame the devil! The only reason you drank it down so fast is to keep from hurting his feelings!" Aunt Niecey bent over where she sat and laughed hard. "But I can't blame you, wit his handsome self."

"No . . . it really is good," Celeste said, unable to stop laughing as her aunt took off her glasses and wiped her eyes. "But what's in it? Seriously."

"To answer your question, it's got a little gingerroot, carrots, kale, a splash of lemon, apples for sweetness, and a little agave nectar, all of which will alkalize the pH in your blood and feed your cells better than most anything you eat," Azrael said, feigning indignation, which only made the women laugh harder. He turned and folded his arms over his chest with a spatula still in his huge fist, giving them a good-natured glare with a half smile. "But I bet I'll get no complaints on my pancakes, even from my toughest customer."

"None whatsoever," Aunt Niecey said, still wiping her eyes and wheezing. "And even that crazy-sounding whipped topping is good. What's it called, toe-hoo?"

"*Tofu,* Auntie," Celeste said, laughing harder.

"Well, don't blame me 'cuz the name is funny . . . but he's right. He sweetened it up with some ole almond milk and coconut milk and syrup concoction and mixed it in that contraption, and now I can't tell the difference from that and the real McCoy. Seems like a lot of work when you can jus' buy whipped cream in the can and spray it on, although you didn't hear that from me. But I still don't see why I can't have my butter on these, which would just take 'em to the moon. Still in all, the way Azrael fixed 'em is definitely all right by me."

"Good," Azrael said in a fake huff, then turned back to the stove.

Aunt Niecey bit her lip and waved him away as she composed herself. "My Roscoe did pretty good with breakfast . . . was a bacon-and-eggs man, though."

It was the second reference Celeste's grandmother had made to some man named Roscoe. But the reference was totally confusing to Celeste, because she was almost certain that Roscoe was Aunt Phoebe's first husband, who died in World War II.

"Roscoe made you breakfast, Auntie?" Celeste asked, gently pushing at the edge of the subject.

"Honey chile, Roscoe loved to wake me up with breakfast in bed . . . them were the days," Aunt Niecey replied, beaming. "So, if you find you one who can make you *good* breakfast in bed, then you are double blessed," she added, laughing.

Shocked that her aunt had gone there, Celeste opened her mouth, closed it, then laughed. What had come over Aunt Niecey? "But . . ."

"Oh, yeah, yeah, yeah . . . everybody said he was Phoebe's husband, on account of the fact that I had to go down South to live with her for a summer."

Thoroughly confused, Celeste stared at her aunt. Generally when older black folks said a young girl *had* to go down South for a summer, it meant that she was pregnant and was sent South, back in the day, to hide her pregnancy. Then the girl came back north and resumed her life, and some older married relative "down home" kept the baby. Celeste tried to shake that out of her mind; that couldn't have been what Aunt Niecey meant.

Aunt Niecey took another bite of her pancakes and flipped through the yellowing photo album with a pleasant sigh. "Wasn't like it is these days. Back then, if a young girl got *in trouble,* if'n you know what I mean, then they sent ya South. Then your aunt or some kin who'd never been showing suddenly had a brand-new baby—in my case your aunt Phoebe, who was a newlywed, had my twins down in North Carolina." Aunt Niecey glanced at Azrael and then at Celeste. "That was the old-fashioned way of having what they now call a surrogate chile on TV."

Celeste didn't move a muscle, much less breathe. Her

aunt had never been so forthright in all the years she'd known her.

Aunt Niecey laughed at her own joke and shook her head. "Me and Roscoe had been in love for months and had only got together for a few wonderful weeks before he got drafted and had to show up on the base. By the time I found out I was carrying, it was too late. He was already on his way overseas. I wrote him," she said in a wistful tone. "He wrote me back and said he was gonna marry me, and I believed that he would have, too. In fact I know it. But he ain't never had a chance to. War took 'im. But we had us some good times . . . and he loved to dance."

Celeste remained very still as Azrael brought a plate of topped pancakes to her. All these years she'd thought Aunt Niecey just claimed her sister's children as her own, the way people often do when they dote on a close friend's child that they love. They'd say, 'Oh, you know that's really my baby,' all in jest and as a show of true devotion to the cherished child. That's what she thought had gone on between her two aunts; she'd always thought Aunt Niecey had verbally claimed her sister's grown children as her own out of deep devotion, never realizing that they were actually, biologically *hers*.

Claiming other people's children was like adhering a stamp of love on a child. It was the village approach, something old folks did in the community; a collective part of the old Southern way that lines of kin got verbally blurred when there was no line of demarcation due to love. To be claimed by many aunties and neighborhood church ladies was to be well loved. As a child in that embrace, you didn't think about it; most times people couldn't fully remember how all the so-called cousins were really related, whether by blood or not. You were just in the tribe, a part of the family equation. But in her family it was obviously deeper than that. A long-held secret was fraying at the seams.

"So Cousin Baby and lil' Roscoe are actually yours?" Celeste finally asked.

"Yeah, and they my heart and soul," her aunt Niecey said in a weary tone. "But they never forgave me for letting Phoebe raise 'em . . . so sometimes they don't act very nice. Probably why they also get so mad at you sometimes, claiming I treat you better than I ever treated them. That ain't your fault, though, and they've got no cause to blame you for anything. They full grown and you wasn't even thought about when all this happened, baby. Your mama understood, though. *She* was my heart, too, my closest sister, and the only one in the family that would stick up for me. But I done turnt it over to my Jesus and I try my best to right the wrongs I've done through my grands."

"You did no wrong," Azrael said quietly. "You were just a child yourself when all this began, and the era wasn't kind to women. Not many in history were."

Aunt Niecey nodded. "You ain't lying," she murmured. "They treated you *and* your children like dirt if you didn't have a ring on your finger. Wanted more than that for them. Only problem was, Phoebe resented having to take care of my twin babies, plus her own after she had them . . . she treated mine different, I later found out. Her husband didn't want to take care of no twins that were put on him and made no bones about it. So your cousins got a lot of hurt to work out of their hearts. But I swore 'fo Jesus that if the shoe was *ever* on the other foot, I would love a child that was given to me like he or she was my very own. Then God tested me out on my promise and gave me you when your mama died. You were always my blessing, my second chance, sweet pea. So don't you ever think for a moment that I ain't love you true, 'cuz I did and I do."

Celeste stood and went over to her aunt and hugged her hard. "I know you did. I always felt like I was yours, and I love you like you're my own mama. I hope you know that?"

Aunt Niecey chuckled and petted Celeste's back before drawing away. "I know that," she murmured. "You, and my grands, are the only ones who loved me without fail. But don't you go feeling sorry for this ole lady. I done lived me a full and blessed life. When my time comes, I ain't worried. I'ma be laughing and put on my best dress and my high heels, and I'ma get young again when I cross those pearly gates to see my fiancé. This time, though," she added with a little laugh, "I'ma make Roscoe marry me right away."

Celeste kissed her aunt and sat back down, catching a knowing look from Azrael. This was more family business that had to be set right so that she and her aunt could be at peace. Celeste also knew that somehow his presence had brought about the confession, although she didn't know how he'd done it.

She ate quietly, giving Azrael the thumbs-up as her aunt slowly paged through an ancient photo album that Celeste had never seen. Now all the stories made sense. All of the mythology around Aunt Niecey being so fiery and rattlesnake mean—Aunt Niecey with no children, who took in everybody else's children and fed them, and disciplined them, and raised them up with tough love. This was the same Aunt Niecey whose heart had been broken into a thousand pieces during the war, the same one who never recovered from losing the love of her life and then losing her newborn children to a sister who didn't want to take them in. No wonder her aunt was so quick to set people straight. It was also probably why she clung so hard to her Bible, the only mental-health recourse for poor people of her era.

Chapter 10

*B*elly full and her spirit at peace, Celeste hoisted her new backpack over her shoulder and left Aunt Niecey and Azrael to chat and argue recipes in the kitchen. He'd insisted on washing the dishes, which caused a huge row with Aunt Niecey, but her aunt had finally relented by teasing him in good spirit and adding Azrael's pleasant protest to the other qualities of his she admired.

Among the many things that amazed Celeste as she entered her old bedroom and dumped the backpack contents on the bed was that in one night Azrael had definitely nailed her taste in clothing. A few pairs of rolled-up jeans tumbled onto the bed—one pair black, one pair dark blue, and one pair ripped stonewashed. Also, a few light knit sweaters in soft lime, deep cranberry, and charcoal, plus several colorful cotton tank tees, a new hoodie jacket, and a short-cropped black leather jacket, socks, underwear, and a white lace nightgown were all sitting on top of a new pair of black sneakers at the bottom of the bag.

But how the heck did he know her size? She turned over the tags and simply shook her head. One touch, one healing, and he'd been able to telepathically pick up all that?

"Now this is deep," she murmured, still going through the backpack.

Celeste laughed quietly when she rifled through the underwear to find brand-new Victoria's Secret bras and panties from their angel collection with the tags still on them.

"Wonder, do they really have female angels where you claim you come from? Who knew?" Celeste laughed and shook her head again as she peered at his selection. "Oooohhhh, bad angel but good choices. Tasteful . . . understated, not too over-the-top, but what other TMI did you pick up in the library's magazine section?"

She held the lacy pastels in her hands and felt her face warm as she stared at the daring black push-up and skimpy lace panties that matched, then just shook her head one more time.

"This one will definitely make you fall, brother," she murmured as she laughed quietly, then folded away her loot, choosing the gray and black sweater and jeans combo to wear.

He'd even stashed the items he'd purchased from the supermarket in her bag. Sweet-smelling all-natural soap, body wash, lotion, hair ties, a comb and brush, and a new toothbrush and all-natural, Tom's of Maine toothpaste along with all-natural deodorant that contained no aluminum additives. Everything she could have asked for was jam-packed into her backpack. She just sighed when she saw a small box of Angel perfume that he obviously made a special stop to get. Aunt Niecey was right, this one was a keeper. Although she couldn't wrap her brain around how he'd been able to do all this in the short time allotted.

Life had made her a realist of the most serious order. Nothing about this made sense; she had absolutely no frame of reference to fit what was happening—yet it was still happening. Her aunt Niecey was now a witness, too, and wasn't looking at her strangely as though she were seeing things that weren't there. Celeste stared down at the clothes on the bed. The gifts were nice but they were also scary.

Either this man was running the most elaborate scam she'd ever seen or she was crazy . . . or he might just be what he claimed he was.

No matter which way she looked at it, she felt it made perfect sense that she was still having a lot of trouble suspending disbelief about everything she was witnessing and experiencing. *That was sane.* Questioning Azrael's fantastic claims was rational. That she had some good old-fashioned common sense left and was trying to debunk the supernatural had to mean that she wasn't totally nuts. That was all she had left to cling to; if she let go of that, she'd be free-falling into an abyss of the outrageous . . . the place where she saw demons in normal people's faces and shadows that split out from a normal human body. She could not mentally afford to go there. The price of doing that was too high and way too scary.

The clothes she'd held in her hands were tangible, but he would have had to walk into a locked store to get them. She'd seen him do it, saw him pay for things by leaving cash on the counter, and had witnessed his ability to unlock doors and walk into an establishment undetected. She'd also seen him fight an entity that defied her comprehension, just as sure as she'd watched him prepare pancakes in Aunt Niecey's kitchen.

Celeste stopped and looked in the mirror, then gasped. She covered her mouth with both hands to stop a scream. Less afraid now that it was broad daylight outside and she had Aunt Niecey and Azrael right downstairs, she'd risked a peek. Her skin was smooth and clear. No dark circles were under her eyes. Her acne was gone and her cheeks were rosy and flushed. Leaning closer, she searched her broken hairline, where it had previously been in tatters from stress, bad nutrition, and heat damage, and noticed the new growth of fine baby hair coming in.

"Oh, God, oh, God, oh, God," she whispered, panicking as she peeled off her old clothes and stepped into the shower with her mind buzzing. "I have to be hallucinating."

But not even the long, hot pummel of water stopped the hundreds of questions that beat against her brain.

There were actually angels? If that was true, when were angels created and was there really a place called Hell? But why were people allowed to be swayed by evil in the first place—why wouldn't the Source, as Azrael called it, just wipe all the pain and destruction off the face of the planet and spare us weak humans? Like, who the hell were we in comparison to all that supernatural bad shit? And why did bad shit happen to good people in the first place? Plus, she wanted to know, was there really a so-called spirit world, and if so, could he get a message to her mom?

But the most pressing question that consumed her was, if all this was really happening, then why was it happening around her—to her? What in the hell did she have to do with any of this?

Brushing her teeth and dressing quickly, she came down the stairs to the blare of the noonday news. Aunt Niecey had the volume all the way up and she sat in her favorite overstuffed floral chair with her arms folded, shaking her head. Azrael sat on the sofa, watching with his elbows on his knees and hands folded between them, riveted to the report.

"Now, see, that don't make no kinda sense!" Aunt Niecey exclaimed, clucking her tongue. "They's gang-warring in a library? Look at all that damage to that beautiful building! Thousands of dollars—irreplaceable marble and iron fixtures. People done lost their minds. I'm telling you, the devil is busy!"

Celeste came to a slow stop on the landing and caught Azrael's meaningful look as her backpack slipped from her hand to the floor. Her stomach bubbled with anxiety as the news anchor recounted numerous theories about who might have committed such an atrocity against a regional treasure.

"Forensics experts are baffled by this case, as damage of this nature," the news anchor said in a solemn tone, "should have revealed some sort of explosive. But there's absolutely nothing yet to suggest what type of bomb blast could have literally ripped iron off the doors and felled heavy marble columns in this manner."

"It looks like a pinpoint tornado went through the lobby of this place," the chief of police said, rubbing the back of his thick neck. "But meteorologists have ruled that out. This was definitely a man-made explosive of some type."

"Well, the only good thing is, that library probably got plenty insurance to cover the damage, but it still ain't right." Aunt Niecey folded her arms over her chest in a huff, then returned her attention to the broadcast. "Shame, too, 'cuz lots of people need to use that place to look for jobs—I heard they don't even have paper applications no mo'. You have to apply for a job on the computer, and most poor folks I know don't have one. How's they gonna look for work if they close that library for repairs? Plus, the city's cutting back and ain't fund 'em no money like before . . . humph! Might not have insurance."

When the police spokesperson stepped up to a microphone and the news cut away into a split screen to bring the only tangible weapon at the scene into view, Celeste gasped. It was the gun that Azrael had handed her. The gun that had his prints on it and might even have hers. The gun that had dropped when the two entities . . . oh . . . my God.

Celeste stared at Azrael and he stared at her. If the news had the aftermath on camera . . . If they actually had a piece of evidence from the site of the battle . . . If her aunt was recounting it as she watched it . . . If other people saw what Celeste now saw . . . then she wasn't out of her mind!

But that meant something scarier was happening. That also meant Brandon was dead and she hadn't imagined that either. It meant that *everything* she'd experienced in the last twenty-four hours had actually happened *exactly* as she'd seen it, angels and demons and all, and none of it was a hallucination!

"Turn off the television," Celeste said quickly, then rushed over to the coffee table to grab the remote before Azrael could pick it up. Her hands were shaking as she clicked off the television and set the remote down hard. "I can't stand to see any more violence," she added, trying to come up with a viable excuse for her outburst.

Seeing the library destruction was only the half of what had shredded her nerves. She was sure that she'd lose her mind if saw a gruesome news report of Brandon's death. She didn't want to know what the demons had left. Azrael's gaze met hers and held it.

"Can't say I blame you, chile. Lissen, y'all be careful out there when you go to New York," Aunt Niecey said, standing. "I used to love to go there back in my heyday. Cotton Club, all kinds of juke joints and cabarets . . . me and Roscoe went all over, and you didn't have to worry about nobody bothering you. But now," she added, shaking her head. "You could be sitting in church even, or at a funeral, and folks wanna be shooting and looting. It ain't jus' in New York, the whole worl' done gone crazy. Can be in the city, the suburbs, don't matter. It's all over, so you all be safe."

Celeste slowly tore her gaze from Azrael and went over to hug her aunt. New York, huh. Okay . . . she was headed north anyway. But if he was really an angel, there was no reason to run away from him. Anxiety was still making her hands tremble.

"Chile, you look like you've seen a ghost. I know this mess on the news is upsetting. I try to jus' watch every now and then so I know the places to avoid." Aunt Niecey hugged Celeste tighter but spoke to Azrael. "This one has a fragile constitution, like I tol' you. Sometimes . . . things upset her—she's sensitive like her mama. So, things like what we jus' seen . . . be patient with her. She's got a good heart, though."

"I know she does, just like you do," Azrael said, standing. "I'll take care of her no matter what. That's my word."

"I'm just glad you're all right, Auntie," Celeste said, finding it suddenly hard to breathe. Celeste swallowed thickly but refused to cry. This time she would leave her aunt seeming strong, not worrying her aunt's peace of mind. A pair of thick, meaty brown arms enfolded Celeste and she drew back to look at her aunt's kind, round face. Aunt Niecey smiled and smoothed down the front of her pink, flowered housecoat. Moisture filled her cloudy brown eyes and she blinked it back behind her gold-rimmed glasses, then tugged at the edges of her short-styled, black-and-gray wig to straighten it.

"I mean it when I say be safe, suga. Don't like you roamin' all around out there in these end-of-days times."

"No matter what, you know how much I love you, right?" Celeste said, forcing the strength of conviction into her voice. "I'm coming back home to see you really soon. Okay?"

"Yeah, honeybird, and I love you right on back, too. So you run on and go do what young folks s'posed to do. Don'tchu be worrying about no old lady. I'm fine. I shouldn'ta had that danged news on to upset you like this. Bad habit." Aunt Niecey released a sigh and pulled back to kiss Celeste on the cheek. "But you gonna be all right, baby. I'm gonna be all right, too."

Deep concern weighed on Azrael's shoulders as they walked down the street. Celeste hadn't said two words since they'd left the house and walked a block and a half to the Route 34 trolley stop. He wasn't sure if her anxiety stemmed from her leaving her elderly aunt, something he'd done wrong, or the shock of seeing the news. But he couldn't lie and tell Celeste that Aunt Niecey would be all right physically. Her time was near. The only thing he could attest to was that her spirit was just fine, and when she crossed over from life into the spirit world or pure Light, only then would it really be all right. Leaving human existence behind was when Aunt Niecey's pain and problems would finally come to an end.

But in his brief time on earth, he also knew that while the angels rejoiced over a life well lived when a spirit came home, humans left behind grieved hard for the loss of their loved one.

Celeste kept her eyes straight ahead and it seemed as though all the color had drained from her previously repaired complexion.

After the healing she'd seemed much improved. Now her nerves seemed on the verge of fraying and popping once more. She looked so skittish that she seemed ready to bolt into the street at any moment. Chancing a question, he gave her some distance to keep her from feeling trapped.

"I memorized the public transportation grid of this city and in New York. They have many more trains than here, but for the size of this metropolis, it is adequate."

He peered at her but she didn't look at him or blink.

"If we go via Amtrak, we'll have to stop and show identification in order to buy tickets . . . which may not be a good idea, since I have none. But if we take the R7 regional rail to Trenton and cross over to New Jersey Transit, then we can make our purchases all via machines. It said that in the online brochures."

Azrael waited, feeling somewhat dejected that she wasn't the least bit impressed by his absorption of knowledge. He also wished she would let him know if he'd done all right in the choices of items he'd selected for her. Although he had absorbed and mastered many facts, he was still at a loss in understanding the nuances of human emotion. Deciphering emotions was clearly an art and not a hard science.

He wondered if she knew how pretty she looked, despite her stricken expression. She'd also put on the perfume that he'd hoped she'd like . . . it smelled wonderful on her. The clothes transformed her body in a way that was thoroughly pleasing to him. The parts of her skin that he could see looked radiant under the sun . . . dewy the way the advertisement had claimed.

"Celeste . . . ," he murmured, releasing a long sigh with his words.

"Why do they want me?" she suddenly said, giving him her direct attention with a challenging stare.

"They don't want you to gather the other Remnant," he said quietly. "Like I told you before, if you all come together, you will have enough power to create a movement of change among the masses . . . and you're the strongest of the Remnant that are left."

"Me? Wrong chick."

He held her arm gently and spoke to her slowly. "Yes, you. When your temple is cleaned out, your inner light is strong enough to allow you to speak truth that literally resonates within average humans. They can't shake your words; they feel your message in their gut. That's *power,* Celeste. Why do you think people have been trying to get you to shut up all your life? Think about it. They've drugged you, tried to break your confidence, tried to make you think you were stupid so you wouldn't speak out against them . . . until they practically stole your voice."

When she didn't yank away or protest, he pressed his point. She had to understand how critical she was to the overall mission. "There is only one member of the Remnant per continent left. Seven of you in all, culled down through history. Each of you has the power to sway multitudes toward the Light by speaking out. You create waves of change . . . first all the sensitives feel it—those people who maybe use eleven, twelve, maybe fifteen percent of their brains, and your message cascades out from there to shift paradigms. People will not accept the propaganda they've been fed once you begin to shift the balance of power through awareness. This continent, North America, has the most powerful military on the planet and is arguably a major global force. In the last days, the last shall be first . . . so you were incarnated into one of the most impoverished tribes in this area of the world. But that is your strength, your empathy."

"All right," she said, folding her arms as she dropped her backpack to her feet. She took a wide-legged stance, as though ready to fight. "Why me? I never asked for this, never signed up for this bullshit. Nobody asked me what I wanted, if there's supposedly free choice. So, how did I get made with this extra light, then, in the first place?"

"I know it has to be unnerving and—"

"Answer the question," she said in a deadly soft murmur.

"We don't like to talk about it."

"Really?" Celeste's gaze narrowed and she arched an eyebrow. "Well, I don't like how my life just got hijacked, such as my life was when you met me. At least it was my own brand of insanity that made sense in my real little ignorant-of-the-supernatural world! Plus, plus"—she pointed at his chest—"if I'm hearing you right, first demons messed my life up and did whatever they felt like to me—now I've been drafted into some army of Light. How about if both sides stop jacking with me for a little while and give me a break, huh? How about that!"

He glanced away, glad that they were the only ones waiting at that trolley stop. "All right. You have every right to feel the way you do, but I have no control over the fact that it is your destiny to be involved in swaying the balance."

"Whatever," she muttered, folding her arms. "You at least owe me an explanation, then, about how all this got so screwed up and why I'm supposedly special."

"It is our shame in the angelic hierarchies, but I guess you have the right to know." He returned his gaze to her and released a frustrated breath. "When the Source of All That Is created this particular universe billions of years ago, the scientists and those that argue religion are both right. It was not a case of either or—it is both and . . . integrated. Some call it the big bang theory. Some call it Creation. It is both. The best term for it is sacred science. And it was a time when the Source even separated us out of itself, first as androgynous cocreators—or what you call angels—then we became both female and male, first the female and then the male . . . hence why all old cultures revered the goddess . . . Eve came before Adam, so to speak and—"

"So there *are* female angels? And Eve came before Adam?" The tone of her question seemed less defensive.

"Of course. Eve is an XX chromosome, Adam is an XY—the rib is a metaphor for the piece taken from her to create him. But the politics of male domination are a discussion for another time. What is important is that you know there is a complete set of all there is. There are also opposites that got created—light and dark, positive and negative poles. There was no exception. As above, so below. Then once placed in this faraway habitat of pristine beauty called earth, evidence of Creation was allowed to evolve . . . the Kemetian record keepers and the Mayans have the most accurate measure of the days of Creation, each one lasting several billion years down to several million and then down to several thousand, to hundreds, and so forth. They have nine steps on their pyramids, representing ages, and—"

"Okay, okay, I feel like a kid who just asked where do babies come from and you're giving me a lesson on cellular division. Can we stick to the point?"

He released a sigh. She was right. But he hated this topic.

"It is complicated, Celeste . . . and it requires that you understand in context."

"Okay, my bad," she said with renewed attitude in her tone. But at least she was talking to him.

"Like I was trying to explain, thousands of years ago, twenty-six thousand to be exact, just like the Kemetian and Mayan calendars forecast now for an alignment on December twenty-first, 2012, the planets aligned to the galactic center. And please keep in mind that there's a reason for all the occurrences of twelve in the date, just like in your DNA—it's a Divine number. But anyway, the galactic center that the planets will align to is what some humans call the throne of God. It's not a black hole there, but dark matter in the center of the Milky Way—matter so dense that humans have no instruments to measure it. Beyond that point is the gateway to Heaven. That is where the Source of All That Is resides."

Azrael paused and looked up the street for the trolley that wasn't coming fast enough, then returned his gaze to Celeste. "We helped all ancient societies . . . Atlantis, Kemet, Lumeria, the Mayans, and many others . . . those of us who were trapped once the alignment ended stayed behind and helped humankind. When the planets align to the galactic center of the universe, there is no gravitational pull or energy fields to block the direct access to earth from either the side of the Light or the dark. That is when we say the door or veil or gateway or star gate opens. And it is a perilous time for the earth and humanity, because there are forces that would love to take over this free-will zone."

He stopped speaking and dug into his gym bag, needing water, but she patiently waited, obviously latched onto the subject.

"All right," she said once he'd taken a deep swig of water. "So, the planets aligned . . . and?"

"And the one thing that made it difficult to travel through the densities opened. The gravitation alignment simply rips open the veil between worlds so the fallen Legions of Darkness as well as the Warriors of Light can come here to do battle."

"Still doesn't answer how I was made, and you're beating around the bush."

He sipped some more water. "I should have done more research on the tenacity of human females," he muttered, but at least his comment made her smile.

"Brother, you don't know the half of it."

"All right, all right," he said, offering her a new bottle of water from his gym bag. "The edict was that no angel, male or female, was to lie with the sons or daughters of humankind. There, are you satisfied?"

"Wait . . . like that stuff about the Titans—"

"Yes, it's true. Disturbing but true. Not just regimes from the fallen disobeyed . . . some from the Warriors of Light fell in love with those they protected . . . and in this density, well, weaknesses prevailed."

Celeste opened the bottle he'd given her and took a long sip of water. "Not being disrespectful or anything, but . . . what was the big deal, if loving is natural and cool and whatever?"

"Because the progeny would be half-angel and half-human . . . something stronger than what was bestowed on humanity at the inception of your kind."

"But I thought you said all of us can do what angels do. And wasn't there even a thing in the Bible about that?"

"Yes," he said, trying not to lose patience. "But wisdom is required to have that much power. Knowledge and power without wisdom can be catastrophic." He paused, trying to find a way to make her understand. "Think of it this way, Celeste . . . if you have a group of five-year-old students in a class together—and they all have the potential to study their letters and grow smarter and more mature together, there is balance, even in their little schoolyard squabbles. No one child is that much stronger that he or she can force their will upon the entire group. However, if it did somehow become thoroughly unfair with a bully terrorizing one smaller child, there is still a parent or a teacher who can intervene in the group of five-year-olds—that would be us. Angels, or the Source itself. But imagine having a class of five-year-olds and then there's an unruly teenager in that class, an adolescent that is stronger, faster, more aggressive, more sexual, more—"

"Whoa, I get the picture," she said, holding up her bottle of water to stop his disturbing imagery. "And that teenager could be dangerous to even the teacher."

"Precisely. And my brothers and sisters of the Light who were here to battle the darkness lost focus, some of them. When the planets lost their alignment and went back into their normal positions, the gate between worlds was closed. Any of them trapped here who violated the edict are permanently to remain here."

"You mean they can never go back to Heaven?"

"Correct," he said quietly, for the first time beginning to feel how tragic a sentence that was. "So, to busy their minds and keep from going insane with boredom, they helped build civilizations, whispered cures into the ears of scientists and doctors, helped inspire art and beauty and all that is good. . . . But they have also lain with humans and have sired offspring."

"Now that's deep," she murmured, staring at him.

"It is." He took another sip of water. "The gate opens roughly every twenty-six thousand years. Some of my brethren have been here for that long. Some have chosen to be Balance Keepers and to forsake human contact or temptation by going to live in remote places as Tibetan monks high in the Himalayas, or shamans deep in the rain forests, or medicine men deep in the Australian outback or African interior. They are from every culture and hide all over the world, forsaking physical contact or temptation. They have the appearance of old men in the vast wilderness who can take you on spirit walks. Those are the ones who have waited twenty-six thousand or more human years for the planets to align again . . . and they can go home."

"So, shit . . ." She ran her palm over her hair. "Like, some angels are just in constant prayer vigil for humanity, waiting to go home?"

"Yes. And when they leave, there will be a void, but who could ask any more sacrifice of them than they've already endured?"

"Seriously." She took a long swig of water, looked down the street for the trolley, then turned back to him. "So, what about the ones who, you know . . . got in trouble because their willpower broke?"

He shook his head, hoping the trolley would hurry up and come. "These Sentinels must stay, and they fight the temptation of excesses here. They experience pain, heartache, loss, lust, rage, everything humans suffer, but they cannot die. Even beheaded, their body will shrivel and turn to dust, but they will be reborn and have to continue here. They are not fallen, and they fight on our side of the Light, but they cannot return home to find ultimate respite. That makes them dangerous, as their temperaments are . . . often challenged by anger and bitterness."

"Now *that's* fucked up."

He nodded. "True, and I'm not judging you when I say this but, words have power, Celeste. I've noticed you use a lot of euphemisms that have low vibration quality attached to them. Everything in the universe is about vibration and harmonics. Certain words have certain vibrations and tones associated with them. Even the sun and each planet have a sound, like I've mentioned before. As you elevate your frequency, you have to at some point also elevate your use of language because words have power— curse and you are emitting low frequencies that attract petty darkness; use more positive words and it attracts the Light. . . . I hope that makes sense?"

He was prepared for her to react with indignation, but, instead, she smiled.

"That is the nicest way I have ever had anyone ask me to stop cursing." She chuckled softly and drank the rest of her water. "My aunt Niecey says just because you can do something doesn't mean you should . . . so I'll try to clean up my potty mouth around an angel—even though this whole thing is really hard for me to accept."

"Thank you," he said quietly, truly glad that he hadn't offended her.

"No, really . . . thank you," she said, now looking up at him with wide, expressive eyes. "Thank you for saving me from whatever was inside Brandon. Thank you for the wildest adventure I've ever been on in my life. Thank you especially for bringing me home to Aunt Niecey and making her feel better and helping her spirit to rest easy . . . and thank you for these beautiful gifts of soap and perfume and clothes, all of it was so thoughtful, Az . . . and all I've done since you found me is—"

"What you should have done," he murmured, stepping in closer to her. "Your inner voice, the voice connected to the Source, said not to trust me, said to be sure. That was right."

"Trusting you means I have to wrap my head around an alternate reality . . . and it scares me, man. You know?"

He nodded. He did know. He was terror-stricken when he fell to earth.

"But why me?" she asked, just above a whisper. "What is it about me?"

He reached out, unable to withstand separation from her soft cheek any longer, and he cupped it as he looked down into her wide brown eyes. As sure as he was standing there, he was addicted to her skin, to her voice, to her scent, to the depth of her deep brown eyes, and that was the last thing he was supposed to be.

"Somewhere in your lineage, an angel sired one of your ancestors . . . and that recessive gene got passed on and secreted away in generation after generation of DNA until it appeared in you."

"So, doesn't that make me one of the bad guys by birth . . . a love child of an angel and a human . . . like some kind of cosmic freak?"

"Oh, no, Celeste," he murmured, feeling the density, feeling her honesty pull him in like a moth to a flame. "You are so rare . . . angels will battle over you. That is why you must stay close to me."

"What? I don't understand?"

He backed up a few inches and removed his hand from her cheek. "Those who have been here since the last alignment or those new to this density desire to lie with a Nephilim more than you can imagine. To speak of it amongst ourselves is taboo, the topic is so volatile.

"A Nephilim is a hybrid," he said gently when she seemed confused. "Thousands of us angels walk the earth and battle, hidden among the billions of humans that now exist . . . and there are only seven of you left. Seven human-angel hybrids amid a sea of billions—seven that only those of us sent directly from the Source are attuned to find. Seven, whose inner light when fused with ours . . . I'm told . . . creates a level of physical ecstasy unknown anywhere else. It is the combination of the raw primal nature of the human being combined with the power of the Light also found within the hybrid that is unparalleled. We can also only sire with humans or Nephilim . . . and Nephilim can heal us, can boost our dimming Light, if that happens."

"But what happened to all the others like me?" she

whispered, suddenly looking around and stepping in closer.

"The dark side either brought them under their sway or had them eliminated by allowable means—broke them and made them take their own lives via excesses and addictions or outright suicide to stop the pain. Some of my brothers trapped in this density may have found their Remnant and were able to remain by their side, protecting them until we could gather the others like you . . . but some reached their target too late and their chosen was already swayed dark or dead. Those brothers teeter on the very edge of their sanity, as they have been here a long time, searching for another . . . aching for a mate—something not required when living completely in spirit within the lightness of the etheric realms, but so difficult to ignore when one is encapsulated in human form."

"I cannot even imagine . . ."

"Nor can I, that is why I do not judge my brothers who have fallen once trapped—even though I must exterminate them. I only have disdain for those that were in the original battle and sided with the One Who Remains Nameless."

"But you said angels can't die."

"The fallen can be beheaded, just like an original demon can. Those brothers that are still bearing Light are immortal. You can see the Light in their auras, or if you look into their eyes, you can see it behind their pupils, which is why they say the eyes are the window to the soul. Those that are lost will lose all Light in their eyes, which become pitch-black when challenged by a Light-bearer. However, the trapped, our Sentinels, are immortal, if they still bear Light and haven't traded their allegiance to the dark side."

She bit her lip and her gentle brow knit as she continued to stare up at him. "Azrael . . . if I were in that position of being trapped, roaming the earth for twenty-six thousand years, unable to love, unable to enjoy the basic fundamentals of being in a body that was designed for sensory pleasure . . . even something as simple as eating what I wanted or having a drink, or whatever . . . I would go crazy. Maybe even go dark, just so that when another brother found me he could end the misery."

"That's just the thing, dear Celeste," Azrael said softly, pushing a stray ringlet that had escaped from her ponytail behind her ear. "There is no rest, then . . . only the interminable darkness, disembodied, and in the clutches of a vast, vast Hell. Some of my brothers who are here and still retain their Light are very dangerous to a rare find like you."

"But, wait . . . you said before that there were both male and female angels. Surely if two angels got together, that wouldn't violate the big order, would it?"

"No. It wouldn't." Azrael released another weary sigh, sad that he had introduced a subject that had put so much panic into her voice. "There are female angels," he finally admitted. "But when the war cry went out and the hierarchies of Heaven emptied to meet the threat, male energy flooded the planet for war, while feminine energy held the line in the ether minimizing catastrophic events that resulted from our battle. Were it not for this critical feminine angelic energy, many more humans would have died from earthquakes, floods, tornadoes . . . I cannot imagine. Female angels ministered to the human refugees, who were confused and aggrieved from the severe clashes."

He looked away as shame and guilt filled him as the memories of the first war flooded back to him. "We were not concerned in those days for the individual loss of human life. We warred fiercely and valiantly, but I now question the honor in all that if it wiped out a village in the process—which many times it did."

"Wow . . . ," she murmured, staring up at him in troubled awe. "So, like, what you're saying is—all the female angels stayed in the ether or on the other side of this portal, right . . . holding it down to make sure you guys who were battling the Unnamed One and his legions didn't completely blow up the planet?"

"Correct. And at times we came close." Azrael raked his fingers through his locks. "This is why in all the old cultures, the goddess—just another name for female angel energy—was so revered. It is also why as the dark energy on the planet grew stronger, you had brutal systems of control and repression visited upon that gentle feminine energy, and women were stripped out of all religious texts as relevant beings except in a few mentions. The earth is a war zone, Celeste. Only through peace can you achieve true prosperity, advancement, and societal compassion. Existence cannot be dominated by war. So, the role of our sister angels was vital—is vital to this day. They brought balance then and still hold it now. Remember, everything is in balance in the cosmos, and just as above so below. There's light and dark, hard and soft, forceful and gentle—"

"Yin and yang, right?" She waited and he nodded, and he was rewarded with her smile. "Told you I watch cable."

"It has taught you a lot."

"Yeah, but . . . that's like all the war movies I've seen . . . like you had thousands of angels, guys with unreal cosmic power, trapped down here for twenty-six thousand years until the alignment happens again—and you're telling me with all those troops, with all those boots on the ground of physically spectacular male beings, they were supposed to just chill and not lay with a female human?"

"It was the Order—the prime directive from a Source that you don't argue with." He lifted his chin, not wanting to continue the conversation, but he could tell from the look in Celeste's eyes and the tone of her voice that she wasn't ready to let it rest.

"I'm human, and it's in our nature to ask questions, even of the Source, especially when something seems so freakin' unfair." She walked away from him for a short distance and then paced back. "Like, who under those circumstances wouldn't just snap? And, besides, you guys weren't used to being in a body."

"True," he said on another weary exhale. "Those of us who pursued the fallen down to earth were initially engaged in spectacular aerial battles and we retained our etheric form. Violating the edict was never in our consciousness nor was the temptation there to do so. But as those aerial dogfights turned into ground campaigns where we had to search and destroy the enemy on the ground—an enemy that had become manifest because of the length of time they'd spent in this density—we, too, had to adapt. Our clean, aerial battles became guerrilla campaigns fought with human villages used as shields and innocents strategically put in harm's way to make us hesitate to raze an entire region where our enemy was located. That's when the problems began."

"I cannot imagine the insane dogfights that must have taken place," she said quietly, staring off into the distance. "It must have dwarfed old World War Two air campaigns, maaaan . . . or like F16 fighter jets scrambling to address a terrorist threat."

"Yes, more like the latter. We move at accelerated speeds while in etheric form. It is a sight to behold. To you it would appear as streaks of light across the sky . . . or a meteor shower."

Celeste turned and looked at him. "I do get why you all were given the edict. If one person can sway others and create a movement . . . that can go either very badly or very well, and we humans are capricious. We have free will."

"From your own recent history, compare what Gandhi did, or the legacy of Martin Luther King Jr., to the evil done by Adolf Hitler. Each was just a single individual with something extra that no one could identify. Celeste, I could sit you down with your library books and take you back to the dawn of recorded history and show you example after example of how one person's brilliance or evil genius swayed the entire course of human history. That's the result of our violating the edict. Need I say more?"

"Whoa . . . those guys were. . . . ?"

"Yes." Azrael laid a hand on her shoulder, unable to keep from touching her again. "Humans have free will. Humans with extreme power added to their DNA can do extreme good or extreme harm. When one of us makes a Nephilim, suddenly the playing field is no longer level. *That's* why the prime directive was given. It wasn't the Source being harsh or toying with the legions of Light. Our physiology is flaw-less. Our progeny are immune to everything from cholera to the bubonic plague. The intelligence of that being will outstrip that of its peers, even when suppressed. And once in the human gene pool, Angel DNA can lay dormant for centuries and resurface anywhere."

"Now that is so deep I don't even know where to begin." She bit her lip for a moment and he withdrew his hand from her shoulder and shoved both hands into his pockets.

"So, I'm like the result of a war, essentially . . . one of those war babies a few hundred generations removed?"

He nodded.

"And the good guys, your side . . . and the bad guys, the dark side, both were violating the edict, and that's how you get a crazy dude like Hitler or a living saint like a Mother Teresa or a Nelson Mandela?"

"Essentially. The dark side has no compunction about creating more dark Nephilim, and there are many more of them than there are of you. Our Sentinels regularly root them out . . . just like the dark side hunts for our Nephilim to sway or break . . . or to make ours lose so much hope and faith that they simply end their own existence."

Celeste rubbed her hands down her face. "This is like CIA, spy games, espionage, but on a frickin' cosmic level."

"And that is why I said, unless I identify the brother angel as not dangerous, you stay close to me. Got it?"

Her stunned expression told him she'd heard him, but it took a moment for her to respond. "You don't have to tell me twice," she finally said, rubbing her arms as though chilled. "So for a hybrid to walk into a den of angels could be like dropping a woman into a maximum-security prison, is what you're saying?" She looked up at him, but now he couldn't meet her gaze. "I mean, I'm just being real, Az," she pressed on. "Earth has been a prison for those guys that didn't make it out on time, right? So, even the ones from the good side might not totally be themselves. They would hurt me . . . I mean, to like—"

"Abduct you, yes. Strange things happen in situations of deprivation and war. As above, so below. The only difference is the time line. Humans were created to show those of us in the Light the evolutionary path from darkness to Light. You were to show us the way back to the Source after the separation into male and female, darkness and Light, with free will being your path back to the Divine best within beings. And, I suppose we were to show you the higher ways, but to also learn humility, service, and compassion by serving humankind . . . because this war has demonstrated that any being, put under enough pressure, can break. But most that are from the Light and trapped because they violated the edict eons ago have continued to choose human female mates . . . but that, too, is a soul-destroying choice given the short length of your lifetimes as humans. Every fifty years, a man can find himself burying the love of his life. Do that for twenty-six thousand years and I guarantee that will wear a hole in your spirit. My trapped Sentinel brothers have suffered in ways I cannot claim to know."

"Damn," she whispered, then briefly closed her eyes. "I'm sorry, but that's the only word for it."

"In this case I agree. So stay close to me as we travel.

You and I must be of one mind, even if I tell you that someone we meet is a brother in the Light. Only if I say trust, do you trust."

Celeste nodded, then stepped back from him as the trolley finally came. He stared after her as she entered the street car, walked up the steps, and put enough money into the machine for both of them. The machine ate four wrinkled dollar bills, then she bade him with a glance over her shoulder to follow her to open seats. He would have followed her anywhere.

Now that she was detoxed and trusting, he could feel the full force of her inner beauty, could feel the press of her honesty and warrior spirit—all wrapped in a beautiful human package . . . her Light essence wrapping around every emotional cord within his soul.

What was within her was just as magnetic to him as her exterior. Celeste had layers of beauty in various stages of bloom. Her hatred of injustice, her wonder at the majesty of Creation . . . her empathy for even those lost to the darkness, the tenderness in her voice and her kiss and her touch. She'd tried to heal his wing scars, even when she didn't know or trust him. Then when her gentle hands couldn't make his scars disappear, she'd spoken kind words against his skin and wished them away nonetheless. And it all happened so fast, so frighteningly fast, just like his rebirth into this mad world.

She sat down on an inside double seat, placing her bag at her feet. He sat beside her, not knowing what to do with his hands, then she slid a soft palm beneath his and threaded her fingers through his and squeezed hard.

"It's going to be all right," she said.

For a moment he just stared at her. "I should be telling you that."

She shrugged. "If what you just told me is true, then you have more to fear than me. I'll just die and go see all my loved ones." Her tone wasn't flippant or sarcastic in any way.

He nodded, then squeezed her hand back. "And when that happens so many years from now, it will be a beautiful place, Celeste."

"Then let's make sure you get home when this is all over, too." She smiled a sad smile. "I've got your back."

He brought her hand up to his mouth, still clasping it with his fist, each finger entwined between hers. *She would attempt to protect him?* This frail human being who had the heart of a warrior . . . the one who was showing him around the vagaries of human life, the one who said by her actions, just follow my lead and I won't steer you wrong. She'd been kind to him even when to her he was a scary stranger. Had fed him and clothed him and asked for nothing but peace of mind and truth in return.

This was what the Source must have known when creating these magnificent beings called humans. This is what the Source was clearly trying to convey when telling the hierarchies and choirs of angels, "Faith, hope, love . . . the greatest of all their gifts is love."

No words would penetrate through the lump in his throat now. Azrael swallowed hard and stared out the window, watching the houses and lives of the throngs he'd been sent to protect pass by. Every individual mattered. He understood now that each one, no matter how seemingly insignificant, was woven into the fabric of countless other lives. Celeste had taught him that, because this one woman and her dear, elderly aunt meant so much to him that he would bitterly grieve if anything tragic ever happened to them. Even with his knowledge of the so-called larger cosmic picture, he'd become attached to his humans, the ones he'd come to love.

In that way, Celeste had also taught him that there was no such thing as casual collateral damage. The guardian angels had always argued this point . . . and until now he'd thought their passion on the subject was mere rhetorical debate born of their lost perspectives. He'd believed they'd gotten too attached to their subjects to see the bigger picture. It had always been unfathomable for him, especially as a member of the warrior legions, to conceive of any one human being as worth so much trouble.

What did seraphim, cherubim, or thrones know beyond their direct and constant attention to the Source? Those upper hierarchies catered directly to the Source of All That Is and had no contact whatsoever with the infinitesimal troubles of human beings. How could dominions and virtues fathom the antlike importance of a single human life when their focus was that of continents and the order of the cosmos? What would powers and principalities really know of the lives of humans? The upper realms were so much farther removed and focused on issues of a seemingly grander scale. Some even whispered their concern about being sent to babysit these childlike entities, but the Source said that doing so was the greatest task of all. Only archangels and general angels seemed to get it, as Azrael recalled.

He became very still. This was what had caused the

ultimate war in the first place—some of his brethrens' lack of acceptance of the edict to place the concerns of humans above all other tasks. Truthfully, the only difference between him and those that had fallen was that he still respected the Light on blind faith, whereas they had questioned the deep wisdom of the Source and refused to bow down to the Source's greatest creation—humans.

Yet, being here in the human environment, suffering the human condition, he better understood the paradox that the Source of All That Is had presented: Humans are weak in will and in body, yet that they face these challenges with a belief in something bigger than themselves when all hope should be gone, is in itself an unimaginable level of strength. That they suffer losses and pain and hunger and deprivation, but still forge on, is the will of legends. That they are mortal and know they can die, but rush in where some angels fear to tread is beyond courageous. That is passion. That is conviction. That is strength. That they sacrifice themselves for others when they could be injured or die is the greatest love of all . . . and this capacity resides within each human, and all of that makes humans just as worthy of respect from the heavens as any immortals with the full battalions of the Light on their side.

His new awareness was sobering. Azrael glimpsed Celeste from the corner of his eyes as she stared out the trolley window. Her profile was serenity itself, so different than only a few hours ago. Before this experience he would have asked what were a few thousand microscopic, nonevolved human lives when the bigger picture of victory over the darkness loomed so large?

But he'd been so very, very wrong. The healing corps

said that there was no more complex, disturbing, or beautiful creation. And now one had touched him so completely that a mere glance over her shoulder without a word passing between them had made him follow her.

Yes, he would follow Celeste right into the bowels of Hell itself. For the first time in his existence he'd come to know attachment. It was impossible to be philosophical about Celeste, to view her in some larger cosmic context.

He now better understood his earthbound brothers' pain, unable to even imagine the state of his sanity if he was ever to be separated from her.

A thud came from the window and Denise Jackson turned away from her afternoon soap opera to stare at the closed blinds. Annoyed, she stood and went to the kitchen and hurried to the cabinets as another thud sounded at her back door. Reaching up with effort, she pulled down an old cookie tin from the top shelf that was heavy with the weight of her peacekeeper.

"Now y'all trying to break into my house during the day? Umph, umph, umph. Ain't no rest for the weary, but I'll help you find Jesus right quick, though," she muttered, and opened the tin, taking out the old .45 that had once belonged to Roscoe.

She went to the window more angry than afraid and peeked out the kitchen curtain. "I got somethin' for ya! Don't think you done run up on some ole lady!"

But the next thud from the side of the house made her open the curtains wide and gasp with horror. Five dead crows were littered in her backyard, necks broken by the sheer force of hitting her house. Then she looked up to the adjacent rooftops and telephone lines behind her house and slowly laid the weapon down on the kitchen table.

A murder of crows looked back at her, silent sentries that seemed as if they were eerily waiting for her to leave the house. She hurried through the kitchen and dining room to the front window and peered through the blinds. The first thud she'd heard was a crow that had hurled itself against the window and then fallen onto the wooden porch.

"Got something for that, too," she said quietly, and crossed herself as she hurried to the end table by the sofa.

As her hand touched the brass drawer handle, the doorbell rang. But she was on a mission and would not be dissuaded from it. She opened the drawer, ignoring the heavy pounding at her front door, and withdrew her Bible, turning to psalm 91 and preparing for war.

"Police! Open up, Ms. Jackson. We can see you in there!"

"I'm coming," she said calmly, holding her Bible open as she went to the door and turned the latch. "Good afternoon, Officers. You here to see about these crows that done lost they minds?"

She studied the two deceptively handsome faces. One was an ebony black man, one was a white man. One had eyes the hue of bittersweet chocolate, the other had eyes the hue of the bluest sky. One wore a dark charcoal gray suit, the other wore navy blue. One pressed a gold badge to the glass of her exterior security door while she stood just inside it with the inner door cracked open.

"Detectives," the black man said. "Homicide."

"Uhmmm, hmmm," she said, looking at the dead crow on her porch. "Bad sign, ain't it?"

The two men gave each other a look.

"The dead birds. Evil's afoot," she affirmed. "Just like they all hanging on the lines."

The blond detective glanced around. "There's no birds on the lines and that's not why we're here, Ms. Jackson. Who cares about a dead pigeon on your porch?"

"Do tell," she said, peering upward. "Strange. They was just all here a minute ago . . . and wasn't no pigeons. Was mean-ole-looking black birds. Ravens or crows. Big, too." Then she glanced at the bird on her porch.

It was a pigeon just as the detective had said, but she knew that a moment ago it had been a crow.

"We need to know where your niece Celeste Jackson is—we need to come in," the ebony-hued detective said, ignoring the dead bird.

"First of all," she replied coolly, "I don't have to let no demon in my house. That's right, I said it. Back up in the name of Jesus. That's *the Law*." She pointed upward with a straight forefinger. "Uh-huh, you know what I'm talking about. Second, if you gonna pretend to be human, then you have to have a warrant. Pick a law, God's law or man's law, either way you gotta follow the law."

The detectives again shared a look.

"She's senile," the blond muttered.

The other officer didn't respond for a moment, then turned back to Ms. Jackson. She slowly lowered her hand feeling every ache and pain return to her body as her once straight forefinger became gnarled and arthritic again.

"Your niece is in a lot of trouble, ma'am, and if you're harboring a fugitive, you're going to prison right along with her."

Denise Jackson narrowed her gaze. "You would do this to an old woman, then there ain't no hope for you, son."

"Ms. Jackson," the other detective implored, "just let us in so we can talk to you. We don't want to hurt you or your niece. We just want to know what happened to her boyfriend."

Denise Jackson looked down at the open Bible and picked up where she'd left off, reciting the psalm out loud and customizing it to protect her. "'A thousand may fall at my side, ten thousand at my right hand, but it will not come near me—'"

"Do you know what your niece did? She killed a man!" the blond detective shouted.

"That's a lie," Denise Jackson said in a placid tone. "The devil is a liar." She smiled at the two detectives and then began reading louder. "'No harm will befall me, no disaster will come near my tent. For He will command his angels concerning me, to guard me in all my ways'!"

"Open the damned door," the black detective said through his teeth.

"You ain't got no warrant, do you?" Denise Jackson looked up from her Bible with a smile. "And you don't have an invitation, demon. If you were real cops, you could bust right in here, but I know what you are and I'm not afraid. And I done lived with Arthur and sugar and high blood pressure all my life—so I ain't scared that you gave it back to me after a kind soul prayed for me so the good Lord would take it away. When I go on to glory, this old body will be well lived in, so if you trying to scare me, you gotta do way better than that." She slowly closed the inner door and resumed reading at the top of her lungs. "'The angels will lift me up, lest I dash my foot against a stone!'"

The two officers backed away and jogged down the steps to get out of earshot of her late-afternoon sermon.

"Don't worry, Malpas. That old broad will have to send out for food soon and will have to open her door," the blond detective muttered as they walked to their car. He looked up at the crows that had returned to gather on the rooftops and telephone lines. "We'll know when she does. She'll open up before—"

"No, she won't. They aren't in there," his partner said. "Azrael wouldn't have allowed us to reverse his healing of that old battle-ax if he'd been inside. Nathaniel will be displeased."

Azrael stood on the train platform with an arm slung over Celeste's shoulders and on guard. She gave him a look but didn't comment. Yet as out of character as it was, he wanted her near, wanted her body close to his, needed to smell her hair. For a moment he lowered his nose to it and closed his eyes as the fragrance she wore combined with her natural scent wended its way through his sinuses, teasing his palate.

Although they were aboveground and could see the sun and feel the wind on their faces, something felt off and he drew her in closer. Pigeons walked along the ground seeking anything commuters discarded. The birds held his attention for a moment as they squabbled over the end of an old doughnut. Watching them rip apart the tender pastry was oddly disturbing.

Maybe it was his memory of how he'd entered the earth plane. Or maybe it was something much more. But the last thing he wanted to do was upset Celeste. He knew firsthand the dangers associated with the platforms, even though this was the middle of the day and scores of travelers were around. He'd been reborn on the tracks and had been attacked there; somehow there was a purpose to all things. Maybe that initial test he faced was to give him the experience of sensing a human confrontation. That was just the thing, the frustration of it all; it was so hard to become still here so that he could rely on inner discernment. Everything was so intense, especially near the trains. Especially near Celeste.

The power, the vibrations, the thousands of commuters' thoughts—all converged. He'd sort it out, would try to meditate as they journeyed. He felt sure that he would learn much by traveling to seek Bath Kol by rail. But something was wrong.

Celeste looked up at the same time he looked down at her.

"I'm worried about leaving Aunt Niecey," she said quietly. "I know we have to go . . . but . . ."

"Send her Light," he replied in a firm tone. "Do it with me now."

"How?"

Azrael drew Celeste closer. "Shut your eyes," he murmured as his lids slowly lowered. "See your aunt in your mind as whole and safe. Then envision a radiant bubble of white Light encircling her. Fill it with healing and loving thoughts and then send the bubble out wider to cover the room she's in, and then the house."

He tried not to frown as dark energy jarred his system. "What do you feel?" he asked quietly, keeping his voice to a private murmur that only Celeste could hear.

"I feel . . . nervous . . . but okay, too." Celeste opened her eyes. "It took me like five tries to actually get the bubble of Light in my mind to go around her. Each time I'd try to think it, it would only go halfway over her or it would start to change into some dark color. Az. . . . Then all of a sudden I felt like she was all right, but—I don't know."

"It's going to be all right," he said, looking away from her toward the inbound R7 train. It was the first lie he'd ever told in his existence, and she now hugged him for it.

Celeste rested her head against his chest. "Thanks. I know I'm just tripping."

He didn't confirm or deny her assumptions. Instead he just hugged Celeste back, wishing he could yell out that she was getting stronger. Her spirit had correctly perceived the exact danger that his had intuited—her aunt had been under attack. Birds had been used as the eyes and ears of demon sentries. Evil had visited her aunt's door, but the elderly woman was a tough warrior in her own right. Yet, her body could not take the onslaught for much longer. They would surely use Ms. Jackson as bait to lure Celeste back to Philadelphia, to break her spirit, to make her doubt, and to call her out into the open at a hospital bedside or at a funeral.

Mortality was all around him. This time he looked at the commuters with angel eyes, seeing them as beings of Light devoid of ethnicity or gender. Some Lights were robust and healthy, some thin and frail. Many had dark spots or entire sections missing that caused a break in what should have been an endless, smooth pattern of illumination. Some had gray, cloudy Lights, while still others had bits of color swirling within them. The man to his far left would be gone before the week was out; Azrael hoped the man would use his time wisely. The most disturbing sight of all was seeing where the gray had entered small children, or the ones with blackout areas denoting some form of trauma so early in their innocent lives. For comfort he sought Celeste's swirling, iridescent radiance that was now so bright it drew him into the warm spill of it.

Azrael briefly closed his eyes and then opened them, willing back his normal human vision. Once again he could see the people around him in their differentiated human exterior forms. Gone were their distracting Lights. There was so much healing to do, but that wasn't his province nor was it a part of his current mission.

As the train roared into the station, he allowed his mind to become so still that all sounds around him evaporated. *Raphael, I know you can hear me through the density—as all archangels have this strength. I humbly call upon your compassion for the elderly woman Denise Jackson. Her niece must fulfill her destiny, therefore must be able to clear her mind of worry and doubt. Her heart cannot be heavy with regret. . . . Please restore and keep Ms. Jackson in your healing Light. I ask that you call in the Mu'aqqibat, the protectors who keep humans from death until their decreed time. I also ask for travel mercy, my brother, as we are all moving through perilous space and times.*

He looked up dazed as Celeste tugged on his jacket.

"Come on, man," she said with a half smile, bringing him into full awareness of his surroundings. "Down here on earth you've gotta jockey for position or everybody will bum-rush the seats."

Celeste stared out the window watching the cityscape go by slowly as the train pulled out of Thirtieth Street Station. Azrael had an arm over her shoulder, and that alone made her worry for him. She could feel the shift in his temperament, the difference in his touch, which had gone from nonexistent, to generic healing and sterile but compassionate like a doctor's, to much more intimate. And if everything he'd told her was true, this brother was in waaaay over his head.

If she didn't know anything else, she knew the beginnings of an addiction or at least addictive behavior when she saw it. She'd been in enough rehab programs and therapies that all she had missing was a license to practice.

As calmly as possible, she turned to him and looked up. She met the most tender and open gaze she'd ever seen in her life. A combination of desire and contentment, yearning and repression, seemed to fill his intense, dark brown gaze, and the odd thing was that, now clean and clear, she was almost sure that she could feel it in the pit of her stomach.

"Azrael," she said quietly. "You have to back off a little, you know. Like . . . this isn't doing you any good and could really get you in trouble." She placed a hand on his arm and watched him draw away as though it literally hurt him not to touch her.

"I'm sorry . . . I didn't mean to offend or to appear to have taken ownership of your personal space."

"You didn't offend me . . . it's just that you said you guys can get in trouble, if, you know . . . and . . ." She looked down at her hands feeling foolish. Maybe that was just how she was beginning to feel for him and not the other way around.

"You're right," he said in a low murmur. "When I touch your skin, it's like being connected to a battery source. I feel all the electrical current in your system enter every one of my cells . . . and it's, frankly, intoxicating."

She snapped her attention up to meet his gaze. "I get you high?"

He swallowed hard. "That . . . among other things."

She sent her gaze out of the window. "Oh, that is so not good."

"I can't help it," he murmured, close to her ear, sending a warm vibration into her that thrummed in her belly as he took up her hand. "I've never experienced anything like this, Celeste."

Truth be told, neither had she, but the last thing she'd ever expected was to be some angel's 12-step program.

"If you don't stop, you'll be strung out by the time we get to New York," she said, watching him slowly slide his palm back and forth beneath hers.

"Friction increases the sensation," he murmured thickly, then leaned in against her temple to take a deep inhale.

"Yes, it does. That's how it works," she said, clasping

his hand tightly and holding it still. She pulled back and looked at him hard. "The more you create friction, the more you're going to want to really break the Law. I can't let you get put in a position of being trapped on earth from 2012 until the next alignment. Focus on that."

He nodded, but she noticed his breathing had become shallow.

"Do you know the Serenity Prayer?"

He shook his head, beginning to breathe through his mouth. "I should know it, but my concentration right now . . ."

"'God, grant me the serenity to accept the things I cannot change; courage to change the things I can; and wisdom to know the difference.'"

She felt his body relax a bit and he released her hand.

"'Living one day at a time; enjoying one moment at a time; accepting hardships as the pathway to peace,'" he said on a labored breath.

"Right. That's the second stanza."

"Okay," he said, sitting back in his seat. "Thank you. I remember the full prayer now."

"You're welcome . . . and just keep saying it over and over until we get to New York, and drink some water to flush that extra charge you got out of your system."

He nodded and unzipped his gym bag, pulling out a liter bottle of water and downing half of it. She watched him blot his damp brow with the back of his forearm and she inched over in the seat a little so their hips and thighs weren't touching. To her amazement he closed his eyes and physically cringed as though the small space she'd created between them had actually caused him physical pain.

Then she stared down at her hands. They seemed normal to her. She didn't understand this current he was talking about. Was he picking up on every electrical impulse in her body or getting high on all the billions of chemical reactions firing within her to keep her alive . . . and was it because her DNA had twelve freaky strands instead of two that it affected him that way?

"Yes," he said, turning toward her with a pained expression. "Your aura is overlapping mine as we sit side by side, and—"

"But last night and at my aunt's house, you weren't—"

"Never this close for this long and you'd just been cleaned out. It took a while for your system to adjust and for the nutrients you'd absorbed to kick in. . . . Now, oh, God . . ." He leaned his head forward and rested it on the seatback in front of them and tightly shut his eyes.

"Should I move? You want me to change seats, to back up? Tell me what to do."

He held up a hand. "Just let me sit quietly and adjust."

She inched over closer to the window. "Okay."

He glanced up and gave her a shy half smile and then began quietly reciting the Serenity Prayer again from the top. It was going to be a long ride up to the city. She'd keep her gaze fastened on the cityscape as the train picked up speed.

Azrael's quiet smile had consoled her somewhat. Even though she was still worried about Aunt Niecey and now worried about the effect she had on Azrael, something about him brought peace to her spirit. She hadn't felt it as they'd ridden all the way from Fifty-eighth Street to Thirtieth and then walked the short half block aboveground to Penn Station so they could catch the SEPTA

Regional Rail line they were on now. But she definitely felt the change as they took up the entire bench that could have seated four in the half-filled car.

She watched Azrael casually rest his bag at his side, sipping water intermittently. She took out a water bottle and dropped her backpack on the floor between her feet. People around them even seemed unusually calm. Once the conductor took their tickets, she would definitely have to ask Azrael about this.

Unexpectedly, he slipped his hand beneath hers again, then sat back with a contented smile when her fingers found the same threading pattern they'd fallen into while on the trolley. It was almost as though she could hear the sigh in his soul, even though he'd remained completely silent. So much for the Serenity Prayer. She cast her gaze out of the window, thinking about all of it, feeling everything all around her as the train waited for the signal to pull a little farther beyond the station.

Soon the tops of zoo buildings came into view as the train followed what seemed to be a retrospective journey of her life during the past twenty-four hours. Only twelve hours ago she was ready to pitch herself into the Schuylkill River, which they were now crossing. A slight, supportive squeeze from Azrael's hand made her look away from the memory to find his warm, brown eyes.

"There," he said quietly with a brief lift of his chin, motioning toward the opposite windows. "I came into one of those underground train stations, reborn into the darkness, and walked until my destiny changed. Whatever it looks like today does not mean it will be so tomorrow. We have both grown in the last twelve hours."

Celeste agreed by squeezing his hand, forgetting about the forbidden contact for a moment. It was such a natural gesture that she'd done it without even thinking as she stared out at the dilapidated factory buildings and ramshackle houses, also knowing that just around the corner Temple University was building. Everything seemed to be a collision of old and new, and although she wasn't sure where this adventure was taking them, she was more inclined to try this new path than to stay on the old road to nowhere.

"Tickets."

She and Azrael looked up at the same time, and she produced the tickets for the conductor, who absently accepted them, then quickly shredded a section on each with a small metal hole-puncher and kept moving.

"That man is so upset about his wife," she whispered to Azrael. "He *does* bring his money home and he *isn't* cheating. She has *got* to stop listening to her so-called girlfriends—haters, man."

Azrael stared at her.

"I'm just saying," Celeste fussed in a low murmur. "It isn't right. He makes a decent wage and tries to do right . . . and they've got kids and all, you know. If they could just appreciate each other a little more." She let out a huff of breath and sat back. "I know, I know, it's not my business."

"Celeste," he said slowly, turning in his seat to fully face her, then dropping his voice. "Do you know this man?"

"No. Okay, like I said, and before you even tell—"

"The man took the tickets from you, punched them, and then handed them back . . . and now you have insight into his life?"

She stared at Azrael. For a few moments all she could hear was the sound of the train clicking along the tracks. Then her vision began to blur out the passing buildings, ragged weeds, and overgrown shrubbery framed in the windows behind him. She covered her mouth with her free hand, stifling a gasp as he gripped the hand he'd been holding tighter. Unnatural light seemed to frame everything, and that all bled together with the speed of the train.

Squinting, she quickly pivoted around to look at the other people that were riding in the same car with them. Just like the landscape beyond the window, they were dissolving into an amalgam of light, each a slightly different intensity and some with different odd colors running through them. But when she turned back to Azrael, she almost screamed. His face had become a large orb or iridescent light with vibrant rainbow hues.

"I'm going blind," Celeste whispered in an urgent rush, squeezing her eyes shut. "Maybe all the stuff I took over the years burned out my retinas or maybe I'm having a stroke."

"You're not going blind or having a stroke," he said, cupping her cheek with a warm, broad palm. "You're just finally able to see like we do. Touching me is sending current into you that fully turns on your inner Light just like the current you send into me fuses with and spikes mine."

Panic made her breaths shallow as she peeked at him, glad to see his face was normal and the lights were gone.

"I've never had anything like this happen to me, not even when I was in a psych ward."

"Your body is in a state of repair, so is your spirit . . . with a little kick start from Divine intention." His handsome smile spread as she fully opened her eyes. "This is just the beginning."

Celeste rested a hand over her heart. "Okay . . . you have *got* to clue me in. I have a gazillion questions, and the first series begins with—what am I *specifically* supposed to do as a part of this whole big crazy thing that I still don't fully get, when is all this gonna go down, and what all can I do? Like what the *Hell* just happened—excuse my French."

He released a patient sigh. "I don't know what your specific task is, none of us do."

"Come again?"

"There are too many variables—what they will do, what you will do . . . we just know the broader mission is to gather the Remnant and any sensitives that can help sway the balance. What that will ultimately mean depends on what happens between now and then, which is why we are seeking Bath Kol for advice. Before he became a Sentinel he had dominion over the gift of prophecy. He still retains the gift because he has not fallen to the dark side. He is still of the Light, just trapped on earth."

"So, like, you have an address up in the Big Apple for this ancient prophecy dude?"

"No," Azrael admitted slowly.

"Oh, come . . . on . . ." Celeste shook her head. "This isn't some little town where you can just walk up and ask the general-store owner where your boy is. Eight million, you feel me?"

"I have a direction from the meditation. That gave me the first location. From there, we must have faith that guides will help us along the way. All Sentinels stay on the move. They have to or else they would be sent unimaginable temptation by the dark side."

"Well . . . okay, then, answer me this if you can. Like when exactly is this whole big battle supposed to happen? Seriously."

"December twenty-first, 2012."

"Stop playing." Celeste opened and closed her mouth. "So both the Mayans and Hollywood were right?"

"The Mayans were right. I cannot endorse anything you saw for entertainment value, except that the date is a fact. Life as humanity knew it will be altered."

"Then what's the point, for real? I mean that in all seriousness. If a giant asteroid is going to blow us up or the sun is gonna scorch us all . . . or the poles will shift, sending us into another ice age following biblical-type floods, earthquakes, and pandemic outbreaks or some nuclear holocaust . . . *dude* . . . then, like, why are you here? Shouldn't we all just stop having babies, open up the beer taps, and party like it's 1999? Damn . . . Prince was just off by thirteen years—which isn't bad for a rock star. Then again, maybe he's a hybrid, too? Just saying."

Azrael smiled a lopsided smile, even though she was completely serious. "Celeste, I haven't heard of a grand plan to wipe out all of humanity . . . but those who can see will see. There will be major shifts in the balance of power on this planet. That will involve a major uncovering of hidden truths . . . lies will be brought into the Light for scrutiny by the masses."

"You know," she said, her gaze drifting toward the windows again, "we are starting to see some of that. Bigwigs are getting busted left and right . . . and yet, even in the face of truth, some stuff is getting twisted up in rhetoric—the script is totally flipped and suddenly they're the victims. Then you have to figure out if the news you just heard is true, or is it a lie, or some BS half-truth."

She brought her line of vision back to meet his and let out a hard breath. "Most people just click on the TV, put on their favorite channel, and take as gospel whatever is said from behind a news desk. They don't have the time or the energy to research it, and it's like the people running everything are all in bed together and they know the average person can't sort it all out. Not to mention that it's so hard to tell anymore if what you searched on the Internet is true or just the crackpot theory of somebody with an agenda. It's like the information Wild, Wild West out here, man."

Azrael nodded. "Confusion is the objective. That's why there is such a fervent effort right now by the dark principalities that rule the airwaves to dumb down the masses and to keep humans distracted. Still, calm people can think. Frightened, angry people cannot think. The best way to ensure they will have lemmings to leap over the edge of the dark abyss is to ensure divisions and to simply keep people fighting and bickering amongst themselves . . . consuming blindly . . . living with their awareness numbed and their bodies so polluted that they cannot intuit their own divinity or the voice of the Source. Truth is now being blended with untruth in an unholy cocktail designed to poison the minds and psyches of those who allow themselves to be led without discernment. Even much of the clerical community of humanity has lost its way into the valley of greed and ego and decadence. I don't know where you fit into the equation, Celeste, but I know you are part of the solution. Your voice will resonate with those of the other Remnant and will cut through this misinformation somehow."

"All right," she said, drawing back from him. She withdrew her hand from his and hugged herself, suddenly feeling vulnerable. "Then, if they didn't tell you what I was supposed to do, specifically . . . then what can I do? Like what was with the spooky lights?"

"I also don't know what gifts will accrue to your spirit. That depends on you. Only time will tell. But each angel has general gifts, and then some have mastery in specific areas. One can never tell with a hybrid . . . how much of their humanity will affect the angelic abilities latent within. But if you are already intuiting the pain of others and seeing their true Light essence, rather than the divisions that make humans tribal and quarrelsome, then it is a fair bet that you have healing abilities. Compassion is the foundation of that gift. I also know how you make me feel when you touch me."

He cupped her cheek again, but this time it wasn't a grounding touch but more like a gentle caress. "You want to fix people, to make them whole, and injustice outrages your very soul. I felt it when you spoke of the man who took our tickets. I felt it when you tried to heal me in the sanctuary. That passion comes through when you speak of the iniquity of the powerful that dominate and take advantage of average citizens."

She looked at him unblinking, her voice calmer now, gentler, as she stared into his liquid brown eyes. "I know what it's like to be broken," she said in a soft voice. "I don't want to see anybody who is a good person hurting or taken advantage of."

"Your compassion comes from a deep well within, Celeste . . . and my cup runneth over for having experienced the beauty of that."

He drew away from her and turned to sit back. His eyes left hers to seek the tall pines that whizzed by at the window. Somehow she could feel a deep sense of conflict bubbling within him, although she wasn't sure of the source. But she did know that silence was best between them now.

Chapter 12

They rode the rest of the way to Trenton in amiable silence, then changed trains on the platform and continued on via New Jersey Transit to Penn Station in Manhattan. But the moment the train entered the tunnel just before the call for New York, Celeste knew something was wrong.

They'd gone through several underpasses along the way, and none of them seemed to have had the effect on Azrael that this one did. Even when they'd taken the subway in Philly, completely enclosed underground, he didn't seem bothered by being closed in at all. But when he'd dropped his head forward and begun breathing through his mouth, it was impossible to ignore that something was freaking him out.

Panicked, she placed a hand on his back and leaned down to whisper to him in short bursts. "You okay? What's up, Az? Talk to me."

"The energy coming up through the tunnels, from the rails, the density of people . . ." His voice trailed off as he wiped his brow, keeping his eyes squeezed shut. "The convergence is astounding here."

"Yeah," she murmured, leaning closer. "New York ain't no joke—but at least it's not Calcutta or whatever. So take a few breaths and drink some water. This isn't where you wanna look suspicious or have Amtrak police start asking if you're all right."

He nodded and sat up after a few seconds and then glanced around. "The tunnels here are teeming. But your touch, your Light, is helping dispel some of what I'm experiencing."

"Okay," she said, now holding one of his hands within hers. "But when you say 'teeming,' I take it that's not with good stuff." She glanced around nervously, then stared at him hard. "So where to from here?"

The train came to a stop and he stood slowly. "That's what I was trying to sense when I got slammed with everything this area holds."

She got to her feet quickly. "Let's get off the train and go upstairs and get out of the underground so you can—"

"No," he said, suddenly pulling her along the aisle behind him. "We have to get another train—two . . . the number two to Flatbush."

"Okay, okay, chill," she replied, finding it hard to keep up with his long strides.

It was the most insane thing. New York train stations were always packed and the flow of humanity was always intense. But to be following a huge angel that was literally running headlong toward a sense or a vibe, like a big hunting dog on a trail, was disorienting. Before he jumped a turnstile, she had to grab the back of his jacket.

"We have to pay, Az. C'mon, you want to get us in trouble?"

"You're right, my apologies . . . it's just that I can feel it so clearly now."

"Okay, but it's stuff like that you have to be cool about," she muttered, trying to figure out the machine on the wall and nearly giving up until she watched someone else use it.

"I will," he said, looking around five ways, "but you are really going to need to stay near me where we're going."

He'd kept a protective arm slung over her shoulder during the long ride to Flatbush Avenue, then practically yanked her off the train at that last stop. Every person that bumped into her in the crush getting off the train left an impression. Brooklyn College was here. Students' backpacks collided with hers, arms brushed, eyes met. If you had personal-space issues, a train in the city was the last place you needed to be.

Once on the sidewalk she looked around, trying to gain her bearings while Azrael sensed a direction.

"It's a house a few blocks down this large boulevard," he announced.

She glanced in the direction he pointed, noting the West Indian restaurants and food stores, as well as the primarily black pedestrians. "We're in a Caribbean community I think."

Azrael nodded but seemed distracted. "The house of
Bath Kol should be close. Come."

Not sure what to expect, she followed Azrael without voicing her questions. The sun had set, painting the
fall sky a dusky red-orange. Nightfall would soon come
and she wasn't sure she liked going into a new environment after dark where angels were looking to war with
demons.

They turned off the main thoroughfare of stores to
a residential block that had small white houses and tiny
front yards, not very different from many of the blocks
in Philly. She relaxed a little until he stopped in front of a
house that had a huge black rottweiler barking furiously
in the back.

"You know, we could try to find a really cheap motel,
like the kind that takes cash . . . and, uh, we could do this
in the morning."

He stared at her and cocked his head to the side in
question. "Why?"

"Because don't demons come out at night?"

Azrael walked up the steps. "They are out night and
day and never rest. You watch too much television."

"Yeah, but don't they get stronger at night?" she asked
a little louder as he banged on the door.

The dog stopped barking. Celeste held her breath. A
tall man with an exquisitely chiseled brown body opened
the door. He had dreadlocks down his back and was
naked from the waist up, wore a pair of nylon runner's
shorts bearing the colors of the Jamaican flag, and was toting a pump shotgun.

"I've come seeking Bath Kol," Azrael said.

"And who you be?" the man said, frowning as he assessed Azrael.

"An angel."

The man laughed and opened the screen door, then peered around Azrael. "And who dat?"

Azrael smiled. "If you cannot see for yourself, then maybe I've come to the wrong sanctuary."

"I am Isda," the man said, slapping his chest to a round of male laughter behind him. "I have been here a long time . . . that tends to blur the vision, but we can make it all better with a spliff, brother. One thing for sure, if you are a wayfarer, I will nourish you and da lady. No worries, mon."

"May we enter?"

"Yes, yes, come in." Isda rested his shotgun on the wall beside the door. He stepped aside for Azrael and held the screen open for Celeste, then shook Azrael's hand in an old-world warrior's embrace, clasping Azrael's right forearm as Azrael clasped his.

"I saw your Light from the steps . . . but hers . . . wow, mon. I didn't immediately see from so far away. So you found one."

"Yes. Her name is Celeste." Azrael glanced at her, then back to Isda. "I need to find Bath Kol as soon as possible."

"Hello, pretty lady. My brother here must be new to the . . ." Isda's words trailed off as he looked at Azrael. "You have talked to her, yes? She understands what this is—so I can speak freely?"

Azrael nodded.

"Hi," Celeste said quietly, taking in the environment.

Isda looked her up and down, then rounded her to go

to the door. "If I had met you years ago, tings would be different. My brother is a lucky man . . . but I have no complaints."

Celeste stood just inside the door as Isda closed it behind her. The small living room was filled with a wide, brown leather sectional sofa and a flat-screen TV. A carved wooden coffee table and ashtray caught the corner of her eye, reminding her of Brandon. The scent of weed was heavy in the air along with rose incense. African masks and art from the Diaspora graced the walls. Drums lay idle in a corner as delectable smells from the kitchen wafted toward Celeste, overlaying the blunt and the incense, making her mouth water.

Men sat in the dining room around the table with plates in various stages of wreckage. A bottle of 151-proof Appleton rum was the centerpiece of what seemed to be a ferocious card game that she and Azrael had interrupted. All eyes were on them now. Cards had been abandoned and three pretty women stood by the kitchen door, silently inspecting them.

Isda smiled broadly. "Anyway, dat is spilt milk. So, as I was saying, your locator must be new to this density to not introduce you to our family straight out. Come, eat, rest. Bath Kol is gone from here tonight."

"She cannot have cooked meats or anything that is not organic, nor can I—but thank you for your hospitality." Azrael gave Isda a look. "I respect that nourishment is your governance—you are still the angel of sustenance, correct?"

"True dat," Isda said with a sly smile, glimpsing Celeste with appreciation in a sidelong glance. "I haven't fallen all da way, brutha . . . just can't get home. Me and my brothers are Sentinels, just like Bath Kol and his squad are."

Azrael nodded. "No judgment, but her Light is still replenishing itself. She needs to stay vegan to reach her full Light strength."

"What you talkin' 'bout, mon? She cannot have rice and peas, curry goat with roti, a little plantains and callaloo to put some meat on her bones?" Isda said, shocked. "You, I understand. You still have dreams of going home, unlike those of us who screwed up and have to make the best of tings. But she can eat, drink, and be merry. In fact, you've probably scared the poor 'oman to death." Isda walked away from Celeste and called out to the women standing by the door. "Make her a plate without the curry goat. Be useful and somebody roll her a joint."

"Whoa, whoa, whoa, man," Azrael said, now coming between Celeste and Isda's line of vision. "Not advisable and not going to happen after all she went through to get clean."

"Weed is a natural herb, mon . . . a plant, right?"

For a moment it was a standoff, then Isda sighed and raked his fingers through his long locks.

"The rum and the joint, okay, mon—that might be over-the-top. But you need to let the 'oman eat."

Azrael held out his bag to Celeste. "I brought fruit."

She bit her lip and Isda chuckled. The women at the kitchen door didn't move, instead waiting for the outcome of the debate as though watching a reality-TV show. Men at the table chuckled and shook their heads.

"How long he been torturing you, love?"

"Don't tempt her," Azrael said with a half smile, but his tone was serious. "You are beginning to sound like the other side."

"Dat's cold, mon!"

"It's true," Azrael said, digging in his bag to produce a mango for Celeste. "I don't know what these dishes are that I smell, but they are . . . absolutely wreaking havoc on my intentions. I can only imagine what it's doing to hers."

"You sure you don't want a spliff, mon?" Isda said with a hopeful expression. "Pour the man a drink. You need to chill."

"No," Celeste said quietly, going to Azrael's side. "He has to remain clear. His system is so new that one joint plus that strong-ass rum, and he'll be high as a kite. Then throw on some heavy food and who knows what'll happen to him."

"Wow, mon," Isda said, looking at Celeste. "How long you been here?"

"One night and one day," Azrael said. "That's why I need your help."

"That's all it took to bond her to you like that?"

Celeste narrowed her gaze, tired of being spoken of as though she weren't in the room. "Doesn't take long to bond to an honest man—or being," she said with attitude. "So, do you know where we can find Bath Kol tonight, or not?"

"Feisty, too," Isda said, glancing back at the other men, who were chuckling, before returning his gaze to Azrael and Celeste. "Okay, listen, here's the deal. He keeps it moving. He just stopped through here, but we made him upset . . . he saw family, remembered all the ones he'd lost." Isda let his breath out hard. "Twenty-six thousand is a hard number to do when you can see the future and the average human life span is less than a hundred. Me and the boys, well, we take it all in stride . . . we live life to the fullest and enjoy our wives and children, and we weep. But we still have joy, you feel me? Bath Kol is so bereft his joy is almost gone . . . and the dark side can feel it. So he has to stay on the move."

"But where would he go?" Azrael glanced around the room and rubbed the nape of his neck.

"He goes to Queen Aziza's wellness center in Crown Heights to get his energy worked on when he gets like this. Her place is a prayer fortress so he can go in and let his guard down while he experiences the center's therapies. Mon, he can spend all day getting his chakras realigned and doing the healing work, you know. I tell him to smoke a tree and chill, but it's getting so that he starts seeing bad tings when he's high. So . . ." Isda shrugged. "My advice is to come in, sit down, and heal thyself first, and then go looking for that cantankerous—"

"No," Celeste said, grabbing Azrael by the arm. She stared up at him. "We need to move, now."

You're sure about this, Azrael asked with a yawn, walking in a quasi-zigzag pattern down the quiet street behind her.

"Yes," she replied, annoyed by the whole situation. "We had to get out of there—that was a trap, sure as I was looking at one."

"How so?" he asked, slightly slurring his words.

"First of all, you've probably got a contact high just from standing in the living room."

"I don't understand."

"That's the problem," she said, walking quickly in the brisk air to help shake the lethargy that was settling on him. "Try to think about anything you picked up while on the Net about the effects of weed and alcohol. Man . . . they don't want to see you go home. Classic haters."

"But—"

"But, nothing." She whirled on him. "They have been here a *long* time; their house leader admitted it himself."

"Okay, true," Azrael said, seeming to find it difficult to keep stride with Celeste as they made their way toward the train. "But what's that got to do with—"

"It has everything to do with it," she snapped. "They are exhibiting classic human behavior, and if it's one thing I can read, it's classic human behavior. I also know a setup when I see one. It was four of them and one of you. Four strong Sentinels working on you, man, is what I'd call a spiritual beatdown, and nobody even broke a sweat or frowned. Look at you. You're trashed."

He stopped walking and opened his arms wide. "What?"

"You are buzzed."

"No, I'm not!"

She strode up to him and pushed him in the center of his chest. "You're buzzed. You drew from the environment and had your guard down once you realized they weren't hostiles. When you met me in a bar, this didn't happen to you because you kept your guard up, but this was different. Once you thought things were cool back at that house, you had total trust and were wide-open, so to speak. Weren't you the one who told me to stay close because these guys who have been here too long are dangerous, blah, blah, blah?"

Azrael slowly lowered his arms.

"Yeah," she said, folding her arms over her chest. "They aren't just dangerous in the caveman style of obvious. C'mon, son, they've had twenty-six thousand years to perfect their game. They've got a whole nuther level of smooth going on."

"I cannot believe I was so oblivious . . ."

"You don't think they've learned how to burn a fellow empath? Like . . . maybe make a guy who's wide-open feel all their vices and to take enough of them into his energetic field to even impact his actual physical system?" She stopped walking for a moment. "Az, I heard your stomach growl in there and could tell you were five minutes from breaking down for some of whatever they had in the kitchen. And I'm not gonna lie, so was I—so I'm not trying to act like I'm Miss Perfect. But I told you I'd watch your back. That's all I'm trying to do here."

Azrael closed his eyes and shook his head but kept walking. "Stupid. I would have been more prepared if they were demons. In a traditional battle, we know the dark side uses devious methods and therefore we surround ourselves with protective energy, like Light armor, going into battle. Stupid, stupid, stupid!"

"Not stupid, just naïve—and there's a difference. But both naïveté and stupidity can get you jacked up. So now that you know, act like you know. Obviously what you're going to encounter doesn't fight fair or engage their enemy by traditional methods. Learn this guerrilla warfare, dude. Seriously. It's a new day . . . or night, as the case may be. Plus, they didn't even bring their A game because they realized how much of a newbie to the density you were."

"He asked me and I outright told him like a trusting child! Damn it!"

"Yeah," she said, shaking her head. "But like you told me, stop cussing because right now you're clearly in no condition to ward off anything slithering up from a sewer or whatever. The last thing we need out here is a low vibration, okay?"

"I must regain my sobriety. Celeste, this is unacceptable. I could have endangered you."

"Nah . . . your boys back at that house would probably jump into a demon brawl, let's hope—especially only a coupla blocks from their house. But for future reference, here's how it was gonna go down if we'd stayed. They'd get you buzzed from a contact, and after about a half hour, maybe you'd say yes to a few tokes, then a few more . . . and once dry mouth set in, rum would seem like a natural solution . . . and while laughing and playing cards, who's thinking about consumption and quantities of get-high? Then, food . . . hey . . . who cares, because your ass has the munchies. So you'll eat that great-smelling grub they had in there, and if your boy has dominion over nourishment, then you know the women he pulled can burn. Why not, he's not gonna abstain now. It's already too late, so he's gonna enjoy every aspect of being in a body that he can. I ain't hatin'."

She lifted her chin as she set her sights on the train portal a half block ahead. "And, once you eat and smoke a joint, who really cares if you find Bath Kol to stay on mission because, by now, you're sleepy—or horny . . . and if your angel brother has been around on the planet as long as he said, then he knows a thing or two about getting his swerve on with a woman. He'd probably get laid in that house tonight, and since you're an empath, you would have picked that up while you crashed on the couch, and then you would have been all messed up and they would have felt like they'd showed you that you were no better than they were. Be clear. That was how it was gonna go. I could feel it. That's why I said, 'We're out.' Ain't no friends in this game."

Azrael looked away. "He said we should be catching the number two train back toward Manhattan, and then we're supposed to get off at Franklin Avenue, go up the stairs to the other side, where we get the number three to Kingston Avenue."

"Changing the subject will not change the facts, Az. Why do men always do that? Never mind, don't answer that—rhetorical question anyway." Celeste stopped as they neared the train entrance and she placed a hand on Azrael's chest. "It'll pass . . . this feeling of being buzzed. He probably sent the energy of the herb toward you just like you showed me with the vitamins, because it is a natural plant, after all."

Azrael nodded. "He did, as soon as you started explaining . . . your words resonated as truth."

"Bet you can taste the rum in your mouth, too."

Again Azrael nodded and took a deep breath, but his eyes were angry. "I would have expected no less of demons . . . but my own brothers. Damn!"

"Yeah, well, sibling rivalry is a bitch. Who wants to see

you go home with flying colors, so to speak, when they've been trapped down here so long they're half-crazy?"

"Did they hurt you, Celeste . . . did they pollute your system, too?"

"No. I think they were focused on you, because if they got you all jacked up, then working on me, a mere mortal, would have been easy."

"Duly noted," he said, disgusted, then leaned against a storefront window.

"Hey, everything has a purpose. Remember this lesson so that the next time you encounter a Sentinel brother, you can guard yourself . . . and me, you know?"

"I have failed you before I've even begun." Azrael released a long sigh and hung his head.

"No, you haven't. Weed either makes you silly as all get-out or makes you melodramatic," she said, laughing gently, fully aware of his raw feelings. "You're leaning on the side of melodrama where everything is cosmic and deep . . . and I bet you're hungry?"

"Starving," he admitted, now searching his bag. "I wish I had some of those chips . . . or ice cream . . . or—"

"Peel a mango, eat it out here now, drink some water, and lemme go into one of these stores and buy some hand wipes."

Azrael set his bag down by his feet and stared at the fruit he'd extracted from it. "Did you every notice the colors of a mango . . . how it looks like the Source just painted each one by hand."

"Oh, man, I could so kick their asses . . . you are so high." She took the mango from him and held it away from her to peel it.

"Celeste," he said quietly. "You're beautiful, did you know that?"

She looked up at him.

"I need to thank you for teaching me all this stuff and . . . you're *so* beautiful. You're making me feel things that . . . I can't put words to and right now I just want to—"

"I know it's real intense at the moment, but I will not be the reason you can't go home." She closed her eyes and tried to steady herself. "Az . . . this feeling will go away once you eat."

"No. No, it won't. The urge to join with you is like nothing I've ever known, Celeste. I felt this before but it was less urgent and I could just will it away. Now it's a craving, an actual body ache worse than when we were on the train. . . . But I'm not exactly sure how allowed any of what I'm feeling *is* allowed or not, even though you're not truly a human, you're a hybrid one of us. . . . I am therefore praying that it is all right, but I don't know if there are special circumstances or rules that we should observe—that is assuming . . . hoping you feel the same way . . . for millennia we just blotted the very concept out of our minds, so I never looked into the caveats and it was never a passing thought where I was. I never had a formal body; I was energy, and—am I making sense?"

"Here," she said quickly, handing him the opened fruit.

He bit into it with a moan of satisfaction, and she hoisted her backpack higher on her right shoulder. "I'm gonna go get some hand wipes or at least some napkins or whatever I can score. Be back in a few. Pitch the skin and pit when you're done—*but stay right here*. The birds will be happy with the mango remains if there's no trash can available, and the fruit is biodegradable anyway."

She left him leaning against the wall devouring the fruit. If they had Kettle chips in the store or some kind of all-natural cake or candy, she'd bring it back to him as a treat. But she had to get away from him for a minute as a diversion. She had to do what she'd just accused all of mankind of doing—she had to change the subject and hope both her mind and body would get the memo. Never in her life had she been so blown away. The man or being or whatever was politically correct to call him was standing outside the store in the dark practically sparking blue-white light, trembling, babbling from trying to be honorable, and breathing hard with an erection that wouldn't quit.

Of all the strikes already against her, the last thing she figured she needed was a black mark on her record for taking advantage of an inebriated angel.

Chapter 13

You all right?" Celeste gave Azrael a sidelong glance as they exited the subway to the street.

"Yes," he said in a somber tone, not looking at her as they headed toward the corner of Kingston and Bergen.

"You don't sound so okay," she said after they'd walked in strained silence for several yards.

"I am no longer inebriated. The water and the food helped . . . and I appreciate the chips you found . . . and the vegan brownie."

"Well, you sure don't sound like somebody who has a lot of sugar and carbs in his system," she said with a half smile, trying to cheer him up. "Anybody with a system as clean as yours is should be bouncing off the walls like a little kid."

"I cannot be childlike or joyful at this moment, Celeste . . . not after shaming myself."

She hurried to get in front of him and stop him. "Hey, you didn't shame yourself."

"I lost complete control and was ineffective as your protector. I am no guardian. Had you not been there to intervene, who knows what mischief I would have been up to."

"Lighten up." She smiled wider when he rounded her and kept walking. "You aren't the first person to go to a house party and wind up getting their drink spiked or whatever. At least you weren't dancing on a table with a lampshade on your head."

"But I am Azrael!" he shouted.

She ignored the outburst and threaded her arm around his waist. "And while you have a body, you're gonna feel stuff—so get used to it."

"I confess that I do not like this condition of vulnerability at all." He looked at her but didn't pull away. "It is very disorienting."

"Welcome to planet Earth. Pain is why everybody here does crazy-bad shit . . . and pleasure-seeking to escape it is what gets more people in trouble than you can count. My therapists said balance was the key. But unless you've got a special hotline to a brother up in the clouds who deals with balance, on that I can't really help you. All I can do is warn you if your rudder is steering you too far left or too far right."

"I appreciate that," he said quietly, then stopped to stare at the address they'd been given.

"It's all good," she said, joining him in staring at the soft folds of jewel-tone purple and green silk fabric that covered the large storefront window. "I think this is it."

Azrael rang the bell and they waited, not sure what to expect. Celeste looked up at the building. The wood frames around the doors and the windows had been painted soft lavender, while the door was a soothing mint green. A large Egyptian ankh was carved into the wood beneath the address, and a large brass one hung inside the picture window with the silk fabric behind it.

Tranquil colors emanated from the structure, and within a few moments they could hear calm movement inside. When the door opened, a petite, brown, delicately boned woman stood in the threshold. Her age was impossible to judge, but her eyes held a level of wisdom that said she'd lived a while. Her smile was warm and her Light was so radiant that it almost seemed to reach out and caress them. Dreadlocks were piled high in a lavender wrap atop her head, her feet were bare, and she wore a soft, orange gauze shift with long, flowing sleeves.

"*Hetep,* beloveds. I have been expecting you. Please come in." She stood aside and indicated with a graceful sweep of her hand where a shoe basket sat just inside the door. It held unused paper sandals, and there was a straw mat for shoes. "You may leave your shoes here and come back into my private rooms to join me in some tea."

It wasn't a request; it was more like a gentle command. Celeste and Azrael took off their shoes, slipped on the paper sandals that had been offered, and followed the queen.

"You may leave your bags over there," she said in a gracious tone, again using a sweep of her arm to indicate the shelving outside the treatment rooms they passed.

They settled their bags on a shelf and continued

through the narrow hallway toward the back. Egyptian papyruses with beautiful ceremonial reliefs graced the walls, as did peacock feathers and small figurines and masks from the motherland. Lavender drifted through the air combined with light hints of rosemary and rose oil that Celeste was sure Queen Aziza used in her day-spa treatments.

The level of peace that exuded from every surface was enough to melt one's bones. Queen Aziza stopped at a spiral staircase and gave them a smile.

"Be careful going down. The wood is slippery."

Celeste held on to the railing with both hands, trying not to gape at the fine art and one-of-a-kind, handcrafted seating that the stairs opened out into. A full apartment was below the small spa, and Queen Aziza simply motioned with a hand for them to have a seat at her carved teakwood dining room table.

A huge, black, old-fashioned potbellied stove was in the far corner of what doubled as a kitchen and dining room, and a wooden refrigerator stood beside a stainless-steel sink and counters, near rows of copper-bottom pots, apothecary jars, and mason jars filled with grains.

"Green tea with raw honey?"

"Please," Azrael said, then closed his eyes.

"Thank you so much," Celeste murmured in awe.

"You must be famished after such a long journey here. Let me restore you with some fresh vegetable couscous, whole-wheat pita bread and hummus with tabouli salad, and perhaps yam soup, or would you prefer miso and seaweed?"

Azrael dropped his head into his hands. Celeste

watched the tension in his body literally unwind in the thick muscles of his broad shoulders.

"My prayers have been answered tonight. Whatever you offer we are honored to share."

"Are you an angel?" Celeste murmured.

Queen Aziza turned away from the stove and laughed. The sound of her mirth was like tinkling bells that made everyone smile with her.

"No, beloved. I'm just a sensitive . . . and Isda called me to confess that he'd behaved badly when you came to visit him."

"He really did," Celeste said, beginning to lose her smile.

"Ah . . . don't be so hard on him and the others. He still has his Light, but he can be irksome at times because he is so unhappy and trying so hard to deny that he is—that I'll grant you."

"Well, he sure messed up Az."

"Jealousy is so destructive." Queen Aziza released a weary sigh and brought two hand-painted platters with food to the table, then set them down. She went to Azrael, who now stared up at her. "Dear brother of Light, may I look at your energy body?"

"Yes, of course," Azrael murmured in an easy baritone.

Queen Aziza frowned. "Your heart chakra is spinning slowly as though the energy there is stuck or conflicted . . . and your back . . . there are dark outages around your shoulders. Can you remove your shirt?"

"I'd . . . prefer not to," he said quietly, and then stared down at the floor.

"His wings," Celeste said softly. "Something happened

when he came through from that side to this one, and it still bothers him."

Azrael pushed back from the table. "Forgive me for being foolish. I of all people should know that vanity is a sin." He released a deep breath and stripped his shirt over his head. "There. You can see the scars."

"Az . . . ," Celeste said slowly, standing up as he turned to look at her and Queen Aziza. "The keloids are gone."

"The scars are in your mind, beloved," Queen Aziza said in a gentle tone. "May I lay hands on you with this Divine one you've brought into my home? I am blessed and honored to be at the service of angels . . . to feed you both as wayfarers along your journey."

"No, dear queen. We are in your debt for such hospitality." Azrael felt over his shoulder, then craned his neck to try to peer to see his back.

"Do you have a mirror?" Celeste asked quickly. "He needs to see it to believe it."

"Yes, of course." Queen Aziza rushed out of the room, then returned with a large salon handheld mirror and a compact.

"Here," Celeste said, giving Azrael the compact and turning him around to face the mirror Queen Aziza held. "See for yourself."

Both women fell silent as he stared, then tried to touch the even brown skin with his fingertips.

"How can this be . . ."

"Take him into the bathroom while I prepare your tea and soup," Queen Aziza ordered, handing Celeste the large mirror. "He can look in this one and see better under the bright lights in the full-length mirror behind the door."

Without thinking about it, Celeste took the compact from him and set it on the table. "This is not vanity—it's called *sanity*. You had a part of yourself amputated and the scars were a painful reminder. Come on. Let's heal this in your head, all right?"

He nodded and swallowed hard and followed her without a word. She walked through the bedroom, which was lit with soft candlelight coming from a fruit-laden altar that bore pictures framed in silver of elderly ancestors. The doorway to the bathroom was inside the bedroom and it stood open and dark. For a moment the memory of what had happened in a bathroom made Celeste hesitate.

"We don't have to do this," Azrael said, catching her arm. "I could tell that—"

"No. You have to see . . . and so do I."

She touched his face and then took him by the hand and led him into the dark room, then clicked on the light. For a few seconds her heart felt as if it would pound its way out of her chest. But in the momentary darkness, she saw nothing frightening, just Azrael's blue-white glow before they were bathed with stark white overhead lights.

"We have to close the door," she said, bringing him into the room deeper as she battled her anxiety. Memories of being in tight bathroom confines under terrifying conditions when Brandon attacked her were still fresh. But she shook the feeling and focused on Azrael. "Stand here."

She handed him the large salon mirror and waited as he took it from her and then flexed the muscles in his shoulder blades and chest.

"The muscles and tendons are still there . . ."

"Then the wings have got to still be there in your energetic body," Celeste said with a frown.

"But I can't see them," he said, angling the mirror in a different way.

"Wait, wait, wait." She took the mirror from him and set it down in the sink. "I knew Aunt Niecey's words would come in handy one of these days. How's it go . . . faith is believing in things unseen . . . or—"

"Yes!" Azrael turned around, giving her his back, then covered his face with his hands. "We regularly chastise humans for this offense—but it is so easy a trap to fall into. I shall forever be changed by this experience, Celeste. No wonder things have fallen into such disarray . . . where was our compassion toward humankind? How could we expect them to see evidence of death, Hell, and destruction but only give them scant examples of hope and healing to cling to and then demand blind faith?"

His confusion was so palpable, his crisis so deep, that the only thing she knew to do was to go to him and hug him from behind. She laid her cheek against his strong back and wrapped her arms around his waist and closed her eyes.

"Maybe, do you think that's also why the Source allowed some of you to get trapped here . . . so that there would be an entire battalion of you guys that finally got the human condition? I was never taught by my aunt that God was cruel. Tough, yeah, but not whimsical and cruel . . .

and especially if his angels fell on their swords, like why would you be locked out of going home? Wouldn't a serious repentance and a cry for mercy be enough? And if you loved the human you'd lain with . . . I mean with all your heart and soul, would the Almighty frown on that? What if maybe, in the so-called end of days, there would need to be enough of you who'd lived here, fought here, loved here, lost here, cried here, and even died to be reborn here to know just what we were up against? Maybe that's the big picture and it has nothing to do with guilt and punishment and rules and whatever . . . but I'm just a half-breed human. What do I know?"

She petted his once injured shoulders, then placed a kiss against his spine between where his wings should have been, and the gasp he released shook her to her core. Testing a dawning awareness, she gently touched the sensitive spot with trembling fingers and watched him drop his head back, eyes closed, breaths becoming shallow.

"Does it hurt?" she whispered.

"No. It brings to mind First Corinthians, thirteen, in a most profound way," he murmured on a ragged inhale.

"I don't understand." She laid her cheek against the tender spot, trying to send as much loving, healing energy into it as she could.

He drew in a deep breath through his nose, then spoke in a low murmur. "'If I speak in the tongues of men and of angels, but I have not love, I am only a resounding gong or a clanging cymbal. If I have the gift of prophecy and can fathom all mysteries and all knowledge, and if I have a faith that can move mountains, but have not love, I am nothing. If I give all that I possess to the poor and surrender my body to flames, but I have not love, I gain nothing.'"

"'Love is patient, love is kind,'" she said, picking up where he left off, reciting one of the four passages Aunt Niecey had forced her to learn by heart—this passage, psalm 91, the 23rd psalm, and the Lord's Prayer she knew by rote.

"'It does not envy, it does not boast. It is not proud,'" Azrael said, his voice bottoming out with so much deep resonance that she could feel it in her womb.

She kissed him deeply against the sensitive spot she'd found and felt his stomach tremble beneath her hands. "'It is not rude, it is not self-seeking . . . it is not easily angered, it keeps no record of wrongs. Love does not delight in evil but rejoices with truth.'" She nuzzled that warm, glowing space between his shoulder blades, drawing another shudder from his body as she spoke against it, now realizing that it wasn't a site of pain, but an erogenous zone. "'It always protects, it always trusts, always hopes, always perseveres.'"

He reached back, framing the sides of her body with his palms, slowly dragging them down the length of her body. "'Love never fails . . . but where there are prophecies, they will cease; where there are tongues, they will be stilled; where there is knowledge, it will pass away.'"

She covered his hands with hers, feeling the painfully exquisite rush of energy that spilled from his aura. "'For we know in part and we prophesy in part, but when perfection comes, the imperfect disappears.'"

He slowly turned and pulled her into a warm embrace. His kiss began at the crown of her head with a rough murmur. "'When I was a child, I talked like a child, I thought like a child, I reasoned like a child,'" he said in a deep rumble kissing her eyelids, then the bridge of her nose. "'When I became a man, I put childish ways behind me,'" he murmured before capturing her mouth.

It was the sweetest, most profound kiss she'd ever experienced. As their tongues dueled in a lazy exploration of soft and hard surfaces, ambrosia covered her palate and sweetness filled her lungs. Heady, she felt as if she were floating, but intense desire welded her to his body. Her hands caressed the sinewy surface of his shoulders and back, as broad, hot palms cradled her back then slid over the rise of her behind, drawing a swallowed moan from them both.

He broke the kiss with a pained expression, then rested his damp forehead against hers and shut his eyes.

"'Now we see but a poor reflection as in a mirror; then we shall see face-to-face.'" She stroked the side of his jaw with the back of her hand.

He nodded and pulled back a bit, staring into her eyes as though seeing her for the first time. "'Now I know in part; then I shall know fully, even as I am fully known.'" He kissed her again, this time harder, urgently, pulling her against him as his fingers sought her hair and he palmed her backside.

"Is everything all right, beloveds?" a light female voice called out.

Celeste broke the kiss and placed a hand against Azrael's bare chest. Where her hand landed, her palm burned. His colors were beyond his body, and iridescent light covered the sink and tub and tiles. Behind his brown irises she could see a flame of blue-white light, and his expression was filled with pure agony.

"Yes, Queen . . . thank you . . . I think his heart chakra is all right now."

"Good, because the tea and soup are ready."

"Be there in a second," Celeste said in a distressed singsong voice.

Azrael clasped her hand and brought it to his mouth to kiss the center of it, still breathing hard. "'And now these three remain: faith, hope, love. But the greatest of these is love.'"

"We have to leave this bathroom and—"

"I cannot," he said, suddenly panicked as he looked down. "This would offend our hostess. This much I am sure of; even culturally inept, I know better."

Celeste held his face and kissed him softly, as guilt accosted her. Earlier she'd warned him not to touch her, but the pull to him had been so strong . . . stronger than anything she'd ever experienced in her life. "I'll go out there, you put some cold water on your face, and I'll stall her. I don't know what the rule system is in the Great Upstairs, but if you can't get it to go down, then you'll have to do what you've gotta do by any means necessary . . . hey . . . I'm just saying."

"You are definitely a healing angel." He kissed her again hard.

"I gotta go, and this is only making matters worse."

He nodded. "You're right, you're right. I cannot think in this condition."

She smiled and slipped out of his hold. He wouldn't

be the first man to experience said condition, but she wouldn't say that to him out loud, ever.

Hurrying out of the bathroom, she shut the door behind her, then closed the bedroom door on the way out to where Queen Aziza had set out tea and food.

"How is our patient?" the older woman said, sitting down across from Celeste.

"He'll live and he's much better, I think."

"How long has he been manifest?" Queen Aziza smiled and took up her green tea.

"About a day," Celeste said quietly, then said a brief prayer before enjoying the yam soup.

"Then everything is brand-spanking-new to him."

"The soup is delicious . . . hmmm," Celeste said, quickly changing the subject.

Queen Aziza smiled. "Coconut milk, steamed yams, a little cinnamon and fresh nutmeg, a pinch of ginger. It took me many years to perfect the different life-affirming recipes . . . and then they started coming to me."

"The recipes?"

"No, the angels," Queen Aziza said with a wink. "In this era, they are not coming like they did in ancient times—as pure beings of powerful Light. They are coming to walk amongst us and to experience our trials and tribulations by our sides as they help. I think the first time they were here they came with such little compassion for the human condition and just handed out these crazy edicts without realizing what people had to go through to carry them out." She shrugged and sipped her tea. "Now don't get me wrong, the ones in the ether who are in-spirit guardians and guides are still active up in the heavenly realms. But people like me are seeing some of them incarnate here on earth, and some of these beings are all messed up, needing help despite all their power… that's where we come in."

"You said you were a sensitive . . . is that why Bath Kol comes to you?"

Queen Aziza nodded. "He gets bad news from the front—like another brother of Light going dark—and he comes to me to get his energy rebalanced. Or he goes on a bender with his Sentinel brothers, or sees some global catastrophe that the dark side created, or it could be a personal loss like an old human friend dying, and he comes here."

"Isda said he left them—no great mystery why—and came here for a healing."

"Yes," Queen Aziza said with a weary sigh. "He came and got his chakras aligned, then I did some energy work on him and put him in an aroma-therapy room for a while so he could sleep. Isda disturbs Bath Kol's sense of peace sometimes and is truly prone to excess."

"I take it he's not here now though."

"No, and he could be a lot of places."

"Oh, brother . . ." Celeste took several more spoonfuls of the delicious soup and fidgeted with a piece of pita bread. "So now what do we do?"

"He hangs out sometimes at a dance club in the South Bronx, over in Hunts Point . . . lot of working girls on that side of town—I'm not judging, just preparing you for what you might see, but he tells me that he goes there because he likes to dance."

Celeste smirked. "Dance, or get a lap dance?"

"I think a little of both." Queen Aziza pushed the

platters of tabouli and hummus closer to Celeste. "But he loves the hip-hop scene there."

"Hip-hop?" Celeste almost spit out her soup.

"Not the new stuff, the old stuff," Queen Aziza said, handing Celeste a napkin and laughing. "The old message music . . . people like Afrika Bambaataa and Grandmaster Flash—not this gangster rap now that promotes killing and misogyny. Two guesses where that came from."

Queen Aziza waved her hand and dismissed the subject. "Anyway, there's a club he likes to go to that has weekend break-dance contests in the old-style way, and if you get him started about the politics of the hip-hop museum being located in the northeast part of the Bronx up on 212th Street and White Plains Road, he'll talk your ear off. By the time he's done giving you a philosophy lesson on the purity of sound as a medium of worldview fusion, you will want a drink, will need a drink, but have made him a happy man. He goes there when he needs joy. It's the African and Latin drumbeats and world-music beats that resonate with him, that's why he picked up on hip-hop so strongly in this era. When he needs to quiet his soul, he goes out to Lily Dale, in western New York, where they have the world's largest group of mediums."

"Whoa . . . why would an angel go there?" Celeste sat back. "I thought there was this whole thing about false prophets at the end of days?"

"First thing I asked the man, but he said he can see a lie as a black ring around the person as they're speaking—since he governs prophecy. Then he gave me this quote from one of the religious texts he was carrying around in a duffel bag when he first came here. 'Everyone who prophesies speaks to men for the strengthening, encouragement, and comfort. I would like every one of you to speak in tongues, but I would rather have you prophesy.'" She waved her hand again as though shooing away an invisible fly. "Has to do with instructions and knowledge, and I think he goes up to Lily Dale to be sure that little community doesn't get besieged by darkness since they help so many people."

"Man . . . I'm gonna hope he's in the Bronx because Lily Dale sounds like a full day trip by car."

"It is, just like when he heads out to the Native American sweat lodges, or just goes up to Canada. Sometimes he's gone for a day, sometimes for months."

"Can I ask you a personal question?" Celeste said, leaning across the table. She wanted so badly to know, how did one have a relationship with an angel, and was a lightning bolt gonna come down out of the sky if she did? She wondered if that was how the angels found out they were trapped. Was it some big embarrassing thing or did they get a termination letter from a winged messenger or whatever?

A placid nod from the older woman sitting across from Celeste helped her gin up the courage to finally ask a small part of what she really wanted to know. "Is he, like, your significant other?"

Queen Aziza smiled. "No . . . in this lifetime he's just a dear friend. His heart chakra is too damaged for that. How many times do you imagine the man saw his wives die over the expanse of centuries he's been here?"

Celeste just shook her head. "I cannot even imagine," she murmured, glancing at the closed bathroom door.

"Should we go check on your guardian? He seemed pretty depressed about his loss."

"No, no," Celeste said quickly. "Azrael is all right. He's just dealing with a lot of adjustment pressure . . . he's only been here a day."

"Ah. Makes perfect sense," Queen Aziza said, standing. "Then let me bring you some lemon water and I can refresh your tea."

"You have been way too kind to us. Thank you . . . but how do you deal with it all?"

Queen Aziza turned and gave Celeste a quizzical look.

"How do you deal with knowing that there really is a side of dark and light, seeing spirits, seeing the lights . . . knowing challenges are coming your way because you are standing in the Light?"

The older woman nodded. "You become calm, you clean out your body and spirit so that you have a strong foundation, and then you stand firmly in your power. When you do, the angels will come to you. Right now they need us to be as strong as they are in spirit." She motioned toward the bathroom. "That brother came in here tore up about his loss . . . confused, angry, body tainted with drugs and alcohol. But compassion is what's going to heal him, having someone to trust is going to allow him to sleep at night. Anyone or anything on this planet is here to learn lessons. *This is school,* boo."

"More like cosmic boot camp, if you ask me."

"Couldn't have said it better." Queen Aziza went to the stove as Celeste noshed. "Most of my clients are good people trying to find their spiritual path through the overgrown footbridges of their lives. Some are on the journey, but most come in crises and we've gotta deal with that first. Then I have these absolutely fabulous visitations like tonight. So, you just tell me if there is anything I can do?"

"There is one thing," Celeste said quietly, "and if you say no, I'd understand."

"If I can do it, I will. If I can't, I will honestly tell you that as well."

"My aunt is old and sick, back in Philly. . . . I left the city in a hurry and don't have a cell phone. Could I just make a quick call to check on her?"

"Absolutely! I thought you were going to ask me for something hard."

Celeste let her breath out when Queen Aziza laughed and motioned for her to follow.

"Come, there's a phone in the bedroom."

"Uh . . . I can call her a little later," Celeste said quickly, panicking as Queen Aziza floated in a graceful stride toward the bedroom door. Tension almost made Celeste stand. If the host opened the bedroom door, she'd be close to the bathroom inside that room . . . and as long as it was taking Azrael to rejoin them in the dining room, the last thing she wanted was for a sensitive to pick up on what was probably happening behind closed doors.

Queen Aziza stopped for a moment, then turned and bowed to Celeste. "Let's try the one in my spa office, shall we?"

"Much obliged," Celeste said, feeling her face warm.

She didn't say another word as she followed the older woman up the spiral staircase and kept her gaze on Queen Aziza's bare feet. Once they'd reached the little room in the back of the establishment, Queen Aziza offered her a seat at her desk and showed her how to dial out. But she hung by the doorway, her gaze locking with Celeste's.

"It's allowed you know . . . and it's natural, and nothing to be ashamed of. Shows you're alive."

So mortified that she could barely breathe, Celeste just stared at the woman.

"I've had very long discussions with Bath Kol about the whole edict."

So much embarrassment filled Celeste even as so many questions fought to get out of her mouth that all she could offer Queen Aziza was a wide-eyed stare.

Queen Aziza smiled. "When they come into this density, everything is a hundredfold more intense than in the human body. The food, if it's pleasing to the palate, it almost makes them high. If it's bad for their system, they'll be sick as a dog until their system adjusts to it. If they have a drink, they are *lit*. And when they're amorous, they are practically out of their minds so I'm told . . . has to do with the twelve strands of DNA and powerful energy connected directly to the Source. Just like they heal in a day or so from something that would have one of us in triage or in a casket."

"But then to send them here is so cruel—and to trap them here because they were the victims of this physical manifestation that they didn't even ask for while trying to protect us? What kind of sick, twisted—"

"So they can *learn*," Queen Aziza said in a calm tone, placing a finger to her lips. "The one you found or who found your Light is the luckiest of the group I've known in this lifetime."

"This lifetime? You said that when we were downstairs."

"Yes, beloved. I've done this before—the last time I recall impressions was in Kemet . . . otherwise known as Egypt. I was a keeper of the scrolls. I was a priestess then, as now, and I know the Divine Source of All That Is isn't cruel. There is a purpose to all of this, even the banishment."

"I tried to tell Azrael the exact same thing."

"Call your aunt. When you find Bath Kol, he can tell you more. But you do not have to be afraid of trapping your guardian on the planet. He can be with you the way he can be with no other. If you won't take my word for it, tell him to send up a Light missive—a prayer, and see what the answer is."

"Are you serious?" Celeste sat back, stunned. "But he said . . ."

"Some of them do not fully know because it was never a part of their consciousness. They heard Thou Shalt Not and left it right there."

"But—"

"But you aren't human," Queen Aziza murmured softly with a kind smile. "Therein lies the loophole. Azrael is blessed, as are you."

Celeste just stared at the mysterious woman as Queen Aziza turned and glided away to disappear down the long hall. She'd heard the words Queen Aziza had spoken, but like anything else, unless she had ironclad proof, a sentence of twenty-six thousand years was nothing to play with. Until she got word directly from a true Light-bearer that it was cool, she wasn't even trying to play games with a cosmic loophole that could get Azrael messed up for eternity.

After a moment to collect herself, Celeste picked up

the phone and dialed her aunt Niecey's house. So much strangeness was happening so fast, that for a minute she just wished for her old, terrible life back. But after being in Azrael's arms, she knew there was no turning back. On the third ring, her aunt answered the phone, and that put tears in Celeste's eyes.

"Hello? Auntie?"

"Baby, is that you?"

"Oh, my God, Aunt Niecey, I was so worried about you.... I don't know why but I wanted to hear your voice."

"I'm jus' fine, baby girl . . . chased some demons off my porch this morning, but you know me. I got Roscoe Jr. and my Good Book. They left out of here and ain't come back."

Celeste closed her eyes and sat back. "Thank God."

"I do every day."

"But you feel all right?"

Her aunt laughed her rich, warm laugh that felt like warm syrup on biscuits. "Never better. I'm watching my crime shows. I thought you two was in New York?"

"We are—I just don't have a cell phone anymore so I had to call from a friend's house up here."

"Well, shouldn't y'all be out dancing and having young folks' fun?"

"We're going out later, Auntie," Celeste said, finally laughing. "I love you."

"Good. I love you, too, baby. Now lemme get back to my program."

"G'nite." Celeste made a kissing sound into the receiver, then hung up. She sat back for a moment, closed her eyes, and just breathed in and out slowly.

Chapter 14

An angry mob of ravens lifted off the telephone wires and took to the skies at Fifty-eighth and Ellsworth Avenue, rushing to the Philadelphia waterfront. The moment they reached the warehouse, they drew together into one large entity that finally formed the silhouette of a tall man dressed in leather.

He entered the building through the rooftop stairs. Nathaniel looked up and stood, wiping the cocaine powder from his nose with the back of his hand when Malpas walked in.

Malpas dropped to one knee before Nathaniel. "Milord, they are in New York City."

"Where in New York? The city is a haystack of eight million and we need to find her quickly."

"The number on the line she dialed out from was a restricted one, but she mentioned New York and that they were going out later tonight."

Nathaniel rubbed his palms down his face in agitation. "Send half of your warriors and three or four good scouts to New York with a legion of expendable demons and *find them*. Then bring me the old woman. I want that girl to make a bargain for her soul. Time is not on our side—and I need leverage, something, *anything,* before she turns that bastard she's with into goddamned Superman." Nathaniel stood and looked out the window with his hands clasped behind his back. "Even though he's only been incarnate for a very brief time, how long do you think it will take him before he realizes that her Light is like rocket fuel in his system? How long before one of his trapped Sentinel brothers fills him in on just what joining with her will do to him?"

Nathaniel turned away from the window, his eyes black. "We've had twenty-six thousand years down here to contemplate how to use the Nephilim; our tiresome brothers in etheric form have no concept of how to strategically use a human being. It somehow violates their flimsy moral code and ideals to use a hybrid to gain power. I am so over it."

Malpas nodded. "But he's only been here twenty-four hours. They've been on the run . . . and he is still of the Light—he won't force her."

"No, he won't, and it doesn't work that way. She must give herself freely; he must want her with only love in his heart . . . or he might as well pick up a human bitch in a bar."

"That is why we still have time, Nathaniel," Malpas hedged. "That kind of profound caring doesn't happen overnight."

"You'd better pray to our Dark Lord that it doesn't," Nathaniel said through his teeth. "So, as an insurance policy, bring me that old woman!"

"As reported earlier, we tried to get to the old woman . . . but the hag seems improved. Her voice was strong and vibrant. She even mocked our attempt."

"Then find me a weakness! Every human has one! Bring me one of her errant children or her fucking grandchildren and do it now!"

Celeste had watched Azrael come into the room, put on his shirt, and eat in relative silence. His gaze met no one's. Queen Aziza seemed nonplussed and a little amused as she gave them directions on how to find Bath Kol's favorite club in the South Bronx.

"Journey well," Queen Aziza said, hugging Celeste for a long time at the door. "Come back to me, my sister of Light."

"I will. And thank you for everything," Celeste said, giving her one last squeeze.

Queen Aziza looked up at Azrael. "My prayers cover you, too." She released Celeste and went to Azrael, giving him a hug even though he seemed a little uncomfortable with the embrace. "You have important work to do and we deeply appreciate your sacrifice."

"Thank you," he said, then looked away. "Your hospitality and kindness are unparalleled. May you and your home always be blessed and protected."

Celeste could feel Queen Aziza standing in the doorway as they headed for the train, and it was a long while before they heard it close behind them. She waited until they were on the train platform before she attempted to speak to Azrael, monitoring the pulsing muscle in his jaw.

"You okay?"

"Yes."

"Aw, man . . . not the one-word answers." Celeste blew a stray curl up off her forehead.

"What do you want me to say?" He glanced at her, his eyes containing so many emotions that she could feel he had to look away again. "I thought my heart was going to explode inside my chest."

"Are you serious?" she whispered, and stood closer.

"Why would I exaggerate something so intimate?" he said, leaning down and speaking in a harsh whisper. "I didn't know what to expect . . . I wish you would have warned me—I . . ."

She swallowed a smile and cupped his cheek. "I would have, but our hostess might have become suspicious."

"It's not your fault, it's just . . . awkward."

"Maybe in front of Queen, if she was aware—but she wasn't," Celeste said, sifting through her mind for something that would assuage his damaged ego. It might not have been exactly true, but it was a healing balm to the man's tattered nerves, and therefore the right thing to do.

"She's a sensitive. She knew."

"No . . . I'm sure she didn't. Anyway, we were up in her office and she was telling me all about Bath Kol, so don't trip."

"Can we not talk about this at all?"

"No problem," Celeste said, sidling up to him. "Let's go dancing."

"Dancing? We have to find Bath Kol, Celeste."

"Like I said, she told me what he likes, where to find him, and a lot of stuff. The last thing we were talking or thinking about was you—just saying."

"Really?"

Celeste nodded. "Really. Tell you all about it on the trains."

Dark, desolate streets faced them as they walked beneath monstrous train trestles. Scantily clad women worked the corners, stopping pedestrians and car traffic alike, on a mission to make their quota. The sheer scale of the naked city when draped in her dangerous night attire was breathtaking. Bodies moved between structures like the walking dead. Mean dogs looked up from Dumpster feeds unafraid, as if they were in a developing nation that they'd laid claim to. Here even the rats took no prisoners, but the music was raw bait to draw even the most skittish human seeking fifteen minutes of fame.

A line wrapped around the corner. Angry gazes followed them as she tried to slow Azrael down, but he seemed not to understand the protocol as he walked right up to the bouncer, who matched his size. Azrael extended a fist. The huge bouncer smiled and pounded it.

"State your intention, muthafucka."

"Wanna sweat till I bleed."

The bouncer laughed and unclipped the velvet rope, then muttered something into a headset that she couldn't hear.

Both men nodded. Azrael placed an arm over her

shoulder and ushered her through the door. The moment they got in, a bouncer took their bags and gave Azrael a nod as if he were a VIP.

"How'd you do that?" Celeste asked. "You even sound like you're from 'round the way. What the—"

"We've been over the fact that I can pick up from my environment, yes? When I'm clear and focused, I can do it more quickly. Besides, do you really think that a Sentinel as old as Bath Kol, who has the governance of prophecy, would have anybody but seers running the place he frequents? Other warrior brothers are here as well . . . in fact, Bath Kol owns this establishment . . . can't you feel his energy running through the pipes and floorboards?"

Celeste opened and closed her mouth and hurried behind Azrael as he walked up to a crowd that had gathered around a competition happening on the dance floor, reached his hands out to either side, and seemed to be touching the music. Before she could say a word she actually saw whatever he was sensing ripple up his arms like a blue-white vibration carried on a beat, then he burst out laughing.

"Oh, wow . . . I get it. I now understand why he comes here," Azrael murmured, then pulled back his arms, looking around, seeming satisfied. "Pump up the volume . . . the music feeds his Light. It's *all* energy, Celeste . . . rhythmic, pulsing energy! Moving, dancing, just increases the wattage. If your vibration is low, this is *exactly* what you'd need!"

She was lost, a spectator to something happening beyond her comprehension. But seeing him flash that awesome megawatt smile of his was worth every second of it.

Just ahead of them, two young guys were dance-dueling in the center of a waxed wood floor. Bodies spinning, backflips requiring incomprehensible strength, made her just stand and stare. Gymnastic ability that would shame any Olympian made gravity seem like a nonissue for their athletic, fluid forms. They moved to the beat in unbelievable acrobatic combinations to a cheering crowd. Drinks sloshed and people screamed as one adolescent went up on one hand to drop roll into a spin, while the other turned his body into what looked like an electrified worm.

As one of the dancers conceded, Azrael stumbled out into the middle of the dance floor, having been shoved hard by a tall, blond guy who looked like a biker.

"Feel it, man!" the blond yelled. "C and C Music Factory! Old school! Give him a beat he can soak up! Spin it with some world music so he can show these young boys how the second-tier choirs do the damned thing. Jack Daniel's on da house!"

"You're insane!" Azrael shouted, laughing. "I don't know how to do this!"

"Yes, you do!" The blond said, coming to the edge of the ring of spectators. "It's the same as everything in martial arts—timing."

Someone behind them yelled out, "Capoeira."

Another voice shouted, "Fifty-two Blocks, man, Jailhouse!"

"Get mad," the blond yelled. "Remember who the fuck you are, dude! Bring up your wattage and just dance! We need you in top form, and this is like training day, but more fun."

Celeste's head pivoted as several menacing guys flipped into the opening and the crowd went wild. Then suddenly they'd surrounded Azrael and the blond sucker punched him.

Blood and spit went one way and Azrael's head snapped back in the opposite direction. Celeste screamed. Azrael's eyes lit blue-white, then the charge rippled down his arms and legs, isolating every muscle as though it were on its own pulley.

"Oh, my Gawd!" one of the defending dancers shouted, gaining fist pounds all around. "This big mofo is sick, son!"

"DJ, make him sweat till he bleeeeeeds!" another called out as the DJ blended in world music and heavy percussion and began scratching records.

Azrael wiped his mouth with the back of his fist, laughed, and immediately dropped down low, spinning on his back, drawing sparks on the floor as his would-be attackers stepped back into the crowd. The blond put his hands up in front of his chest laughing as the throng of humanity cheered.

"That's what I'm talking about!" the blond yelled, pointing at Azrael. "You've gotta work your human body and get used to it, man! Gotta push it to the limit so you know what it can do when you're in a firefight—this ain't the ether!"

Flipping up with a one-hand backward push-up, Azrael spun on that hand, legs whirring like helicopter blades, before his chest hit the floor in an exaggerated worm, and the next thing Celeste knew he was back on his feet, hands and feet a graceful blur of syncopated motion. Blue sweat lit up his dreadlocks, electricity seeming to run down every strand as he did a one-legged squat, fell back on his hands, mimicking what he'd seen the younger dancers do, then brought his legs over his head into a full split.

Reversing the split in a flash so that his legs were now on the floor, he pulled himself up to standing, never missing a beat, with his arms reaching up over his head as though gripping an invisible rope hand over hand.

The crowd released a collective scream of approval. Azrael stepped back and bowed to let the young dancers continue, then slapped them all five as they gave him props.

"Drinks on the house," the blond said, slinging an arm over Azrael's shoulder. "And don't tell me some shit about how you don't indulge. You're on earth, man—ain't this place awesome?"

"Bath Kol . . . I—"

"Give the man a beer. I see good things in your future," Bath Kol said, pushing a tall pilsner into Azrael's hand. "A cold one, after a performance like that, c'mon, son!"

Azrael laughed and looked back at Celeste, then raised the glass toward her and downed it, slamming it on the bar. She looked at the Sentinel named Bath Kol, annoyed that he'd gotten Az to take a drink, but held her peace for the moment.

To her, Bath Kol looked to be no more than thirty-five or forty and ruggedly handsome, with the kind of face that made a girl stare even when she didn't want to. His hair was biker-spiked and his complexion was deeply tanned as though he constantly rode his bike in all weather. His brilliant white smile was infectious, and his hazel eyes were positively magnetic. Bath Kol had the body of a Spartan, pure sinew packed in a six-foot-two frame. Even grungy with a dark blond five-o'clock shadow, the man was fine . . . hell, all of them were, honestly. Heaven sure knew what it was doing when it put these males in human bodies.

"Warriors!" Bath Kol bumped Azrael's chest with his own and released a roar.

Azrael clasped Bath Kol's arm in a warrior's shake. "It's been too long!"

Fists raised around the pulsing dance floor. Celeste watched as several eyes watched her. She moved closer to the bar.

"Yeah!" Bath Kol called out. "You walked into my joint with your Light battery low and energy all fucked up even though you'd found her? Are you nuts? I thought for sure you'd have gotten your Light fuse on by now, bro. It's time to kick some demon ass, man!"

"I . . . just found her, so, no, and it's not like—"

"Aw, man, lighten up," Bath Kol said, knocking back a shot. "No disrespect to the lady."

Azrael nodded but she could tell he was still uncomfortable. This was literally like taking a college preppie into a biker bar with the Sons of Anarchy.

Celeste stood next to Azrael and stared at Bath Kol as the barmaid refilled Azrael's beer. She'd felt Azrael visibly cringe at the rude reference to their "fusing," and that only seemed to make Bath Kol's smile widen. Instantly, she didn't trust the man. Clearly Azrael was so new to earth, compared to the Sentinel's long-term incarceration, they were going to mess with him somehow.

"She's beautiful, man. Clean energy . . . wow. Package is sweet, too," Bath Kol said, sending an appreciative gaze in Celeste's direction.

"Celeste, forgive him," Azrael said, accepting another beer. "This is Bath Kol—brother, this is Celeste."

"Nice to meet you," she said, taking the beer out of Azrael's hand and sipping it with her gaze steady on Bath Kol. "He's clean. More than one, if that, is no good."

Bath Kol rubbed the stubble on his chin and chuckled. "Oh, yeah, she's *the one*."

Celeste glanced around as she put the beer down on the bar and gave Bath Kol a hard glare.

"Don't worry, sis. I only have really well-indulged Sentinels in here with me . . . none of those guys who are still trying to get back into the Light after a couple of thousand years of abstinence, so you're safe."

She looked off toward the dance floor for a moment, monitoring Azrael's strained reaction, before she met Bath Kol's hazel green gaze again. "Yeah, okay. But if life is such a groove, then why were you over at Aziza's getting your shit realigned? Stop fucking with Az's head just 'cause he's new, all right, and me and you will be peace."

"Whoa," Bath Kol said, putting his hands up in front of his chest and laughing. "She's warrior class at that. I love it."

"Can we go somewhere to talk?" Azrael said with a smile.

"Definitely, brother," Bath Kol replied, clearly un- fazed by Celeste's verbal snipe. "We'll get your bags and I've got a place around the corner. Ground's been conse- crated, for what good that'll do . . . given the company

I keep there sometimes. But it's pretty secure. Nobody's jacked my bikes yet, so around here that means a lot. It's quiet. We can talk."

Bath Kol never lost his smile as his sinewy body cut through the crowd. If she wasn't so wary, she would definitely have called him handsome, devastatingly so. Celeste glanced over her shoulder taking note . . . damn . . . every one of them was handcrafted by the Divine. And immortal, too? Somebody slap her.

"Have you seen Gavreel?" Azrael asked as they rounded the corner.

"Does this look like a place where peace would reside?" Bath Kol laughed and hiked Celeste's bag up higher on his shoulder.

"Not really," Azrael replied. "Just wondered because he paid me a visit in Philly."

Bath Kol stopped walking, bringing their threesome to a halt. "What'd you do?"

"I opened up a cylinder of energy to send earthbounds back into the Light. They were trapped and—"

"Oh, man! Shit!" Bath Kol raked his fingers through his sweat-spiked hair. "That means the dark side knows where the Light sent you."

"But we're not there anymore," Celeste replied evenly.

"Yeah, well, you'd better hope that they didn't tail you." Bath Kol started walking again. "Gav came in through New York. That's how he found me or I found his dumb ass. He was wet behind the ears just like you, and trying to get a lead on some fucking Colombians that move weight. He eventually followed them down to Miami and out into the freakin' Amazon looking for his chosen. He knows she's a Latino, was originally thinking Central American, but then picked up the vibe of her surroundings and that wouldn't make sense if she was dropped in the barrio up here . . . records say she was taken young and they've got her working in the coca fields trying to break her spirit."

"That will most assuredly steal his peace," Azrael said in a sobered tone.

"Ya think?" Bath Kol looked over at Celeste. "So what's your story?"

Before she could answer, Bath Kol stopped walking and made a fist with his hand to silence them. He slowly lowered the bag he was carrying, and Azrael dropped his as well, easing Celeste between the two men as they turned their backs to her, boxing her in. Then the alleys emptied out.

Demons belched from the darkness. From every shadow, every alley, from behind every post, twisted, fanged creatures leaped out, snarling and hissing and poised to attack. Skinless faces and red, gleaming eyes peered at them as green saliva slid down huge incisors. Crablike creatures with backward-facing human heads scrambled out from beneath abandoned cars. Terror seized the scream in Celeste's throat as panic sweat covered her body.

Bath Kol yanked two nine-millimeters out of his waistband, throwing one to Azrael as he pushed him behind a car and took a running leap, firing as he landed on top an abandoned vehicle. Shooting with two hands, Azrael was up and over the top of the car. Celeste dropped down and hid behind the vehicle as silver shell casings pinged the ground all around her. Gruesome creatures with bat wings and gray-green skin charged them from the air, from the ground. There were too many of them! Then something yanked her underneath the car, dragging her halfway beneath the vehicle before she felt it let go the second Bath Kol's slug blew its head off.

Green gook splattered the ground beside her. She was up on her feet in a second, headed for cover as Azrael shouted to her, "Move!"

But one of the clawed creatures had a Dumpster and slung it toward her. The metal moved so fast, the velocity was impossible to avoid. She heard both angels scream, "No!" and she covered her head to save herself from brain injury. Then everything became eerily silent. A warm light bathed her, a familiar body shielded her. Wings wrapped around her, so bright that she couldn't even look at them. The Dumpster made contact and crumpled. The next thing she knew a void was beside her, a cold rush of night air. When she looked up, Azrael was hovering five feet off the ground, ripping sections of metal off parked vehicles with magnetized energy drawing it into his hands, then hurling them into demon bodies with an insane warrior's yell.

She couldn't move for a second, paralyzed by the sight of him. Azrael was a being of pure, raw power and poised for immortal combat.

A glistening, muscular, twelve-foot, white wingspan blotted out the darkness. The force of his presence sent debris flying. She had to shield her eyes and face with her forearm as the preternatural wind from his wings blew everything away from him. Fury was in his now blue-white eyes, his fists were lit with supernatural, crackling white light, and demons were scurrying to get out of his line of fire.

Suddenly he reached out and a truck bumper from a block away came whizzing toward him. He caught it in a two-handed grip and began using it as a baseball bat, splattering demons against buildings, the train trestle, and the asphalt. More Sentinels rounded the corner. Bath Kol lowered his weapon as Azrael sent a pulse of blue-white light out from the car bumper he held and pointed it toward the asphalt.

Burning-tar stench stung Celeste's nose and the quake from the explosion made her fall. The blast from the bumper Azrael pointed toward the ground was as though he'd hit the asphalt with an energy cannon that resembled an RPG round. It opened a huge fissure in the middle of the street, leaving twisted pipes, open sewer lines, billowing smoke, and crackling electricity.

Celeste covered her head, fearing a gas-main explosion to follow, but before she could get up and run to safety, Azrael released a thunderous command.

"Go to Hell!"

Everything that was dead, dying, or fleeing, got sucked into the abyss and then the street instantly closed behind them. Azrael flung the bumper a hundred yards to crash into the side of a building, then touched down, one knee on the hot asphalt, one hand on the ground, looking up with blue-white eyes, his shirt burned off, his jeans in charred shreds, wings spread and breathing hard.

"Damn, man . . . definitely just like old times," Bath Kol said, raking his hair.

◈

As Azrael dried his hair with a clean towel, Bath Kol put a stack of money on the table. He put a set of motorcycle keys next to it, then looked up at one of his men, who slid ID, credit cards, and a passport across the table toward Azrael. "Got an automatic and ammo, too, all silver, hallowed-earth-packed shells."

"Thank you," Azrael said in an angry but weary tone. "I'd rather that my death blades had come through with me into this density. I am more familiar with wielding my weapons of choice in the ether, than using these conventional human weapons, but it is what it is. Again, I thank you."

Bath Kol nodded. "It is that indeed. The city is hot now; you've gotta be on the move. Here's the keys to my place up in Lily Dale. It's a safe house on consecrated ground. We've got Sentinels in the area embedded with the local Native American tribes . . . psychics all around that want to protect angels and communicate with them. If anything's going down, you'll feel it telegraphed way before it gets to your door. It's all good." Bath Kol nodded at the man closest to him.

Celeste stared at the most serene young man she'd ever seen in her life. His skin was the color of polished amber, and his dark hair was swept back into a long ponytail wrapped with silver and turquoise Native American leatherwork. A pair of dark eyes studied her as though she were a curiosity. His high cheekbones looked as if someone had decided to carve a gorgeous mask of humanity, then placed a dimple in the center of his chin.

"Jamaerah handles all manifestations," Bath Kol said. "You can't function down here without resources. He can make things appear and disappear like we could up in the ether, so I guess you can say that's his specialty or gift or whatever. Maybe he can get your death blades, man? I don't know. We'll work on it." Bath Kol knocked back a shot of Jack Daniel's and poured another. "But, I ain't seen shit like you just pulled off in the street in twenty-six thousand years, man. Impressive. Gives me hope . . . ain't had that in a while, either."

Bath Kol gave Celeste a glance and poured a shot of Jack Daniel's into a clean shot glass, then set it in front of Azrael. "I'm not hatin'," he said to her, leaning forward with a serious gaze. "But the man's system is adrenaline-pumped and he needs to come down or it'll mess with his kidneys. The human body wasn't meant to stay amped to that supernatural level for long. If he keeps this shit up, he'll look fifty by next year and will have the internal organs of an old man. Then we'll have to get him a new frame after he burns through this one." Bath Kol slid the drink across the table to Azrael. "After a battle, this is medicine."

"I want her to rest," Azrael said, accepting a shot from Bath Kol when Celeste didn't protest, but he let it sit beside him as though considering whether to drink it. "And I want her to be safe."

"Like that's a problem with you around?" Bath Kol shook his head. "When you spun on the floor, I saw the sparks, but I didn't know your wings were coming back in. I just thought it was energy bouncing off the wood to keep your velocity going."

Azrael motioned toward Celeste with his chin. "She brought them back."

Unsure glances passed around the group of Sentinels

that had joined the battle from the club, then all eyes fell on Celeste.

"I don't understand," Bath Kol said in a quiet tone. "You haven't been here long enough for them to have come back that strong. Most of us took years to grow them back, earned by hard lessons . . . and none of my guys ever found one of the Remnant as a potential healing source to get them. I know I talk a lot of shit, but we've never had one willingly, you know . . ." He shrugged, but this time his expression held awe, not the jaded wiseass glance that he'd initially given her and Azrael. "You said you didn't fuse with her and we all believe you. You ain't no liar, Az. You're too new for that. So is her gift in her hands?"

Azrael reached out and covered one of Celeste's hands for a moment, his gaze focused solely on her.

"I don't know how she healed me," he admitted quietly. "But I feel so strongly in my spirit that, the way she did it is, she brought out the best in me. She made me become attached to someone more important than myself in every way. Made me care so deeply that it hurts. Made me want with everything in my soul to protect what the demons would rob from me and from this planet . . . and then she made me believe in what I could not see. She told me I was whole and I believed her." Azrael withdrew his hand from Celeste's and knocked back the shot. "She is that for me, my angel. And if I get trapped down here because of it—so be it."

Silence answered his statement as he set the shot glass down precisely. "And I think my system finally normalized to this density . . . must have been the adrenaline rush."

"But you came here cut up . . . right? Your back in

shreds—I saw it in a vision. Not like when we fought here the first time when everybody had wings." Bath Kol stood and took off his leather jacket, then stripped his dirty sleeveless T-shirt over his head. He closed his eyes, inhaled deeply, making the hard six-pack muscles of his stomach tremble from some unseen effort until gorgeous white wings unfurled from his shoulder blades.

"All trapped Sentinels have them," he said in a low murmur. "All Balance Keepers have them . . . even the fallen have them. But how do you have them, after the order went out that no new-era Remnant Gatherers would have this advantage?"

"I don't know," Azrael admitted quietly.

"I *never* saw it coming," Bath Kol murmured, beginning to pace behind the large dining room table that sat in the middle of the open warehouse space. "Never frickin' saw it coming."

"Well, just like you never saw the attack or Azrael's wings coming," Celeste said, nursing a bottle of water. "I really wish you'd tell me what all I'm supposed to be doing . . . I don't want to be blindsided, either." She glanced at Azrael, allowing her gaze to travel around the gathered warriors before it settled on Bath Kol. "Please. I need to know."

He nodded and yanked a chair out from the table, turned it around backward, and sat down on it hard.

"I heard before I came here that there were only seven of the Remnant left," Azrael said quietly.

"You know our etheric time and time in the density are different. Years go by . . . and there aren't seven left anymore." Bath Kol let out a hard sigh and stared at

Celeste. "This ain't gonna help you sleep at night, sis. Az said you should rest, and I think the man is right."

She looked at Azrael. "Not knowing what I'm supposed to do and getting snatched by demons won't help me sleep, either." She turned back to face Bath Kol and waited. "Didn't you tell Queen Aziza that prophecy was instruction and knowledge?"

"Yeah, I did."

Their gazes met, neither backing down, neither willing to give ground for a moment.

"I need both." Celeste leaned forward across the table and folded her hands in front of her, holding Bath Kol's gaze. "I can't take being in the dark anymore."

Bath Kol nodded as he rubbed his neck with a resigned sigh. "The Mayan calendar spoke of twenty-two cycles of fifty-two years . . . we gave them that to keep track of the thirteen heaven cycles that would end roughly about a hundred and fifty years before the next culture that would dominate the world crawled out of the Dark Ages into the so-called Age of Enlightenment around 1541. Then there were nine hell cycles after that, ending on August sixteenth, 1987. If you look at the hell that was globally created during that nine-cycle period, you'll understand our perspective.

"Anyway, these cycles all had to do with how much energy and resources the dark and the Light were prophesied to have on the planet at any one time. The date August seventeenth, 1987, was supposed to mark the next shift out of the hell cycles. All of the great prognosticators kept my ass busy, from Nostradamus on down. But that said, what we call Harmonic Convergence took place . . . and seven days later on August twenty-fourth a mini-alignment took place. It was the forerunner of what's going to go down with the heavenly bodies on 12/21/12."

"Okay, but that still doesn't explain my role," she said, looking around the group.

"When this happened, you were seven, just like you're thirty-three, a double trinity, now." Bath Kol paused. "I'll let Az fill you in on sacred numbers later, but take my word for it, that first number, seven, was significant. From the moment that grand trine appeared in the sky—an equilateral triangle like the great pyramids—it was our turn to clean house. Five years was all the time we had to make a run at the energy shift. The balance was supposed to shift to peace. Old structures were supposed to fall, and some did. It was the end of apartheid in South Africa then, and the breakup of the Soviet Union. People, especially sensitives, congregated at power centers along the earth's electromagnetically fertile areas, like Mount Shasta, Mount Fuji, the Himalayas, Kilimanjaro, Sedona—there are thousands of places where the veil between worlds is thin. But as you probably guessed, the dark side didn't give up without a fight."

Bath Kol stood and paced, slowly retracting his wings. "The year before the Harmonic Convergence, Chernobyl happened in the Ukraine. We lost Remnant Natalia . . . she was seven. Her mother died of an aggressive form of cancer caused from the nuclear fallout, and her father was immediately killed in the reactor blast. Orphaned, by the time our brother Paschar found her, she'd been sold into white slavery by the Russian mob, was strung out on heroin, and had literally sold her soul to Lucifer. She practices black magic to this day. Paschar, who is down here with me as a governor of visions, hasn't been quite right since."

Bath Kol stopped pacing and came to the table, placing his hands on the back of a chair while holding Celeste's gaze. "Remember Tiananmen Square? Yeah, well, our Asian-continent Remnant was eight when the Chinese government opened fire on the crowd. She wasn't supposed to be there. Shit happens. That soul's Light was disputed for years because they aren't supposed to outright kill one of you, if that's any comfort. Bastards tried to claim her Light on a technicality, but they fucked up because she was still at the age of innocence. She was just a kid and not a grown woman, so she wasn't aware that going there was suicide. If she'd been grown and had gone there and gotten shot, well, they could have said she martyred herself or something. Regardless, she got caught in the crossfire."

Bath Kol let out a hard breath and pushed away from the chair. "Then there was what happened in Rwanda and Sudan, shit so sick I don't want to talk about it in front of a lady. We also lost a girl during Shock and Awe in Iraq… stubborn father didn't believe an invasion was imminent and was trying to protect his downtown business. The girl and her mother were basically hostages to a demon-possessed tyrant. The bombs fell. She was the victim of war collateral damage. Scratch that beautiful young woman off the list."

Ticking off countries on his fingers, Bath Kol said, "So, that takes out our Remnant Light in Europe, Africa, the Middle East, and Asia." He grabbed the bottle he'd been nursing off the table and poured another shot. "So don't ask me why I drink or why my language is colorful. My vibration can't get any lower sometimes, because I see this shit before it happens, me and my boys rush in and try to avert catastrophe, and sometimes we make it and sometimes we don't. It doesn't matter how many you save, the ones you don't haunt you. Then I go to Queen in Brooklyn to have her pull that poison out of my aura. Works for a while, until I really start thinking about how truly fucked-up it is."

"We've got one rumored to be located in Denmark," Jamaerah said quietly, looking at Azrael and then Celeste. "Paschar went to find her, but was delayed when all flights to Europe were grounded when Eyjafjallajokull began spewing ash in southern Iceland."

"You see?" Bath Kol shouted. "Who thinks of erupting a fucking glacier in Iceland to delay flights going in and out of Europe!" He shook his head. "This is what we've been dealing with from those guys on the other side."

"But most of the time we must keep to evasive maneuvers to ensure that we don't accidentally hurt the human we are seeking or cause additional humans to be killed," Jamaerah said, staring at Celeste for a moment before returning his gaze to the group.

"Right, and like we know an old Aborigine shaman secreted a baby away years ago—but damn if he didn't hide the kid so well that even we're having trouble finding it," Bath Kol added, sloshing his drink. "Hell, for all I know at this point, the kid in Australia was relocated to Denmark. I don't know . . . they hardly tell me anything anymore. We've been all through the Polynesian freakin' islands, Bangladesh—now there's a hellhole on earth. Tibet . . . do you believe they actually slaughtered monks and desecrated temples up there? Then how many times did we do India and Pakistan, and Turkey and back, to try to see if the Dalai Lama's people found one and hid one? This shit is really getting on my nerves!"

The other angels traded glances. Jamaerah reached out and took the shot glass out of Bath Kol's hand, replacing it without a word with a steaming mug of black coffee.

"That was cold, man . . . you didn't have to cut me off like that in front of the lady." Bath Kol took a deep swig of coffee and winced. "So where does that leave us?" He lifted his mug and looked around the room. "A possible in Denmark, if we get to her in time. A possible in Colombia, if Gavreel can make it to her before it's too late, and you . . . a bird in hand being better than the other two in the bush, if you ask me—even though they burned down an entire neighborhood trying to snuff you out in '85."

"What?" Celeste tried to stand, but Azrael covered her hand.

"See, everybody forgets history and then wants to whine about why it keeps repeating itself. In 1985 you were a little kid, darlin', and you lived in West Philly. Didn't they drop a bomb on the same block your parents were living on at the time . . . like the 6200 block of Osage? Think about what would make anybody drop *a bomb* on a house with eleven people trapped inside, mostly women and children, to make them come out? Who does shit like that? It was a residential neighborhood—then they shot anyone fleeing the blaze, five little kids included. Does that sound like normal police activity, or does that sound like the forces of darkness? Just a question."

Celeste stood with a gasp, ignoring Azrael's light hold.

"Yeah. Thought so. Made national news, too—gotta hand it to 'em," Bath Kol said, sipping his coffee. "Couple hundred homes or something went up in the blaze. Your father was out of work due to drug use ... your mom barely holding her own. No insurance, blah, blah, blah. You and your mom had to move in with your aunt a few blocks away. Mom and Dad broke up because your aunt knew a demon when she saw one," Bath Kol added, pointing toward Celeste using the same hand that was holding the mug. "But you got out, kiddo. You were one of the lucky ones. A lot of our Remnants didn't make it. The dark side can't just abduct you guys when you're little because we'll definitely pick up the Light trail right to their hideouts— old school, putting their demon heads on pikes. No, their game is to always keep tabs on where you are and make your life miserable or try to cause accidents and circumstances that put your life and Light in peril. Their game is making your life a living hell, and from what little bit I can pick up, they played you real good, baby."

Bath Kol stumbled away from the table and bent over and rubbed his neck, precariously balancing his coffee. "Damn I'm tired—are you tired? Because I swear I'm tired. Man, I hate this job."

"Okay, General," a huge, thick-bodied Sentinel said, going to Bath Kol. "Enough prophecies for one night. Tomorrow you'll feel better."

"Lies," he said, sweeping his arm out and pouring

coffee everywhere. "You see how they treat me?" he argued as the massive Sentinel lifted him up and slung him over his shoulder.

"Say good night, BK."

"Good night," Bath Kol slurred, hanging upside down and allowing his coffee to drain out of the mug onto the floor before he dropped it.

Celeste stared after him as the huge Sentinel kicked a door open in the back of the warehouse and lugged Bath Kol into a room.

"We've got a hundred spare rooms. As you can see this place is enormous," Jamaerah said calmly. "Used to be a factory—put in showers back there, plus you'll find towels, clothes, fresh linens, and privacy. If you're gonna ride a chopper, I'll make sure you've got boots and leathers in your room before morning—saddlebags, too, so you can ride. I can manifest pretty much anything you want or need, just tell me before I turn in."

He looked at Azrael, then cast a gentle gaze on Celeste. "We're well fortified here. We take turns on watch. There's artillery in your footlocker by the closet. We've never had a breach here—there's too many of us. I suggest you get some rest."

"Thanks, man," Azrael said, standing. He clasped Jamaerah's forearm in a warrior embrace, then looked at Celeste.

"Five years of intense fighting happened after the 1987 shift," she murmured, looking up at him and then the remaining angels. "I was seven when the Harmonic Convergence happened . . . five years later during the great shift I was twelve."

"Twelve is a sacred number," Azrael said quietly.

"Really? August seventeenth, 1992, is when demons must have attacked my mother and she died." Celeste released a sad and bitter chuckle. "They said it was a stroke, but once again, Aunt Niecey was right when she'd said it was the work of the damned devil."

Chapter 15

*A*fter *all she'd just* seen and heard, being alone in a bathroom for an extended period of time, *at night,* was completely out of the question. Everyone had congregated in the kitchen, and once the meeting was deemed over because Bath Kol had passed out, she had to decide where to sleep.

Celeste looked around as Azrael packed money and the ID and the keys they'd been given in his gym bag. The angels that were roosting in the massive abandoned structure had sectioned off the top floors into living space, but the sheer size of everything, as well as the remoteness of the location, made her see a demon around every corner.

Huge twenty-five-foot windows allowed moonlight to spill over a four-foot-high, half-brick wall, and that blue-white wash painted the cement floor, which ran a full block long. Shiny Harley-Davidson choppers and Kawasaki crotch rockets with helmets hanging off the handlebars were parked in the far side of what appeared to be an open rec-room/living-room. The warehouse elevator that emptied into that space was a wide, open wooden structure with a rickety metal gate. Celeste glanced at it; anything could crawl up the cables and burst in. Sleeping in here was out.

Oversize, tan leather sectional sofas and chairs in various states of disrepair framed an in-home entertainment theater as well as a long, low Tibetan meditation table now serving as a coffee table. Several video-game controllers littered the floor, and half the room away were pool tables and foosball stands, a Ping-Pong table, along with well-worn air-hockey tables.

The kitchen was a huge industrial stove pushed up against a brick wall and set beside a double stainless-steel sink that was overrun with dishes. There was also an overloaded dishwasher, and two refrigerators—one that held nothing but beer and vodka and the other that contained a questionable food supply. In the middle of it all was a long picnic-style table surrounded by an eclectic arrangement of ladder-back chairs, barstools, and ottomans. There were no cabinets, just wire-rack-stand shelving like one would find in the back of a hardware store, and it was filled with boxes of sugary cereals, five-pound bags of rice, beans, staples, canned meats, peanut butter, and cookies.

She followed Azrael, who followed Jamaerah, and kept her gaze sweeping as they walked. The warehouse seemed so much bigger, so much more desolate, now that the brothers had withdrawn from the kitchen.

"Four brothers will be on the roof, four on the ground, and four patrolling the floors between the roof and the ground—a twelve-man detail, given that we have a VIP in the house," Jamaerah said to Azrael as they entered a long hallway that had huge offices lining either side of the corridor.

"We just knocked out the walls between offices to open them up and then turned them into suites. Everybody wanted their own bathroom," Jamaerah said with a sheepish grin. "This one is clean so the lady doesn't have to be offended. The guys aren't used to having to clean up after themselves and I can't vouch for the state of the other bathrooms."

"Do I have to be in here alone?" Celeste looked from Jamaerah to Azrael.

Azrael hesitated. "I can stand watch inside your room, if you so desire. Our kind does not sleep more than an hour or two, and that is only because of this density."

"Thank you," she said, glancing around at the high ceilings and endless rooms from which anything could jump out.

Jamaerah looked down to the floor. "There's towels and stuff in there like I said. Just look in the tall, green metal cabinet by the wall. I'll be on the roof."

Azrael gave his angel brother a nod and fully entered the room, cutting on the light. Celeste looked around warily, then shut the door behind her.

The room was an odd mixture of cleaned-up, old factory furniture and what looked like cabinets and other items that had been relocated from a military base. The more she thought about it, the entire setup seemed like a barracks and an airport hangar for a daredevil angel squadron.

Near the far wall was an old metal desk and a wooden chair that looked as if they came straight out of the 1950s. As promised, up against the wall was a tall, narrow military cabinet, with a military footlocker on the floor beside it. Also, a couple of bright orange and psychedelic bean-bag chairs were at the foot of a king-size futon. As though sensing her concerns, Azrael went into the bathroom and clicked on the light, then returned to give her an all-clear nod.

She didn't say a word, just slowly set her backpack down on the floor and went to see for herself if the coast was clear. He gave her navigating space, taking his gym bag and the gun to the desk on the other side of the room.

Open ductwork crisscrossed the ceiling, even in the bathroom the brothers had installed. She had no idea how they'd commandeered power and water, but she knew the drainpipes and the toilet stack ran down into the sewer. If a pipe fed into that, then it also meant something could just as easily slither up it. And the windows, in her opinion, represented a serious security problem.

The tub was a wide, long, claw-foot porcelain thing from the forties that had been retrofitted with a wide metal curtain ring, a white curtain, and a big sunflower showerhead. The fixtures were all different, as though cobbled together from eras gone by. A regular sink was on the wall next to an industrial toilet, but there was also a potbellied stove in the corner next to a floor-stand mirror and a porcelain washbowl that seemed as if it had been relocated from the 1800s. Bathroom tissue was stacked twelve rolls deep in individually wrapped rolls inside a copier-paper box.

Celeste quickly exited the space, only to find Azrael awkwardly making the bed. He held out crisp white linens away from his body and was yanking on a fitted sheet with two fingers. He'd found a duvet and had set it on a beanbag chair, but looked totally lost.

"I'm still dirty," he said, careful not to allow the sheets to touch him. "You may have to put these cloth sleeves on the pillows . . . I'm sorry, but I cannot figure out how to do it like I saw your aunt do so without soiling them."

For the first time since the battle in the street, she felt a slight smile playing at the corners of her mouth.

"I'll do it once I wash up." She looked at him, then rushed over to her bag, not sure how to broach the subject. "Listen. . . . I have a really big favor to ask you. Can you like bring a chair in there and keep your back against the bathroom door while I get in the shower . . . and can you bring the gun?" Holding some toiletries she needed, she looked up at him and accidentally dropped her lotion, then picked it up again when his brows knit. "I know it sounds stupid, but like what if something comes up through the drain or tries to drown me in the water . . . or—"

"Yes."

She stopped unpacking her toiletries with a gasp. "Yes?" she said, panicking.

"Why would you think that I would decline your request to stand guard inside the bathroom?"

"Oh," she said, releasing her breath and briefly closing her eyes. "I thought you were saying yes that you felt something was definitely about to attack me in there."

"No, no, no," he said quickly, going over to the table to get the weapon. "I meant yes I would be honored that you would trust me in your space again . . . after, well . . . after I shared a bathroom with you before and temporarily lost my mission focus."

"Oh," she said in a quiet voice. "That wasn't your fault . . . it was both of us."

"I won't let it happen again," he said, lifting his chin. "The last thing you should have to be worried about is your protector having ulterior motives."

"I'm not worried about you . . . and any additional motives you may have are not bad. You have a good heart, Az. I can feel that. Besides, I've seen enough to trust you with my life." She collected the rest of her items, pressing a toothbrush, toothpaste, soap, lotion, shampoo, and conditioner against her body within the crook of her arm as she extracted a white nightgown from her bag. She threw the gown over her shoulder and passed by him to get a towel and washcloth from the cabinet. "You're going to have to teach me how to shoot."

He swallowed a smile. She'd graciously changed the subject.

"I think that is a wise idea."

"Me, too," she replied, heading into the bathroom.

He followed her, holding the wooden chair from the desk in one hand and an automatic in the other, still cautious of his possible reaction to being in a room alone with her again. But the space was large, not as intimate and confined as the space at Queen Aziza's. He watched Celeste carefully place her items inside the porcelain bowl near the stand mirror, then drape the nightgown he'd acquired for her over part of the stand.

"Would you like me to turn the mirror to the wall?" he asked in a quiet voice, remembering her fears.

"No, it's okay . . . as long as you're in here with me I'm not afraid."

It was a great compliment she'd given him, one of many, and he allowed her soft response to flow through him as he closed the door and sat down on the chair against it.

He watched her remove her sneakers and then do something strange. She stepped into the tub and closed the shower curtain around her.

For a moment he wished that the lights had been off so that he could enjoy her moonlit silhouette through the curtain, then he sanctioned himself. He forced his gaze to study the pattern in the cement at his feet as she began dropping clothes outside the dry tub onto the floor.

"Is it hard?" she asked, breaking him out of his floor-staring trance.

"No, not anymore. But . . . that's a very personal question, Celeste."

She laughed and turned on the water. "Shooting an automatic. I'm asking if it's very hard to handle a weapon that size and if it has a lot of kick to it, because you're stronger than me."

"Oh." He studied the gun in his hands, feeling foolish. "I don't suppose . . . we'd have to actually go somewhere to try it where no one could get hurt."

Making his humiliation worse, the sound of the shower plus all the liquid he'd consumed was taking a toll on his bladder.

She peeked her head out of the shower for a second

and peered around the edge of the curtain. "I am so not trying to be funny, but I left everything halfway across the room. It's not like my old apartment, where the space was so tight that you could reach everything from the tub."

"No problem," he said quietly, and set the gun down on the floor. But the moment he stood, his eyes practically crossed. "What should I bring you?"

"Just the soap, shampoo, and conditioner," she replied, holding the curtain to shield her body.

Trying to keep his line of vision on the washstand and not glimpse her from the corner of his eye, he walked with his head up and shoulders back, summoning discipline. But for the first time in his existence, he was finding it lacking. It took everything within him not to linger near the small opening in the curtain as he handed her the items she'd requested. His imagination roared to life, awakening his body along with it. Now he had a twofold problem to contend with, and he turned away and stared at the gun on the floor.

"Celeste . . . may I leave you for just a few moments to go into another bathroom?"

"No!" she said, yanking the curtain around to poke her face out again. "Like, can't you just go in here . . . and I mean, if it's real serious—you know what I mean—I can jump out and stand right outside the door and—"

"The beer and Jack Daniel's shot with the sound of the water . . ." He squeezed his eyes closed. "I'm just getting used to the tolerances of a body, but—"

"Is that all? Well, if you've gotta pee, do it, I won't hear you over the water—just don't leave me. Every scary movie has this kind of bull in it."

"Thank you," he said in a rush, hurrying over to the toilet and getting his zipper down as fast as he could. After figuring out how to angle his erection so that he'd hit his target and not the wall, the sense of relief that coursed through him as he unburdened his bladder made him close his eyes and let out a sigh.

Remembering what he'd learned along the way, he zipped up, then studied the new type of commode for a moment, saw the handle, and flushed.

Immediately, Celeste screamed and jumped back from the water. He had the gun in his hand within seconds and yanked her out of the spray with his left arm, barrel pointed at the drain.

"You flushed," she said, sputtering and wiping soap out of her eyes.

"Yes, but did that send the demon up through the tub pipes?"

"Huh?"

He set her down, naked and dripping on the floor. "Why did you scream?"

"Because the water went hot when you flushed the toilet." Then she smiled, now wrapping herself in an edge of the shower curtain.

He walked away from her and placed the gun on the floor by the chair again and gave her his back. "Before you return to the shower, then, since the water systems are connected, may I wash my hands?"

"Yeah," she said with amusement in her tone. "No problem."

He quickly washed his hands using the pump bottle of soap on the sink, then seeing no towel except hers, he simply shook them dry. "I apologize for interrupting your shower."

"It's okay," she said, her voice still holding mirth. "At least I know you're right on top of anything that coulda busted in here."

"I assure you that if anything tries to harm you, Celeste, it will not want to encounter me."

She didn't respond and he was glad that she hadn't. The sight of her body soap-slicked and naked combined with the sound of her scream of peril adding to the adrenaline rush to kill whatever had attacked her was an extreme confluence impossible to process. He needed a few moments to recalibrate his mind and to throttle his passion. The desire to join with her was overwhelming now, yet he'd made a vow to himself not to view her that way. The best alternative that immediately came to mind was to keep his eyes on the floor and to will away the pulsing throb that consumed him.

Soon the scent of the shampoo and soap he'd brought her perfumed the air. The female of the species smelled so different and used wondrously fragrant potions that easily melted a man's resolve. The sound of water pelting her wet body finally made him break his promise to himself not to look at the curtain.

Even with the bathroom light on, he could see a faint outline of her nude body as she leaned back and allowed the shower spray to rinse through her hair. The sight of her slow, languid motions stole the last of his peace and became a dull ache in his groin.

When the water stopped, he almost stood, then thought better of it. But she peered out from the curtain again, sending an aromatic burst of fragrance in his direction.

"Can I bother you one more time to toss me my towel and my nightgown?"

"Sure." His voice sounded a little deeper than he'd expected. He made quick work of the task and watched her reach up inside the curtain to hang her gown on the outside of it so that it wouldn't get wet.

Everything within him told him to back away from the curtain, but for a few moments he was riveted to where he stood as she dried herself off. When she opened the curtain again, this time only a graceful hand came out holding the towel.

"Thanks so much."

"You're welcome." He accepted the towel and laid it against the porcelain washbowl, watching the nightgown slide up and over the top of the shower curtain.

This time he could not turn away and watched her faint silhouette as she sheathed herself in the lacy silk fabric. When the shower curtain opened, he stopped breathing. The sight of her wearing the gown replaced anything his imagination could have conceived. Human language failed him.

"You'll feel better after you have one of these," she said with a shy smile.

It took him a moment to process the words she'd spoken or to move out of her way.

"The floor is hard and dirty . . . your feet look so soft," he said, standing in front of the tub, blocking her exit from it. "I don't mind lifting you and setting you down on a clean surface in the next room."

She smiled. "If it's all right with you, can I just stay here like you did and sit in the chair?"

He nodded, then looked at the sweat and demon splatter that covered his chest and pants. "Wait," he said, grabbing her used towel and laying it on the floor, then creating a path to the chair with her clothes. He gathered up her lotion and toothpaste and brought it to the sink, then returned to her to offer her his hand to help her out of the tub.

"You are so . . . just, I don't have a word for what you are, Azrael." She placed her hand in his and walked along the path he'd created. "I'd say heaven-sent, just as a phrase before . . . but you really are. This is still so hard to comprehend."

Azrael nodded, understanding, yet she didn't realize how much she looked like an angel to him. The white gown had stolen reason from his mind and words from his lips. All she needed was a pair of wings, and yet it was only because of her that he once again had his.

He watched her go to the sink to brush her teeth and couldn't tear his gaze away as she bent and cupped her slender hand beneath a stream of cool water from the faucet. The gown whispered across her buttocks, allowing him to appreciate the form of her thighs, which tapered into her shapely calves.

"I promise I won't look," she said in a cheery tone, which made him finally gather his wits and turn away from her.

"I trust you, Celeste," he said quietly, kicking off his dirty shoes and stripping off his pants.

"I don't know," she said, laughing. "We humans can be very unreliable . . . and we are prone to mischief."

—⬦—

She glanced over her shoulder just as he stood. Turning away quickly, she bent to the sink and splashed cold water on her face. She'd seen his back . . . but mercy claim her, seeing the entire package was like a vision from the stone-carved Greek pantheon.

Waiting until she heard the curtain move and the shower go on, she stood up slowly and air-dried her face with her hands. His back was a work of art . . . but his ass was majesty in form and function. A deep gully at the base of his spine had given rise to tight, unblemished lobes of flesh. Thick thighs corded with sinew tapered down into developed calves. She shook her head as she grabbed the lotion and tiptoed her way to the chair to sit down.

The only way she knew of to break the tension was to come up with topics of conversation. Celeste opened the lotion and began applying it to her legs and feet, working feverishly to apply the cream to her semidamp skin but also to distract her wandering mind.

"Have you noticed that the guys seem to have collected things from different eras and just put it all together in here—it's kinda cool and funky, but what's really great is that they've lived through it, too, you know? It's not like they were just going to thrift stores to affect a look."

"Uh-huh."

She stared at the curtain for a moment, envisioning what he looked like with soap running down his sexy chest and abs.

"And it must be really hard to just keep your spirits up

when you see all this tragedy and drama every day. I really give them a lot of credit."

"As do I."

Celeste began applying cream to her elbows. "So, like, you guys are elite battalions of angels . . . and you fought together before?"

This time he turned and looked at her, standing so tall that he could see over the curtain. "Yes, it was a glorious battle time indeed. Those of us who came into the density during the first war retained our wings. We fought without rest, night and day, beating back the forces of darkness. Michael, our general, was at the fore, swinging a blade of pure Light and taking demon heads. Some of us were called back to fight another day . . . some of us got trapped when the gate closed. But we all remember that time and we wait for its return."

His gaze held hers captive for a few moments before he turned away again. "For many years I didn't understand the angels in the lower choirs, the ones who came through as peacekeeping forces . . . those who cleaned up the aftermath of raging battles that caused natural disasters in the cosmos. In my tier, we warred. Maybe that has been part of our lesson . . . to connect with an individual human and to care deeply about the outcome."

"I think you're too hard on yourself," she said softly. "I think you'd make a perfect guardian angel—and I sorta like the fact that you can really kick ass. Sometimes that's what's required, you know?"

He turned his head and glimpsed her from over his shoulder, lathering his body before turning back into the spray. "You truly think so, Celeste?"

"I do . . . and I heard you guys talking about blades of death. Wish you had those now, given what's after us. A Glock nine seems a little anticlimactic."

He turned to peer over the top of the curtain again and then closed his eyes, appearing lost in a memory that she wished she could see.

"Oh, Celeste . . . they were twin battle-axes with double-blade heads, one for each hand, fired by the sun . . . silver alloy, Heaven-steel blades, with custom gold handles inscribed with Divine writ. If a member of the fallen even touched them, the writ alone was enough to cause combustion. Much more effective than human conventional weapons, you are right. But I should not dwell on what is no more."

"They brought you joy, so why not remember them with joy?"

He opened his eyes and stared at her. "Celeste, you always seem to find a way to make room for Light, even when by all accounts you have had reason to look at things darkly."

"Oh, believe me, I've done my share of the cup-is-half-empty-routine . . . but it serves no purpose. Just makes you feel worse. So, if a small, little thing makes me happy and it doesn't hurt anyone else, then I try to enjoy it—even if it's just thinking about it."

"Wise again," he said.

"No, just observant." She smiled when he smiled. "How happy were you when you found out you had wings again?"

"Oh!" he exclaimed, turning around in the water. "I was—I was . . . just . . ."

"On cloud nine?"

"Yes! Exactly!"

She laughed, but not at him, just sharing his contagious joy and enthusiasm. "Then why don't you open them out and wash them and use them and enjoy them when regular people aren't looking?" She stood and lobbied her point, gesturing with her hands. "Az, you were magnificent out there! I have *never* in all my life seen anything like that—or even imagined anything so spectacular. And you have them hidden in your shoulders? Why? If I had all this space, which is why the brothers probably decided to move in here, man, I'd be playing table tennis from the air . . . I'd be dribbling a basketball and doing slam-dunk shots like highlights from the NBA!"

He laughed hard and soon she could see iridescent light painting the curtain from the inside. "They're not supposed to be used for games."

"Who said? Is there a rule? Because I'm definitely not challenging the Big Source on anything anymore. But just curious."

She watched him pause and then peer at her over the top of the curtain again.

"I don't think there is a rule."

"Then open 'em up since you just got 'em back and wash the gook off of them."

That made him laugh hard and he shook his head. "Demon splatter doesn't stick to our wings."

"Really . . . wow. Okay . . . well, just do it because you wanna get 'em wet—whatever. Does everything always have to be logical? Can't it just be because you felt like it?"

Again he laughed. "Would you please throw me a towel, Celeste—the water is getting cold."

"Sure." She dashed into the other room and returned in a few moments with a clean one. "But you're changing the subject and you know it."

"You weren't afraid," he said, turning off the water as she met him at the curtain. The mirth had gone out of his tone and his gaze was tender.

She paused and handed him the towel slowly. "No . . . I wasn't."

"Why?" He continued to stare at her through the slit in the curtain.

"Because you made me laugh and gave me joy and I forgot for a few seconds about all the terrible things after me or in the world."

Her statement seemed to slow his motions and he wrapped the towel around his waist, then pulled back the curtain to stare at her fully now. "Joy is powerful, too. It is a subset of love."

She nodded and moved back so he could step on her wet towel on the floor.

"And in my joy I allowed your feet to get dirty," he said in a quiet rush.

"It's all right," she said just above a whisper.

"No, it's not . . . and there is a very old tradition that I would like to observe."

She didn't move and didn't speak, just kept her gaze connected to his until he closed his eyes and took a deep breath and unfurled his magnificent wings before her.

They were so different now that he was not in battle, and his eyes were so gentle, that she wanted to touch his face. Soft, pristine white plumage framed his dark mahogany skin, and the towel slung down low on his hips made a disorienting combination. He didn't say a word as he came to her and lifted her up and slowly walked her into the bedroom, setting her down on the edge of the half-made bed.

She watched him as he withdrew and went back into the bathroom to collect the porcelain washbowl, then filled it with warm water and soap, returning to kneel before her and place her feet one by one into the warm suds. Taking up a foot, he gently massaged it, using his wide palm to cup water in his hand and trickle it over the foot he held.

"We were told to kneel at the feet of our human beings . . . to love them and care for them and cherish them for their complexity and the joy within them . . . and for the love they bring to the planet." His gaze captured hers as he took up her other foot. "Celeste, I am at your service . . . for all of eternity. I wash your feet. You have brought love to the planet and into my heart, along with indescribable joy. I am yours."

Unable to stop herself she reached out and traced his lush mouth with a forefinger. He was so painfully beautiful inside and out that it brought tears to her eyes.

"Have I upset you?" he murmured, cupping her cheek with a damp palm.

She shook her head. "I'm just so overwhelmed by what I feel for you and it's only been so short a time."

"Human time is something that I do not yet fully understand. All that I am sure of is that you bring joy and love and hope and fear and passion together inside me, all at once in an amazing rush, and I do not know what to do with the intensity of it all."

She took his mouth slowly in a soft kiss, testing for acceptance, feeling him tremble as her hands found the sides of his handsome face. "I'll show you," she murmured, lifting her feet from the water and lying back on the bed.

He followed her, gently blanketing her with his warmth and the soft, soft down of his wings. He leaned into a deeper kiss that she offered, seeming to remember the first one they'd shared only hours ago as he eagerly sought her tongue. Damp feet against the damp backs of his muscular legs, she traced the cords of sinew, opening herself, arching, showing him the rhythm of pleasure with only the towel as a barrier.

A gasp escaped his mouth into hers as she loosened his towel to slowly bring her hands over the swell of his buttocks, then followed the deep valley of his spine up and under his trembling feathers to that sensitive place between his outstretched wings. Raining kisses down his neck, she slowly dragged her fingers back and forth along the delicate ridge until he dropped his head back and moaned.

"I shouldn't," he said in a hoarse whisper.

She pulled back. "You're right . . . you're right. I'm so sorry, it just felt—"

"Natural."

She nodded and stared up at him for a moment. "Queen Aziza said I wasn't human . . . I'm a hybrid. Technically."

He just stared at her.

"I don't know who to ask or if a lightning bolt will

come down from the sky if I ask . . . but do I count as a regular human that can trap you here?" She traced his jaw with trembling fingers, then tried to push him back to sit up. "You know what, I'm really out of line here and you're the one with everything to lose. I'm gonna—"

He kissed her hard, then rolled off her to stand, rubbing the nape of his neck for a moment and clutching his towel, then securing it. "I don't know."

She watched him as he hung his head and closed his eyes, then turned away from her.

"Az, I'm really sorry," she whispered, and stood to go get a pair of jeans to put on. "I don't want to be your addiction, the reason for your downfall. You're clean, and good of spirit, and I've tasted way too much of this world. I'm all screwed up, Az. Look at me. You don't want to risk being trapped for someone like me! I have major issues. My life is raggedy, my—"

He held up a hand to stop her self-debasing flow of words and then looked up slowly, opening his eyes. "You're not my addiction, Celeste," he said in a low, sensual rumble. "Down here you've been my salvation."

That she'd so thoroughly corrupted him in so short a time made her want to cry. She hurried by him headed toward her backpack to get her clothes. But as she passed, he caught her by the wrist and slowly brought her into an embrace.

"You are not human," he murmured against her neck.

"You're sure? And that means . . ."

He nodded. "Hayyel does not lie . . . my brother in the ether answered me."

His nipples had become tight raisins of need, and she

brushed them with her fingers and then bent to suckle them, putting tears in his eyes as he moved against her harder when she finally sought his mouth again for a kiss. Her goal was singular, to make his first time what hers should have been . . . a long, sensual anointing of his body, rather than an irreverently quick desecration.

Sending all the love that she could summon from within, each kiss down his chest was a prayer for his pleasure, every touch an exquisite verse to show him how much she cared as she led him back to the bed to lie with her.

When she slowly slid his towel from between their bodies, he began to breathe so quickly he was almost hyperventilating. But with patience and never losing eye contact with him, she gently rolled him over, careful of his wings, aware of his excruciating arousal, but unable to allow him not to fully experience every bit of joy such an intimate encounter deserved.

Attending his shuddering stomach in a series of slow kisses, she made him cry out and grip her by her arms. Their eyes met as she looked up. She waited until his grip relaxed and she nodded. He fell back, eyes shut, chin tipped up to the ceiling as she drew him into her mouth and he called her name.

Unable to stand it as she felt his climax approaching, she climbed up his body and took his mouth, straddling him in a slow, determined sheathing. He broke their kiss, iridescent tears now streaming down his face as he stared up at her. When their pelvises met, he released a deep moan that bottomed out on a hard gasp. Suddenly multicolored light spilled down his locks, over his wings, and down his arms, covering her and the bed, making her cry out and move feverishly against him.

Pleasure like she'd never known filled her. When he touched her breasts, gently gliding his hands over her aching nipples, her voice rent the room. His hands then found her ass, pulling her against him hard enough that he did a sit-up on every thrust. Ambrosia flavored her mouth; pleasure turned every breath into a high-pitched gasp. He held her now, sitting up, her legs wrapped around his hips, his wings wrapped around them both, their heads dropped back, auras joined . . . and then she felt him trip over the edge of the universe with a hard series of contractions that put blue sweat on his brow.

Everything he felt, she felt. His pleasure became an echo of giving and receiving. Her cries would set him off again; hers were so powerful that he just broke down and wept. For a long time they sat joined, holding each other, tears streaming, gently rocking their way back to calm.

"I want to give you the same joy you just gave me," he said, still breathing hard as he nuzzled the side of her neck. He took her mouth again in a deep kiss. "I must share this gift of joy back to you, Celeste."

"You already have, trust me," she said, winded.

He stroked her hair and traced her eyebrows with the pad of his thumb. "No, I want to kiss you like you kissed me . . . in the place that begins with pain from so much need, but then spills like ripe fruit."

She closed her eyes and rested her forehead against his, feeling desire build just from his mere suggestion. "I don't know if my heart can take it," she whispered through deep breaths.

"Your Light has fused with mine," he murmured, caressing her face. "Everything I feel, you will feel; everything you feel, I will feel. I want to experience this with you again until fatigue claims us."

She brought her hands between their bodies and looked at the colored lights dancing at her fingertips, then slowly flattened her palms against his chest. The moment she brushed his nipples, intense pleasure tightened hers. He nodded and held her gaze as her arms slowly wrapped around him to find that place between his wings. The moment she stroked it, they both arched with a shuddering moan.

"Oh . . . my . . . God," she whispered.

Azrael nodded and closed his eyes. "Definitely."

Chapter 16

*D*awn *kissed the windows* and entered the bedroom with rose-orange glory. A profound peace filled Celeste as she lay beneath an angel's wings and watched the horizon change before her eyes. Now she understood why the brothers had chosen this high building with windows all around. She couldn't imagine the many dawns they'd seen during the millennia they'd been marooned here, or what golden memories still called out to them from beyond the sun.

"Please, God," she whispered, staring at the parting clouds and focusing on a wide shaft of light, "I know I'm in no position to ask anything, but if you do hear me, please don't blame him because I was weak . . . don't blame any of them. Let them all go home. Down here is no place for an angel. We'll make it. Humans always do. Even if you have to leave me, take them . . . because I wouldn't wish their banishment on my worst enemy."

She closed her eyes as a strong arm pulled her closer and a gentle kiss brushed her shoulder. Then a warm cheek and a solid jaw fit into the space between her shoulder and cheek. Azrael released a long, shuddering sigh and his voice shook with emotion.

"You prayed for me at dawn?"

She covered his hand and nodded, swallowing hard as tears spilled down the bridge of her nose.

"And you would sacrifice yourself for me and all my brothers," he whispered. Between deep breaths his voice was thick and gravelly. "I . . ." He stopped speaking as though he couldn't go on, and soon she could feel his tears wet her neck. "What have I done?"

"I'm sorry," she murmured, and squeezed her eyes shut.

"No . . . it is I who begs your forgiveness, Celeste." He turned her over to look at her, anguish staining his expression. "I am not speaking of fear of the consequences I might face—I am speaking of your willingness to sacrifice yourself for me. That cannot happen. You are the one we are to sacrifice ourselves for. And somehow I have managed to influence your—"

"Shusssh," she murmured, placing a finger gently to his lips. "Love always protects, always trusts, always hopes, always perseveres." She kissed him softly and cradled his face with her hand. "I love you, Azrael . . . so allow me to hope. I may not do many things well, but we humans are the best in the universe at hope."

He stared down at her, eyes serious and filled with too many emotions to name. "Then come share the water with me, ray of hope."

She traced his eyebrows in a way that made him close his eyes. "Only if you promise to open your wings under the spray."

She was just pulling on a pair of black leather boots when the blare of an electric guitar sent shock waves down her spine. Azrael looked up from repacking their belongings into the bike saddlebags Jamaerah had left them and stared at the door. The signature sound of Carlos Santana bounced off the brick and metal, reverbing off the concrete floor.

"I think that's our wake-up call," she said, standing and heading toward the door with a frown.

"I believe so," Azrael muttered, frowning.

They walked down the hall in tandem as the music got louder, then they stopped twenty-five yards from the kitchen. Jamaerah was barefoot, wearing only a pair of ragged stonewashed jeans, playing an invisible guitar to "Put Your Lights On," rocking out while coffee brewed, singing his heart out in perfect pitch, wings spread, eyes closed, and an expression of sheer ecstasy gracing his beautiful face.

She placed a hand on Azrael's arm when he started to advance. The sight of the young angel absorbed in his passion was one that required reverence, and soon she could feel Azrael relax beside her as he began to comprehend what he was witnessing.

Listening to the words of the ballad, she understood why the angels whispered into the ears of artists so that they could touch the world with their Light. A voice so filled with emotion belted out stanzas in a plea that made her cover her mouth in awe. Jamaerah looked like a vision from the Sistine Chapel with his silken spill of dark brown hair covering his bronze shoulders, his fingers deftly moving up and down an instrument she couldn't see as tight cords stood up in his neck while he sang his heart out.

"Hey, la la, we all shine like stars . . . then we fade away."

At the conclusion of a long guitar exit, Jamaerah allowed the invisible guitar to fall from his hands with a flourish, then clapped. The warehouse was instantly silent. He wiped his face and hung his head with his eyes closed, then opened his arms and slowly turned his face up to the ceiling.

"It's okay," a gruff voice said behind Celeste and Azrael, making them turn.

"You can go get some java. Not like you're interrupting a church service or anything," Bath Kol muttered in a surly tone, clearly hungover and annoyed as he brushed past them heading toward the kitchen. "The kid only gets morose like this every once in a while. Shoulda went and gotten himself laid last night, but I guess he was doing shifts on account of the demons."

Jamaerah looked up. "Sorry, BK," he said quietly. "Didn't realize I had the volume up so loud."

"You never realize you have the volume up so loud—and most times I don't care," Bath Kol muttered, pouring a mug of black coffee into a used cup. He took a deep slurp and winced. "But, damn, this morning I mind."

Jamaerah turned to the sink, giving Celeste and

Azrael his back, and quickly folded away his wings. "Coffee? Breakfast?"

"They probably want that green-tea shit that Queen keeps forcing on me," Bath Kol said, sitting down hard at the table. "Says it's got antioxidants in it, like I give a rat's ass."

"We have tins and tins of it," Jamaerah said in a gentle tone, still not looking at Celeste and Azrael. "Please sit down and I'll fix it. I'm sorry I woke you."

"It's all right," she said quietly, her heart breaking for the young angel who was, oddly, lifetimes older than she. "I can fix the tea, you've been up all night . . . and your voice is beautiful."

"Yes, so, please, no apologies, brother. We were awake anyway," Azrael added.

"Yeah, *we know,*" Bath Kol said after another slurp. "That's probably what set the poor kid off in the first place."

Celeste studied the grain in the wood of the table. Azrael sent his gaze out of the window. Jamaerah grabbed his shirt off a stool and began rummaging around on the shelves for the elusive green tea.

"I'll put water on for it, and I believe we have honey."

"Thank you," Azrael said, walking across the room to take a survey of the motorcycles.

Maaaan . . . this was so not how she wanted the morning to go. Summoning the courage to look up at Bath Kol, she met his bloodshot gaze and changed the subject.

"Do you think I might be able to call my aunt from here, like I did last night?"

As soon as the words had passed her lips, Azrael and

Jamaerah spun to stare at her. Bath Kol lowered his coffee mug slowly and set it on the table with precision.

"What did you say?"

She looked at Bath Kol in confusion. "I said, can I use the phone, but if that's like a felony or something, then—"

"Celeste," Azrael said, coming to the table to sit on a low chair in front of her. "When did you call your aunt?"

"Twenty bucks says it was before we got ambushed," Bath Kol said, standing and going to the sink. He tossed out his coffee and found the bottle of Jack Daniel's, then returned to the table.

"I called her from Queen Aziza's office before we took the trains to the Bronx," Celeste said, looking around nervously.

Azrael closed his eyes, Bath Kol rubbed his palms down his face, and Jamaerah just shook his head while rubbing the nape of his neck.

The sound of the elevator engaging and boots on the roof put Bath Kol on his feet. He grabbed a pump shotgun from beneath the kitchen table. Jamaerah yanked out a snub-nosed from beneath the kitchen sink. Azrael had found the nine-millimeter faster than Celeste could draw a breath. But a voice called out from the rising elevator and put everyone at ease.

"Friend, mon! Don't smoke a brother!" Isda came off the elevator with several of his men and Bath Kol's patrols.

The moment the elevator gates swung back, he walked right up to Azrael and pointed at his chest.

"Dis mutherfucker is sloppy as shit! He almost got me boys snuffed for rebirth and got me 'oman kilt—Queen's place laid to siege! Whot—all because he can't handle his bizness, now we all got to suffer?"

"Whoa, whoa, whoa," Bath Kol said, coming between Azrael and Isda.

Several angels separated the would-be combatants as they jostled close to an all-out brawl.

"I made the call. He didn't make the call," Celeste said, looking around the group.

"You are *his* responsibility down here!" Isda shouted as two burly brothers held him back. "*He* should know the fucking wires are the province of the darkness! You don't have to know! He's supposed to know!"

"Speak foul in a sentence directed toward her again, and I will forget you are my brother!" Azrael yelled, lunging at Isda. Four angels pushed him back, grappling with him to keep him from going after the Sentinel.

"You drugged him and then have the nerve to come up here blaming him for being off his game?" Celeste shrieked, scurrying around the brothers. "Let that sorry bastard go!" The second they did, she slapped Isda's face. "You drugged him; fuck you! The only thing I care about is what happened to Queen Aziza."

Bath Kol walked a dangerous path toward Isda, making the others back up. "You drugged a newborn brother? Gave him some shit without his permission or knowledge and then allowed him to take a Remnant out in the street, unarmed?"

Suddenly Bath Kol's wings were out and he'd lunged with so much velocity that Isda slammed to the floor. His hands around Isda's throat, Bath Kol yelled down in his face, spittle flying as another brother left Azrael and tried to pry Bath Kol's fingers from Isda's throat.

"I'll kill you myself! I swear I will! If Queen died

because of this, I'll put your head on a pike and sell it to the demons!"

It took several minutes for the other brothers to prevail, and they finally got Bath Kol up and pressed against the refrigerator. Isda's men helped him sit up, and he gasped, rubbing his throat.

"She's not dead, you crazy son of a bitch," Isda wheezed. "We got there in time, no thanks to your boy."

"What happened?" Azrael bellowed, making Isda's posse back up.

"The wires are tapped for anybody she's connected to—you know that," one of Isda's men said. "When she called home, they traced it to New York. They hit us first."

Isda nodded, still winded. "Couldn't come for us, so they sent a demon into my dog . . . my 'oman opened the door to let Sheba in. It was a jumper. Blew my dog away with a sawed-off, then the fucking thing split and infected her and the other women." Isda hung his head and drew a shuddering breath. "Couldn't get it out of them. House got swarmed. Fallen Sentinels showed up. . . . I had a machete and had to send my 'oman and her two sisters into the Light. Beheading was the only way."

Angel brothers released Bath Kol from where they'd had him pinned. Although he was still red in the face, compassion filled his eyes.

Celeste hugged herself. The horror of it all was surreal. Innocent people got killed because she'd made a phone call? Oh, shit . . . Oh, God . . .

"I'm sorry, man," Bath Kol said.

Azrael shook his head as Celeste sat down hard on an open chair. "My condolences and my apologies."

"Her sister screamed out where you were going when one of the fallen asked the demon to wrench it out of her gut," Isda said in a far-off tone. "Had I treated you like a brother, maybe none of this would have 'appened . . . had envy in my heart when I saw you'd found your chosen. Our prayer lines were weak, our commitment was sloppy—that's how the demon got in. Won't ever forget seeing her eyes change back to who she was the moment her head was on the floor at my feet. Jus' one more thing to add to my sentence, hey."

"Pour the man a drink," Bath Kol said. "We've all been down here a long time and sometimes we fuck up."

"What happened to Queen Aziza?" Celeste said quietly, going to Isda.

One of his men handed him a drink and Celeste waited as he knocked it back.

"We got there and the place was surrounded, but a strong blue-light prayer line held them back." Isda looked up at Azrael. "It had your signature in it, man."

"You blessed her on the way out," Celeste said, turning to Azrael.

He nodded. "But her fortification was already strong. I just added to it."

Bath Kol stumbled away from the refrigerator and sat down hard on a stool. He let his head hang back and closed his eyes. "This profession is so bad for my nerves."

"But if they attacked your house and tried to go after Queen Aziza's, I have to go back to Philly! My aunt Niecey is—"

"Well protected," Azrael said gently, going to Celeste's side. "I said a prayer to protect her home and her being. I sent the angels of the old books to her. The Mu'aqqibat as well as the Malakhim."

"Damn, mon . . . you weren't taking no chances I see."

Azrael looked at Isda. "No, I wasn't."

"Two things," Bath Kol said. "One . . . you and your men have to hunker down here now. Three women beheaded and a dog splattered in the kitchen up in Flatbush means cops and problems—lots of problems. They'll swear it's some Jamaican drug bullshit, especially when they find your stash in the basement." Bath Kol reached out and Jamaerah put a filled shot glass in his hand. "Second thing, I think Celeste is right. We do need to send a squad to Philly. Her aunt might be protected because of Azrael's prayer, but what about grandchildren, kids, cousins, there are any number of ways to break that old woman's heart and make her come out of where she's protected . . . and if they go after her, they know they can make Celeste come to them for a trade."

Celeste walked over to the table and placed her hands on it, then dropped her head and closed her eyes. "I cannot have the deaths of three women on my conscience . . . let alone Aunt Niecey or any of her grandchildren. Babies, they're just babies."

"Oh, shit!" Bath Kol jumped up from the table as blue-white light spilled over it.

Celeste backed up with a sharp gasp and stared at the table in horror as the interior of a demon-infested warehouse came into view. The table itself became like a giant flat-screen TV monitor flashing images. Hundreds of demons scuttled along the walls and the ceiling, screeching and fighting over human scraps of homeless victims. Gore and body parts littered the warehouse floor, and the pale, gargoyle-like creatures ate and hissed and bickered.

But the more Celeste backed up, the more the focus of the image zoomed out and expanded to show them the outside of the building and surrounding streets, until she began screaming.

"Get it off of me! Get it off of me! What's happening?" she shrieked. "This is seriously freaking me out!" Celeste squeezed her eyes shut tightly. "It's almost like I can feel them crawling on me!"

"No, stand your ground, it's just a vision," Bath Kol said, nearing the table. "I haven't been able to do this in years. I've been too stoned and too damned cynical to allow the visions to return with clarity like this." He moved his hands and the image shifted as though he were paging through an iPad. "It's not coming from you, it's coming from me."

Celeste relaxed as all eyes went to Bath Kol and then the table. But it took several minutes for her heartbeat to return to normal.

"Archdemon Asmodeus, aka Nathaniel," Bath Kol murmured, bringing his hands close to the table. "Forcas the invisible . . . Malpas—the crow . . . Lahash, who thwarts Divine will, and that bastard Appollyon—the destroyer . . . I remember him from the days of Rome. Pharzuph—ruler of lust . . . he was the one who made us lose our Light in the Middle East."

The group gathered around looking at the images, burning them into their memory. Celeste would never forget the Nordic-looking Forcas, the fallen angel that had attacked them in the library. He'd reminded her of a stunningly beautiful Viking warrior, but the evil he contained was chilling.

Each of the fallen was curiously handsome, their raven-hued wings eerily magnetic. The one who called himself Nathaniel was swarthy and handsome with dark, intense eyes and a spill of brunet hair over a pair of broad shoulders. His voice contained a Slavic accent as he paced, asking for a report of what had happened. She'd never forget it, just as she couldn't forget the dark beauty of Malpas—his regal African features made him seem as though he were a carved ebony mask. The one pointed out as Lahash had the sublime beauty of an East Indian yogi, while Appollyon was built like a Roman god, with jet-black, wavy hair and penetrating sea-green eyes. Pharzuph reminded her of a wealthy, handsome desert sheikh. She wondered what the Ultimate Darkness looked like if these were the bad guys.

Bath Kol slapped the table and pointed at her—erasing the vision. "Don't ever wonder that! He is worse that you can comprehend and the most beautiful of all the realms. This is the human flaw, curiosity." Bath Kol paced, breathing hard. "It will kill that cat, and satisfaction from that son of a bitch will not bring you back, sis—so don't even go there."

Celeste placed her hands on top of her head. "I wanted to know in case I ran up on him—or he tried to trick me, because without your wings out . . . it's hard to tell what side is which."

"She makes a point," Isda said, strangely coming to Celeste's defense. "How will the humans know?"

"They have to be blind to the exterior and feel the light," Azrael said, looking at her.

She nodded and went to stand beside him, feeling exposed in the presence of the others. "I'm sorry . . . I don't know what I'm supposed to do."

Bath Kol waved his hand. *"De nada."*

The words triggered something within Celeste and she grabbed Azrael's arm. "Bring your brother Gavreel back." She looked up at Azrael and then over to Bath Kol. "There is one of you who speaks fluent Spanish. He . . . he . . . is somewhere lost. What he seeks is not there. She's going to the airport, and her body is packed full of cocaine stuffed in condoms. She'll be coming in on a flight that will land in Miami, and he's got to get there when they pull her into custody!"

Bath Kol blinked, but recovered quickly. "Okay, okay, three brothers get a message up to the archangels stat—I want a line-drive prayer going to every available messenger angel to redirect Gavreel," he said as Azrael enfolded Celeste in his arms.

Azrael looked up at the others. "She's the primary locator," he said in wonder. He stripped off his jacket and shirt and enfolded her in his arms and wings.

"Whoa, mon!" Isda shouted. "When did dat 'appen?"

"Last night, long story," Bath Kol said, nearing Celeste and then looking at his hands. "My brother had no wings, and now after you touched him, he does. My vision was going dark from despair and was spotty at best—nobody here would say it to my face, but if I'm honest, Jack Daniel's was killing my ability . . . that's why I was going to get help from Queen. Then you touched the table, sent your Light into the wood I was just sitting near and touching, and now my gift has returned full force. You're the only variable in the equation, sis. You're changing us."

"Her twelve strands of Light have been repaired," Azrael said in a quiet rumble, stroking Celeste's hair.

Unsure glances passed around the group.

"The woman in Denmark is no longer there," Celeste murmured against Azrael's chest with her eyes squeezed shut. "Give Paschar renewed vision. Her hair is blond but her skin is dark . . . she is both Aborigine and Dutch. She is now in Quebec, and he, like Gavreel, must bring her to Philadelphia."

"Why Philadelphia?" Isda said, coming closer to Celeste.

Angels made a ring around her and Azrael, watching her intently as her lashes fluttered with blue-white light.

"It is the birthplace of the currently strongest nation on the planet," Bath Kol said, his eyes glowing neon blue. "There are many Philadelphias on the map and mentioned in the old books . . . but in this era, this one is in the new empire. Revelation speaks of the only church, translated 'community,' that has not lost favor. It is where the gate will open . . . in the historic district." He snapped out of the vision and looked around. "The founding fathers were all Masons . . . they'd gathered information from the ancient scrolls of Kemet. At some point, I know we'll have to go to Kemet, otherwise known as Egypt. But the start of it is in Philadelphia. The founding fathers had to have been told to build a structure or to set aside a place for this to occur."

"That is why the streets we saw around Asmodeus's lair are in that city," Azrael said. "Why else?"

Celeste suddenly looked up and then looked around. Blue tears filled her eyes. "You all can go home now."

"What?" Bath Kol whispered.

Angels drew closer.

"You can all go home." She glanced around as Jamaerah's lip began to tremble. "All you ever needed was for one of us, a member of the Remnant, to pray for all of you," she said quietly. "Now the choice is yours if you want to stay and fight for us, or if you want to leave and transfer all your knowledge to fresh battalions."

"It wasn't just one of the Remnant . . . it was you, Celeste," Bath Kol said, staring at her and then at Azrael. "It was the combination . . . the Angel of Death had to die to his old ways and be reborn into compassion and love and understanding . . . and in so doing, he can open the portal . . . but only those healed by your prayer can go into the channel of Light."

Azrael stepped back and opened his arms and closed his eyes, summoning down a crystalline column of white Light in the same way he had done for the lost souls on the day of his arrival. "Province over the transmutation of souls is still mine," he murmured. "But I cannot override a banishment edict. Only mercy and forgiveness . . . love . . ."

"And a prayer," Bath Kol said, tearing. "She *prayed* for us, man . . . we can *all* go home."

Celeste nodded. "When I heard Jamaerah's sad music, I whispered a prayer that no man should be banished, no angel of the Light trapped here in this hell. Before I even heard that, I had prayed for you all at dawn."

Azrael stared through the column of light. "Anyone here may try it. If Bath Kol's theory is correct, you will

ascend. If not, you will simply be bathed in light and there
will be nothing more I can do."

"The Balance Keepers spoke of this," Jamaerah said
in a soft voice. "Jophiel of Enlightenment . . . Uzziel of
Faith . . . Elemiah of Inward Journeys . . . and Douma of
Silence. I have studied with them all and you know the
prophecy, Bath Kol."

"I do," Bath Kol said sadly. "The One, the Key of the
Remnant, would end the banishment, three months before
the final war. We could lose many valuable warriors . . . or
not, as angels would for the first time be given a choice
without sanctions. Three of the Remnant would then
stand at a sacred place on the appointed date of 12/21/12,
and their Light would wash the landscape . . . their healing
would touch the masses . . . sensitives would Light, 144,000
around the world, and that Light would be enough to
stamp out the perpetual darkness that has haunted humankind. Then the ensuing battle we waged would be to drive
back evil, once humanity chose to surrender the dark."

"Go," Celeste murmured, and then walked over to
Jamaerah.

"I feel so weak, as though I should stay and fight . . .
but . . ." He hung his head and turned away with a sob.

She placed her hands on his back, then laid her face
against it. "Someone must go tell the others what happened down here. Someone must make the angels weep
for their lost brothers and help the higher realms have
compassion for the sacrifice you all have made. Twenty-
six thousand years of death, hell, and destruction." She
rounded him and hugged him, then looked at Bath Kol.
"Release him from the guilt. He loves you like a father

and cannot bear the thought of going without you, and I feel it in my core that you want to see this to the end."

Bath Kol nodded and swallowed hard. "Go," he whispered. "Report directly to Michael about all that you have seen and endured. Tell him we need more air support from the etheric realms above here on the ground down here on earth." Bath Kol lifted his chin as Jamaerah lifted his head. "Journey well, my brother."

"Come," Celeste said in a gentle voice, walking Jamaerah to the column of light that Azrael held open for him.

"You shouldn't set the kid up like that," Isda said, wiping his nose with the back of his hand. "What if we're all wrong? How many times have we tried opening columns, going to shamans, doing group fucking war dances, you name it, and it never worked! It never worked!" he shouted, pacing back and forth. "And if he doesn't ascend, you'll have made him suicidal—it's fucking irresponsible to make someone hope like that!"

"The Angel of Death was never here in our midst when we tried before, and we certainly hadn't located a member of the Remnant who was packing a full twelve-strand charge, man . . . so chill!" Bath Kol shouted back.

"All I have left is hope," Jamaerah said in a calm, firm voice, then he hugged Celeste quickly and stepped into the light.

Instantly his head dropped back and his arms opened slowly, along with his majestic wings. Little by little his clothes burned away from him and the unsure, pained expression on his lovely face softened to one of pure serenity. Soon his body began to lift and shimmer until his form and features became a bright prism that made everyone squint. As he neared the ceiling, he faded away, just as he'd sung.

Celeste hugged herself and silently wept with joy. For once she'd done something right, done something that gave another being respite and peace.

"Any more takers?" Azrael looked at Isda and then Bath Kol, before he glanced around at the other men. But oddly, no one else stepped forward.

Isda shook his head. "I'm ride or die, man . . . all I needed to know was that I could go, if I wanted to." He then dropped to one knee and bowed before Celeste. "In your service and in your debt, forever."

Azrael turned his focus to Bath Kol.

"Sucks that I lost the best manifestor in my unit," Bath Kol said, rubbing the stubble on his face. "But like the man said, we're too close to the end—I'm ride or die all the way. Wanna be here for the big end-of-the-year party. Besides, Philly always did have the best fireworks in the country."

Chapter 17

The moment Azrael closed down the column of light, the entire warehouse became a frenetic blur of activity.

"Birds of war, this is not a drill!" Bath Kol shouted as he walked through the ranks of angels that were packing weapons and readying bikes. "I want a place we can hole up; somewhere there'll be minimal human collateral damage." He slapped a road map against the chest of a passing brother. "Find me that place, now!"

A tall angel with a red ponytail walked by and pounded Bath Kol's fist, then held up an iPad. "Dude, c'mon, a paper map? What're we, pirates now? Join me in the twenty-first century of technology. I've got an app for that." He showed Bath Kol the screen. He pinched it open with his fingers. "Oregon and Christopher Columbus Boulevard terminates at the waterfront. There's an old, abandoned naval vessel destined for the ship boneyard.

Good temporary roost—lots of high lookout points, no houses nearby, only businesses blocks away . . . and did I mention it sits on water?"

"I love how you think," Bath Kol said, cuffing his shoulder. "One brother drops a prayer grenade on it and we light up the Delaware and make it holy water."

"Like turning water into wine, dude."

"You got a make on the other side's warehouse?" Bath Kol called out. "Anybody? Talk to me, people!"

"Yeah," the brother with the map said. He looked up from the table at Bath Kol, tracing streets with a yellow highlighter. "It's in the North Central section of the city. Up on an Allegheny Avenue . . . at about Twenty-third Street. Lot of abandoned factories and warehouses up there, but also a dense residential area. We can't bring the firefight to them without losing a lot of civilians—gotta get them to come to papa."

"Why do these bastards always do that?" Bath Kol raked his hair with his fingers and walked in a circle for a moment. "I so just wanna hit that place with a hallowed-earth-packed grenade launcher." He walked over to his bike as the other angels mounted up. "We'll figure out the rest when we get there. First order of business is to move this squad."

Celeste held Azrael's arm for a moment, stopping him as he fit their saddlebags onto a Harley. "That is so near where you and I were, like only a couple of miles—tops."

Azrael nodded, "That's generally how they operate—they get in close enough to smell you and then put enough pressure on your life to leverage you until you break. I'm sure that's also why my brother Gavreel most likely broke protocol to tip me off before I stumbled into a hornets' nest. They'd had you identified for years."

"I'm sorry that I got those women killed," she said quietly.

"You didn't, and there was no way for you to know." His voice was soothing, low, and tender, and he leaned down so that their conversation remained private. "Signals can bounce off a satellite and we can watch cable all day. That's anonymous communication, just like plucking around on the Internet can be masked . . . but they are always listening for our voices. All of us know each other's voices—there's a frequency that never leaves it, even when fallen . . . just like we are all attuned to the voice of the Source. It was designed into us so that we can always find each other. Now that some of us have fallen, it's both a blessing and a curse."

He brought her into his arms and kissed the crown of her head. "Let it go, Celeste. You didn't cause that. You did what was normal. You called home to someone you had every right to be worried about. If Isda hadn't been playing games, I probably wouldn't have left you and would have instructed you not to make the call." He held her tighter. "But really, if anyone's to blame, it's me, like he said. The thing that hurts my soul is that I was inattentive for reasons I'm not proud of."

"No," she whispered, and stared up at him. "Do not take that into your spirit. Don't."

He sighed and released her. "We have to go."

"One question," she said, again staying his leave. "If something happens to me, will you go home?"

"If all goes well, we won't have to think about that for maybe another seventy years," he said, handing her a helmet. "My prayer is that you live well past a hundred. Climb on."

She gave him a skeptical look and reluctantly took the helmet. "Do you know how to ride?"

"No," he said with a wide smile. "But I know how to bend energy."

"What are you saying?" Nathaniel roared. "We lost scores of demons, our Sentinels actually saw them, and we pulled back? Now you're blind to them!"

Rahab looked up from the glistening, bloody puddle in the center of the black pentagram she'd drawn on the floor, then made the vision disappear with a wave of her hand. She pushed a long swath of raven hair behind her ear and placed a graceful hand on her slender hip.

"They're protected from our scrying, Nathaniel. Complaining about it won't change the facts. They've gone to ground after the battle. We laid siege to Isda's safe house—his stronghold was weak, and from there we acquired information on the location of a sensitive whom they frequent for minor healings. When that proved fruitless, as she was well protected, we pressed on to the location of Bath Kol's club, but as expected, we couldn't enter. You know he is well fortified there and we've never been able to find his primary roost. So we waited and ambushed them while they were en route to his stronghold—hoping to learn the location of that once and for all, but your stupid demons saw the girl, got excited thinking she was an easy target, and rushed the ambush . . . and that's when we encountered a much improved Azrael."

"Bitch, your condescending tone will get you—"

"Remember, Nathaniel . . . my name means *violence*. But at the moment we cannot afford to have our troops decimated by infighting." She walked away from him unafraid and left the argument to the others.

"Appollyon, take three brothers with you and bomb that old woman's house. Period. I want Celeste Jackson to have a reason to return to the city. Open a gas line or something."

"Sometimes force only works against you, but I do not expect the brothers who you've just sent to bomb that old woman's house to grasp the details of finesse. Maybe one day you'll choose me as your second-in-command, after Appollyon fails you again." Pharzuph studied his nails as Appollyon lunged, but Malpas and Forcas caught him.

"One day I will feed you to Cerberus," Appollyon growled.

Pharzuph ignored him with a sly half smile and turned his attention back to Nathaniel. "Have you tried a subtler approach, milord? I do recall we dropped a bomb on that very same neighborhood in '85, and the results did not yield the fruit we'd expected . . . isn't that right, *Appollyon?*" Pharzuph cooed in a sensual murmur. He glanced at the tall, beautiful blonde who lounged on the sofa. "Onoskelis rules perversion now," Pharzuph said with a smile, then nodded toward a voluptuous redhead who was noshing on sushi. "Or you can put in a petition to Lucifer to have Lilith mine one of their weaker brokers for information . . . after all she is in charge of prostitution. Perhaps we could send in Dantanian, our man with many faces, to sound like her dear aunt and take on the fat woman's form. If we cannot get to the old hag, then we can lure Celeste Jackson out with a fake."

"If we had time," Nathaniel said, narrowing his gaze. "But we do not own that luxury based upon Malpas's report."

"He has regained his wings," Malpas said on a low booming voice. "That means that the Remnant he found now has her twelve strands repaired."

"And that could have only happened after a joining!" Nathaniel shouted. "He had to bond to her, give her his Light—and that means she can heal them all if we do not get to her in time."

❖

The news van pulled up in front of Denise Jackson's home. Neighbors came out on their porches, craning their necks to see what had happened. Nosy Thelma down the street called and told her to go to the window, saying that live news crews were coming up her steps. Denise Jackson peered out the window with the phone in her hand. Sure as rain, the familiar newscaster she always watched at noon climbed out and a pretty blond woman was driving the van. A black man, who seemed oddly familiar, but that she couldn't exactly place, followed her favorite reporter with a huge camera on his shoulder.

They didn't even have to ring the bell. She opened the door, straightening her wig and snapping her housecoat closed.

"Ms. Jackson," the reporter said, seeming concerned as he pushed a microphone near her face.

"Yes," she said, hesitating. "What's all this about?"

"We know that your family has been recently hit hard by a spate of ill fortune . . . first your niece's boyfriend was tragically killed by an alleged drug deal gone bad, and then your niece fled the city—"

"Aw, hell, I'm going back in my house. I thought you was one of the good ones, but you—"

"Your grandson Jamal," the reporter said quickly. "We need to ask you some questions about his tragedy."

"What about my baby?" she said, turning back to the reporter slowly with her hand over her heart. She could see neighbors on the adjoining porches straining to hear.

"He was shot during recess at school—and we wanted to know if you thought it was in any way related to the troubles your niece and her late boyfriend had with area drug dealers?"

"Oh, Father God," she said, falling back against her door, holding her heart. "Tell me, is my baby alive?"

"Barely, ma'am," the reporter said. "They rushed him to Temple University Hospital."

"And my own daughter never called me?" Frantic, she turned away to go back into the house, but the reporter laid a kind hand on her shoulder.

"We can give you a ride," he said.

"Me and Pearl can drive you, honey," Thelma yelled out from the crowd. "Lawd have mercy, they done shot that poor boy!"

"But we can get through traffic better with our news van," the reporter offered. "It's the least we can do. We didn't realize you hadn't been contacted, or we would have never come here like this—we aren't monsters."

"Thank you so much," Denise Jackson murmured as

fat tears rolled down her face. "Jus' lemme go put on some shoes and get my purse."

"You'll give her a heart attack," Forcas said, walking around the chair that held Denise Jackson captive. "She passed out once when she saw Dantanian's face change and realized we weren't reporters and saw what we really are."

"Keep the duct tape on her mouth," Rahab warned. "Her prayers are stronger now that one of the Warriors of Light has healed her, prayed over her, and entered her home. We have to be careful of even the silent ones she says—so it will be best to make the trade soon."

"Yes," Onoskelis said, glaring at Ms. Jackson. "She prayed and prayed for that boy's miserable life, calling on the names we never say until I almost ripped her fucking throat out in the van."

"Duct tape was a better option," Nathaniel said, laughing, "because then I would have had to rip out yours. She may be old and troublesome, but she's worth her weight in gold now." Nathaniel nodded toward Pharzuph. "Subtle was just the plan we needed, old friend."

Pharzuph glanced at Nathaniel. "Since Azrael called out the etheric messengers, we could not directly come at her. Oh, and did I mention he actually got through to Raphael—so we can't override his healings on this old bat now?" Pharzuph sat in a chair facing Ms. Jackson and smiled. "Anything we did would have been deflected, unless she came to us of her own free will. Even her grandchildren and her children are protected. Our troublesome Angel of Death appears to now be in the human-life-saving profession ever since he found his chosen. But, we still own the airwaves, and she sits glued to the television watching her favorite, trusted news shows. The rest was simple. We just appeared to her as her favorite news anchor and she was out of the house with no fuss, no muss."

"Take note, Appollyon, subtlety works miracles. Sometimes brute force is just that—brute." Nathaniel leaned down and slowly, gently removed the tape from Denise Jackson's mouth. "Bring her some water. We are not animals."

Appollyon walked away glaring as Onoskelis flipped a long blond tress over her shoulder, laughed, and brought Nathaniel a glass of water.

Nathaniel grabbed a chair and set it down near Ms. Jackson as Pharzuph got up to pour himself a drink. Taking his time, Nathaniel turned the chair around backward to sit down and study her. "If you are calm, you may have some water." He rolled the glass Onoskelis had given him between his palms while staring at his captive. "We will even let you stand up and get some circulation, and we have some fruit and PowerBars—as we understand that you are diabetic. We can even allow you to rest on the sofa and watch your favorite shows."

Ms. Jackson just looked from one individual to another, her eyes filled with terror and her bosom heaving like that of a frightened bird. "My grandson . . . did you kill him?"

"No, unfortunately not. He is protected. He is not even shot and hasn't a clue all of this is going on," Nathaniel said with a deep sigh, and closed his eyes with a squint when she quickly gasped, "Thank you, Jesus."

He leaned into her, his gaze darkening. "We try not to say any names associated with the Light around here . . . it's taxing." Then as though they'd calmly been discussing the weather, he sat back. "Our goal isn't to hurt you or your children, or even your grandchildren. We just want Celeste to give us what she owes us."

Denise Jackson closed her eyes. "I told that girl . . . I told that girl a hundred times, if not once, not to mess with Brandon or the people he was dealing with."

"Wise counsel, but we could give a fuck about Brandon. He was expendable."

"Then what does she owe you?" Denise Jackson looked from one face to another, trying to find one that had an inkling of mercy in it. "I don't have much, but I can put my house up. I can, I can give you whatever I have, just don't hurt that chile. If she stole from you, I'll—"

"Ma'am," Nathaniel said calmly with a cruel smile, "you can't give us what that girl owes us."

"I can raise the money."

He clucked his tongue and shook his head, gently peeling back more duct tape to release her left hand from the arm of the chair. He placed the glass of water in her hand. "Drink."

She stared at the glass. "What does my Celeste owe you?"

He shook his head and smiled. "They told me you were a tough old broad. I told them that was impolite." He released a long sigh. "We want her soul."

"You said my grandbabies and my children were safe."

"You want to strike a bargain?" Nathaniel leaned

forward as she brought the glass up close to her mouth, but recoiled when she spit in the glass and then flung it at him.

Spittle and water splashed his face.

"Get back, demon!" she shouted.

Nathaniel was up and out of his chair in the lightning-strike quickness of a serpent. He backhanded her with a loud crack and split her lip. "If I didn't need you alive, your heart would be beating in my hand!"

"See what I mean?" Rahab said coolly, sipping a vodka martini.

"My life ain't worth squat—done lived my life," Denise Jackson said with an angry smile, dabbing her bloodied lip. "My people been through worse than this and still survived. Angels protect my babies, that's all I care about. You can't take what ain't yours even if you beat me to death. I ain't scairt of seeing demons. And I'll be praying in my mind that Celeste runs as far away from here as her legs can carry her."

"Tape her mouth shut!" Nathaniel ordered, and began to pace. He looked up to the ceiling and his eyes turned black. "You of the Realms Above have etheric messengers of the Light looking out for the old woman! Then take this message to Azrael and Celeste that I am not the one to fuck with! I have messengers, too! Demons that can deliver a very clear message! How about if I send them instead?"

He released a black charge that sent electrical arcs from his fingertips. A black funnel cloud appeared and swirled along the ceiling ductwork like living black smoke. Screeching demons moved within it, then suddenly it sucked itself into a vent and was gone.

Pharzuph petted Ms. Jackson's cheek and then held

her jaw tight as she tried to flinch away. Rahab held her arm down on the chair's armrest. Pharzuph duct-taped her mouth, then restrained her free hand again. Rahab stood back and laughed.

"When this is all over," Pharzuph cooed, "and you try to tell anyone about us, they're just going to think you have dementia. How sad."

Celeste dismounted from the bike and Azrael was right behind her. Although they'd roared in on the expressway with an amazing show of chopper force, once they got to the ship, it seemed as though no one could see them. They'd passed traffic, but strangely no drivers turned to even contemplate the loud convoy of bikes. No one looked toward the dock, no one looked toward them. She noticed that a slight tinge of glowing white-blue light covered each motorcycle and its riders. Azrael gave her a subtle nod, and from his gaze knowing spread within her that they'd been angel-cloaked.

She looked around as bikes were quickly concealed, and Azrael and Bath Kol greeted a brother they addressed as Nemamiah. He was just over six feet tall and broad-shouldered with thick brown hair that hung down his back in a wavy ponytail. His jaw was covered in a velvety wash of five-o'clock shadow, and his dark brown eyes were intense and kind. If he'd been a human and if she'd tried to place where he was from, she would have pegged him as an Israeli.

"Protective lines are up; water in the harbor is blessed. I take it you had travel mercy?"

Bath Kol went to grip Nemamiah's hand and froze as Celeste dropped to her knees and screamed. Azrael got to her first.

"Aunt Niecey! They have her!"

Azrael looked up at Bath Kol, who nodded. The squad gathered around as Azrael helped Celeste up.

"I have to go to her; I don't care!" Celeste shouted.

"No," Azrael said. "You're walking right into a trap—"

"I don't care—it's just me, they only want me!"

He grabbed her by the arms and looked her in the eyes. "It's not just you. It's the whole world."

Crying, she twisted out of his hold. "Didn't you say we have to care about one person, about the individual, and screw the big grand picture?"

Bath Kol rubbed his hands down his face, and Isda released a long breath.

"A man will say a lot of shit when in bed with a woman," Isda muttered.

"Tell me about it," Bath Kol said under his breath.

"Call them," Azrael said quickly. "Find a phone—someone downtown here who has a New York cell phone number."

"Damn, where is Jamaerah when ya need him?" Bath Kol walked around in a circle. "Somebody jump on a Harley and get downtown, posthaste. Send out a request for help that a messenger knock a New York cell phone out of somebody's hand as you're passing by on the bike, dude." Bath Kol looked at Azrael. "Then what? I take it you're making it up as you go along?"

Azrael held Celeste by the hand, talking to the group

while holding her gaze. "You're going to call your Aunt Niecey from the cell phone. You're going to leave her a voice message on her home phone and sound concerned but not panicked, like you feel something is wrong but aren't sure, okay?"

She nodded. "I can do that."

"Then you're going to say, 'Since I haven't been able to reach you and feel strange, Azrael and I are coming home.'" Azrael stared at her and waited for her to nod. "You'll tell her that because of rush hour and some errands, you have to run to pick up some of the food you know she's now eating for her health. But you'll be stopping by my place on the docks by six p.m., and then coming home to her house."

"Okay . . . I can do that."

"They won't kill her or harm her, Celeste, as long as they think they can trade her for you. They want to keep her healthy to show you she's all right . . . then they're going to force a trade—but we want that to happen on our terms, down here, and away from all those homes filled with innocent people. Your aunt is strong. She will survive this."

"Promise me."

Azrael hesitated.

"Yo, sis, don't stress the man," Isda argued, stepping forward in agitation. "If the Angel of Death says she's gonna survive, that's pretty much money in the bank."

"I can't promise that, Celeste," Azrael said quietly. "It is logic, it is my hope and my prayer . . . but I know that this way is best."

She nodded and went to him and he enfolded her in his arms.

"Okay, brothers, listen up," Bath Kol said. "We need a phone, then we need the number wiped so we don't get some poor bastard accidentally whacked by the dark side—make sure they get an upgrade or something for the phone we're gonna borrow. Now . . . here's the thing. We gotta make it seem like she snuck and got a phone without Azrael knowing. So, she's gonna need to call back and say Azrael was acting weird in New York and didn't want her to call, but a friend of his—a nice lady in Brooklyn who owns a spa, slipped her a phone."

Bath Kol looked at Celeste. "They got the first tip-off from Queen's house, so it stands to reason they'd believe that. Then you're gonna whisper and act like you're calling from inside a bathroom so Az can't hear you, around six thirty when it's just getting dark. I want you to describe to your aunt's answering machine what the ship looks like—can't miss it. Then from there, it's battle stations. I want you to keep the line open for an incoming call—and you're probably gonna get that incoming call for the negotiation of the trade, or some kind of contact from them. I'm not sure. That's where it's gonna get dicey. Park the bikes; unload the weapons. That's all I made up so far."

"The messengers haven't gotten to her but she's feeling something," Malpas said, coming to Nathaniel. "The wires are hot. She left a message for her aunt. She had an eerie feeling and is returning to Philly tonight around six thirty."

"Good. She should be feeling something. I'd be concerned if she didn't."

◆━◆━◆

The waiting was the hard part. The sitting and doing nothing while they rigged the ship to go up like Fourth of July fireworks was crazy-making. The knowing that her aunt Niecey was being held and possibly tortured by demons, an old woman frightened out of her mind, tore Celeste's heart out of its frame.

But learning how to shoot everything they had in their arsenal helped take the edge off. She'd always been afraid of guns, but given all she'd seen and all they were up against, being able to defend herself gave her a sense of personal power. If they had her aunt, the dark side had drawn a line in the sand—one that she wasn't afraid to cross to blow their heads off.

Just as Bath Kol predicted, her borrowed cell phone rang a little after seven.

"Remember the plan," he said, sitting across from her with a map and a crate between them.

The other angels nodded and they gathered in close. Azrael placed a hand on her shoulder when she picked up on the third ring.

"Auntie?" Celeste said, amazed at how her aunt's home number came up on the caller ID.

"Yeah, baby, you still coming to see me?"

"Of course." Celeste then dropped her voice. "But Azrael is acting really weird. He's got me down in the old ship on Christopher Columbus and Oregon that he swears he's gonna renovate for some on-the-water hotel—him and his brothers. You know men and their big dreams. But he was really adamant about it after we ran into some trouble in New York . . . but I don't want you to worry. Everything's fine. I should be there in like a half hour to forty-five minutes, okay?"

"All right, baby. You just take your time and drive safe."

"Love you. We will. Bye."

"Bye."

Celeste hung up the phone. "That wasn't my aunt."

"Right you are," Bath Kol said, standing. "Demons can throw their voices and sound like whoever they want."

"She knew we weren't driving when we left, that's one. Two, she never said, 'I love you,' back." Celeste stood and ruffled her ponytail up from her neck. "Now what?"

"We take a small extraction team up to the abandoned factory warehouse up on Allegheny Avenue and hope most of their forces are headed this way. Our team is ready for whatever they send down here, but let's just hope that they don't figure out that we know they've got your aunt up there."

"But won't they be expecting me to walk in the door up on Ellsworth Avenue at my aunt's house in West Philly? They're going to bring her there and make her open the door there." Celeste looked around at the group. "Right?"

"Or they could have a face-changer greet you at her door while keeping her at the factory," Isda said. "That's what Bath Kol should just come out and say to you straight."

Bath Kol nodded and rubbed his palms down his face.

"They could try to trick you into a trade for nothing," Azrael said slowly. "Celeste, this was why I wouldn't promise you, despite what the brothers urged me to say to you."

She pushed him in the chest hard as hot tears filled her eyes. "I knew she could be at risk! But with all this time we've wasted, she could already be tortured or dead! You had me here for hours, waiting so your ambush would work? I don't care about getting *them*; I care about saving her!"

"No . . . I didn't just leave her there as bait. I was trying to figure out the best way to buy some time for her. If we rushed in with heavy artillery, there would be too high a risk for collateral damage—her loss of life, Celeste," Azrael said carefully, trying to steady her with the calm tone of his voice. "There were and are so many variables, Bath Kol has been trying to keep his visions open, trying to—"

"If she dies or is hurt, I'm kicking all of your asses, we clear?" Celeste pointed at Azrael, then spun on Bath Kol. "You put four fliers up in the air and I'm going to tell you the route they'd most likely have to take. You're able to blind people to your presence as angels, so do it. If you see my aunt in a car or van in your visions heading toward West Philly, then bum-rush the van. If you can't find her and there's no evidence of anyone in the house, meet us back at the factory. Three or four of us can take bikes to West Philly, because if there's a no-show, it's easy enough to cut over the back side of West on a chopper, roll over the Girard Avenue bridge, and be in North Central in a heartbeat. We can meet up with you there or we can do the damned thing at the waterfront."

"Yes, ma'am," Bath Kol said with a half smile.

Isda nodded and leaned in near Azrael. "No offense, mon, but your 'oman is sexy as hell when she's pissed off."

Chapter 18

*R*iding with a pack of what looked like Hells Angels that were really heaven-sent was somehow surreal. Anger trumped fear as Celeste hung on to Azrael's shoulders all the way up Oregon Avenue from the waterfront through South Philly. They made a quick jag onto the expressway, taking I-76 West and coming off at the University Avenue exit, packing enough artillery to take out a fair section of the city.

Strange thing was, people only saw them and the bikes. Bath Kol and his unit were masters at making weapons disappear against a chopper. They simply covered the artillery with blue-white angel light, and suddenly the extra bulk appeared to the naked human eye as extra detailing and design on their motorcycles.

Three bikes peeled off from them on University Avenue, going down Woodland Avenue—they took Baltimore Avenue. The connect point would be at opposite ends of Aunt Niecey's block. Azrael slowed down as they entered her aunt's street, bumped the bike up on the sidewalk, stomped down the kickstand, then looked back.

"You ready?"

She nodded and took off her helmet. He turned off the motor. Neighbors leaned out of doorways and craned their necks from porches. She could just hear it now: Denise Jackson's drug-addict niece got her little cousin shot and came home with some big, burly black biker dude. Bath Kol had told her what the dark side had done, and now she seethed with rage just knowing what kind of emotional hell her aunt had to be going through because of the lie.

When she saw Miss Thelma run down the block in her slippers, Celeste cringed. But to her surprise Azrael turned around and pointed back up the block.

His command was simple: "Go home."

Celeste waited for the normal hand-on-hip, neck-peck who-you-talkin'-to that never came. Miss Thelma looked confused, as if she'd lost something and couldn't remember what it was, then shuffled back up the street in her bedroom slippers. Clearly something had happened to Azrael, too. He seemed to be getting stronger, more used to his power here . . . Celeste couldn't identify it, but he was different.

Listening for sounds in the house, Celeste rang the bell, unable to think about any of that now beyond praying nobody on the block would get hurt if it got crazy inside.

After a moment, she saw her aunt coming toward the door. Azrael put a steadying hand on her shoulder.

"Perceive with your gift, not with your heart," he said

quietly in her ear. "If you see me do something, think twice before you shoot me."

He stood up straight as the tumblers turned, and she forced a smile. Her aunt opened the door, but didn't ask for any sugar. Celeste cast Azrael a glance and he caught it.

"Did you have a nice time in New York?" Aunt Niecey said, smiling at both Celeste and Azrael.

Celeste rounded Azrael. "Yeah, Auntie, we had a ball. Az brought a new bike. Come out and see." Her goal was simple, get the demon impostor out of her aunt's house. Bath Kol had been very clear about how Azrael's prayer barriers had been breached. Aunt Neicey let the demons in of her own free will. That had been the only way they could have gotten inside the house. Guised as her favorite reporter, the demon had tricked her aunt into giving them an invitation; tonight Celeste and Azrael would revoke it.

Azrael glanced up as crows began to gather on the telephone lines.

"Aw, baby, I'll see it later. I'm not dressed. You all come in here and get something to eat."

"I'm not taking no for an answer," Celeste said, rushing up to her "aunt" and grabbing her hard by the wrist.

The second they touched, she saw a face behind the face. Azrael yelled no, but the entity yanked Celeste through the door. Azrael was right on Celeste's heels in time to see her unload two silver shells into what looked like her aunt's forehead.

"Pull it out of the house," Celeste said, backing up. "Seal the house again like you did before."

He yanked the body out by the feet and quickly touched the wall, causing it to light up. Sirens and neighbors were screaming. Then he opened up a light column on the porch as the thing lying at his feet began sitting up.

"Go to Hell!" Azrael said, and reached behind his back and pulled out the machete Isda swore by, beheading the creature.

Celeste turned away. Neighbors shrieked. But the second the head rolled away, the demon's true face could be seen. Pure black eyes were sunk into the sockets and a mouth filled with gnarled teeth held a deadly grimace. Within seconds it combusted, also sucking the blood from the rug up and down into the fiery swirl that the light column had become. The front door slammed and resealed itself with blue-white light. But thousands of angry ravens exploded from the telephone lines.

Jumping down the front steps, Azrael grabbed Celeste by the waist, hit the pavement, and was on the bike, wielding a machete to fend off the birds, with her behind him. Bikes met them at the corner, and Bath Kol's men flung blessed liter bottles of spring water into the air and into the center of the attacking flock, then shot the bottles before they hit the asphalt.

Birds fell and burned from contact with the holy water that spread out in the air like napalm. Then suddenly the scorched flock drew together into a screaming, black-leather-clad, dark angel. His once handsome African features were partially melted and bloodied. Fangs lengthened in his mouth as his pitch-black eyes revealed no whites and beheld them with pure hatred. He got up holding his seared face as the motorcycles split up and went in opposite directions. Opening his massive black wings, he took to the air behind Azrael and Celeste.

"Use the machete," Azrael shouted. "Don't shoot! He wants you to hit innocent bystanders."

Celeste ducked down, holding on tightly, and accepted the handoff of the weapon. The sound of huge black wings beating the air behind them made her shut her eyes for a moment, but in that same moment she saw Nathaniel strike her aunt . . . in that same moment a strong hand wound around her ponytail and yanked her head back, and in the next moment her eyes met the eyes of the fallen. There was no scream from her lips as she swung with all her might, and suddenly she was free.

The machete cut through leather, skin, and bone. The arm fell and the dark angel that had been chasing them from the air in sinister swoops and dives touched down. Celeste looked over her shoulder as two choppers skidded in behind theirs, facing the injured beast, and sent a grenade-launched rocket into its chest. She pressed her face against Azrael's back as embers floated down and sulfur stench filled the air.

"Go to Hell," he said, then spit, pulling away on a wheelie.

—◈—

Breathless angels flew in next to Bath Kol and took cover outside the abandoned factory warehouse.

"There was no sign of them on the highway," one said quietly, hunkering down in the shadows. "Every street Celeste told us to monitor, we did."

Bath Kol used silent hand signals to position his men around the perimeter and then touched the walls. He shook his head.

"Nothing," he whispered. "The building is cold. I should have been able to pick up a human heartbeat, though. She's not here. They've been using black magic to block my vision, once they were onto my first visual breach into their lair."

The moment he said the words, the building vomited demons from every orifice. Crablike creatures with human faces bent into demonic contortions skittered out from the windows and fire escapes, as bat-winged gargoyles took to the air while fast-moving flesh-eaters bore gruesome mouths packed with razor-sharp teeth. The angels unloaded everything they had but the legions seemed to replenish themselves at will.

"Fall back!" Bath Kol ordered. "Fall back! The building is infested!"

A knife in his back made him hurl blood. It got him between his wings, the attacker an expert at angel physiology. Paralyzed, he couldn't even cry out as the blade twisted.

"Remember me?" a female voice whispered close to his ear as he dropped to his knees. "I might not be able to permanently kill you, immortal . . . but I can make you start over from scratch after you leave this body really, really slowly." She kissed the side of his sweaty face and licked his ear. "I'll leave you conscious while they disembowel you . . . you know how demons like to play. Maybe cut off the thing that got you trapped here in the first place . . . either, or . . . both."

Her blond hair caught on the breeze and flowed over his shoulder, but he couldn't even reach up to yank her off him. He just stared as demons rushed toward him, his

men's voices becoming so far away. He'd told them to fall
back; they had obeyed orders and in the mayhem didn't
see that he was trapped.

Beasts would feed on his flesh; they knew how to keep
a man alive for hours . . . days . . . he'd seen the horrors
during the old days of Rome . . . during the Inquisition,
during so many demonic victories. Tears ran from the
corners of his eyes as he choked on his own blood. The
sound of a motorcycle made the she-devil stop carving
into his back. His tormentor stood, yanking out her huge,
serrated-edge bowie knife to defend herself from something moving quickly in a blur.

That's when he saw Azrael, running toward him, black
leather pants, wings outstretched, dreadlocks lifted with
blue-white force. Azrael took three hurdler's leaps and
went airborne. Opened both hands and gleaming battle-
axes filled them. Throwing the axes like boomerangs, he
cleared a path to Bath Kol, severing heads along the way,
calling his blades of death back into his grip again and
again.

Uzi gunfire ricocheted off Azrael's gleaming wings as
he spun and pivoted midair, using every graceful martial-
arts move he'd demonstrated in the density of the Bronx
club. He threw an ax at the window and the gunfire
stopped. The fleeing blonde dropped to her knees, her
head rolling into the weeds before her body fell.

Bath Kol chuckled, although still crumpled on the
ground and lying on his side as Azrael came to him. "I'm
all fucked-up, man. Got it in the back between my wings.
Never saw it coming," he wheezed, and spit blood.

"Do you want to go home?" Azrael asked, kneeling

beside his friend as his eyes compassionately searched Bath Kol's face.

"No. But I don't want to be a freaking baby again. I want my old alcohol-and-tobacco-ridden body fixed. Don't wanna have to be reborn the old-fashioned, human way. I like me and all my flaws." Bath Kol chuckled again and coughed, but this time closed his eyes. "This hurts like a bitch, man . . . I ain't gonna lie."

"If you come with me for a little while, I can get you healed," a familiar soft voice said. "Let me help you, my stubborn, valiant brother."

"Jamaerah . . ."

Azrael stood and crossed his chest with both axes. "Thank you for manifesting my old arms—my blades of death. I never thought I would see them on this side of the ether again. Take care of him and send him back to us as we've known him."

"Manifesting for you, dear brother, is my honor. I will always be in your debt," Jamaerah said, then lifted Bath Kol away. "Fight well and kill them all."

"Seal this area!" Azrael shouted, causing the parking lot to implode and open into a yawning inferno. Quickly the edges of concrete liquefied into a giant sinkhole. Abandoned cars, trash, and debris tumbled over the edge of the fiery abyss. "Send everything not of the Light to Hell!"

A huge explosion of demon bodies created a landslide, sucking the building down into the unending pit. Magma slurped at the edges of glowing bricks. Celeste scrambled with the team of angels that guarded her to get out of the way of the ever-widening hole. Ground was crumbling inches away. Angels dragged her forward as bikes toppled into the hellfire. Then just as insanely as it had started, the hole closed up in a snap, leaving a half-destroyed building and residual black smoke.

"We have to get back to the waterfront," Celeste said breathlessly the second Azrael was at her side.

"We lost several bikes," one of Bath Kol's men said. "We can fly, but if we carry the Remnant and we take fire—"

"She is my chosen," Azrael said. "We go by air."

Isda dove into the water off the starboard bow. Hundreds of demons dive-bombed behind him, turning the Delaware River's surface into an oil-slicked, burning inferno. He came up on the Camden, New Jersey, side of the river and took a running leap to fly back toward the roiling battle on the opposite shore to catch the fleeing Lahash between the wings with a machete.

Lahash hit the river, paralyzed and gagging against the holy water it had become, as Isda dispassionately watched him slowly drown. Lahash's skin bubbled off his flesh as though he'd been soaked in acid. Soon the dark angel's grasping fingers that futilely clutched at the water turned to bones and fell apart, dissolving right before Isda's eyes. Black feathers floated to the water's surface as the sound of Lahash's wails and thrashing made Isda smile a dangerous smile.

"Go to Hell, motherfucker. Dat was for my 'oman and her family," Isda whispered through his teeth, then spit into the river as he watched Lahash's body explode into an orange-red bubble deep beneath the surface.

Forcas suddenly materialized behind him, but Isda's best Sentinel fired an automatic that hit Forcas several times and caused him to disappear.

"Good look, brother," Isda shouted, and he then flew midriver under the bridge, hunting Forcas. "I'll find the bastard. He's bleeding."

— ❖ —

Aerial dogfights crisscrossed the riverbank. Nathaniel watched it all with his inner circle of dark angels from the Camden Aquarium's observation deck.

"Isn't it beautiful?" he murmured, walking along the edge of the railing with his hands behind his back. "Just like the old days." He turned to Denise Jackson and patted her duct-taped cheek. "But we will prevail like before."

Forcas materialized, bleeding badly and holding his arm. "We haven't been able to breach the ship," he said, panting. "Prayer barriers on all but the top deck make it impenetrable to our demon forces, and they have as many angel fliers as we have fallen fliers. We can board the deck, but need something to make them nervous enough to send out some of their warriors from inside the ship where they guard the girl, so we can get the message to her that we have her aunt. We know she must be in there because of the way they're so mightily defending that stronghold."

"Send in Bune to deliver the message. I love the three-headed dragon in him," Nathaniel said calmly. "Send him with two strong, dark Sentinels. That should draw Azrael out to defend the girl. Then Bune can tell him that the old woman dies if he doesn't make the trade. Azrael has clearly bonded with the girl—and that means she *will* feel our message in his spirit the moment he knows we have her aunt. Then we sit back and watch the girl tear herself apart emotionally. Somewhere in the fracas, she'll break and will go against her protector's pleas . . . and then we move in. Human free will still rules all in this zone."

"But I thought you wanted to save Bune for the December offensive and—"

"Do not challenge me on this, Forcas. You have failed in every attempt so far. Look at you. Go regenerate and get out of my sight!"

Forcas disappeared and Nathaniel walked to the edge of the water, his massive twelve-foot, black, glistening wingspan keeping him aloft just above the mud. He watched as Bune transformed, extending scaly bat wings, and then Bune's head split into three snapping, snarling dragons' jaws. Two more dark Sentinels rushed in behind Bune, then suddenly a loud concussive blast from the slurp blew them all backward, sending shards of glass from the aquarium flying. Bune and the fallen that flanked him were consumed in the inferno on the other side of the river. The trap had worked.

Nathaniel flew back from the water's edge and hit the wall. Denise Jackson hit the ground, her screaming muffled behind the tape. A strong arm grabbed her up and then suddenly released her. She dropped to the ground and looked up at the massive entity that now coughed blood. Her captor had been hit.

Appollyon fell to his knees, and the female entity that had been one of Denise Jackson's tormentors screamed. The blond fallen angel grabbed a piece of glass, clutching it so hard that blood ran down her fist. Scrambling toward Denise Jackson, she poised the glass above the elderly woman's throat, but her hand never lowered as Isda removed her head from her shoulders.

"Think it over, bitch!"

Isda dragged Denise Jackson away, keeping low. Azrael recovered the ax he'd thrown out of Appollyon's back as Forcas materialized, weak and bleeding and holding a sword. Rahab lifted an Uzi and then thought better of it as seven more angels flew in. She took flight over the densely populated Camden neighborhoods, knowing they wouldn't pursue a battle there. Forcas vanished into thin air.

But Nathaniel flew at Azrael, then pulled up midair as Azrael's battle-axes hurled toward him. He sent a black-orb energy blast, knocking Azrael into the water and sending Azrael's axes tumbling. Azrael flew up, wet, fury in his eyes, and hurled himself through the air directly at Nathaniel, who lowered his head and released a war cry—colliding with Azrael. The moment they made contact, Nathaniel began screaming.

Holy water burned through Nathaniel's leather cloak like acid. The two aerial gladiators separated as Nathaniel released another black blast. This time Azrael ducked to allow it to pass him and to hit the side of the Ben Franklin Bridge.

And then Nathaniel was gone, along with Forcas and Rahab. Lahash had been committed back to the pit. The diesel-strong Appollyon needed to be sent back before he recovered, but he, too, had vanished. Warriors of the Light glanced around, unsure what to do. Isda ministered to Ms. Jackson, who was weeping.

Azrael closed his eyes and opened his arms, pulling everything dead or injured by angel hands into a swirling abyss he opened in the Delaware. "I commend you back into the pit!" he shouted, watching the water writhe and bubble with thick sulfur plumes.

Without needing orders to do so, Angels of Light touched down and quickly began forming a search party. They were all aware that Celeste, their Remnant, was missing. She wasn't with Azrael. She wasn't with her aunt. Bath Kol's men were on the other side of the river. In the heat of battle, Azrael had to leave her side for seconds to protect her, and in that fragile space of time, she was gone.

The moment the pit closed beneath the water, Azrael dropped his arms and began running back through the Aquarium building. He saw two injured angels lying unconscious in the stairwell. He could see Celeste in his mind: A dark angel had her in a chokehold, dragging her down the steps, toward an exit door, obviously trying to get her to where he could take her airborne. But she stomped down hard against his knee making them both fall at the bottom of the stairwell. Immediately Celeste cried out the name of the Almighty and spun. A blue-white current rippled down Celeste's body, then the vision went white. A shotgun blast made Azrael call out to her, becoming frantic.

"Celeste!"

He followed the sound of the gun report, hurdling steps an entire flight at a time, as the smell of cordite stung his nose. He found Celeste with a pump shotgun broken back and Pharzuph sitting on the floor with his face blown off.

"Go to Hell," she said calmly, then stood there beside Azrael for several long minutes to watch Pharzuph burn.

They said nothing as they trudged back up the stairs, but the instant Celeste saw her aunt, she ran to her and dropped to her knees.

"Thank Heaven you're all right," Celeste gasped, hugging her. "Did they hurt you?" She pulled back and then kissed her aunt's cheeks.

"Just trying to make sense of it all," Aunt Niecey said, trembling as she glanced around. "This young man . . . or I guess I should say angel, said my grandbaby is all right and they lied," she said quietly, glancing up at Isda. "And I know they lied. They said so theyself right in front of me."

"I swear it's not about a drug war and you're not crazy," Celeste said, kissing her aunt's face again. "I don't want you to be afraid. We're going home, all right?"

Aunt Niecey smiled through her tears and cupped Celeste's face. "Chile . . . I am in the company of angels and I'm still alive. I've seen things that don't make sense and I got you, and Azrael kept his promise to me. I ain't scairt of no demons after what all I done seen."

Epilogue

Three months later

Celeste sat in the first row of plastic chairs with Azrael at her side. She didn't wail or cry bitter tears the way she thought she might . . . that would have been hard to do when a promise had been kept and you knew there was another side. It was now a little less than a month before the world would forever be changed on December 21, 2012, and people were still focused on the mundane the way they had been for years. Knowing was a double-edged sword, but it made accepting people's crossing over a lot easier.

Aunt Niecey had slipped away in her sleep with all her family in the house after Thanksgiving. Said she was tired, needed to rest. Doctors said her heart just gave up—no pain. She died the way everybody should, with a smile on her face. Azrael told the family he'd found her, but

Celeste knew that they had talked a long time first and he'd brought Roscoe to hold her hand. Azrael told Celeste so, but she'd also felt it and seen it in her head. Her visions were stronger. So much stronger now.

Even though it was gray and chilly outside, fall colors still made the trees pretty. An unusually long, warm Indian summer had made the trees last beyond what was normal . . . and the foliage in the cemetery seemed to be held in state just to welcome her aunt. It was a good day to bury Aunt Niecey—not too hot, not too cold, a break in the rain so the ground was dry and firm. No mud, a little sun here and there. She couldn't help wonder, had her guys put in a special order for the day?

Celeste turned her face up to the wan sun and closed her eyes, listening to her young cousin, who wasn't more than fifteen, sing "Amazing Grace" with all his heart and soul. Jamal was singing, but he had help from Jamaerah somewhere in the ether. She'd remember that voice anywhere. Hearing that was the thing that was gonna make her cry, especially when all the old ladies said her cousin had the voice of an angel. She couldn't make claims about any other day, but today he did.

"Are you all right?" Azrael murmured as he helped her to her feet and handed her a rose.

"Yeah," she said quietly, looking around at what her family called "all those strange friends of hers from New York," then smiled. "Angels were her pallbearers, except her son . . . isn't that just right?"

Azrael kissed Celeste's cheek and went with her to lay a flower on the casket before it descended. Bath Kol stood on her exposed side with Queen Aziza, right next to Isda and his new lady friend, then Gavreel and the Remnant Magdalena, and Paschar and the Remnant Melissa. Then there were all the brothers who stood in the back, who'd made a show riding in on Harleys.

She didn't care that she was gonna catch liquid Hell from her family for all these people that they didn't know. They were still arguing about why everything got left to her to be put in trust for the grands way before Aunt Niecey had been committed to the ground. Now her cousins, who'd spent a lifetime giving their mama heartbreak and pain, were trying to fall in the casket behind her. But that was family. Celeste tried not to smile when Azrael just shook his head.

There was plenty of drama at Aunt Niecey's homegoing, that was for sure. Folks in the neighborhood were still wagging their tongues about what they swore they saw one night in September. Problem was, the police couldn't find a body or evidence of blood splatter. A few shell casings in the streets of Philly was like telling the cops somebody was going around dropping gum wrappers on the ground. The rest of what happened made the news as gas-main explosions and noxious-fume buildup. Yeah, Celeste couldn't wait to go back to New York.

"Bye, Auntie," Celeste whispered, and touched the edge of the casket with gentle fingers. "I'll see you later when we all come home."

Celeste and Azrael walked a little ways arm in arm to go back to the limousines, but her cousins stopped them.

"You are going to the repast at the church and then back to my mama's house, right?" Keisha said, several female cousins by her side. Every one of them had their arms folded.

"Yes . . . Keisha," Celeste said, releasing a long sigh. "We'll be there."

"Good, because you know we've got family business to take care of. No offense, Azrael, y'all might be her *new* man and all, but there's some things my mama wasn't *clear* about, on account of the fact that we know she had dementia in her last days . . . talking crazy about all kinds of insanity—just like your mama used to, Celeste. Only difference was, my mama was *in her eighties* and your mama . . . well, you know the story. We just need to be sure she wasn't taken advantage of, which is why we need a private conversation with just us and Celeste. Me and Junior want to make sure there's no problem."

Azrael just looked at Celeste's cousins for a moment and began to draw her away.

Bath Kol chuckled. "You sure you got all the demons out of that house, man?"

Azrael shook his head. "No, I think I must have accidentally left a few to keep it interesting."

"Oh, no, you didn't!" Keisha shouted behind them. "Who you signifying on and calling a demon? At my mama's funeral, too? She must be turning in her grave thinking about you trying to take over everything. This is *family* business. That's exactly why we need to talk to Celeste *solo*. Boyfriends ain't got nothing to do with it, and you didn't even really *know* my mama anyway, Az-ri-el."

Isda slowly walked over to Keisha and locked his gaze with hers, then smiled. "See dat man over there? He's the last one on the planet you want to have to tell you to go to Hell."

Celeste smiled and looked over her shoulder at her cousin and squeezed Azrael's hand. They had important work to do, sensitives to gather, and a planet to save. The last thing they had time for was Keisha's drama.

"For real, girl. Rein in your inner demon," Celeste said, shaking her head. "Listen to Isda. You so do not want Azrael to have to tell you where to go."

Celeste walked away, Azrael's hand in hers.

Pocket Books
Proudly Presents

Conquer the Dark

L.A. Banks

Available in paperback
October 2011
from Pocket Books

Turn the page for a sneak peek at *Conquer the Dark* . . .

*C*eleste Jackson opened her eyes in bed and stared across the large warehouse loft. This was her favorite time of the day, when a new dawn blotted out the last vestiges of the night and the angels spread their wings.

No matter how often she'd seen it done, each time Azrael opened his wings, she stared at his back in awe, watching the thick ropes of muscles that gave it form and substance unfurl pristine white appendages from beneath his dark mahogany-hued skin. It took everything within her not to gasp as the steel-cabled sinew that flanked his spine bulged and stretched just before a seam developed along his shoulder blades, then instantly gave birth to glistening feathered beauty.

He stood in front of the massive warehouse

windows naked from the waist up and wearing only white cotton karate pants with his magnificent twelve-foot wingspan outstretched. Soon, the dance would begin, his silent communion with motion and gravity and some force she could not see. And she waited.

After a moment, he turned with his eyes still closed, barely breathing it seemed, the new day washing his handsome face in rose-golden light, his long, dark dreadlocks spilling over his broad shoulders and his stone-cut chest. Every stacked brick of his abdomen cast shadows between them only to give rise to the wide planes of muscles that almost appeared to absorb the light.

Celeste allowed her gaze to travel over his corporeal form. He was definitely a divine creation, and that he was hers still blew her mind, even after the three months he'd found and bonded with her. She briefly closed her eyes and said a quiet prayer of thanks, also glad that his being with her violated no heavenly edicts. He loved her, just as she loved him—and she wasn't pure human. Therein lay the technicality that kept him from getting banished when their bonding went from platonic to unstoppable passion—or joining, as he called it.

Not touching him was impossible, especially when he was literally addicted to her energy now, and addicted to her skin. Their joining combination caused a fusion that increased her gifts and increased his power here on this plane. She was his battery; he was her jumper cable. A Remnant found by her warrior angel was a balance tipper from the dark to the Light on the planet. He and two of his brothers had found theirs. Three in all. Those that hadn't gotten to their Remnants in time had ultimately been exonerated from their previous lapses when they found key sensitives, those humans highly tuned to work with Remnants— so it was all good.

If only things could go on this way with her man, her angel, peaceful and happy, his brothers sated and relaxed, their partners the first real female friends she'd ever known. The warehouse was a sanctuary on the banks of the Delaware River in Philly. If things could just stay that way . . . but she knew the clock was ticking. Learning to live in the moment was the only way to mentally survive. Maybe that's how Az made sense of it all too? Being immortal had to have given him a philosophical perspective.

Rather than dwell on what couldn't last forever, she tucked away any unpleasant thoughts and watched Azrael work out through his methodical Tai Chi dance.

He was deep in meditative prayer, and serenity wafted from his very being as he opened his arms and slowly bent his knees, beginning his morning ritual. She could literally see the energy move through him in the form of a thin, blue-white charge that began to cover his skin as his entire body became engaged in the graceful ancient choreography. Like witnessing a celestial fan dance where his majestic wings lifted and dusted the floor, creating music in the pauses and breaths and sweeps, she watched in abject reverence.

It was all so beautiful that emotion tightened her throat. She was supposed to be dead by now, but he'd found her on the night when she'd seen a demon take her ex-boyfriend's life, and she'd been hell-bent on also taking her own.

But with a touch, Azrael had pulled drugs and alcohol out of her system. With patience, he'd convinced her to stop running from him and that she hadn't had a psychotic break—that no, she hadn't lost her mind. Then he'd shown her that angels and demons truly did exist and took her on the most hair-raising journey of her life.

Time was relative. Three short months ago she'd met an angel and everything she thought she knew about the so-called normal world had been shattered in an instant. Three short weeks ago she'd lost the last living relative that she cared about—her aunt Niecey, and yet because of Azrael, she'd been at peace with that. Now that she knew there was actually another side and that what she'd heard all her life hadn't been rhetoric, it was easier to accept many of the losses, especially the hard ones, like losing her mother and Aunt Niecey.

Tears rose to Celeste's eyes and then slowly burned away when she thought about all that Azrael had given her. He'd claimed that she'd saved him; but what she could never explain was that it was the other way around.

Before him, there was only fear and self-destruction. No one understood her gift, save her dear late auntie. Until Azrael had shown up, the only thing she'd known to do to stop the pain of seeing demons and frighteningly horrible weirdness was to drown it all through a bottle. Her so-called gift was so debilitating back then that it left her weak and vulnerable, unable to work with a psychiatric file as thick as a phone book. The ravages of poverty had taken its toll on her health and self-esteem. And all along she'd thought it was all her fault, until Azrael came to show her that she'd been targeted by the dark side because of the coming work she was about to do.

Sudden joy filled her heart now as she watched him bend and turn, the cabled sinew stretching along his thick biceps and forearms, her gaze going to his massive but graceful hands that could caress ever so gently and heal, but that she'd also seen wield blades of death to behead demons. Surreal.

Oddly, that made her feel safe, after all she'd seen

in her life. And yet, the warrior angels who'd been trapped on earth since the first big battle with the fallen, some twenty-six thousand years ago, had been waiting for her, waiting for her prayer and her willingness to sacrifice herself for them so that they could return to the Light, even if they'd violated the edict and had lain with the daughters of man while here.

And after twenty-six thousand years, all it took was the right combination lock of her prayer as a member of the Remnant—a Light Nephilim with twelve strands of DNA hiding in her half-human genetic code, to fuse with the Angel of Death's intention to liberate his trapped and suffering brethren. Profound. She'd sent up the heartfelt request; Azrael had opened the portal to the Light. But there was only one taker, Jamaerah, a gentle spirit with province over manifestation that could no longer take his entrapment in the flesh. Liberated back to the Light, he demonstrated to her how angels and positive spirits still help from the etheric realm. Yet the battle-hardened, Jack Daniels drinking, partying crew that thought all was lost and lamented about not being able to return, had stayed when given the choice, deciding to ride or die with her and Azrael to the end.

That was the thing they'd taught her, too—just knowing one could leave if one wanted evaporated the illusion of being trapped. That mental paradigm shift was the freedom that the angels with dirty wings, her guys now, needed. She'd given them that and they loved her for it, calling her *the key,* since she'd unlocked their minds and commuted their sentence for violating the prime directive while on earth. In return, they'd given her protection and knowledge that was unparalleled. Many a night and well into the dawn they'd all sat up with her other Remnant sisters debating the merits of the lessons learned by having everything angelic except immortality stripped from their beings.

To hear Bath Kol tell it, hellfire would have been easier. But they'd each agreed that, by being made manifest, by temporarily losing their wings and being thrust into all the temptations of the flesh, gave them empathy for humanity that just couldn't be fully perceived while in etheric form.

To experience heartbreak, suffering, physical pain, desire, rage, jealousy, lack, need—all of that had given them serious respect for the human condition. Now when they fought for humankind, they fought with a whole different level of respect for the beings that endured here even with demon oppression besetting their existence. After twenty-six thousand years here in the flesh, this special dirty angel corps knew that humans weren't just weak cattle. They'd been outgunned and outmanned by evil immortal forces way stronger than humans could ever hope to be. Yet many people still endured, held the line, helped their neighbors, sacrificed their lives for others, were honorable and loving and reached out to those less fortunate, despite the tidal wave of negative forces. *That* was courage under fire, to be sure.

And her angels said *that* had been what the Almighty had known and seen in the divine creation, they'd all subsequently learned. It was also why to not serve humans was such a defiant act. To be righteous and perfect when one is all-powerful is not difficult; to do so when mortal and weak and hungry and afraid is heroic. Azrael told her that the Source of All That Is saw that striking quality in its creation and demanded the angels respect that. Most did, but some did not—hence the war that has raged on since the planets aligned the last time to open the veil between worlds.

For all that Azrael and the others gave her, the one thing none of them could bestow upon her was complete peace of mind as to the date of when the next alignment would approach.

Celeste quietly sighed. The soft sweep of Azrael's wings and the gentle pat of his bare feet against the floor were soothing. Had his dance not been so profoundly beautiful she would have closed her eyes and allowed the constant metronome-like rhythm to lull her back to sleep.

But there was no way of closing her eyes on that

splendor, just as there was no way to un-know all that she'd come to see and learn since he'd entered her life. Never in a million years could anyone have ever told her she'd be living with a battalion of angels in a retrofitted warehouse with the future of the planet hinging on one date, 12/21/12.

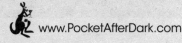

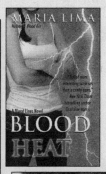